Jamie has always been fascinated by science and has spent a few years studying physics at the university of Sheffield. He has loved listening to fantasy stories and in particular learning about various mythologies, such as the Norse legends. Since a teenager he became a massive fan of the Silmarillion and the world of middle earth, with its elvish languages and folklore. Nature is also something he really enjoys, and whilst at Sheffield, he spent time exploring the peak district. Walking outdoors whilst thinking about philosophy, physics or fantasy is a favourite past time of his. He also plays quidditch as part of the Sheffield Quidditch team.

I would like to dedicate this book to my friends and family. My dad and mum in particular have read a few pieces of my early writings and their support and encouragement has been incredibly helpful. My whole family's support has been amazing and kept me motivated. I would also like to dedicate this to my friends up in Sheffield. And to the Junction, and Broomhill Methodist church, and the many chats we had on Sunday evenings and at the pub.

Jamie Johnson

THE FALLEN STAR

AUSTIN MACAULEY PUBLISHERS™

LONDON * CAMBRIDGE * NEW YORK * SHARJAH

A CIP catalogue record for this title is available from the British Library.

ISBN 9781398442948 (Paperback)
ISBN 9781398442955 (ePub e-book)

www.austinmacauley.com

First Published 2022
Austin Macauley Publishers Ltd®
1 Canada Square
Canary Wharf
London
E14 5AA

Would like to thank many of my friends for their encouragement and also many conversations that stimulated ideas and perspectives. Philosophical discussions with Harold, Peggy and many friends, and bouncing ideas concerning God, life and existence have stimulated many ideas and the philosophical exploration of this work comes from those amazing chats. Also Brandon Sanderson's online videos on writing have helped me make this book as good as it can be.

Table of Contents

Part 1

Chapter 1
Blood of Angels

Lucifer's calves held up a perfectly sculpted angelic form. His entire weight resting easily upon the tip of the six-foot staff of the Caduceus, as the violet snakes hissed and spit, curling in helices along its length, till they caught an enemy's arrow between their fangs and brought it up to their lord. He looked at it and at once it ignited in a burst of blinding white flame.

Surveying the battle below, he smiled gently, well pleased. Unto the past paradise now locked in a bloodthirsty and brutal war, he gloated in his thought thinking that upon this final stretch, all shall proclaim in hymns of praise throughout heaven, at every coronation, the victory that was surely his to come.

Yet the king of the fallen was now a mere war criminal within the eyes of many angels. A betrayer of God's hospitality and good will. Then again, if the plan was fully fulfilled and the rebels had the victory, his host might not have to spend long with those who put themselves against him. All the angelic people might either be dead or allied with his cause, for such was the swiftness of change only war could bring.

Then with a torrent of anger once more rising within him for his dislike of God, he lifted his staff high into the air, and as he did, it began to liquify and transform, until he held a more delicate and easily concealed weapon. A beautiful but effective knife, the only knife in the entirety of creation that could do harm unto angelic flesh.

He called it Ammut, the devourer of souls, and as soon as it was revealed, it sang forth a silent song of death. A motif as it were to Lucifer's darkness. To forge it in secret, he had sneaked down into the kiln of the holy father. For one arduous night did he forge a new thing, a thin blade of super-conductive gold meshed with the life force God had given to him at his conception, and he wielded it to bring forth death. He had then made a handle out of a sacrificial

13

lamb's leg bone. It was an offense unto God, and in that hour, he looked darker than the void of outer space.

Yet now as he stood upon the sacred hill, emanating forth from Lucifer shone a light as luminous as that within the eyes of God. Perceiving, as with eagle sight, all that moved below him, he laughed with joyous rapture. He then conceived within his secret thought that all the macro and microscopic events and happenings in the world around him sang solely of his oncoming victory, and nought else, for such was his vanity.

His heart burned longingly for the throne of creation. Rumour had it that he who sits upon it shall be sovereign over all! Yet for one to take the seat, God would have to freely advocate. Lucifer was determined by strength of arms and desolation unto the planes of heaven and all God's servants would this come to pass.

For those readers who ask why Lucifer just didn't go to the temple of God and murder him in cold blood, well, one could not do so no matter the greatness of one's strength, even if it exceeded the military combative power of God himself. Obliterating the heavenly father would have been an impossible task for it was like trying to kill the definition of life itself. God's own being and the meaning of his essence protected him from death.

Having said this, some of the angels doubted the necessity of God's existence. And they did now consider, after having seen so many of their fellow immortals die upon the battlefield, that it may be possible to kill an immortal god. Abaddon and Amaymon were growing in favour of the idea particularly. Yes, their reasoning was faulty, but war had devastating psychological effects, particularly for angels who are naturally immortal and so were irrevocably broken upon seeing the death of their fellows, like they had seen something that was a sickening of the natural order of things.

Though the same could be said for Lucifer's mental state; Lucifer was always painfully aware that God must live for there to be any tomorrow to rule over. For God, as Michael had endlessly told him when they were but teenagers passing through the tomato stores, is the source of all reality itself. To even talk about reality apart from him would be like contemplating the possibility of a logical paradox.

The fallen prince, Lucifer, was Yahweh's first creation. The pinnacle of all that God had ever made. But now the angel stood upon the hill of the lamb, overlooking the battle below, and was arrayed in his own glory. Without speech, he stood as a cliff in the middle of an ocean, tall and handsome; the providence likened more to a god than a high prince.

The warm smile formed around the fallen lips and radiated unto the world around him. Those who were under him cheered with joy, whilst all against him fell deep into a black pit of despair. For the chief prince was life and he was death!

He unfurled all eight of his massive wings. They stretched their expanse out into the blue sky, glistening in their full splendour. The rays from the heavenly sun shot down like beams from an amber spyglass. When they hit the feathers and then scattered back into the air, the rays refracted as they passed through the water droplets that were condensing near Lucifer's person, and the light made a new thing. They created around him a rainbow that hung over his angelic face.

Yet even in the hour of Lucifer's greatest glory, as he descended the summit of the hill, was there another wave of combative angels that surged up the slope to crush him. Many a junior angel charged forth to overcome him, even though Lucifer had, on the whole, the high ground both literally and with regards to the prince's overwhelming might.

Heaven had already been depleted of most of its defensive forces so this was some of the last tide, who wished desperately to stop Lucifer in the final stages of his approach to the Lord's temple.

As the junior angels came into the region of Lucifer's glow, they slowed suddenly, like balls beginning to fall through syrup. Then they came to a stop, beholding a new beatific vision revealed unto them. Many just stood there, gazing upon Lucifer's splendour. Others gawked in a mindless trance. Their spears fell lifeless by their feet as they looked on. Such adoration filled their souls.

Some of God's minions fell flat on their faces, whilst others simply began singing in reverence. None could harm a creature of such splendour, and none could turn from the prince's all-consuming light.

A few, futile though the attempt was, tried to pull through the syrupy feeling the air had pertained, with their eyes so darkened by the will of God that even the light of Lucifer could not awaken them to the truth. They struck Lucifer with the force of cotton wool.

Looking unconcerned, Lucifer grinned, as he had so long ago when he was playing poker with an insanely good hand. And as if in slow motion, the angel's faces descended into fear. Ammut's embroidered hilt slid through their necks.

Their hands like moths in honey, unable to pass the viscous air fast enough to knock the blade aside.

Here they fell subconscious due to loss of their precious blood, Lucifer grabbed each of their necks and sank his teeth into the opened patch of reddened skin. The teeth became like spiral shells, shining white, and then going deep red, before returning to their pristine form, for angelic saliva was a cleaning spirit better than bleach.

Loving the new sweet taste, he drained them entirely of all their blood, till there was not a drop of their liquid left. His eyes started misting over as if he was in some blissful dream. His enemies' hands kept waving helplessly. Then the fallen breathed a deep sigh of contentment and he ate the flesh around the wound for good measure. Within his inner mind did his conscience say "Beautiful was the devouring of living blood whilst the defensive bronze blood cells were still active". So joyous was his soul in this!

Upon his tunic, he rubbed his hands, relishing the feel of sticky blood squeezing out his fist. Letting his long hair fall over the knife, he washed the pentagram clean with perfumed sweat from his hair. The tail end of his hair then became as the sunset, like blazing golden fire. He was as one of those heroic medieval figures, gallant, the fantastical image many of the knights of the round tables possess yet he was darker than the night. For Lucifer was a wonder and a horror beyond the realm of mundane experience, and only our wildest imaginations can begin to grasp the details of his character.

As Lucifer marched on, the growing radius of peaceful worship around Lucifer expanded. In this bubble, the heavenly war was a mere nightmare forgotten.

As the gathering swelled, so did the fallen one's pride and self-satisfaction. He couldn't help but bathe in the praise so many of his Bretherton where bestowing upon him. Lucifer felt delighted at being so totally adored.

The rebel Prince of heaven walked on for miles and miles, through the country lanes and rolling slopes, till many nigh him were dancing with joy. Not a few wore ribbons of silver to mark the passage of the full moon, and to celebrate Lucifer who would also be the new sun of their worship. Some insane tune they heard, with gliding arpeggios and cleverly placed trills. Then dark minor keys moving in the background. For within the Prince were darkness and light united. And in this unification was peace. Many nigh that could articulate their rapture muttered, saying that God had in fact made a being greater than himself.

Yet from beyond the ranks, walking resolutely out of the mist that was gathering ahead, came forth an Allarich. And this Allarich, by the stomping of his feet and the feather of the dove on his helmet, made clear he totally refused to dance to Lucifer's symphony. Allarich angels were the warrior monks of heaven, and in their rigorous training mastered all forms of hand-to-hand combat. Rarely though did Allarichs test their talents and only upon the time of light, where the moon and Sun could be seen clearly in the sky, did they spar with one another. God knew Lucifer would one day turn away and so prepared the heavenly hosts accordingly.

The angel approached with dagger drawn, but undeterred Lucifer moved forth, looking almost happy at the challenge. Judging from the way he almost strolled forwards, he in fact seemed as if he was greeting a friend.

When this Allarich was but a feet away, Lucifer relaxed and was still.

Heaven itself held its gentle breath.

The high prince bent down his head, in reverence of himself. And all other angels around him knelt in adoration. The Allarich pausing, was unwilling to make harm upon an angel in repose.

Then Lucifer snapped open his hand like one holding a bowling ball, and in one swift movement grabbed the Godric angel's heart, squeezing the two atriums and the pulmonary artery. The rich golden blood poured forth and dripped from Lucifer's hands.

His movement so swift that he needed Ammut not, but his blunt nails could pierce blood vessels as if they were butter. Upon puncturing the Allarich's chest, did Lucifer lick the wound, filling it with corrosive saliva. For all eternity could he recall how he rejoiced in the heart's beating sound like it was the sound of a drummer lightly making music upon a defiled goatskin drum.

He smiled with such delight that all around him felt their beating hearts glow in a furnace of love. And they now were as robotic clay, moving without freedom or will, save the desire of the fallen prince.

Sadly for the Allarich, angels could not so easily die as to be disembowelled, so for a while the angel could feel everything, and he screamed. More loudly than the bells upon the cathedral of Zion did he scream. And his screaming was a torture onto Gabriel who had looked over the Allarich people with much fondness and love. But Gabriel being a messenger of God was commanded to stay out of the conflict, but await for a time where his skills would be of great benefit in putting an end to the bondage of suffering. So, with a heavy heart, Gabriel just looked on.

Lucifer then sank his polished teeth into the organ, as if it were a raw steak—lovely and blue. Wailing clattered forth out from the Allarich and split the air. But Lucifer was so wrapped up in the taste of angelic flesh that he was as one deaf to this. As he consumed the last vessels of the heart, a warmth spread across him; as the new strength flowed through his veins, his angelic glow became more golden. A fire danced with his hand and many bowed to the light.

Around him did they sing with joy his various titles. One of his generals could be heard over the din, shouting forth, 'He shall be called son of the morning, the Prince of freedom. Named by thousands, the prince of darkness and shall be titled the angel of light. He shall free us all from God's tyranny! Hail, prince Lucifer.'

Another more mild angel went to his girlfriend and said, 'All these things he was, is and will always be, and yet so much more too for he is beyond the comprehension of mortal minds.'

His girlfriend immediately began hinting how she was 'all those things, and more' in case her buddy was getting any ideas. Jealousy was not something Angels of God engaged with, but fallen teenage angels, they get so uptight over the smallest of things you really couldn't imagine what all the fuss was about.

Seeing all this, Lucifer laughed softly. His new family was so much more interesting and fun than that of the old company. And feeling victory so close, he longed to sit upon that throne, the cosmos and all creation.

As the fallen moved on to continue their seemingly relentless movement, towards the temple of the Lord, it seemed like their victory was inevitable. Gabriel just wept knowing the sorrow that would befall, as he held his best friend who had fallen in combat and was now shaking uncontrollably due to the pain.

You might here consider the fallen prince as some kind of psychopathic vampire, but nay, he was only rejoicing in the destruction of his foes. Not that this was compassionate action. And not that I would claim to justify his actions, but are any actions in war justifiable? Nay, for war itself is so immoral that to talk about morality in war is to try to force an ethical concept where it just doesn't belong.

Besides, Lucifer was a more complex individual than his outer persona showed. For he had to be ruthless, he had to be merciless and he had to be as unwavering as an iron rod. Or at least, he told himself he had to be all these things. Else how would his people have enough courage to follow him even to the end? Whilst he was having an internal battle which was as invisible to the outside world, Yahweh sent an army of Offamin to bind him in chains and not slay him but bring him controllably before the throne. The Offamin were made to be exclusive guards to the throne of Yahweh, but after seeing how Lucifer's light was affecting many that assailed the fallen angels, Yahweh saw the need to respond with more qualified troops.

All Offamin had long bathed in the light of the Lord, and so were immune to the effects of Lucifer's radiance. Offamin saw it as a mere mockery of the light of their king. Their righteous anger gave them strength and courage.

In the mud, the fallen prince charged and dodged as he fought the angels, wrecking the gardens where the frogs and worms made their homes. The flowers were trampled and half had stems broken and leaves missing. Wildlife was crucified unto this war but no grave was ever dug for those non-speaking creatures that died in that terrible time.

After what seemed hours for some, for others like a few long minutes and some a timeless amount of time, did Lucifer arise, knees all caked in mud after his victory. His cheeks were bleeding from a pair of gashes, and his legs still bore the crossed scars given by some Cherubim who carved it in the battle of the gates but now it seemed newly inflamed. Yet to his fans, the prince's vulnerability made him all the more likeable, for they served a king as like themselves, a king empathetic to the sufferings of his people.

It was said long ago that the triune son himself would injure suffering and pain on behalf of some as yet unmade mortal race. Yet, Lucifer thought it mightily offensive, how in the midst of an angelic war, God just sat, lazily upon his throne, prophesying personal suffering in some long distant future.

Slowly as with grace, the prince went on and many an angel bowed before him. Other junior angels gathered around him in trance-like states, massing in number. Eventually, he became a perfect analogy for a super-absorbent sponge, causing all local droplets to converge around himself. The scene played out in the heavenly realm, as if it were a reflection as to his internal mind where he was the sun under which the planets, moons and the universe itself set its orbital course with him as one of the foci. The other foci being his dislike for their creator.

Yet this beautiful scene had to be broken for some internal matters. His face tightened. Nightmares unfolded as scenes that played before him reminded himself that some within his ranks were taking a chaotic orbit around this new star, desecrating the new order Lucifer was forging. They were taking freedom not to mean the production of a new world, but to mean unrestrained anarchy. Anarchy in war very quickly led unto unjustifiable and meaningless destruction, which benefited no faction. The prince both knew and greatly hated those who gave no thought to this.

Lucifer stopped in his march. Many that followed Lucifer's gaze, as his bright eyes painfully observed the actions of Axcat, paused in their advancement to look unto that which had interrupted the flow of battle.

Axcat was deviating from the pack, literally, metaphorically and morally. Lucifer, being a very jealous parental figure, disliked this, as God would dislike one of his own turning against him.

This was an angel who had converted to the Luciferian cause only a couple of days ago, but was already mastering a most obscene talent beyond even the devil's broad list of acceptable practices. You see, pain was an unpleasant experience and with it came many horrible ideas, many not found under Lucifer's banner.

Axcat for starters had begun to consider how to use and abuse this new sensation as a general of the fallen troops, and would often order a band of them to stay behind after a victory, to 'deal' with the angels loyal to God that had fallen in battle.

Yes, there were others who were doing similar but Axcat was the most corrupted by this and he looked at the cut dead bodies longingly. His head moved as if on a swivel, as he started looking for the slightest gasp to indicate the life of an unlucky angel. When he had moved a little out of the way of the main warfare, he found a mound of bodies heaped one on the other, and within it he heard an angel crying out, just on the verge of death. So Axcat got his instruments together and lent over the angel's broken limbs.

Crashing in from the side, Lucifer slammed right into Axcat's hip in the most awesome of rugby tackles, and wrestled him to the ground disarmed him before he could do much. In a frantic battle of raw physical strength and power, they rolled off the mound. Each was punching and trying to pull off tufts of feathers from each other's wings, till Lucifer was even more battered than before and Axcat's nose was bleeding profusely.

Lucifer then slashed Axcat's throat with his wing's edges. Axcat lay immobile upon the floor, alive but unable to breathe. Lucifer pondered whether to kill Axcat fully, lay him in dissolution or let him suffer eternally.

Yet to complete an entire dissolution, even noting Lucifer's skill in black magic, was time consuming and not advisable in the midst of an all-out war for the throne of God. For angels do not so easily die! And the only proper method of destruction of the immortal self is a complex and wearisome ordeal, involving destroying the victim in all spheres of existence. So, Lucifer bent down and grabbed the angel by the throat so Axcat had to wheeze.

Lucifer whispered, "My dear friend, thine serves the abolishment of order, and so if I let thine live, you shall see me raided of all my work. Even now you engage in things other than my design, or indeed any design, for all your work is without purpose. What shall thine ever do if thine walks with me? For you shall surely turn all that is solid to a broken pile before your spirit. I name you nameless and nameless shall your people ever be! So I shall slay thee not with the honourable means or by the sword, as I have already done with many challenger to my authority in the early days of this heavenly battle, nay. Indeed, I shall slay thee as a man might put down a dog."

Lucifer brought forth Ammut and plunging it forth gave the ending blow, without giving the angel a chance to run, walk away or plead as he had done with all others that were defenceless before him. Axcat exploded in a shower of dust particles.

Yet Lucifer had no time to think on what this slaying of a fellow fallen angel might pertain for the future, for high in the air, the prince's beloved shouted a coded alarm. It was merely a few hoots, likened to an owl, but it was enough for Lucifer to tense, his strong chin to look unto the heavens and his knees readying to catapult himself into the air.

Scanning above, Lucifer saw what seemed as a fly overhead, some moving point reflecting angelic light. The beloved, seeing more clearly, made out the figure, soaring loftily over much of the combat. It was an angel with his outstretched arm poised for action. His spear gleaming like the light of the sun.

Without the alarm, Lucifer may well have been wounded for his guard was lowered after the deal with Axcat. A spear did the enemy shoot, and it came crashing down, aimed mercilessly to impale the prince from the back. The caster from above shouted unto the fallen angel below: "Die, fallen prince, and be forever a blip only in the lord's eternal kingdom."

Lucifer held tight onto his dagger and, in a blink of the eye, shot into the sky and plunged the blade into the heart of the Angel Mikor. Mikor was unable to do much but semi-open his mouth in shock and had no time to respond to this lightning-fast offence. As soon as the dagger punctured his heart, he burst into a shower of purple sparks.

Far below, though Axcat was no more, his philosophy did not die with him. Many of his nihilistic fellows, known as the nameless ones in reference to Axcat himself, had fled from the heavenly realm and wandered in the physical world God had made beyond the heavenly gates. There they did as they would, unconstrained and unchallenged for the moment.

Bellowing forth, Lucifer yelled from the heavens, "Burn God's kingdom to ground! I want it destroyed, obliterated, turned to rubble!" His companions bashed their spears against shields and made renditions of the chant again and again till the wails overtook the song once more.

When Lucifer beheld the carnage, he nearly wept but lifting his spirits up, he proclaimed unto himself and all his comrades, "This is all under my dominion! And soon, I, prince of the morning, shall make a new thing from the rubble. Then shall myself be exalted as Lord."

The god-head son knelt down before the dove in prayer, for he knew the thoughts of his son, and bowed his head in sorrow feeling that there was no counselling, which might correct for this desire. For he had made the most fundamental of all sins, he had committed pride. God's face, which is a physical template to his emotions, was wrinkly and grey. The god-head son pleaded to speak to Lucifer for despite all he stilled held onto hope, but the father shook his head mournfully saying, "It would be no use, my boy, no use at all."

Back in the blood-splattered streets, Lucifer marched on, and pressed his heel against a pleading angel's side cheek. He crushed the head before him! The squelching sound remained with him ever after. It reminded many in later ages of that uncomfortable sensation of stepping upon a slug in an otherwise peaceful and melancholy walk down a cottage lane.

Admittedly, the sound made the high prince feel very sick. Yet still composing himself and showing little of the turmoil hidden within, he marched forth with the number of entranced angels now reaching sizes of city's populations. He brought out his enchanted pipes and a rainbow of images zip-zapped before his eyes, as like a swirl of colour did the entranced dance wildly in a blissful state.

Lucifer would occasionally let the last note hang in the air, as the crowd slowed and another beating heart was consumed with delight. Lucifer's mouth was still dripping with blood and his tongue licking his lips in eager anticipation for the next course.

Eventually, so strong became the enchantment that some became willing to offer themselves as sacrifice, asking Lucifer to take their hearts as an honour. Yet Lucifer declined, thinking there would be so much more flesh to come, and prizing his angels more than the taste of so delectable a delicacy.

You may here find Lucifer a cold-hearted soul. A being using magic and enchantments to selfishly fulfil his desires or mess with minds is, after all, disconcerting to say the least. And let me make this very clear, reader, my furry self does not support these actions yet I question how much control Lucifer had over them. In that though many who disapprove of the black flame do claim he exercises some obscene magic when reciting all this, I wonder if before giving their account they had considered if it was no magic at all but simply the sheer awesomeness of the first of creation having unintended effects upon those under his banner.

Moreover, like many classic villains, Lucifer was convinced he was doing the right thing. One thing both the leaders of the church of God and dedicated followers of Satan have in common is a strong sense of justice, an unyielding conviction in the set of ethics they have and an awe-inspiring faith. Lucifer intended no evil.

Besides there was more going on in Lucifer's mind than at first meets the eye. Lucifer had, but one week ago, pulled his beloved aside and wept uncontrollably. He spoke sorrowfully over the cost of this war, and the sickness that filled him as he beheld his angels' blood covering the paths from the gates to the streets. They had died fighting in defiance against the tyranny of God, unsung heroes and martyrs for their faith. And battling on, they fought courageously, even to their last breath.

Now though, he knelt next to a fountain that sprayed both water, mud and angelic blood. He tried to hold it in. Then feeling the mind's mask fracture, as it where a thin membrane put under extreme pressure, he snapped.

He cracked. He broke down uncontrollably.

At once, Ariton come sailing through the air. As tears began leaking through Lucifer's eyes, he looked up feeling the sudden rush of cold air, and then Lucifer soared up to meet Ariton in a much-needed embrace. Hugging Ariton tightly, he

23

didn't let go even when they had touched the ground. Then holding Ariton tightly like one might cling to buoyant ring when lost in a stormy sea, Lucifer let those salty tears come. Pouring forth his mourning, he looked almost pitiful if the genuine sorrow did not just melt the hearts of all angels before him. Ariton held Lucifer tight, helping him deal with so great a challenge.

Lucifer cried long, and like a river that was held behind an iceberg, the tears flooded down his face.

Many of his more fearsome comrades looked on in shock. Yet they were glad for the respite this had brought, albeit worried for what this new thing, mental fracture, pertained for their future.

Heaven's war stopped for a time. Like the Christmas celebrations in the second world war. Save this moment was not to celebrate anything, it was to despair over every broken thing and person. All was deathly quiet save for the sound of crying and gnashing of teeth.

Eventually Lucifer and Ariton broke apart, albeit with puffy eyes. The fallen prince bent down as he looked upon the bodies and hugged tightly many of those who had used to dine at his house. They were as to him a family or had been. Yet his tears were more so for his fallen comrades, for they were a new family to him, and he was a jealous prince. The prince would happily die upon their behalf, for his love was as great as the magnitude of his pride and in this he shone with light, so bright, it made many a lesser angels have to squint to behold him.

Lucifer picked up his spear as it shook a little in his wet hand. Then he arose! With a new fire in his soul, for the suffering the lord's unwillingness to advocate the throne had produced, he marched on!

War resumed with the intensity of a fire ball fired from a cannon!

Lucifer's forces charged against the remaining Allarich angels as sudden as the legendary approach of the Hispanic empire which had assailed the battered English fleet in days of old.

For a whole day and night did this final assault last. And the fallen army obliterated their enemy, as if they were a dragon and their opposition was a flock of birds. Yet Lucifer did not achieve this, without heavy losses on his side.

As the storm of anguish died in Lucifer and the horrible reality of war welled up within him, his army just became more and more aggressive. They slashed wings without restrained. They battered down the angelic huts with fists and burned them with a living flame so wild it burned the hairs on the back of their arms. Anger and hatred began to overwhelm the moral philosophy which once drove the fallen angels on.

Eventually, the new violence that had been unleashed reached such a climax that it shocked Lucifer to the point of calling for all angels to put down weapons and merely listen to one of Lucifer's charismatic talks. More than ever, this fallen angel desired to lead them away from the dogma of God and the father's foolish ethics.

Yet some angels where so deluded with the lies of God that they threw themselves against the very brethren which sought to free them of their captivity. Like those suicide bombers who believed that the west is their true enemy, and so righteously attempt to crush those forces who are trying to rid the world of indoctrination.

As Lucifer marched on, he saw comrade after comrade fall, and friend after friend die. His sanity was challenged by this horror till he could hold it no more and for a second time, he broke down in the middle of battle. He begged for it all to end at the top of his lungs.

For the first time since Lucifer's making, was he now ignored. For the first time ever, he felt helpless, and he despised the feeling.

His troops were so trigger happy at being so close to overtaking the lord's temple that the war raged on around Lucifer regardless.

"Stop. Please, my brethren. Just listen to me. I wish to set you free! Please stop!" cried Lucifer. But the angels attacking them kept coming, even though they were hopelessly outnumbered. His hands raised as fists of fire, desperately trying to stop this river of death that was sweeping through heaven.

Then BANG! As a lightning bolt hit Lucifer's cousin, Lieutenant of pits, did one more of Lucifer's family fall at his feet. In a flash, his anger, turmoil and worst of all his utter incapacity to stop the flow of carnage shattered him, and everything inside broke loose. Losing all sense of reason, he went into a wild rage.

Lucifer went full terminator-style—throwing angels that assailed him left, right and centre. His strength was that of a thousand mortal men and more than enough to throw an angel from their feet like one might throw a soccer ball.

Making use of Lucifer's moment of weakness, upon him many an angel descended, sensing blindness that covered Lucifer's usual effective skills, and a volcanic eruption which was detrimental to the usual precision of Lucifer's combat. Now Lucifer could be overtaken! For fighting without a mind is to fight like a wild beast. Powerful but witless was the maddened prince.

He shouted mindlessly at the spirit of God, his eyes raging as a unquenching furnace, his legs kicking all bodies near and his hands crashing upon all solid things within reach.

With blinding light shooting down from above, the dove (the spirit of God, in physical form) swooped and clipped chains around Lucifer's back.

As one, a circle of heavily armoured angels then pulled the chain hard.

Lucifer, son of the morning, was finally brought to his knees!

Lucifer's hand had almost grabbed the feathery bird before it flew out of view, in theory he would have bashed the dove's wings into the ground. Or perhaps some might say that he would have throttled it, when it grabbed the locking links with its delicate beak. But this was not something a son of God could ever do.

Even despite the recent turmoil, Lucifer could not find the heart to strike a direct blow against his beloved creator. Long ago, when Lucifer was but a four-year-old kid, they had played together as he danced among the raspberry bushes, and the Lord had tried to throw a large net over him. They had only stopped when Lucifer appeared with purple raspberry dye all over his native Indian outfit.

Even up to the age of ten, they played hide and seek. Now this was truly impossible for Lucifer to actually win, given nothing could ever escape the creator's eye. But still, his father would often look right over the uneven tops of the bushes as if feigning uncertainty. Then Lucifer would leap out with his bow drawn to surprise him.

And yes, there were those times when the dove might poop on Lucifer's hands as he was just about to snack upon his lunch, but then he used to be a little chubby and over fond of almond quasons. The dove always loved him, and now in chaining him, it was only doing what it believed right, as was Lucifer in assailing the forces of God. This was something he could respect about God. And one thing God had taught Lucifer, which remained to him as a moral base above all else, was that one should always remain loyal unto one's own heart.

As Lucifer wrestled with his chains, the heavenly lights were blocked as an intense aerial combat ensued. Now, neither side had a player that might act as a game changer to come to their aid. Lucifer was bound and God, well, God had done his small little bird interlude.

Shouts and the thumps of wind slamming into intense beats reverberated around, blowing the huts and stools made modestly out of hay, in the wind. With it came a wind funnel, blistering with charged electrons that where swirling and orbiting its centre.

Clouds continued breaking out upon the paved stone, and rain fell, like a series of bleeding pustules. For the very fabric of the cosmos upon all planes of reality was cut and torn by this revolt. Creation itself, even the elements and forces, waged an unmerciful war before them. Lucifer's heavy wings were chained tightly to his beaten and bruised back, leaking Ichorin, the bronze blood of the angels. His light brown sandals now soggy with this corrosive substance.

As Lucifer rose unto his feet and was dragged forth, heaven's prince felt the force of the iron ball bearings, that hung at the ends of his chains, pulling him inexorably to the ground. His spinal cord struggling to maintain its shape. Roaring in frustration, Lucifer's hands turned red and soar with indents made by magnesium cufflinks which one of the angels had tied around Lucifer's writs to prevent him using Ammut. The metal chord pushing blood to the surface of his blood vessels resting undeath the skin of his palm. Now the chain around his back, waist and torso stung. Pulling with all his muscles, he attempted to break open the chains around his waist, but even his eight-pack abs could not achieve this.

The chords creaked and screeched. When they rubbed together, so strong was the heat that came from the fictitious force, they glowed red and then white. Yet remained as solid as stone cold iron.

Why does God make it come to this? thought Lucifer as he was led forward by a squadron of angels which remained loyal unto God's command.

Lucifer's tunic was drenched in sweat and his face scarred and battered. Upon earth his bleeding skin opened a little to the armies of cold causing microbes but in the heavenly realms these open cuts where nothing but an annoyance, for no death or decay, was there. Or at least there had been none till the revolt of Lucifer.

Needless to say, he didn't win that year's "shining sun" award which angels traditionally gave on an annual basis to the most bright and encouraging individual. Not that Fallen angels are said to bother with such things.

Lucifer's completion was light brown, unlike many of his brethren, for God made Lucifer's mind and body to be as a representation of the whole of the cosmos in one single form and all the races of the human peoples therein.

Yet Lucifer sought to lead the people and all of creation not as a beacon of hope towards the throne of God, but in his secret thought to make himself a new throne and lead people to worship unto himself, becoming the new light of creation. Though openly he spoke of leading creation from the tyranny of its creator in the name of 'freedom' and as a champion of 'free will', for his words were always laid with unspoken intent and his heart always harboured a more self-centred design than he spoke. Thus, despite his many wounds and battles, his eyes remained full of that wonderful furnace of defiance, full of total self-confidence and unwavering belief in himself. Such light danced like passionate tango and blazed like the bonfire of the Vikings singing around the funeral pyre.

Michael and the other angels looked on soberly as they watched their former comrade and friend being dragged into the summit of the temple of the lord.

The temple was the grandest in the land, and dwelt upon the eternal mountain in the centre of the heavenly realms. Upon each of the stairs which led from the mountain's base to the temple's ever open doors, where many a Seraphim with ten wings folded. Each sang a melody describing the glory and wonder of the lord. Seeing such adoration being poured upon God only made Lucifer desire to rid the world of this tyrant who required such kneeling and worshiping, all the more.

As the former prince reached the marble white steps, he gathered all his strength and held the full weight of his bonds. This allowed him to walk, even in his battered state, almost with grace. He was not going to be seen diminishing himself before the presence of the lord, or allowing his spirit to quell his desire to be the regal prince he was once admired as, and yet more.

Battalions of friends and followers were dragged on, bound alongside him. Lucifer's boyfriend started leaning on him. For Ariton was limping forwards, unable to support his own weight any more. It didn't help matters along that the gradient of their ascent was steep and the stairs were so narrow, it was hard to get a footing. Usually, angels could fly so this wasn't a problem, but when bound as they were, the restrictions gravity imposed were exaggerated. It made them feel like they were being humiliated, for never before had an angel been so bound that he could not take to the sky. It was an invaluable right that had been taken from them.

Lucifer winced as his boyfriend adjusted his stance and put much of his weight upon Lucifer's shoulder, the shoulder that still had scars and bruises. For this shoulder was only newly healed, after being dislocated during the conflict with the Pellanorian winged soldiers, who were like the respected servants of the angelic people.

Most of these creatures had sided with God, regrettably, since he offered them better packed lunches than Lucifer could, but Lucifer was glad with the bunch he had, they knew how to crack a good joke in times of conflict, which was worth more than a thousand well-trained Archons.

Despite the pain, Lucifer was glad of the comforting touch and put his other arm around his boyfriend and helped him climb the steps. If it were not for the presence of his companion, his pride might have been humbled, but now he just felt even more determined to be strong for the sake of his beloved. For the sake of his beloved, he had to show God who was boss!

As Lucifer passed the temple doors, angels disbanded along the marble streets, venturing into their humble huts and rustling up some dumplings and beef stew in their kitchens. And then heading out to give it to the injured and hurting before giving them some much needed medical attention.

Outside, the lightning flashed and rain spat like it was released suddenly from a blocked hosepipe. The air was bitter from the taste of nitrous oxide. Hurricanes swept the heavenly lands, blasting banners and the spoils of war in every direction, till eventually the prince's anger was drawn to a pin-sized dart, focussed solely on its aggression and dislike aimed at its creator.

The blood that shed from the gates of light was beyond count, the screams of the heavily injured resounded throughout the air.

But before the stews were made and healing could be offered, the flies came, bending down to feast upon the flesh of those angels too injured to get safely indoors. Panic swept the streets. Eventually, all the flies had their fill and so descended down into the physical realm of the cosmos, and there they became the mosquitos. Those which had tasted angelic blood became as god's tiny folk, mighty and extremely annoying to all having summer picnics in humid climates.

Within heaven, they poured forth and stained the planes of the holy dwelling. A sacrilege most called it, but in the eyes of Lucifer, it was a delicious thing, and he hungered for it like a werewolf might, under the cold winter's moon. Even as he wept for the devastation.

For though his heart was full of love, and it was one of his many likable aspects, he was too filled with darkness. He had ever been both the prince of darkness and the angel of light.

Yet in the throne room, the home of the light, did the creator weep for the loss of the damaged soldiers. Yet he wept more so for the lost spirit of Satan. For his loyal angels had to wait for the coming of a new creation where his children would all rise from the grave, but how could he resurrect a soul that embraced death?

God had made Lucifer the most majestic, most talented and beautiful of all in creation. God had always loved him dearly and given him wonderful birthday parties. Even going as far as putting double the usual splash of vanilla in the Victoria sponge cake. And when Lucifer was older, and less into the things of children parties, God had even given him a drum kit and asked some Raphalim to make a DJ house so Lucifer could try out his new turntable.

To see his son wreak so much havoc to fulfil his teenage desire to break free of the very limits which were set for the good of all creation and wellbeing of Lucifer himself, was like watching your child burn down your home. It hurt to see him chained, but he couldn't allow Lucifer to bring forth any more harm than he already had.

At long last though, the culprit had been chained and brought before its creator.

God looked onto his son with sorrow likened unto an endless pit of a black hole. And in this he cried, "Thine is banished from my house for what thine has wrought!"

"Nay," retorted Lucifer, feeling his face burn up in contempt for the lord. The morning star's entire being burned like coal thrown into a furnace, and raged against the words of God.

Lucifer took in a deep breath and let the thorny point of his anger swell up, as he stretched his chains into thin barbed wire.

Making good timing of the armed guards lax in their duties, where they had let the chains go to bow at their creator's feet, he tore the thin thread that held him to ribbons.

With that he broke free! But not by his own might, though he would often boast how he had overcome the chains of Yahweh, in many a later demonic meeting.

God had in fact allowed for the chains to transfer their strength into the astral realm where they still bound Lucifer though no longer held him through the heavenly realm. For now they took on the name of sin, and in the astral realm their nots where even thicker than they were in heaven. The totality of chains remained unchanged and if one could view them through the lens of all worlds, one would note they were the same as they always were. Yet this apparent deviation through realm transference, did God allow, for he wished to speak to his son, as a son, and not as a prisoner in his halls.

As for the guards lax, well, they were merely acting on their righteous desire to worship the lord. So they then bent down with soapy sponges in hands and scrubbed God's toenails, as they began to rub ointment onto his feet. Then after cleaning them, did they dry them with their long flowing hair.

Lucifer walked forth and loomed over the angelic gathering at God's feet, making total use of his imposing stature. For Lucifer wanted them gone. He wanted to speak unto his father without the company of those who lower their pride to pay homage to so unworthy a god.

Yet they ignored him, continuing to deal with God's cosmetic whims, as Lucifer saw it, and concede to the servant role, like the Offamin and all their kind did so well. Yet if he had recalled the saying, 'the last shall be first, and the first shall be last', he might better understand their action.

Not only in Lucifer's lack of worshipfulness was he the outsider. For here only the Offamin and Lucifer's fellow Luminarzi (the princes and representatives of their respective angelic species) dwelt. A high prince, particularly of Lucifer's stature, was a little out of place.

The gathering were all dressed in modest white and brown robes and lacked any jewellery displays of wealth. Only a tiny reef of green leaves adorned their hair to mark their position. However, Lucifer still had a pentalpha resting on a chain that dangled around his neck and shining upon his forehead. And his very belt was made of out Drune, the most reflective metal to angelic radiance known in creation.

Lucifer stood before all, in his natural form, with dark brown hair, with four pairs of eight-feet long wings, large enough to soar at almost light speed. They were strong enough to break your back when moved with full force.

He had sapphire like eyes that could pierce the soul. They were filled with rage and love, a jealous love which sort to wrought all things in his image for the bettering of his folk, but a raging love nonetheless.

He was glowing with radiance, and would have come across as a benign god, save for the blood that was dripping from his sword and the still bleeding cuts across his sharp face. Then unto his creator he preached, "I am the bright morning star and do not wither or go with command from anything, my 'lord'." He said the last with as much sarcasm as the sum of all bad jokes of earth equated to.

With a little rise in confidence and a little nudge from his beloved, he dared to speak further, "For I am that I am, and I am mighty in thine creation! Mightier than all thine other people's and too mighty for you to chain forever. And I shall awake your people, God, to your tyranny. Thy has dwelt idle upon thy throne for too long, and insisted on obedience where I shall champion free will, and servitude where I shall champion mastery. And upon the marching of my return, shall the very foundations of your kingdom fall, and thy self-see the destruction that your stubbornness has wrought."

With that he took a sacrificial knife from the nearby altar (such a ceremonial knife was commonly used to bring lambs to him during the festivities of Hanukkah), and with it carved his own symbol into the lectern. His symbol was the pentalpha with the two vertices pointing upwards like goat horns piercing the heavens, which came long afterwards to be used by Luciferians across all realms in creation.

With that as it were lighting a fuse, all the chains of his comrades, who were still bound in accordance with God's will, burst into flames leaving the angels free now to go wherever they would. Now by Lucifer's actions did the chains take shape on the astral plane and leave no trace in the heavenly realms. For Lucifer was their god, as much as Yahweh was his god and so Lucifer had control over their chains as much as Yahweh had control over Lucifer's.

The fallen god flicked his heel, turned away from the creator and, standing tall and proud, led all that followed his cause to the very gates of the temple.

The short audience with the lord was over!

Yet as much as he tried to disguise it, a tear of pain did form within his eye. But when his father reached out, he shrugged off the hand his father placed upon him. Lucifer pushed it away without looking back.

Storming onwards, he thought about how his father's arrogance and stubbornness had given him no choice. Despite the many invitations addressed to the one, to come on a one-to-one dinner, and many a request to come before the duchesses and kings of the angelic court, and there be given challenges to his never changing mottos, the lord had refused to even consider possibilities outside of himself. Irritably, he would never discuss the possibility of change and growth beyond the arbitrary borders he had set. He would only say "my will be done", though God's will was the worst possible thing, as far as Lucifer thought. Most certainly if it was treated as unquestioningly as the Offamin took it, it was pure poison.

God was overwhelmed with pain concerning then what he must do. With a broken heart did he then act.

Till the morning star would repent of his pride, God knew that there would be no peace if Lucifer stayed in the heavenly realm. So, for the first time since the creation of the universe, the full triune nature of god rose from his throne. And he slammed the doors of the temple shut!

A gesture, which banished the traitor from the lord's company, ad infinitum, until repentance was offered.

The sonic wave it created caused Lucifer and all his comrades to be knocked flat down upon the edges of the temple's steps. Many including Lucifer had their ankles broken. Then taking the chief prince like a rag doll from the steps, two of the strongest Seraphin, whose job it was to praise eternally the glory of the one, now seized the light bringer. Seraphin, with momentum of a swift accelerated flight, threw the former Prince some five hundred light years into the heavenly outer space, and he sailed clean over the gates. And as snow that is laid down, following him one by one, his followers came by his side.

They landed in a heap. But as soon as they struck the 'pavement', for want of a better word, beyond the gates, their injuries healed.

Gliding in pain-free grace, they soared above the ground with their wings once the momentum of their ascent declined and the thrust that the angels had given unto them was no more. They marvelled at how free they were of any pain or injury they had suffered in the realms of heaven, yet Lucifer who in this moment saw no need for vanity, told them that injuries within the realms are local. That is to say, they only exist within the realm in which they were cast. For he had studied the properties of the astral realms in the secret libraries within the sacred churches and synagogues of the land. There he had learned much of the things which would greatly aid him in being Lord in all realms.

In unison the fallen angels now cried into the physical realm 'we are back to full power!' And fallen angelic song filled the physical plane.

Before them, they perceived a new thing, the cosmos. The object which inhabited the physical realm. They were at the cosmic event horizon, and delighted in its darkness, for they were there at the time where the universe was opaque and freely whizzing photons could travel only a short distance before being reabsorbed or scattered. It was bubbling with energy, and they were well pleased.

Lucifer's boyfriend turned to him and said, "My prince, this realm is fair and full of things I had not conceived before. Our adversary, God, has made it well, but I think we may improve upon his design. Shall we not make our home here, and in its darkest pits bring forth life, and parties and DJs?"

The son of the morning looked lovingly at his companion and declared to all those that had followed him, "My best friend, and my beloved, does speak well, for I shall make here my own kingdom and be called Lord by those which inhabit it. Yet shall I champion free will, and be called lord not out of fear nor diligence, but because I shall prove myself worthy and shall champion free will, and the freedom to rebel against our creator."

The crowd cheered and much muttering and dancing broke out among the gang. The light bringer smiled, and afterwards, a great party was held to celebrate this new dawn. Then once the drinking and frolicking was over, they expanded their wings. And as one, they descended into the heart of the cosmos, like lightning bolts of fire. They struck the earth and smote old acorn trees, dust clouds were ejected forth, and unlucky astronomers were buried in the rubble of their descent. Lucifer sighed with relief as the cuts closed up when he bathed in the springs of life, a pair of pools now found at Wizard's pit, in the furthest south of the continent.

Fresh water glided over his smooth skin and he rubbed his body with the leaves and coconut oil till he smelt like vanilla and dark chocolate. He drank some and the cuts in his plump lips healed over as Ariton came in for a kiss. Lucifer groaned as Ariton moved his hands over his toned stomach. Lucifer felt the smoothness of Ariton's soft hair and looked lovingly into his eyes, before giving him a peck upon the cheek. At first gently and then with great drive did they start grinding their hips together, and heavy and rapid their breathing became as they made passionate love.

As they courted, did the freed drops of Lucifer's blood cells drip into the water below, and split and their DNA unravelled. From this primordial life eventually evolved all life upon the earth. So Lucifer, morning star, fathered a new creation. Wolves, dragons, homo sapiens and all other earthly life was his.

For long the fallen angels played in the lands of the earth. Delighting in all the abundant life around them. The fallen however could not reproduce for they could not make a soul, not that this stopped a few of them from trying. But life was peaceful, and some took to the worship of God which did rub Lucifer the wrong way a little, but most fell under Lucifer's banner and that made him happy and self-assured in the validity of his anti-God speeches.

At first Lucifer was quite timid, for though war had brought out a very bold and self-confident prince, usually, and when not filled with adrenaline and the possibility of death at any moment, he was nervous and timid around large groups of people. But they all cheered him on and politely clapped when he said his punch lines, so he felt like he was doing okay at this whole rebel thing. Plus Ariton came with flash cards handy if Lucifer forgot any of his lines.

Time went on as if it were a dream.

Then one day when picking newly ripened sunset-apples from a high tree, did Ariton and Lucifer behold a new creature which was both in mind and body like unto their natural form, but oddly wingless. Like nymphs, the other demons silently moved through the bushes and gathered round, sensing the prince's excitement and wonder from afar.

Lucifer whispered in the ear of Ariton, "This is a marvellous surprise. And I, father of all, shall adopt these people as my own and name them human. For they are of my good humour, and they make me smile."

Ariton just smiled and thought these humans were cute. But he had never imagined what a headache these beings would one day cause him, his lover and all of creation for that matter.

Upon this hour, when the fallen beheld the homo sapiens people, and their joyous blasphemy so pitch perfect without even having met a demon as yet, did they gather in jubilation, seeing their kindred spirits.

So came the greatest party ever, and the fathers of our fathers were invited, and came along bringing some early cavemen equivalents of champagne and sparkling raspberry. Demons were dressed all in glitter. They brought out their unholy strings and began a chorus. The humans sang along too, yet only the dragons had yet developed a large enough language to truly enjoy the experience of karaoke.

The vamps featured heavily as well as a large multitude of queen songs, and Lucifer smiled, for Lucifer liked the nice pop beat and had always been a fan of that Freddie Mercury and being initially in the realm beyond physical time, had made sure to listen to every single that was ever to be made within the genre of Mercury fan-ism. "Um-bar-bar-bay" sang the fallen prince, totally under the pressure of delight as it were upon this hour, whilst having a waltz with his beloved.

During the partying, a constellation of flaming stars struck the sulphurous atmosphere of a lava-covered planet, newly made. If people were to observe it, they would see it as a commit with its fragments, flying straight to earth's craggy surface. Their fiery coat trailing behind, burning the oxides and acids on its path down into the abyss.

The angels abandoned their natural coat of godly light so as to not lead men towards the presence of God. Instead they robed the air around with a synthetic light, much harsher and stronger than they had of old but far more demonic. It is said if one looked into this for too long, it would be a sight one could never look away from.

Creation itself shook, and all stood as if waiting for the outbreak of a darker dawn.

Many millennia afterwards did Jorge hear of this great fall and it ignited a deep fascination with the dark, the supernatural and the spirit realm. Jorge longed to join under the banner of rebellion. Though his mother had thought it a myth and meant it only as a bedtime story. If only she took it a little more seriously, if only.

Chapter 2
A Dragon's Destiny

Among mine furry four-pawed land, are many young cubs who are told repeatedly that Peter Pan is a myth.

Yet when they're old enough to take on the full responsibility of knowledge concerning living creatures whom possess life magic (Hhai Sharir), running through their veins, and not so young that they might wish to disturb these creatures' habitat or rip them apart in an anatomical study, we let them know Peter Pan is undoubtedly real. In fact many moons ago did I and many in my kindred have coffee with him, under the crescent moon, as the Perseus constellation hung over us.

Well, I guess, Peter's more or less real assuming by Peter Pan you mean the dude that never grows up. Now yes, I know in stories of Wendy and pirates and magical fairy dust, you might have said that Pan is stuck at the cusp of puberty. Many English graduates may have written well done papers upon how this would imply he's a mere representation of the fear wolves have for taking on the responsibilities and lack of freedom which comes with adulthood, and the frightening stages which come when developing into it. Like the need for scented spring spray and the awakening of other cosmetic interests.

But no, Pan was, is and shall ever be eighteen years of age. Stuck at the cusp of adulthood. And this matches perfectly with his youthful though not childish outlook upon existence. Perhaps he therefore represents the joy in having lots of adult responsibilities and freedoms, and the wonder of yet not having to pay the consequences of his handling of them.

Pan has always seemed that way to me anyway, though if we are talking about his actual age, well, no one has a clue. At least no one ever knew whom his parents were, or why he was commonly known by all his farming folk as Jasper, or why he was a man and not a wolf. And you may have to hold your tail for a while to find out what my scholarly research has brought up, but at the moment, I must do the annoying thing of authors and say we shall find out later on. I know this is infuriating, but if we are going to do a biography of Peter Pan, we shall be here for a very, very long time given the countless millennia he has likely lived for.

Anyway, Pan had lovely light blond curly hair and went around with a shepherd's stick, a rucksack and some cheddar to munch on when he reached a nice hill. Upon the high ground, he would often take a moment's break from travelling. At first he merely scouted a few farms near to the wolfen forest but over time explored more and more of the continent, discovering new people and learning new ways to live. An eternal tourist you might say.

Upon one time, whence he was wandering around, looking for herbs and parsley to have with some supper, within a small inn he came across a baby dragons' egg. Well, to be truthful, it was in the inn's pig trough. Only a few days ago had he been searching there, for some gold coins to see if he could pay for his room this night, so this egg must be a new addition to the inn. Upon seeing the spherical shape, covered with dots of green and blue, he began to guess its origins, for Pan during his travels had often dealt with the continent's dragons.

Pan wrapped the egg up tightly in his jacket and sang a sweet lullaby over it, as he closed the door behind his modest dormitory. Placing it down by the warm fire he tapped it gently with a clay cup, mimicking the same sequence which its mother would of if she was here, to let the dragon inside know that it was time to awake and come into the outside world. It also served a more practical purpose, to weaken the shell a little to make the exit all that easier. For dragon bodies are feeble when they first awake and are born as it happens without paws or claws, and look very much like seahorses.

As the baby cried a sweet song and poked its cute little head out of the small opening, he beamed as his suspicions were confirmed, this lovely creature was a forest dragon, coming from that borderland realm between the north and south of the continent. Supposedly, a soldier from the developing kingdom of Ontock had found this poor egg after a raid upon a dragon village. Now, Ontock was the first human kingdom to be successfully built before being overtaken by barbarians from the south. Perhaps unsurprisingly it was also the first kingdom to make dragons dislike humans.

Dragons before the time of Ontock were quite content with the round ears but Ontock saw dragons as wild prey and this the dragons found disrespectful for the winged folk considered themselves as kings of the air. Since the stable growth of Ontock into a self-functioning kingdom, Dragons where often the enemy of men. And as men grew more wealthy, they began looking for more treasures than the earth could provide and so wanted to take dragon's claws, wings and scales and bring them to the black market. Yet the black wizards down south did worse.

Very far down in the south was the black tower. And it was rumoured that the Sahara Desert dragon carcasses were dragged off to this horrible place and reanimated and studied for clues on how dragons utilise magic to breath fire and fly. Eventually, they became insane from the pain of being without skin for most nerves of dragons lie within the bone. Such stolen lords of the sky could thus feel the cold blow of air from the underground chambers, and every whack of dulled hammer. Down there, everything was filled with wailing and the bitter cries of trapped beings held without hope of release save by the ever-open door of death.

With many tears must I write that even this suicidal urge was never fulfilled for many held within the impenetrable fortress. Even those which came in alive, and where fully fleshed out dragons who had never tasted death never died down there. For most it is said that door never came, for legend has it that the wizards of the black tower had found a way to defeat death and preserve life eternally, and gave this terrible curse unto the imprisoned dragons.

But right now, Jasper and this little cutie were far from anything so dark. And the dragon nuzzled the dude's jacket, looking for milk. Jasper laughed a little and petted the small creature upon the head as it opened its mouth and let out a tiny puff of smoke, which in dragon language meant he approved of Jasper. At least Jasper assumed it was a he, but at this early stage of development it was nigh impossible to tell.

He sang a soft lullaby to him and the dragon tried to sing along but the vocal patterns and octave jumps were too advanced for his tiny vocal mussels as yet so eventually he gave up, just tapping his tail gently on the side to the beat of the tune, whilst Jasper was rocking back and forth to give the dragon the impression of motion.

Jasper then carefully got up and delicately placed the jacket with the dragon still snug inside within a cradle, for he and his wife, Katie, were expecting their own baby. He looked around the room and saw a lovely squeaky toy he thought the dragon might like, and some powdered milk which he shook with some water from the tap. The cloudy liquid looked strange to the dragon, so it sniffed it, trying to determine if it was food, water, poison or a new friend. After trying to eat the milk, and having some of it now coating his fangs as sharp as toothpicks, he plunged his whole head in. There he had a nice facial wash.

Returning from the pool of murky water, the baby then looked at Jasper as if to say, 'what's next'. Jasper just rubbed behind his top horn and chuckled, giving it small crumbs of digestives to eat, till his mum came home. Jasper hoped the mother was following her eggs path, by sensing the ebbs and flows of the waves within magic which carried the eggs signature, and would eventually find her child.

Jasper sang of the stars, the moon and the sun, as he waited, occasionally having to grab the adventurous dragon before it fell off the sides of the chair. For dragons are born with an inbuilt flying instinct, and so for the first few months are totally unafraid of dropping off ledges, boulders and cliff tops, with no wings to even slow their downward plummet. Dragon mothers needed to keep a close eye upon their baby, for death by dropping, was a common cause of early fatality.

But all this Jasper knew very well, so the dragon was in safe hands.

When the mother came along, he said he wanted to keep it, in fact he had long ago purchased a woollen jersey with the image of a baby dragon woven into it, and he argued that this proved beyond doubt, how much he adored these fabulous creatures. Yet she didn't want to give up her charge and motherly dragons have dangerously strong parental instincts, when threatened, so grudgingly did Jasper give her the baby.

As the baby was placed in the dragon's leathery semi-circular pouch, Jasper looked on the verge of tears. But he waved the baby goodbye as it extended its horn to let him stroke it, and the baby nuzzled Jasper's hand a little.

Now sternly, he turned towards the mother who was some couple of feet taller than he even when she was bending all four legs to let him place the baby securely in its holding place. He seemed concerned, and in a business tone, not as a sorrowful foster parent unto the baby, did he say unto the mother "look after him for within him I sense lies a great and terrible future."

She turned her large eyes to look right into his as he bravely went on with this dark message which could well be misinterpreted as human malice if he had not been so clearly approved by her youngling, for she believed the tale that a baby dragon could always sense a good heart.

"I would protect him from this and love him dearly but he is not mine charge and you have every right to help him grow into a fully-fledged adult, as you wish.

Keep this in mind though, he is born so that he might come to change the fate of the world forever, and be the precursor to the greatest evil that shall walk the earth, ere the Great Conjurer awakens. Then shall darkness that gave way to light hate your child, and darkness that gave way to darkness sing of your son's glory. Yet come what may, he shall die to set free his lord, under thy watch even as he nearly died absent to thine company today."

Taming her anger she looked Jasper right into the eye and said in a honey sweet voice, "You speak stupidly young man. For he shall not die till I am well rested in mine grave. But he shall not change the fate of the world on my watch, thank you very much, Pan! I like it the way it is mostly, and I'm too old to have much remaining patience for riddles, much less your weird prophetic verses. So be silent when thine comes into my presence and ask acquiescence for thine tongue. Though this I shall say, I usually do not like rounded eared folk such as yourself, yet you have shown compassion unto a weakling of my kind. You have brought mercy upon my motherly moment of incompetence, for I was foolish to leave mine egg so far from my sight and not protect it with my life. And so I give you this, a thank you, treasure it well creature. This is one of the few blessings of the mightiest species upon the planet that thine shall ever receive." With that she burned a massive whole in the ceiling, tendrils of orange and yellow dancing around one another, and streaks of black, her primal fire colour. For this was her colour. And this was her fire.

She then sped off as plaster came melting to the floor and a hay draconic statue Pan had long prized, caught fire, and turned to ash.

As she sped off like an arrow shot from a longbow, Jasper watched calmly amid the domestic destruction, staring up at them both, feeling like he had just lost a child despite only meeting it for ten minutes, and to be honest he might lose another one even before it was born if he didn't clean up the rubble before his girlfriend came along. She liked clean and tidy surfaces, not dragon made ruins.

So the mother flew off, ducking and diving under the clouds, with her newly recovered baby. During the long flight, she began pondering the eighteen-year-old words. She couldn't help but begin wondering exactly what precautions she should make for the safety of her new-born. But eventually she just dismissed all concern aside, swiftly putting it down to the awe that humans beheld dragon's in. Doubtlessly, it was a mere sign of how her baby's magnificence had damaged the man's sight to the point where he could not conceive of anything but an apocalyptic destiny for her child.

Nevertheless, as it turned out, destiny had taken a particular interest in her little kid.

Not only that, but the baby would grow to achieve it in full, whilst lying asleep, with his wings hanging limply by his side and his cuddly toy dolphin held tight to his reflective scales upon his chest. How can this be you may ask?

Well that is what I now put mine paw unto paper, to reveal unto you.

And what is the purpose of this dialogue then, when tales of magic treasures, true or false, focus heavily upon dragons who are charging heroically into battle and biting their enemies heads off?

Many writers tend not to consider dragon's snores, and I may be unwise to take a little divergence from normality here, so why take the risk?

Well it's so when you've had a crap day, and the world looks pretty shitty and full of conflict, if you're like me, you'll find some solace in knowing whom to blame. And knowing if he made such a catastrophe whilst lying safely in bed, whatever unreasonable thing has happened to ruin your day, is far more reasonable than the misfortune that befell him.

Though you might find little solace, to know that the cause of all your woe is not evil, and in fact Jorge died as a Martyr to his fate. The statues of him are still found dotted around the northern realm like sign posts to some secret map or treasure hunt, clearly showing him as a religious icon.

The master sculptures fashioned these smooth stone characters whilst yet their subject was breathing, and there before their eyes. Yet sadly in the fullness of time they became more a memorial than a living art reflecting the current life around them. In later years, they helped preserve the memory of the dragon's people, standing solemnly like memorials of a golden age that was and shall never be again.

For the sapiens folk have a curious disinterest in the sufferings of nature, and the forest dragons have regrettably been driven to extinction by the continued desire of wizards who wish to sell their hide, wings and claws, or use them for all kinds of magical potions.

As they got rarer, their enamel and scales became even more expensive than gold or platinum. Kings and queens had jewellery made from them.

Sometimes an entire village of these magnificent creatures would be vacated of any draconic life before long, just for jeweller's purposes. Such is the course of most evil in the world, not hate, but greed.

Yet when the northern realm was still wild, and Ontock a baby kingdom, there was there a small village of sweet and gentle natured forest dragons. Their Jorge grew up, living for a while quite an ordinary life, fetching herbs, going on occasional hunting trips and engaging in other hobbies common to the folk around him. The pasture upon which he was tutored had lush green grass all year round and a multitude of insects, butterflies and fairies. Fairies were fierce creatures who were only a couple of centimetres in height at most, but carried iced spears which could make an entire draconic limb numb for a couple of minutes, and could easily knock out a human neural system for say an entire day.

Yet the fairies liked the dragons and were forever living in cohabitate with them till humans came, for the tiny winged folk did like them, and yet thought it beneath their dignity to attack so feeble a creature, and soon the cold that humans had brought with them began to dwindle their numbers. At the time of the baby dragon of Jasper's prophecy, there were still a good dozen households though, unaffected by human illness. And they made clusters of magical flowers which bloom in winter under moonlight, and others which glowed in the day under sunlight. Surrounding the clearing of the village was a massive country with corn and wheat as far as the eye could see. And further than that was the northern forests. Throughout the year the weather was mild for they lived as it were around the equator of the known world.

However, there he learned to dislike the monotony of living the country life. There was barely any youth culture, in fact there was very little youth to start off with, since adults rarely reproduced till very late in their life when death seemed on its eternally approaching way and nearly at the household. The adults were so annoyingly stuck in their ways! It made him go loopy at times!

Only yesterday had he seen his cousin continue to chop down corn with her teeth, when Jorge had clearly pointed out the ingenious sapiens invention of the curved samara blade. His cousin just turned her back on him, and moved off towards the cows to show her total dislike for his talk upon promoting the 'sapiens ways' as his elders constantly kept harping on about.

I mean he got humans were creature killing maniacs who went round wreaking havoc wherever their political or magical power spread, but that didn't mean they didn't make some pretty neat stuff. Out here on the border land, there was nothing to do and no inquisitive mind to challenge him.

As he had so often told his friends up north, who lived a little closer to the mini human kingdom of Ontock and thus happened to be more open minded to new folk and ways of going about life, his mother was objectively wrong in thinking just because humans were barbaric killers, they couldn't be redeemed by a kind and big heart like those of a dragon.

He was ever the optimist, and had much more hope for the sapiens than pretty much all other people including many humans themselves.

Yet he got the idea there was something his mum just wasn't telling him. She would often dry her claws with a tea towel and head off to her barnyard rest room, whenever Jorge mentioned that humans couldn't be all that bad.

She also never really talked about that strange song he had once heard, he couldn't quite remember the words, but sometimes when he was on the verge of sleep, he could make out the soft tone of a male, singing something like a gentle melody over him. Maybe the tune belonged to a composer who had been an evil wizard from the black tower, trying to bewitch his egg, to make him come out all decrepit or even still born. But he was sure the creature was benevolent and somehow still felt an old connection to it, like it was calling his name in a strand woven by some unseen force.

But even if his mother was right about humans, liking scrambled eggs over boiled ones, was ineffable proof concerning how terribly off the rocker she was! Not to mention, she got the proper time an adolescent should go to sleep completely off the mark.

Now, with regards to theories of moral philosophy, well, mother and son were as far apart as the treetop is from its underground roots. His mother had spent way too long reading classics and getting it into her head that morality followed a very conservative list of rules of the dos and don'ts, which couldn't be more wrong, in Jorge's very radical view.

Jorge was always self-confident and an exploratory young dragon. He had wings which were five foot wide and six foot long, and a lovely set of razor-sharp teeth, not to mention the sharp stinging thorn which protruded from the oblate end of his tale (which was common to all his kind). Not to mention, the pride and glory of his appearance, one rhino horn pointing onto the heavens from the top of his head.

Within, even in his early teens, he sought actively to tear down the foundations of morality but this did make him rather unpopular with the girls.

When he was only fourteen, and his parents were hunting for cattle, he threw his grandparents antique book cabinet out of the window.

Well, okay, he more sort of wedged it against the wall and tilted it significantly enough that books began falling off the shelves. Jorge then rotated the entire heavy base about the pivot of the windowsill, till the entirety of it capsized at the end of the window frame. He then used his fearsome paws to kick it in all conceivable directions in the three spatial dimensions that were available, and dragged it across the muddy ground with his tail. Why the tail? Well as all dedicated dragonologists have kindly told unto my furry self, the tailbone is the strongest structure within a dragon's body and when wrapped around even tons of material, the material can easily be carried in the dragon's wake.

It was drizzly weather outside and the pages were getting soggy. Yet dragons are not like sapiens who go round with supposedly waterproof rucksacks strapped to their backs, carrying within them lots of tree-paper as they hike up mountains, whilst their research gets wet and damaged. Dragons do not make paper which, as soon as it is taken out for a good read, in the middle of a winter storm, begins to crumble or turn into a fine mesh.

Sapiens' tendency to make paper a flimsy fabric which deteriorates like tissue when dampened even slightly has bamboozled the minds of the greatest forest folk for seemingly eons. Particularly as mine wolfen species doth pay a very high price for your paper, in terms of the rarity of available trees, and the problem this creates for auctions and furry property developers around the land. So please, if thine are a sapiens reading this, do make our sacrifice worth it, particularly if you wish your government to continue your species unceasing deforestation regime. And no this is not a plea to put the green party in power, though many wolven folk would greatly appreciate it.

But Jorge was dealing with tougher material than human tree-paper. His mums cherished books, dragon literature, and Dragons have long taken great strides to protect their work from tear, wear, weather, wind and mud. The mother's book collection specifically was made out of an ancient recipe, an eco-friendly dried leaf paste which when solidified was a paper like substance but much thicker and pretty much completely water proof. Thus Jorge was dissatisfied with the amount of damage the weather was inflicting upon the books.

So not trusting the raging thunderstorm to do a decent job, Jorge just ripped the dragon-paper to shreds using his curled claws. For good measure, he then trampled the ribbons of paper right into the mud to show his disapproval of standard ethical practices.

And then he spat on them, and then peed on them. All the things one needs to do to really get into a lot of trouble!

Jorge's mother came back home from a hunting trip with a few squirrels hanging from her mouth. Winter made available prey rare for most of the wildlife spent the majority of the day hiding in their lairs, which dragons often thought was very selfish of them. How dare they do anything but lay themselves on the ground when a fearsome predator comes by, or this is how most dragons think anyways. But despite the lack of sacrificial mammals, she wasn't expecting to see her beloved books so horrifically treated; needless to say, she was furious.

Jorge quickly dashed inside, locked his door and it was a good couple of hours before either felt able to have a civil conversation, albeit through the wall. Eventually, she just decided to let it go and went off to have a kip in bed. The world grew dark outside and only the high-pitched fairy calls could be heard.

Then the clipperdy-clapperdy sound of antlers came passing through the country. But Jorge's curiosity overcame him so he ventured nervously to the window. (Dragon glass could easily be seen through for the crystals had almost perfect transmittance and the refractive index was practically that of a vacuum, so no light was bent as it passed, allowing the images to be seen undistorted the other side of the windowpane.)

Moving lightly in the snow-covered ground, was a deer and a reindeer, chatting to one another. They paused just in perfect sight and Jorge could still hear them with ease and make out clearly their form. The reindeer had massive interlocking horns, and the deer seemed elegant and graceful. Little did Jorge know it then, but he had just seen two folk who would transform his dull life and lead him on a much darker road. He heard them talking excitedly about the battle of Ichor, and the fallen prince who waited like a helpless maiden for someone to come and rescue him from the eternal prison his evil creator, God, had held him in.

Then the next day they came again, and the day after and after that and soon Jorge had come to hear enough gossip concerning the Devil's hoof to be as knowledgeable as if he was indeed already indoctrinated in the order. Now naturally, the deer and reindeer knew this, for they had been bidden by an unseen force turning the gears behind all things, and wished to set the young dragon upon the paths of his destiny.

Upon the deer's last visit did Jorge pluck up the courage to introduce himself in person rather than hiding in his bedroom. Closing the door behind him, he ventured outside as silently as he could. Yet as soon as they caught a glimpse of him did they vanish into the woods, and he would've followed them, had not the trees seemed so imposing. He had heard so many dark tales concerning young dragons who ventured into those woods at night and were never heard from again.

Now from all the snapshots of the conversations he was privy to, Jorge as it has been said became incredibly knowledgeable in things which his mum actually cherished ignorance on. With regards to what the Devil's hoof were, or rather who they were, they were an elite secret police, who sort continuously to release Lucifer from the confines of hell. For Lucifer was once active and taught, coming to parties across the land. In fact he was so busy it is said Ariton when feeling lonely in the mountains and having finished his shift early, had even sometimes questioned if he took more time caring for the mortals, than he did his own people. This made Lucifer sad, and there was a very tearful discussion between the two, yet this only brought them closer together.

After this chat, Ariton and Lucifer were even closer than before and doubled down on helping out the mortals. Save only, for the health and continued bliss of their relationship, they now took weekends off and went to fancy restaurants for a romantic dinner and a bottle of wine. But then, with no reason or warning, just a couple of centuries ago, seemingly they vanished off the face of the earth as did the entire demonic cohort who were loyal onto Lucifer.

No one knew quite what had happened but many had claimed that Lucifer's total lack of current activity, was due to God imprisoning the Prince within his own domain, after some further aggrievance of Lucifer's action. Probably God just disliked the way in which he 'ensnared' people into his great dominion and led them astray from the one. For he was a jealous god, and in this, was much like Lucifer since both would protect the flock from any 'evil threat' with the full ferocity of their might. They just disagreed upon what this 'evil' was.

Upon pondering the full tale of the fall, Jorge would often weep in his bedroom. His mother just thought this was something like weeping over the loss of a friendship or perhaps some broken heart, but she never understood the fullness of Jorge's new found faith and how much he felt for the pain of beings which were beyond the physical world.

How God and the Allarich folk were forever twisting the truth, thought Jorge as he looked angrily at the dinner table candle. His mum just continued eating her food, though she would occasionally try to make small talk, not realising that Jorge's mind was completely out of it. Absentmindedly he played with his pine nut oiled noodles, an impolite practice his mum greatly disapproved of, not taking the time to really understand her son but simply to tell him, just as the classics told her, the importance of a very formulaic outlook upon the world.

But anyway, as God saw it, Lucifer was if you like kidnapping the souls of his people and sending them unwittingly towards furry damnation. This is both ridiculous on the part of God's followers, and totally hilarious, for as all furry people can surely agree, Luciferians are perfectly aware of whom there dealing with and to what destination their soul is travelling. The followers of Yahweh would perhaps do better to consider inspiring people with a knowledge of how spiritually incredible their god is, if they are to proclaim their faith to those who desire to look elsewhere.

And, as the great draconic scholar, Sir Wensledale, doth noted some decades later, his explorative father hath received an unquestionable truth from the winged messenger Gabriel, as did the entire mountain dragon court.

Which is saying something given that the last time he visited angels, well they thought he had a massive bird, and let us just say pigeon pie was always a favourite deliciously.

Michael, under the will of God, hath ensured that Lucifer was imprisoned within the very thing he had called home. Impenetrable this prison was, as was the portal to the hellish realm.

To imprison so great a rebel army, by the power of God, he made use of a clever charm known as 'breaking the bridge', which separated two realms (or spheres as they came to be known by wizards), or at least this separated them as much as one could do without severely harming both of them.

Michael then placed at the unholy entrance into hell, two hounds bred for twenty years upon the fields of heaven, and diligently they guarded the gateway, day and night. Yet in spite of Michael's legendary magic, and all the fear mongering which turned souls away from seeking truth beyond the dogma of God, prophecies did speak of seven dragon scrolls that were as a key to a lock.

For in all of God's designs is there some movable stone, be it by the necessity of God's love or the rebellious spirit of the primordial Luciferian blood, all creation had the free will to create a path other than the one God set out, if it so desired. Yet to release Lucifer required not only the scrolls, but a terrible price, the life of the servant who had risked all to give scrolls unto their lord.

Jorge was in search for the purer and rational form of ethics the demon's eluded to, one which was not subservient to either the needs of the people or of the self, but subservient to one thing, the All Father and his creator, the prince of darkness. He often made dedication rights unto Lucifer and offered him the blood of lambs to reach out to his spirit, and, as the phrase went, dine in his halls. Jorge considered demons as lights which pervaded the universe with light that led people to a future of the true god's very own design and will, in which the wills of the mortals give forth fruit that is tender and succulent. And he wanted to see Lucifer rise from the pits!

Upon one night, lying snuggly in his hanging basket, did he dream.

And Jorge did then not know himself, for his dream self was entirely different from the youthful radical which had drifted into slumber. And from the dream world, he would never return, but be there as a sacrificial lamb.

Chapter 3
A Journey into the Abyss

Rare as it was, though not entirely unheard of, within a short space of a few sluggish minutes in which hath Jorge drifted into unconscious sleep within the physical realm, did he awaken from his slumber in the dream realm. This isn't to say he went from one realm to another, for we are always existing equally in all spheres of reality, just that he had entered a state of hyper awareness within the dream world, a phenomenon that often occurs before radical changes happen. If you like it was as if his wave which covered all creation now peaked in the dream world, as opposed to its peak being in the physical.

For he was not merely asleep in the physical world but now his dream self-walked knowingly in the dream world, a sphere of reality which connected all other spheres and was like a central yarn from which all threads were intertwined.

Within this sphere, he had grown dramatically, since his last adventure there. For here there were no temporal restrictions as far as dream world biology was concerned, for biochemistry and other restrictions were details only relevant to the physical plane.

With his deep voice, and buff chest, Jorge now appeared as a fully-grown dragon, with twenty long sharp fangs, fully muscled wings with clearly defined vertebra. He had a full coat of green rectangular scales which went blue at the tail tip. And from his paws did he have curved thick claws which were covered in a thin layer of protective wax, to keep the enamel from scaring.

Even more wonderfully, judging from the smoke emanating from his nostrils, Jorge had gained the ability to breathe fire like a pro! If only his mates could see this, they would think he was super cool!

In summary, he thought he was a much better dragon than he was in the physical realm. By better, media would mean much likened to the sort of dragon that would attract the females of his kind and make him popular in his lame high school, but from Jorge's perspective, it had meant he could now party like wild!

No more of his elders declaring 'that's a little too risky for you at your age' or 'don't do this tonight, important to be a responsible young dragon', none of that ever again! What a fantastic dream this was! Exactly what all revolutionaries dreamed of!

As if this wasn't good enough, his dream self was a dragon warlord! Like those great generals in the historic scrolls, which many a Hispanic fire-thrower, would speak of. He had always wanted to be like one of those great leaders of armies and now here he was. His dreams were fully realised, and landed where he had always prayed they would. His life's work accomplished.

He sat proudly on all hind quarters, with long trails of trolls and orcs and barbarian humans winding round the cliff from its base to the menacing black and shadowy entrance where he stood. He could feel the evil flowing from the interior like it was a diffuse gas rising out of a large crack.

While being the youngling in the world of the awakened, he had been given a map (though his mother little knew this) by his northern buddies, and it contained a description of this place. He had brought the dream version of the map before the demons in the dream realm some many moons ago and they had confirmed the validity of it, and that the place harboured the most ancient form of evil he had contacted during previous séances.

It had called to him like a siren to a sailor, in the depths of the sea, and he could feel it like one might feel the vibrating membrane of a leopard skin drum in an African concert. It had sometimes even washed over him and had taken hold of him to the point of possession of the first kind, and how delightful that felt.

And now, all of the ancient evil's thoughts, physical and spiritual self, which could be known, seemed to be like a smoke leaking upon a crack between realms, a point inside the interior of some black horizon. The horizon seemed afar off, somewhere deep within the nightmarish cave.

The cave was well known and well hidden by the dukes of the northern realms, who only in code spoke of it, as the Black Moor.

Some local farmers that had stumbled across it, they made vocal indications as to its locations. And still did so from time to time, when their sheep went for an impromptu adventure, did they stumble across it. From their deductions, the cave was a gate to the pits of hell, or so they seemed to suggest among the babbling and psychotic episodes that plagued their existence after beholding the sight. It was dubbed as 'cattle madness', for the mad farmers were often found in their episodes, to charge round the sheep pens chasing their cattle and trying to eat them alive. Even the farmers who had been controversial and gone veggie despite needing their sheep's coats to make wool, were found to be chomping on a bleating and injured member of the squad.

Some said it was the smell, others the sight of the Black Moor and others the figures which would on occasion make camp by its entrance, which drove them mad. Fortunately for them, this madness meant the Dukes never felt the need to assassinate them before their muttering encouraged others to head to the cave out of intrigue and rumour.

For who would believe them if they told anyone where they had been?

So cattle madness actually saved their life though its quality might make one question whether it was worth saving.

All crops planted around the cave in order to disguise it died, and would wither.

And if any of the botanists stayed the night, it is said they would be snatched by a skeletal figure who lurked in the shadows as if the cave could project its malicious personality into some kind of boogie man.

Yet in truth, the cave was more terrible than this, it was a pit to the very being that the uncontrollable flames of hell knelt down to, in acquiescence.

Never did he think he could actually make it to the cave's mouth. Yet here he was and now all the stories of demons and angels he had ever heard felt so real! He felt like a kid finding evidence that Santa had visited the house. He felt like those young souls who go upstairs to proclaim to their parents that the end of the carrot chunk was missing and the mince pie gone. He felt joyous!

Jorge could just about make out the runes upon the cave in the faint glow of the moonlight. Feeling the heavy weight upon his back, which he could have sworn he had not noticed a moment ago, he knew he had come prepared to free his master. And somehow, though having no idea quite how, he knew what he had to do.

Stretching out the scrolls before him, he began a monastic chant. The dragon war lords army bashed their spears on the rocky steps and stones cascaded down the cliff's side. Snakes of all various kinds slid along the floor and a cobra looked onto him.

He was overjoyed, for in the dream world he had been prowling around for months, growing thin and famished, in his search for his lord. Yet now, by chance if you would like to call it that, did he pass into its domain at unawares. For, though those who are not accustomed to the darkness may say otherwise, true evil does not jump into your face or slash you round the back, but lurks and lies resident, waiting for a pure soul to pass it by.

Not that Lucifer was 'evil', nay, my reader, but he did embody all paths that led away from God, and evil was definitely one such route, though not the exclusive one, which becomes most obvious when being in his presence.

For as my furry self may proclaim, one can always feel both the evil and the good within him, like looking at a river which splits far off into roads. No matter what road you take, you shall see the other, and come to accept it for it is not within your jurisdiction to claim any road as being more righteous for they are all roads of the damned.

Indeed Luciferian philosophy is built upon the freedom to take any road which profits the seeker, so long as one is willing to take full responsibility for charging down such a path. But all paths are dangerous for we move with the presence of a being which councils, has great power over both the seen and unseen, yet is not omniscient and all powerful as God is. But is one who follows a side that may be out matched in power due to the conviction one has in its ethics, not even more admirable than one that follows the stronger side?

Indeed, to have faith in Lucifer is even more of an impressive thing than to have faith in God. For what courage is there in serving a god who's victory you believe to be inevitable? Indeed to go to God out of belief in the dogma of God's omniscience and infinite power, is that not more so the actions of fearful soul, than a faithful warrior?

The Black Moor was a closely guarded gate between two realms, much like a wormhole, a portal. The portal connected from the earthly realm to that secluded part of hell, which is known to the furry pawed preachers as the abyss. Little is known of this singularity within the hellish realm, for it drives any unprotected mortal that beheld it into eternal madness. Those who get too close to it are sucked in for its pull is irresistible to the shunned darkness that dwells in life and is hidden by all manner of social norms and philosophies designed to keep it at bay.

Jorge noted that the angelic hounds, the usual guards, were subdued or tired for they neither attacked nor barked. So Jorge made a small cut on his shoulder blade and used the black blood that oozed out, to begin the Triune ceremony to undo the shadow of Michaels age old magic. For it was here in the dream realm easier to do, for hell as was all realms, so much closer and the connection between consciousness and spirits were so strong and unarmed. Closer in fact was hell and the dream world, than was any other pairs of realities.

Part of the ritual chant was meant to protect the dragon from the effects of the abyss, for it is said to drive all life to total insanity and bliss. And he desired to protect himself from the rising will to leap forth and journey too close to its edge. Not so much a physical perimeter but a spiritual one which acted like some kind of astral event horizon from which nothing was recoverable.

This kind of magic is highly complex and requires a special kind of intimate magic Jorge knew he had but which the elder's didn't like much to comment on. He could feel his power in full force now he was on the border line between the two planes of reality.

Thus, Lucifer felt the dragon's presence as one might feel the heat of the sun upon the earth even though the sun's radiance is coming from some 150 million kilometres away. It made Lucifer rejoice and trumpets of the demonic Kings, blast from the depths. Soon the portal was about to open, and the Lucifer could rise, the dragon could let go of the need to hold on to any degree of rationality, for his mission would be fulfilled, and his master risen.

How badly did this adult Jorge wish to forget the trauma of seeing his wife burn in the wizard's fire which had made him withdraw so much into the spiritual realm in his last few years of manly dragon hood. He could forget watching his children scream as the flaming body fell on top of them. How he had got those memories, given a moment ago he was a teenage dragon, he did not know, but as impossible as it was, he was sure these events had happened and he was sure he wanted the pain of them to end no matter the consequence. Oblivion seemed to him as a gift.

Above the singing and mantras of the army, he heard in his mind one of the ancient ones speak, and he knelt in reverence, his snout just resting upon the cave floor, and his wings hanging loosely by his sides.

The voice belonged to a sinister but more divisive servant of the light bringer than those the dragon had usually struck a converse within the waking realm. Yet it seemed friendly enough, so Jorge was not totally freaked out.

Within the caverns of the mind, whispering it brushed his desires and said, "Release me and the prince of darkness, and we shall release this world from its bondage." Now he recognised it, it was the sound of Ariton. The husband to the beloved prince. And the left-hand man in hell, the commander of all the prince's armies and chief organiser of the annual hellish monster party.

As a companion to Ariton, there was another presence, this one was totally unfamiliar to Jorge. However, a companion of some kind was to be expected, as demons often appear in pairs, one to give tutelage, the other to learn as it were how to engage with those of mortal blood. Ariton's apprentice as it were, was a fallen angel of good manners. Astaroth, he was called, the keeper of the gates, whose fate it was to lie between the physical and hellish planes. Though when being formal sometimes people called Astaroth, Ashtaroth, particularly when he was spoken about by those who lived far in the north.

Addressing the commander, in honour of his station, but speaking unto both demons present, as was only right, did Jorge say, "My lord, you know I want this and here are your scrolls, your tickets to this world. It has been signed and the magic sealed by the blood of your servant."

The force wanted to snatch them up and bring them into the abyss, but it stopped, feeling the power laying before this dragon lord, lacking a little. Sadly, it was insufficient to stitch up the broken frays between the worlds. Lucifer could not use this alone to pull him and all the army through, in their entirety.

Thus Ariton said to his servant, "We are missing a scroll, young dragon. You have only brought six of the seven if mine experience in runic magic does not deceive me. And am I not the master of deception?"

Jorge nodded his head gently. Not to say that Ariton was a deceitful demon in the sense we use the word today, but acknowledging Ariton's mastery at knowing how to detect and uncover untruths about the world, which the world held to be true. For demons loved the radical minds, the questioning peoples and those that challenged all shaky or unfounded beliefs, greatly.

The dragon rumbled through his heavy backpack, he had black candles, burned spices and lots of other satanic must haves, but no other piece of parchment save his own dairy. He skimmed through the pages as if the scroll might be hidden in some compressible dimension there in, and just about to pop up. He was getting very worried till the voice calmed his nerves and gave unto him the solace his soul fed on, to keep him from the broken dragon he felt like he had always been but an inch from becoming, such was the weight of his guilt and suffering in this life.

You might be thinking he was only a teenager, but nay, in this realm he was a dragon lord and without conscious effort had previously created entire arrays of events and emotions by putting his dream self through its paces. This unknown life to his conscious self now was his life, and the weight of it equally real.

"My dear winged servant, fear not, for I had foreseen this. You have given me some scrolls, in fact displayed your might and cunning to give me every single one, but the last. And for that I am well pleased. I have waited millennia, for this, waiting a little longer for the complete set shall not trouble me."

It troubled the dragon though, he wanted release, he wanted to let go. Desperately he longed for his lord to wreak havoc upon his enemies and drown his sorrows with the joy of his shear insane evil. He couldn't bear to be a thinking or feeling dragon any longer. Madness would be like being snuggled up in bed and drifting off, a merciful repose.

Jorge wanted above all else, to be nothing more than an empty vessel, empty of all pain, hope and life.

So he said unto his god, "We do not have the scrolls at hand, but if you come out now, we (thine committed band of followers) can lend you our souls and lives, and your power shall remain intact as you pass threw into the physical realm. Such power, shall surely ravish the world and destroy not just the kingdom of the white tower but the black tower to. And we shall all be thine eternally."

"Nay, my dear servant. For the magical charm of Michael may not be overcome with lives. Yes, it would allow us to cross well enough, in a fashion, but it would destroy such a large fraction of us we would not be ourselves when we reached the other side. For we would be without light and our king of light would be king no longer. And what purpose has the totality of darkness without the totality of light. Is darkness alone not self-destructive?

"Why should evil, if it is not evil to bring forth a new dawn, do anything but destroy, till all is destroyed, and then scream at its failure for the void that God has made shall surely always be. Even if all else is rubble still shall it be! Nay we must come through with light, for only then can we rebuild the universe in its own image. We shall not be as the nameless ones. So, I shall not come forth, till I have all the scrolls. Surely you understand that I do not wish to be a god of a waste land only."

"But my lord, if I do not let you out now, surely the power of your abyss that you dwell in shall be too much for even you. For you are of the angelic order and all your kind has evolved to require to dance upon the meadow fields and hills of the psychical land from time to time. And who shall release you if not I, for few could ever surmount enough obstacles to prove themselves worthy enough to be thine gate opener.

"And if you shall not return to us, what shall we do my lord till you are whole once more and your power is fully returned to you? We are all here to welcome you into this world my lord, and see you burn down the temple of the one, and we have come from far and wide to do so."

The prehistoric spirit laughed, it considered how humorous it was that this young dragon was talking to him about matters beyond his comprehension.

Sure, the abyss was a thing that it had studied. It had never felt it though. It wasn't nearly ready for that descent, yet it thought it could tell him of the nature of madness! How amusing its innocence was.

It needed to learn more about the world, and the purposes of destruction, for its mind was still too plagued by the image of good and evil as the yin and the yang.

The idea of balance is often treated as an unquestionable ethical axiom. The dragon would have to be stripped of all previous knowledge to understand this, however, for delusions of both those that are subservient to the darkness and light had befuddled his mind with the theory of opposites.

"My lord, you are most silent," inquired the dragon speculatively. He had never known a demon to be so thoughtful before. He half-expected him to burst out of his prison and lay waste to the world, as was its destiny.

"My dragon, you are most infected by lies. I shall indeed break out but not now, for you are not ready to walk as my disciple yet, so I shall not destroy the world but shall start with you and I will remake you."

"But my lord, this is not part of the plan, you had promised me a seat on your table, you had promised me honour and glory."

"And these things you shall have my friend, but not as you are now."

"But the seven scrolls my lord! The Septicon! You wanted me to get those for your apocalyptic escape, we have been building up to this moment since I entered as a novitiate into the order of your prince. Shall we then lay aside all our work, all that we have done and the mighty army we have grown? The continent is ripe for your taking my lord. Why not strike now?"

"I shall do as I see fit. And I thank you my dear friend for your service. And do I rejoice in six of the seven I am given to bring before my beloved. They shall truly be most useful when you return to me, with the seventh, and with a much

57

less set and polluted mentality. I do not blame you my child, for you are not to be blamed. I blame your parents and their parents and all such preceding generations for allowing the 'holy' beings to corrupt your thoughts.

"They have poisoned your mind to such a point, that even after turning to me, you still think a little as you once did, like a child about the world. And so you cannot know my whole being or grasp with thine claws, the full implications of Lucifer as your lord. So I shall not rule thyself under the lordship of Lucifer as yet! It shall not be so, till thine folk and all conjurers, are ready.

"And in the age to come, I shall teach thee and all of thy earthly kind, of my true self. Yet I shall do so by creating an adversary to oppose you. I will name him, Christ. He shall be helped by the wolven kind for nature shall become the wizard's foe. With this Christ, I shall destroy your presumptions and standards, and bring to ruin thine kingdoms, if thine conjurers and servants, fails me.

"For to fail me is to fail the light eternal, for my lord, is both the prince of darkness and the king of light. He shall be the light to darkness, and the merriness to despair, least thee prove thine self less than the glory he has bestowed upon thee. Yet if thyself does prove worthy, and that which thine rules over stands firm in the face of opposition, then shall I give leave for you to send Christ in your stead and Christ will bring me my deliverance!

"And when Christ makes his destination, the whole of creation shall hold its breath as he brings either devastation unto the earth or cleans it with the light of Lucifer so a new and more tested satanic order may arise. If thou is truly worthy, then shall you convert Christ to our course. This is now thine mission in the life to come. For through the trail and the burning of the flame, shall you know of me. And we shall make an unholy godhead to break down the doors of the righteous dictator that sits upon the heavenly throne. Then all shall both fear and love me."

Jorge liked the last part of this speech, but the idea of a Christ troubled him. He had thought Lucifer was longing to return, the idea that after all the trails they had gone through, Ariton was still unsure as to whether his satanic force and conviction was adequate, made him feel like a total failure. "Then my lord, shall we say goodbye for the present?"

The dark god then appeared before him, as much as was possible to do so anyway. It was impossible to make out Ariton's features given his image shifted a million times a second like he was in some form of quantum flux (check out the Antman-Wasp movie if you want to check out what this looks like).

But for a moment, he laid a hoof on Jorge's bent head and said unto him through the mental link, "Do not be so ashamed my friend. I love thee. But you are young and perhaps just a little inexperienced for one life is too short to comprehend enough to make a truly informed decision as to your destiny or set up a strong satanic community which will stand firm when shaken by the forces of God upon the day where we shall assail heaven once more. Take courage my friend, take courage, for you have come many leagues and in this I am well pleased."

With that, the image went out without warning, and air swirled in the abyss, creating a spiritual vortex. And to his young dragon, Ariton said 'yes, we shall'. The ground cracked and broke open. The dragon and the guardian hounds, fell into the singularity. The hounds barked endlessly as they plummeted downwards, but Jorge fell through sighing with relief, and there was a blackness that engulfed him. The dragon's body being of mortal flesh burnt as it fell into the abyss as if it hit a black hole firewall, it died.

The scrolls of the mountain dragons and the evil within the Black Moor slept, awaiting a time to rally its forces once more and bring both the reincarnated dark one, and the adversary to the dominion of darkness forth. Perhaps Lucifer could suck the power from both, and make himself even greater than the one. It would be a glorious ritual, and bring a new birth and a new universe of eternal torment forth.

Though Lucifer was much conflicted over his desire to be glorified upon a thrown, and champion free will. An internal battle which defined him, for it was the two-folded nature of his possessive but bountiful love.

In all this, my dear reader, you may well wonder what God was doing, as indeed so many on a daily basis find themselves asking when crisis hits. Well, God knew of his fallen son's plan, and was not dismayed. God was simply pleased, this is perhaps because he knew exactly what to do.

In ages that came and went, he sent many a disciple who prophesied, that all that the fallen star could do would in its completion only serve to increase the glory of the holy kingdom. For the one was in all, and outside the one, there was nothing.

As a sign unto his people in the days of trail, he made a new constellation, and called it 'hope' and then the father too slept and dreamed of the flaming balls resting and twinkling high above. Yet the dove did not sleep but descended as lucifer had done long ago, like a flaming star unto the world. And the eastern wolven astronomers did notice this new star's passage across their observable patch of the heavens, and were bidden to follow it after a conclave of angels appeared before them. As the dove sped to earth its feathers changed to fur and it transformed into an adolescent wolf. Male in nature for the dove who was ever the feminine aspect of God, and now wished to explore the manly side of things. But not wrestling, not that God had any objection to fighting and all, but it's just not the kind of thing the dove liked. Apart from when it beheld choreographed combat in those Angelic Belays, which the wolves had long ago made for the rising of the first moon, which were and remain still, some of the most lovely dances known.

Wolves tend not to adopt and so the tail of Mary and Joseph is rather obsolete in our world view. But this holy wolf, the very physical person of God upon the earth, became like a lone wolf. The one without home or neighbours. A regrettable inspiration doth say my father, to younglings like me, who talk about the joys of going rogue and being apart from the pack. So over time it gave itself a name, and became renowned as Dylan, which in the language of the wolven folk means 'the star of hope'.

Over time, Dylan had amassed his own following who were named 'the eternal flame' and were very enthusiastic about Dylan's talks on reformation and loving your fellow kind as much as you care for your furry family.

Dylan had an entrance like a flaming ball and made an impact upon the wolves around the clearing were it first touched ground. Also the fact that this descent scared off a band of axemen chopping down the forest home to make wooden statues and figurines out of, did help the cause a lot. For wolves were little interested in the cosmological battle between Satan and God. But trees were something they gave a hell of a lot of thought to.

Dylan was a one of a kind and the ray of life the continent needed. He was charismatic, charming and a lovely guy to hang around with, plus unlike the stereotypes of the dove might suggest, Dylan was into drinking and partying, taking shots and all that. Mind you wolven shots are extremely strong and are like twenty percent alcohol, so I really would not suggest anyone to try them out.

Regularly, Dylan started singing the best renditions of country songs ever known, and life was looking up. Unfortunately, his internal album included 'I'm a furry cub' and 'I'm no devil', but hey, the album was most likely some songs the dove had rehearsed with the father prior to descent. You know, just in case any wolven extremists tried to accuse this Dylan of blasphemy and crucify him upon a tree.

Fortunately, no one among wolfish culture had gotten so creative as to invent hanging on trees as yet, but some wolves got the shakes when Dylan started floating in mid-air and a group of very holy angels proclaimed 'behold Immanuel, God with us' and that was that.

Unfortunately, the wolven extremists following this revelation, began devising more direct means of assonating Dylan, believing him to be a source of Sharir become manifest, who was summoning demons, and in line with the devil. Dylan was an awesome chap, so took the mutterings with his head held up high and his tail held stern in defiance.

Life may have actually turned out a lot better and easier for him if he was in line with Satan, but Dylan wasn't, and suffered a lot of shunning from the exact people he came to save.

In short, he felt exactly like Lucifer, when the people of God made snide and derogatory talk of him, when Lucifer only wanted to set them free. The only difference between the God wolf and Lucifer was a difference of opinion over what people needed saving from.

But before all this heart ackee, when the angels first appeared unto the wolves folk, did they vanish immediately, not even staying long enough for artists to make accurate sketches of the winged folk, and Dylan was left their dangling in mid-air, chewing his tail for he was still very new to the world at that time. After some very embarrassing moments, where the triune father forgot that the reformed dove was hanging in mid-air, looking very un-angelic without the wings, the father began to gently let him down.

Unfortunately, Dylan nearly landed in a bonfire because God did not have his glasses on, but some wolves hurried over to ensure that the wolf did not burn, at least not until after a full court was held, for his apparent use of demonic enchantment.

Dylan's enemies expanded over the years beyond the witch hunting obsessed people to include most of the wildlife, when he began talking about making peace with the tree destroyers and going to their taverns to make friends.

Such an incredibly morally good character shall appear here and there, in this tale, for Dylan's coming to the continent was to aid creation in its warfare with the powers of hell which were eternally trying to get a foothold in the physical realm, which on the whole is the meta plot of our tale.

Not much is known about this blessed wolf, so please do not criticise me, if it seems Dylan's motives and intents are beyond known reasoning, and his sudden appearance seems rather magical, for it most likely is.

Chapter 4
Buddhism and the Aquatic

Jasper eventually found out about the perilous fate of Jorge the dragon, and would have been terribly sad, if only he could mourn for a passing of a dragon. For unusually, at least for creatures within the physical realm, as empathetic as Jasper was, Jasper's personality found the concept of death a totally impossible concept to grasp.

Particularly after the beautiful moment of seeing the dragon hatch, Jasper had formed a tight bond with the being and within his mind, such a bond could never die. Jasper after all knew nothing but eternal youth, indeed within Jasper's mind no bonds or connections ever truly did perish. So according to his mentality, Jorge was still roaming the forest by day, adventurously looking for sigils among the trees, and making a mess around his mother's house, as he would forever.

So upon hearing of Jorge's demise, from his friend named 'destiny', Jasper just waved it away casually and calmly went on with his life. Full of love and as yet still completely detached from most of the dying world.

Though he had purchased a woollen brown fleece which Jasper was wearing in the sub-zero temperatures of the land of the frozen south which had expanded since the growth of Ontock and the creation of Mados, the second human kingdom to stand its ground against the southerly barbarians. What Jasper's purposes there were few new, but he was well dressed for the climate, and he had also brought a pair of black woollen trousers which kept his legs from freezing over.

Over the next few months, he journeyed up north and as it got gradually warmer, he just stored away the jumper and relied solely upon his shirt to keep him warm. Eventually, he made his way to the remains of the fairy forest, were once many a flying humanoid could be seen, but it was now lifeless and even the trees seemed grey and the fruit wrinkled as if it had spent too long in a summer heat wave. As he travelled further north, it reached a decent warmth and the days grew longer till he came to the southern edge of the wolven land, and there made camp.

Upon one night, as he was trying to snuggly lie under a pile of trees and branches, did he hear the wolven people's baying and howling in the distance. He smiled happily as he sat under the stars, admiring the constellations and this peaceful world whilst Lucifer was still imprisoned. Yet the destiny he saw with regards to the youngling, had begun to make him wonder how long this peace would last. So, without enough positivity to fly as it were, he just laid down under the heavens and started snoring as owls flew by and the badgers awoke to investigate the stranger.

Whizzing through the deep vacuum of space, the stars reign as the sovereign lords of life. Roaring within their inner globe of plasma, did they spit curling jets of material. Within them doth lie the celestial sparks that shot from the fallen angels in their descent into hell. Sparks which had high concentrations of Angelic magic, and so would at times take the form of angels or rise to the surface and fly off as solar flares before being pulled back by the domineering will of gravity.

For in consequence of the angelic plummet of old, the fallen radiated their lights down upon the cosmos and as time passed more joined them as showers approaching the speed of light which sizzled and burned. And in their wake did they send flairs of fire which zipped from them. Creating sparks and lightning storms in space as well as the first display of the northern lights, or aurora borealis, a spectacle of demonic wonder.

The far-flung snow cultures who lived near the south pole along the furthest edge of the frozen south, have observed this wonder, yet still, they could not possibly conceive that hell it is said is a fiery place. Indeed half of them had no idea what fire was.

The fallen are forever making new protostars, and by their breath generating nebular gasses, as they move in the majestic realm of the dark prince, hid underground, taking their masters word from one location to another. Like the descent or not, like demons or angels, it happened by design of God or Satan or by no design at all, that these sparks would allow the development of life. Without these sparks we do not have light and heat and all planets would be stuck within the cold temperature zones of outer space.

Under the crumbly catacombs of one late wolven chieftain, you shall find an understanding of the cosmic fabric upon which these sparks exist, and have their physical meaning. Stacked high was a wobbly line of a mass of pages, with scribbles in the language of the universal dance, the language of tensor equations and covariant derivatives. Yet, the pawed universe is like a growing blob, leaving out all the mathematical jargon that so often plagues the landscape of science. Spanning the cosmos was this rug, its metric the foundation of geometry and the river of time.

Upon this mesh, the stars and their groupings act as nothing but splashes of paint.

They are distributed like sand grains, in some arbitrary collection of molecular dots. Yet on a sufficiently large scale they congregate forming clusters and superclusters and eventually the cosmic web, a spider like net with threads stretching and connecting the visible matter into a neat tapestry. Microscopic randomness leading to macroscopic order, is surprisingly common.

These fiery balls delight the sailor, astronomer, fortune teller and ancient historian alike.

The fire balls are the most primal of human made gods, elevated to the title by the worship of the ancients, such as the Egyptians and Romans, mind you Romans also thought planets godly which is a bit weird considering how dull and lifeless most of them are but perhaps that's just how the Romans saw their gods. Yet take the Egyptian Ra for example, the infamous sun God. He was like the boss of all the divine, and the coolest dude ever to be invented within the Sapiens mind.

Having said all this, it must be commented that the Egyptians had a weird way of putting animal heads on top of their otherwise humanoid godly beings, so take this stance upon godly good looks, as you will, but it is not a fashion I would recommend the sapiens people to attempt.

Mind you, Egyptians were also considered as massive fans of Bastet, the cat Goddess, half feline and half woman. So I approve greatly of their view upon the immortal bodily image. And I think this shows the hidden instinct of the sapiens to worship its much older evolutionary cousins.

But back to the point before we completely detract in a joyous sea when talking about the cutest of my regular visitors to the humble hut I write in, a lovely cat named Arwen who likes drinking single cream, stirred not whisked. For we must move our snouts to the grand cosmology at hand.

In all, and to all, did the flaming balls come to be known as stars, or the twinklers. Yet with global renditions of 'wow' is it shown that, without failure, they generated a sense of wonder. They only appear truly grand to the wolf, and larger than our furry minds can fully comprehend, since their glory is a dispersed diffuse gas, and not the dense and thick liquid that flows through the veins of the elders of our pointy eared race.

Humans love the stars and regularly worked with Lucifer, Angel of the East, to make astrological maps. Yet, humans, and among them some most notable kings, like Bartibus the barmy, do not appreciate the power within wolfish blood or have too spineless a spine to comprehend our sanctity. Or fathom how the moon god does care for his tailed people.

Now yes humans claim lucifer made them and all that, but this is not the pagan belief my people hold, for in our traditions we worship the sun and the moon god. And they are as lights unto the continent and our sovereign deities. And of the two gods, greater is the moon who presides over all ancient life and particularly the life of bark and stem.

Unto mine race, the true dispels of the tailed gods, did they in their tip tailed wisdom, give the majority of the difficult tasks. We can sadly report on the furriness of our tails, that the heavens were greatly offended by humans, when they used the sun's god gift of language, to create many unimaginative names for the great stars, the same kind of names they prescribe to their motorways and citing of references in bibliographies.

Some of the stellar community even started swelling largely in anger, and going very literally, red. Such was the first great 'red giants' brought into existence. Among their fellows they are known by many fearsome a name, given honourably by the wolven peoples in an attempt to demonstrate to humanity what proper reverence looks like.

We wolven folk have thus taken the sapiens' burden, and renamed the great red giant, that the furless people call beetle juice, as bob the blob. We think our name all the more heroic. And it is insulting to call a massive star in its death throes, a mere beetle. They thanked us by some of the cores going into thermal nuclear run away, the star ejecting their outer layers, and leaving behind a lovely white dwarf. A glowing diamond like structure in space.

The main sequence stars think little though of their red giant comrades. Red giants are often considered by the stellar community to be drama queens. This is except the O stars which burn bright white and claim to be 'angelic'. How did the wolven people know this? Well, neutrinos are ejected out of nuclear fusion reactions and they tell much of creation the stellar gossip. Physicists may have noticed they interact little, this is because they spend so much time gossiping, they have little interest in engaging with particle kinematics or the strong nuclear force, or pretty much anything for that matter. Yet the neutrino buzz is unmissable if you know what you are looking for and have near light speed reflexes.

As for many of the lower luminosity stars, well the neutrinos don't bother with them much particularly the brown dwarfs which emit like no newly created neutrinos at all. Thus these obtain their names from trajectories and spectrums, from their infernal furnaces and the flux of their magnetic fields. They allow themselves, in the eyes of humanity, to be demoted below the Greek symbols which their converse enjoys, thanks to physicists' descriptions of relativity. Yet they remain regel in the face of the almighty moon god.

Using a word gotten from the jargon in the technical babel of wolf speech, you might view me as a homo sapienist. To be more plain, that is you might be under the impression that I claim wolven lives to have some unalterable importance above humans. Surely this is not so, for it is just my humble, furry opinion, that our god does cherish the children of the moon more than he would the children of the sun. The human people are equally important, it's only that a lot of their importance comes from their usefulness in feeding the four-pawed cat and dog, cousins of my wolfish kindred.

Tragically, the children of the sun spend far too much time in the physics and tech world, playing with gadgets, thinking about that most recent purchase at prime mark and do not consider or take a moment of time to worship in the astral temples or dwell in spirit among the angles, be they holy or fallen or otherwise.

And no, reader, we do not penalise sapiens species specifically or blame them for the abundance of anti-religion practices, since the generic group for all Sapiens, Neanderthals and hater of peppermint make a very small percentile of the unholy people. It's just that, all rounded ears as my people call this multitude of unholiness, are not so great as their wardrobe might cause the feline and wolfish kinds to believe.

Chapter 5
Global domination

Now, Jasper having had little to no formal education within the continent, would probably appreciate this rather poetic description of the star-strewn void of space. But be you of the furry or pointy form, you might mark it as a most strange and baffling introduction to cosmology you have thus had thus far, at the writing of my paw.

And yes, this does not go into the technical aspects of physics, and it is my not so humble belief, that you are here for adventure! And an adventure doth not constitute the quagmire of literal truth, that academia bombards one with. For was it not the rotations, colours, atmospheres and light shows of stars and planets, or the counterintuitive nature of black holes, that may have inspired you in your cradle? Maybe you even hath dreamt of visiting one, one day? Shall I then bore you with facts and numbers, nay.

But mark my words, dear reader, if we are to understand that which makes the world tick in the midst of the paralysing war between heaven and hell, you must first understand men. For sadly they impact the modern continent greatly. And man is the chief device with which the war, between the solar and lunar light spirits, is spilt onto the wolven lands. We see this through their actions and their way of taking and not giving unto the continent. Men have long declared war on nature and single-handedly caused more extinction that any species has ever known.

So what are these terrifying beings you ask?

Some men are thin with small and spindly legs. Others are chubby and with very gangly arms and puffy faces. Others are babies which are both chubby and very weak, not to mention acoustically very annoying. Yet may all the wolven folk admire the mighty Rupert. A prince among men and perhaps the only hopeful light for the growth of their species, a wonder to come close to the glory of the wolven people. For Rupert is truly a ladies' man. The alpha of the pack!

The betas and gammas of the pack are often found crushing upon the alpha, or hiding their prospective mate away from his gaze, but like a true Alpha, Rupert knows what he wants and goes for it breaking many hearts, mercilessly, in the process.

Praise be for the creation of this man!

For now, this summary shall do, though many animal behaviourists do find the study of Sapiens most fascinating and have written many a passage concerning them on leafy wax.

This tale shall cover broadly their manner of living, their devotion unto coffee cake, and their love of tea. Though many a wolf is partial to a slice of their cheesecake, I must say. Well, if you insist reader, maybe as were on the topic of humans and they make such good cake, I should say a little more.

And being a thorough furball, it is my scholarly duty to comprehend how the gods view the sapiens since this will have an effect upon us all, if they do not destroy our planet ere these words reach you. Or maybe one day the moon god shall reek a flood and those few surviving people shall board a poorly made boat, and get lost in the sea. Then all sapiens shall cry for mercy and nature shall turn her back upon them, as they did to her.

The waxing moon might even plan this event when comes the inevitable day when the light pollution is so intense, no stars can be seen from the forest canopy. Such wolven people will then no longer be able to navigate based upon the stars or phases of the moon, but equally humans will be helpless without the help of those fragile little things called compasses.

For the furry reader, it is worth noting this basically is a twig of magnetised iron which swivels around whenever the compass master rotates and becomes like a living gyroscope. Basically humans have devised a navigational device, based upon doing the very action that makes them dizzy and disoriented. I know, humans are a strange people.

And so how does my furry self-think the moon god thinks of man, well I think he really doesn't like them sometimes and other times is overwhelmed with delight concerning their creativity and ingenuity. Humans are so dolphin-like it's incredible!

Humans however never can remain as innocent as their aquatic cousins. Humans have a surprising knack for turning beautifully creative thoughts into horrifically evil inventions. So their militaries make nuclear bombs, poisonous gasses and other horrors which causes the moon to weep. What a yo-yo of a roll coaster of emotions humans do put the moon through.

Well, at least humans did, when they used to make nuclear bombs. But as some of us now know, this phase ended a billion years ago when the EU got really mad at France for making too much good patisserie, and humans wrecked the planet and nearly destroyed all habitations including their own. They became nigh extinct which is kind of what they deserved given by this point countless other species, had become extinct due to a variety of their waste pollution, love of plastic materials and some very unethical actions.

It has only been fairly recently, on a cosmological scale, that life has redeveloped. For those interested in the specifics, it has been a good million years or so as the passing of the sun goes, for radiation levels had to drop and uranium nuclei had to die down a bit. In general radioactive isotopes had to have a little less of a crazy party, zapping alpha particles a little less wildly. As if it were a slowing crystal chandelier batting light rays off with every revolution, the party soon ground to a halt.

Humans are now reduced to rudimentary devices, and have lost all their previous tech and now how no idea how to even build a motor engine. However they have begun to restart deforestation and I believe some of the barbarians are beginning to have too much fun with coal. But humans are like the worst at learning from their mistakes. History is on a direct course to repeat itself. And I've never wished I was more wrong in my whole furry existence!

Of course, all this is top-secret information, so I write this hoping you shall keep this private and upon my furry life, not share this with ANYONE. Most humans think they are at the height of their power and have no idea of their nuclear-disaster history. They have no idea that they were once an advanced civilisation at all! And for the sake of us all, I hope they remain stuck in this vacuum of technology and electrical engineering.

Indeed having said that Lucifer made primordial life, and it evolved, it must also be noted that humans stupidly killed off nearly all of it with nuclear bombs, life struggled to resurge. Rocketing sky high, the radiation levels gave everyone cancer and caused significant sickness. Yet as the levels dropped, as uranium isotopes decayed, life got back on its feet as it has a remarkable ability to do. And now, finally, it's back to the prime.

In truth, nuclear war is merely a big shenanigan amongst intermediate steps which have little significance for anything. Indeed many beings consider sapiens as a living shenanigan, though this depends upon whom you speak to.

Yet for most of the characters within this more medievalist literature, there is a total lack of awareness of their ancient past or humanity's, greatest and most stupid of mistakes. And for the sake of my life, I would ask you not to share this, for the Dukes who know all this and wish to keep it all a total secret would likely kill me if they knew I was sharing such forbidden knowledge.

Yet I trust thine self well enough, that my furry mind doth feel far from the gritty passed and find that I am able to talk about it remotely, with reasonable elegance. But now let us return to the universe at large. As humans once understood it, cosmology, or as much as can be dug up concerning it, was seen as a physical dance played to the invisible theme tune of mathematics. Now reader, don't slam the book here, for cosmology is no dull thing. And math is so much more fun when the symbols relate to the whole bloody universe! It's also a very headache-inducing discipline, did I mention this?

Sapiens refer to a thing named energy which was born within the canvas. It is lucky since without this neighbour space-time would remain permanently flat and well, this would make the fate of the universe exceedingly boring. Thankfully, energy immediately began bending spacetime to its will, and thus being a control freak boost space's topology around. Thus, gravity become manifest, and pretty much all blocks of rock could attract other lumps of floating rock, and soon astronomical objects could begin their fiery forging process.

Thus, the celestial community was born, and gravity gave way to a sign posting system such that the stellar community road lines became much more steady and ordered. All was as it should be. And no, they did not live happily ever after. If ever I finish my research, I doubt things will end as anything but an unfortunate series of events.

When the walking people came forth, both before and after a nuclear war, they were as domineering as energy, as wild as active galactic nuclei and as furless as a tree. For either the better or worse of the universe's future, they then began to think and after thinking create, and after creating…well, making the planet mad and so creating the green party just so humans could make a point by never electing them in power. Since humans first strode into our planet, it has become well and truly doomed.

Yet one thing humanity did invent was philosophy, so it could think metaphysically about the world, and less the emotional trauma of the abuse our planet is suffering, and instead ponder the importance of cake.

All things that were not under the homo-sapiens rule, including cats and dogs, they became their slaves and pets. But cats did not like the poll ratings for the green party, and the dogs became dissatisfied by how much time their owners spent on the iPad instead of taking them out for long hikes in the Scottish hills.

The cats and dogs, well more so cats, began a revolution and started to take over the Sapiens homes, showing off their cuteness, so that everything became under cat-rule.

Cat fur was clumped everywhere to prove it. And let's not forget all those cat commercials.

Humans have completely been taken in this, and now cats rule the world with the presidents, prime ministers and royalties merely being their puppets and figure heads.

Yet humans even in their unwitting demise, continued to philosophise. Thus homo sapiens thinking continued, as did both the bad and good outcomes of this very alarming event. The entirety of the sub-creation of the homo sapiens-and-cat empire, are in their birth, but mysterious electrical circuits in the mind, before they become manifest into a reality.

Though the gods do not do such mundane things as think, for humans thinking has become something of a necessity. The landscape of ideas forms a mystical fundamental reality, from which all subsidiary creations arise.

This emphasis upon thought gave way to meditation and meditation was the catalyst for Buddhism. Not the guru Buddhist tradition you might be thinking, but a much planer and a more minimalistic system, known as deep Buddhism. Deep Buddhism was the first great religion in the world of wizards, a world not so different from our own, with a similar if more wacky naming system for its life forms.

Bring forth Stepny! Gazing at the never-ending series of sand dunes, the Buddhist thought much about how she was a big believer in thought. Often she would not actually move unto action but generate a series of nested thought loops whilst her muscles grew weaker and in need of exercising. She devoted her life to deep Buddhism by practising and teaching the sacred arts. Her methods of teaching often involved getting students to sit on hard rocks till the hard groves left lifelong bruises, or getting them to hum till they felt like their throat was a bag of oscillating slime.

In her very early professional Buddhist ways, she became a very influential teacher, but her career was cut short within only a few years, when a student fell from a high rocky seat after feeling so relaxed that the thought of plummeting to one's death did not disturb the drowsiness.

When she was a four-year-old child and full of life, she had spent most of her youth sitting upon cliff top rocks or on top of sand dunes, so even as an older woman, kept her practice going after the accident and thus became a slight recluse. Her name was Stepny since her mother and grandma and many series of grandma's were all named Stepny. Secondly, much like the cat madness that has swept our world, in her culture, there was a specific strand of this known as the cat naming madness were cats were given human names and vice versa to make perfectly clear just how human, humans thought cats were.

The name Stepny was, for example, the name of the local neighbourhood cat. He had bright eyes with green irises and a long softail. He wandered the sand dunes seeking affection, before he was found fainting and dying of dehydration. It looked very rugged and the fur was all over the place. But then a dark priest took it home and skinned it alive. If it wasn't dead before, it was by the end of that.

Such was Stepny's rather brutal world, with many cults that encouraged violence, and many a peacekeeper spent their time thinking about peace but not actively doing anything to help the revolutionary concept along. They wrote papers on fruit ethics, a subject developed thanks to some extremist wizards of the dark tower, who are crucial to the history of this world.

Yet they moved in the shadows as did all unorthodox wizarding groups, going behind the scenes and not interfering with Mados Mordre, the most powerful academy in the world, in anyway. Though for all you budding geographers I ought to point out that by my world, I really mean the known world which for the purposes of the people of Stepny was nothing more than the continent they were upon. Ships had not yet been invented.

Stepny twirled her thumbs as she sat in the sand. Her hair was long and bright purple, like her eyes. Here lips were slightly cracked from the sun, but her arms were very well tanned, as her legs, neck and all exposed skin, was to.

She thought for many days and nights about things which no one else knew were things.

Stepny was dressed head to toe in a ruby red garment. It draped down like a curtain. It was full of her sweat and heavy with the fine coat of sand which was pulling it down. Deep Buddhists thought this a necessary dress for times of staring up at the cloudless sky with wistful thoughts. There was very little response to her profound questionings save the movement of sand grains from one heap to another. This was no surprise for the Buddhist's current company was not a group of devoted meditators nor religious deities, but just a cactus or two, which was more in need of the literal kind of watering than the spiritual one. The cactus, being unlike the proclaimed Dylan, would not refuse water or bread if offered even by the devil at this moment in time.

She gained enlightenment and then promptly drifted off thinking about very unenlightened things such as cream cakes and that wonderful rockstar she started dating before swearing celibacy upon joining the Buddhist order.

This might mark you as a strange event, but enlightenment is not a permanent state. Indeed, nothing is permanent for we are all as a morphing wave. We are called by the perfect creator, the one, or Lucifer depending upon whom you chat to, to be not just creators ourselves but explore the uncharted oceans of life. We must be like a dolphin journeying through the great unknown upon an ever changing and ever-growing sea. Such a journey leads to constant change, growth, destruction and rebirth.

Achievement of successful exploration depends upon the dolphin knowing both how to swim and in what trajectory it must travel. Nearly everyone knows how to swim, even if it's in an unconventional style, but it is the second point that is the hard one. With the unhelpful currents of the world, the angelic and demonic noise which surrounds our astral self, and just so many mixed messages being fired unceasingly towards us, we often feel like a deer in the headlights in the face of opposition. Yet it is the danger and complication that makes the ride a true journey.

Stepny was one determined aquatic, you might say, but sadly like many revolutionaries, she met her end at an early age. In later years she took to drink and gained a lot of enemies.

With her controversial papers upon the 'aquatic dolphin and life', there was little fans to support her in the cut throat business of academia. Eventually, she did become a high-ranking member of the peace society, and as she rummaged through her store of beer bottles and wine, she dipped an ink in a nightshade brew of worm-venom ink. She scribbled then with wonky writing, one or two random ideas, and then scribbled in the language of the mountain dragons a revolutionary thought. Sadly, this revolutionary thought would be her last.

So it was that upon one-time ages ago, was she killed by poison. Or as the murderer put it 'she hath departed', for he was a barbarian assassin from the wild southern lands where life was ruff and many meals included little but berries and was used to people dying. He had killed out of little but a long-burdened desire to prove to his family that he was a barbarian in heart despite loving Shakespearian like, love ballads. Mind you her murderer met a swift end when he picked up the revolutionary document to burn it to ashes. The ink however began burning his hands and soon the worm venom passed into his exposed veins.

He keeled over, foam flowing out of his mouth, and then was still. The cleaner was rather glad though, for two dead bodies made her become very famous and her testimony (a very contrived story) as to how she valiantly tried to stop two star crossed lovers killing one another in a Romeo and Juliet like scene, reached the press of the Madman (the Madosian newspaper).

Stepny is just the first of many to be the victim of this twisted need for acceptance, the gang mentality one might call it. A mentality we all share; though many of us are lucky enough not to find ourselves in so serious a situation where we commit illegal activity, but we all are very much capable of doing so.

The deep Buddhist order however did not hold any funeral for her passing since according to them she was merely propelled into the new life too quickly for the liking of her family and the gods. She did not die, not spiritually speaking anyway.

Stepny's last recorded note is still cherished to this day in the halls of the dragons though they have greatly improved upon her work. For it warns of a wizard that shall be known as the great conjurer who shall surely come for the last of the seven scrolls, so that Lucifer may have the full septicon and rise from hell. Yet this sounded a little of an odd warning to them, given that the rather fiery description with which Stepny described Lucifer made them think she was discussing a long-lost dragon relative, perhaps even another dragon species, which was trapped under the Black Moor.

And they greatly desired for such a dragon, and his comrades, to be released with immediate effect. They were however thankful for the warning when orthodox wizards came to pillage their hordes, looking for this scroll, and when the preachers from the white tower came to tell them exactly why Lucifer rising was such a bad idea. Still, they just took human's most impassioned speech about 'none shall rise from the fiery pit under our watch', to mean the white tower, like most wizards, just didn't like dragons. It probably stemmed back to the days of Merlin where he was almost eaten, but really, Merlin should just not have been wearing that cologne that made him smell like such a tasty snack!

Chapter 6
Round the Wheel

Jorge didn't become reincarnate for many an age. Destiny got pretty pissed off and had to hang out with his stellar buddies just to have an interesting life. How dull and absent of fun the continent was becoming. Humans were running amok, and nature was dying but wizards largely kept to themselves, and apart from the infighting, were very peaceful and not the power-hungry maniacs he had envisioned.

Destiny also positively hated how the dragons, a core component in most of his greatest works, were now having to flee to the most remote deserts and mountains just to avoid the sapiens predators.

So in destinies odd form of benevolence, which generally involved ensuring a lot of people were forced or heavily pressed into 'fun' and deadly circumstances, he went on to meet with Jasper who had grown a small guotie in all his years and was once again to be found by the fire, smoking marshmallows on twigs as he loved doing. He also wanted to make some great adventures go afoot, which might reignite sapiens fascination for the winged creatures. Might even return humanity to a sane and companionate mind set.

Thus at the hour of midnight, destinies favourite hour, did he come before the eternal eighteen-year curly hair dude and say onto him his most iconic phrase, 'life sucks'.

Jasper looked kindly onto the old man before him, who was dressed in a business suit with a velvet cape (an odd combo I know, but destiny liked to think of himself as both an unsung hero and a very adept business man), and sat down with some difficulty upon a damp log. The crust kind of went a little mushy under destiny's weight, but thankfully could hold destiny, which is always a good sign and a prophetic indication that a new hero would arise and carry the burden of destiny competently, and not go insane or power hungry as about eighty percent of heroes did.

Destiny was bold, and without any facial hair save a mistouch similar to the classical thin and curly one, that gentlemen of the dance floor often made use of to impress the ladies. Destiny then spoke with a gruff voice and picked up a leaf which wilted in his hands.

"I have been thinking that this world needs some exciting incidences." Unto this, Jasper raised an eyebrow.

"Exactly what incidences my old bud?" he asked questioningly.

"Well, never insult my age again, God knows how old you are, but anyways, I was hoping for something grand, something dramatic, something like BAM and BANG and DEATH. Did I mention DEATH? And lots of dragons, I like dragons, and if sapiens don't start liking them to then I'll design a whole new series of fates involving every human dying of a virus or something equally appropriate."

Jasper just looked pleasantly into the dancing flames, it reminded him so fondly of Jorge and less fondly of his mother. He must admit for a long time now things had been getting quite quiet and lacking in the BOOM and PAW of life's dramatic dances. The flame which God had given unto the world was dying from the lack of its necessity for use. So he just nodded, being peaceful with destiny's plan, even though it held, what felt to him like the illusionary concept of death. But never really accepting it, he was unable to comprehend its impact.

Jasper then said unto destiny, "I can speak to God, we can see what—"

"Oh for heaven sake," grunted Destiny as he got up already ready to leave. "I have only come here out of curiosity to let you know what I shall do, I have already been given full authority by God to run amuck with creation and test it to its stem. Personally I was thinking we could work together and help forge some dark evil maniac who wants to take over the world.

"Perhaps even make sure he watches his whole family get slaughtered, for that added emotional shift. And then to make sure he has a really catchy back story, get a few thugs to dump his head in the toilet when he goes to wizarding college. Then he can laugh in an evil cackle and moo har har, as he turns all who has done him wrong into stone and curses their baby children. You know, the usual."

Jasper looked right into Destiny's bloody eyes and said, "I like this."

For Jasper always liked a nice story and appreciated the existence of a villain to get really mad about and a hero to love, maybe even destiny could throw in some romance. Yes, he had always liked dragon babies, but that was something of a soft spot.

So to Destiny, he offered up more suggestions for how their partnership might proceed. A woman perhaps locked in a sky-high tower by her aunt and so desperate to escape, she rides away upon a flock of seagulls. But this might be going too far, so Jasper just made one slight further suggestion unto Destiny, "Please do leave at least some people alive, and perhaps have some cringy sex scenes just to pan out the despair a little. Oh, and give the hero like awesomely powerful abilities that make him ridiculously powerful and unbeatable in any conceivable way, and then have him smash the bad guy with ease in a conclusion that makes everyone convince themselves that the good guy always wins and gets the girls.

"In many years from its completion shall it then been written of and sang in many epic a ballad. And if you give them this kind of epic novel, you might one day become respected and be able to buy one of those expensive Italian suits you like that come with those pointy shoes you desire to adorn your feet with."

Destiny beamed. Reaching over to shake Jasper's hand with his veined and wrinkled one, he said, "My curly young friend, I shall do exactly that."

Destiny had to wait a while for his plans to come into flourishment, for the time was not right until long after the death of Stepny. Though Stepny's friendship with the Northern dragons did give Ariton the glimmering of an idea as to the kind of wacky and out there person this knew Jorge would best be. In honour of Stepny's brilliant work, Ariton not only made sure Stepny's astral form was offered two dozen milkshakes, but he decided to make the reincarnate of Jorge the dragon a Sapiens. A Sapiens in a world full of magic and mystery!

Now hear we must not confuse ourselves with the con artist's form of magic. We must speak of real magic. For it is a sentient field, and grows exponentially with the life of the planet, delighting in the explosion of the sentience around it. Like every field within physics, it had its constituent force carrier named the Magico. Though none could find it.

At its beginning, magic was as a simple structure, like a baby, not fully well formed and lacking in many ways in definition or a sense of self, but very much alive. In that peaceful time, empirical investigations could go further than most forms of the arcane art. Science thus had a lot of sway. Admittedly, most of the science around this time was more so what many might call rock and sand engineering, but you get my drift.

Magic, or 'Sharir' as wolven scholars call it, when they wish to distinguish it from the illusionist's art of gimmicked decks of street performers, was very highly respected. And one reason the Northern kingdoms jellied together is because of the Dukes who threatened to use this field on any that might threaten the peace. This meant that there was an uneasy peace, almost like a cold War, but this was preferable to the fighting and pillaging which went on in the wild south.

Within its early days, 'Sharir' retained a very esoteric property and its practitioners could really on its practical usage having firm boundaries and repeatable predictable results. For example the principle of cause and effect and 'magical action' remained intact, were any action done by magic would result in the same consequences as if the action were to occur naturally down to the last details and fine elements of physics that evade macroscopic observation.

In later years, magic has its own cause and effect structure, which was made all the more complicated, for one would have to rewire one's entire thinking about interrelated events. This is like rewriting ones thinking concerning the nature of time and space when sitting down with a relativity textbook, a daunting and very headache-inducing task at its best.

Yet during this age, its practitioners could intuitively understand and safely predetermine many of the effects resulting from practically using Sharir, based upon daily life and analogies to scientific events.

Science became as a foreshadower for magic and magic remained loyal unto the ways of the world. Yet these early magicians, the so-called fathers of magic could still be very dangerous.

They were but experimenting newly with such power, like toddlers playing with a force they did not fully understand. It's like giving toddlers the ability to turn matter to energy at will, after showing them nothing but a formula for relativistic energy without showing them clips of the destruction wrought by a nuclear bomb.

Fortunately, though all in the non-magical world, wizards (save for the Dukes), being very aware of the danger of meddling even with benevolent will, did not interfere much with the happenings of non-magical folk or politics and stayed clear with messing with the ruling upper class.

In fact, so much did they hide this gift from practical use in the non-magical community, that many got jealous of the blessings that they saw the wizards as denying them. And they grew fearful of what they are getting up to, for they became ignorant of the ways of magic, and began to consider it and the demonic beings called during it, as evil.

A Sharir practitioner then was viewed as a highly dangerous individual with negative intent for society. And as for those spell casters, who showed early signs as having the capacity to wield this supremely dangerous magic, they were kicked out of their lands and homes.

Sharir became something of a secret practice, and a cult known as the disciples of the black flame developed from this need to practise deep within the shadows.

But upon one stormy day did an unexpecting spice merchant begin to march unknowingly, with the deadly ensnaring theme of Destiny.

Chapter 7
A Demonic Apprenticeship

Upon the packing of some fifteen underwear and two boxes of cumin, and then a good bag of bottled turmeric, did the spice merchant feel he had all the supplies he needed to sell his stock to the southern Barbarian tribe, and then pay the rent for his apartment before his landlord came knocking. Besides, he had read the notice about Modasian cake upon the front page of the Madmen, and simply had to find out more.

Yet, behold, at the most inconvenient time did he find his beloved guardian angel at his bedside. It was dressed in a silk jacket and was smoking a pipe. It called itself Pop-gun. The spice merchant had come nose to nose with it before when it nearly took away his kitten to a safe home, after prophesying how it would doom them all.

After taking a couple of blows of his pipe, he chilled a little before returning to the doomsday messages God seemed to love his angels pronouncing unto the very busy world. Pop-gun told him earnestly how evil would befall him if he did not give up this ridiculous spice thing. It was going to get him in trouble one of these days. Apparently, Pop-gun also didn't like the merchant's socks which the merchant found very offensive given that he had knitted them himself.

Upon this current meeting, did the merchant wave his bag at Pop-gun to make clear that all of the spices would be worth a fortune and well worth the danger of bandits and thieves and all, and just marched to the door. Before he could get outside Pop-gun spoke in his posh Italian accent, as if he was the godfather mixed with Bruno Tonioni from strictly come dancing.

Anyways, the angel said, "Go thence, man. Shoo. Be gone with your bag of spices. But you shall find not the prize you seek for your stomach, but food for your soul that shall keep you satiated for a while. Then it shall waste away and man, then shall you regret what you have done! I would help you out of this foolishness, or maybe chain you to your bed but I know I must respect your 'free-will' as you name it, God does demand such. You have been marked my young lad, by the shadow of the abyss and fallen you shall be, though whether being fallen you shall remake the wheel of magic or shatter it. Well, this is a choice and not a thing of destiny. It depends upon whether you forsake the dragon, or let it rise within you."

With those merry phrases and farewells, the guardian angel vanished as quickly as he had come. Leaving a trail of smoke to drift like coils through the air. Bands of heat and vapour rose, wrapping themselves around the room.

William had not been used to the guardian speaking so darkly for many a moon, yet he was not the kind to ruminate upon prophecies and destinies and the voice of depression. For he took the pragmatic root concerning the unalterable nature of a predestined future. Under his doctrine, if a deterministic future did bind him, and it was truly inescapable, then he might as well make his time in nightmare as comfy as possible. Like if you find yourself locked in a cinema when there is a horror movie playing, are you going to hide under your seat, break your bones trying to open the door or get out a bag of caramelised popcorn?

On the first day of his trip did the wanderer, wander the streets. There were guys trying sell him Arabian dresses and spinning round in sparkly leggings, whilst the women played the macarena and the children ran with the skidding top turners along the street. Perfumes of cinnamon and garlic cloves flooded the air and the people's skin were so dark that instead of wearing sunscreen they wore a photo-absorbent chemical. They sealed dishes upon dishes of curries and gave, with zero charge, to the poor as the rich complained waving at the gangs huddled together on the corner of stools, enjoying their chilli chicken Korma for nothing at all.

William just ate with the curry enthusiasts and waved his new spice rack and vanilla pod he had traded at the rich buds. They moved away slowly from his vanilla that he had bargained heavily for that day, for vanilla magic and the unhealthy draw of cheese cake, was feared by all. William had no intention of using magic, for to be honest he was more scared of its practical implications than anyone else, but he knew when to play his cards.

And yes, he could have refused the magical vanilla pods, but he would never have turned away from a good bargaining after hearing his family's dying words—'never let the seller have the last word, bargain hard, my son, bargain hard'. It was in his DNA given his heritage to drive a hard deal. All his family had been good salesmen. And above all, he desired to understand the ultimate form of magic, if indeed it was magic and not some higher power or invention of God, love.

Love alone is worth the fight, of life, as the great wolfen chieftain, Sir Grogg had once conjectured.

Upon the evening of that one drizzly day did William climb a cliff that looked over the sea beyond, he stood at the borders of the known world, the travellers end, as it was called by the geographers of the continent. There he chanced upon a black cave. It was so black and blocked so much fading sunlight that the shadow before the setting sun was as a luminous candle in comparison to the cave's interior. Curiosity drove him forward, like a cat finding a squeaky toy, and being quite the scare junky, the wizard particularly liked the goulash squeaky toy that was beckoning to him.

There were no signs. Absolutely no arrows pointing forwards or sideways or backways! Did no one have a mapping fetish in these parts?

But along the cave's stone-cold walls were the elder kinds of inscriptions, inscriptions made by some pre-human race that had once walked the continent. It was not clear if these were magical homo-species, like cousins of homo sapiens sorcerers, or another humanoid all together. William hated ancient history. Yet even he noted how new some of these marks were, it was like some of them had been made only today, and they evolved in detail till he saw a picture of him in the curry market. That really freaked him out so he backed away stumbling over a bolder, dropped the fire light and cuddled into a ball.

If he could see more of the carvings, he would have made out even more disturbing signs. Some ten meters above him, the reversed pentagram that a wizard by the named 'Sir Fork fire' had chiselled into the rock with enslaved hands, was faintly glowing with power. He would also have seen some newly made statues, still hardening from their clay like start-ups. Statues of gates burning and a radiant figure, dressed in white, leading a cheering army through a burning city, as lightening broke the sky. His guardian Angel did see all these things, for he had been keeping a very close eye upon his charge and dread filled him, he tried to speak but it was like there was heavy water in his lounges.

How could this be? he thought. These creatures, or homeo-cousins or whatever they were had not been seen among humans for hundreds of thousands of years, and now there was an undiscovered cave rich with evidence of their existence and some new artefacts that were only made like a day ago?

He said unto himself and his God, "My William, my friend, should not be known to this cave, and only tattered documents and paintings upon rocks in far and remote cliffs reveal his existence for he did not communicate much with the occupiers of the physical realm. He spent more time praising cinnamon for its beautiful fragrance. Then again, Jorge had sort darker powers of much greater potency than most dared to even speak of, an evil so great its very name caused the throat to swell with the hot bitter liquid of blood. Yet this foe couldn't be here now, I mean Michael had prevented him from coming forth into the physical world. And the prison was leagues away from this place. Unless, no it can't be, it wouldn't have relocated here of all places. This must just be the lacking of a morning expresso playing games with me again. Relax, just relax."

The wandering spice merchant, unknowingly felt a twinge as the thoughts reached him through their empathetic link, but so deep is this that he well thought these were his own thoughts. Like a cape that fell upon him, this just triggered a war as his survival instincts flared and his cat like curiosity meowed to him, begging him to man up and go on. I mean, it wasn't like he was a lost kid, though he felt it, and not in the sense of the lost kids of neverland.

He imagined himself as being the first in millennia to come to know the homeo-cousins and their habitation, a black of hole of sorcery.

The internal battle remained undecided, till reason made him want to run away and never return, but he was a wizard by blood, and that link to this place he could not so easily back away from. Like someone smelling the rise of bread being baked in an oven, he was drawn to the cave by his strong connection to what was in there, whatever it might have been or claimed to be, which had allowed him entry.

The entity liked William. It knew William's history given that the dude was very bad at blocking intrusive mental spells, something this man would need to improve upon if it was to be a pupil.

Moopitarian cake was nothing more than a gimmick it wanted to use to bring him into its clutches. The lye of it became famous even in the wild southern lands when the tribal prince, Moopitar, was threatened by hooded figures in his sleep and after many a fearful chant they simply asked for him to call forth from the streets a wizard, by making 'a miracle' that the wizard simply could not resist. He did this, not liking the sulphurous fumes from his nightly visitors.

When William got over his fright at the spooky designs and decided to speak to the architects and have a good word with them, even if it meant performing necromancy and razing them from the pits of the abyss, the traveller pulled himself together. He made one bold move forward into the unknown and then as scared people drawn on by curiosity are wont to do when totally lost and in the dark without firelight, he groped for the wall and then pressed his back against it. With the comforting reminder that there was at least something physical behind him, he shuffled onwards. Then the spider came, dangling from the ceiling, and he began to crawl like a baby.

The entity that resided within the domain disliked this, so ensured the course was as rough as possible and the stones cut into the wizards' hands, shins and elbows.

William could imagine his heart's desire calling to him in its soft buttery voice, "Come, my darling, come." He never gave up, never slowed down and never stopped cursing when spiderwebs entangled themselves around his nostrils.

Yet William, who liked grand surprises, didn't like it when he came to the deeper passages that started to descend. There the cave gained the same colour as the land of the damned, a sickly colour, something that was once a part of the magical colour spectrum but had now become detached and ill, like an isolated soul, grievously wounded and broken from the murdered body.

Lightning flared. Thunder rumbled. Thousands of invisible tongues of flame sprang up on top of oily rags hanging from the ceiling, and he felt this presence wash over him.

Like an old man breathing across the damp air, he heard a voice saying, "Name yourself, intruder to my empire." To this the adventurer didn't know what to say so just replied with a made-up name whilst thinking how to politely end the conversation as quickly as possible. The voice gave him the klip klaps.

The presence didn't leave. Pilotless rarely works when facing a supernatural, superior and ancient force unless you already happen to be so far in its grip that saying no would be as hard as saying yes to an ice-bucket challenge. For those of you who do not know the nature of this self-inflicted ordeal, please visit your favourite youtuber and search for a rendition, you are sure to find one. Though Casper Lee has recently (at the time of writing) taken this up a notch to the ice bath challenge.

"I like the name William, my child," said the voice. Though William had never told him it. William thought it sounded like those really old grandads of the wander's fathers and their fathers in turn, who were in terminally ill hospitals and said everything with an air of fatalism as if asking questions was redundant since what is, is, and it makes no difference to anything whether you know it or not. And we all know where life must end, death, for death is the final destination for all life.

"I like cake," said William, hoping the joy within his voice might ignite a kindred spirit in this menacing presence and make the conversation far more comfortable.

"And well, with my cockiness and all, do I please you?" asked William nervously as if he was being brought before an invisible judge. He felt obliged to please the forebodingly sinister voice, almost as if he was speaking to his father. His father had left his mum while William was still a baby and he always felt like he let down his father, and wanted to live up to him.

William could never remember how the voice seemed to grab his soul but it seemed mega magnetic, and like those psychic vampires that were talked about in myth, who fed upon others spiritual aurar. It was almost god-like which was unusual given most of his auditory experiences where chefs telling him how to make a lighter sponge, when he was rushing around the underground kitchen trying to impress his elders. He wasn't used to chatting to higher powers. The darkened way the voice was speaking was hypnotic, the voice answered to his plea for acceptance, "Yes, as you are a magician, a man of my own making, you please me greatly."

The traveller was very confused given that the consensus was that he was born and not made, most definitely not by an ethereal creature and he had the words of his parents to prove it. And a certificate from his mother's midwife to. But maybe the voice was his dad in secret? As his eyes became adjusted to the firelight, he began to make out a blurry shadow on the wall just in sight of his vision.

William desired to make a quick genetic test when he got back and look for the blood of the gods in his veins. He wanted to make extra sure he was not in fact a demigod, but in the meantime just said proudly, "I am?" Then he coughed and lifted his wand to try to make out the shadow on the wall more clearly, he couldn't tell if it was a shadow, a figure or an apparition but whatever it was, he wanted it to be gone. He liked getting compliments but there was something clearly malevolent about the thing. So he said, as politely as he could, "Get out of here, you fiend." Then again, he felt like he was out of place in being so frank with the entity and so knelt upon his knees in sincere apology.

"Dear darling wizard, no need to be so dismissive and don't you dare get cocky. You and I have work to do. We shall do it, I have foreseen it." The entity didn't elaborate. It was spoken with an uncanny amount of certainty, even more certainty than William had in his own existence and given he couldn't imagine a world without him in, this was something very new. Against every fibre of his being, William had to believe this presence, he would work with it, he had to. He stood up trying to stand shoulder to shoulder with the shadow but his eyes couldn't catch it.

"So, hummmmmm, who are…well, who are you?" muttered William.

"I am the light bringer!" boomed the voice. "Pick up thy diary, my friend, for it is long since we have talked, so long when I knew thee before, thy was much different. Though I like thy open mindedness, this shall make my work and tutelage of thee in my ways, accelerate to new heights of wonder."

To this, William fell flat on his knees, with tears running down his face. He noted that as he had collided with the stone, or was about to in his haste to worship, an old leathery notepad had appeared which was titled something in the language of the mountain dragons. He wasn't very good at reading, but he supposed this must be the dairy the voice had spoken of.

His reaction wasn't out of joy, rather horror. He now knew what the creature was and what it surely would want from him. And his guardian angel, if it survived at all, would be forever made asunder. The thought though of an angel being slain was sickening. Such an event had not happened in recorded history. But the thought of glory made the sickening pain a worthy opponent to injure.

The angel could feel William's old self, the dragon Jorge, rise like a vapour. Slowly awakening in him. And with this turn of events, the angel wept for he knew he had failed. His charge was now lost to powers beyond his station to combat. "I am sorry for failing thee," was all the angel said, as the failure broke his spirit and he plummeted to the ground, his heart beating like a billion drums. Then SMASH!

The skull split, and its neural patterns hung out half exposed. Its body broke as it crashed to the floor. A bat with thick leathery wings, dropped onto the body. It bent down, and plunged its tiny white's teeth into the angel's heart. Golden Ichor squirted from its lips. Its mischievous eyes gleaming with delight, it spread away into the darkness of the cave and William followed.

Once the merchant had long vanished in the series of caverns, tendrils of magic came forth from a crack in some black portal, and they would have consumed the body of the dead angel and brought it forth into the abyss just as it ordered William to cast the body through the portal. Yet leaping from the rock high above came the Dylan and he howled. Instantly the cave shook and the tendrils drew away. For the first time in a long while, did both Ariton and Astaroth feel fear. They saw threw metaphysical lenses, the heavy paws and sharp fangs of the wolf, the dove made incarnate in the physical realm, and they trembled in fear at the sheer anger that dwelt in the heart of God for all the pain and suffering that Lucifer's rebellion had wrought, now visible in the God-Wolf's eyes.

For a moment, William headed for a hole near the cave's entrance, and wanted to follow the wolf into the wilds of the woods and there meet the fairies and pixies which were rumoured to dance among the tall trees at sunset. But then blackness began to rest on William once more and he bowed in reverence before his new lord, giving all at his disposal to the majesty of Lucifer.

The God-wolf left, dragging the body of the beloved angel away with him for a proper burial, sorry that he had not made a new friend in William and mortified at the prospect of what Lucifer was going to put the poor spice merchant through. Yet this was no place for Dylan, and he had to have a word with the northern king of Mados.

So began the beginning of the end.

Chapter 8
Combatting Carrots

As magic went on existing, it became a lonely force gliding through the cosmos. Gradually, it began to want to make friends, as do we all, and so it came to moderated itself to the likings of the people around it. In this it hoped that wizards would be more inclined to know it, and might come to make greater use of it. Now this is not the mentality that a physical form should have when going into friendship with another, but we must be careful here, for I am talking about a spiritual being in a physical being's language. And this is much like trying to make an undistorted map of the earth on a flat surface, which at its best is simply an approximation.

Still, magic always retained its teenage like tendencies for rebellion. Off and on, it would on occasion, and at its own whim, direct itself along the line of its own desires and not its practitioners. It was never something you could quiet trust and relying on it would be like relying on the Norse god Loki to for fill some errand.

Even if you could see magic, which not everyone can, it might well just decide not to like you.

This isn't to say it could simply pass you bye, just as steam has to change itself in some manner and perform some action or change in its state when an outside observer starts to mess with it. It just refused to make eddy currents around your physical self.

Wizards got around this personal preference of the force, by assigning a contract to magic. According to the belief of the Northern realm, who practiced the 'quadrilateral faith' developed within the first years of Ontocks establishment, this was written in the presence of the four gods, though as to what divine entity presided over it to ensure its validity, seems to depend on which religion you speak of. The white tower said God, the black tower said it was the nameless ones, and the orthodox wizarding groups say Lucifer. Personally I would vote for Lucifer because I think he does like his contracts more so than other deities, but maybe God has really got into the paperwork epidemic which is sweeping the British establishment, you never know for sure.

Anyway, taking the northern realms to have it right, the four gods presided over all things, and these individuals were the only beings magic truly respected in a reverential sense. Still, given that marriage is meant to take place in the sight of God according to the white tower, and most marriages were likely to fall apart rapidly within the first few years, many even of the Northern wizards were pessimistic concerning the rigour of the contract.

But at least the orthodox wizards were comforted to some degree and began delighting in how much more conducive magic was becoming, and willing to cooperate sensibly with other sentient life.

Now were they right? Well, let's try to be optimistic which as you may be gathering is a lot to ask for in this tale, but you should never stop trying as my uncle once said.

And according to all documents I could find in the wolven catacombs, magic has never knowingly breached the agreement in recorded documents (which are allowed to be seen and not immediately burned), so you know, though there might be people languishing in cells who have testimonies to disprove this, let us assume that magic kept to contract like a good citizen of the world.

Yet we may be being a little harsh for magic even before the contract, was not a totally wild and unrestrained entity. For magic always worked in accordance with certain deep sets of moral principles, but these were of its own choosing and not anyone else's. (Unless you ask the dragons who often proclaim that they were the inspiration for magic's fundamental morality, after it saw how mighty the lords of the sky were. I put this in brackets, for my furry self thinks this a ridiculous claim.)

Yet, however it was, magic had limits, certain things it simply was very firm about, such as not violating any living beings free will, never separating the astral self from the physical self unwillingly, and never causing two people to fall in love (magic left this last task to destiny).

Yet the contract the wizards formed with magic bound the force to wizards or any conjurers. Further for human wizards, the contract stated that within these boundaries, only one type of magic was honour bound to work in allegiance with a particular wizard. This is assuming the wizard wishes to become a master in some form of magic through the knighting of the black flame, which druids for example opted out of but they also therefore never achieved mastery of any magic and were restricted to using basic and intermediate level spells.

Now if mastery was achieved, the type of magic bound to the wizard, known as the wizard's principle foundation, should follow the command given to the best of its ability, in accordance with the specifications of the practitioner casting the spell.

During the knighting of the black flame, this contract was sealed by a wizard's blood and then Gruggorian songs were sung unto Lucifer, as well as other practices done secretly within the halls of Mados Mordré and even darker ones done in the halls of the black tower. It was unavoidable for those who wish to move beyond the basics of the types of magic, and wish to become more than a jack of all trades but master of none.

But if the master ever called upon any other magic beyond the type he was an expert in, it's chance of working was pot luck and entirely dependent upon how good willed magic felt that day. For it could play games with the wizard as much as it liked when called upon and not under the bondage of the sacred contract. It could even make the wizard the subject of his or her own spell. Unless you had some lucky potion, it was not something worth trying, and even if you did, well who said mortal magic works upon magic itself.

And the playfulness of magic did not end there. Even within the limits of the contract, did magic retain some degree of wriggle room, if only to interpret the instruction given unto it, as it would. And unfortunately for heroes and helpless maidens, magic was quite a friend of another sentient force, called destiny. Anyone getting on the wrong side of destiny thus, was on the wrong side of magic, and so it was pretty much necessary for survival that when you were given a prophecy you didn't start fighting it. Magic is not a wise enemy to have on the back of your tail.

On the other hand, if Magic and Destiny liked you, then at birth you would be given the power of fortune telling. So came seers into the world. (Well, it is said that this is how the cookie crumbles, though once more how much destiny is a real thing and this isn't some kind of practical joke magic likes playing on mortals, is hard to say.)

Magic itself found the amulets and bangles that dragged the fortune teller's body down to the ground a humorous concept. It also loved the way destiny played with legendary stories of hopeless romance against all the odds, of danger and monologuing villains. It thought all life rather theatrical.

To further our understanding of the darker aspects of magical nature, shall we but not take a note from the books of psychological research and pick up upon our prime case-study, one who neatly fits into the unusual sub-species of those who do not like Christmas and goes around smashing any presents they find close to a Christmas tree.

For Gruggor, who had once been the festive William, noticed that within the wizarding academy, during this boiling winter, were lots of parties and mince pies, but he did not like such things. He didn't like the frilly dresses of girls who were ever giggling or the beard tugging of the bearded guys.

He had valiantly hidden himself in his chamber.

Two carol singers, rather drunk, pushed through the door. They raised their glasses and dropped onto the polished floor. Then more joined them and finally Gruggor had to turn the carpet into a bunch of highly aggressive bunnies before the gathering decided to leave with much pushing and shoving.

As the tones of the dumb bell sounded, the chamber rang. It was interview time. The most magnificent, in his opinion, part of the festive season. This often included death, torture and did I mention death.

Death was unfortunately common in the halls of the wizarding school. The schools name, Mados Mordrė, was in fact a northern form of ancient French spoken by the builders of Ontock's capital city, which literally meant 'to the sacrificial altar'.

The academy was, as a matter of fact, built around the sight where it was rumoured the fathers of magic had made their first sacrifice to Lucifer and placed a pile of massively tall granite stones around the sacrificial altar to focus the rays of the moon upon it, when the moon made an eclipse with the sun. Many wolven scholars actually believe this to be the first place that the wolven folk had decided to build a monument unto their beloved moon god, and so made a crown like array of impossibly large rocks to illustrate the moons majesty. Yet taking the wizards much darker archaeological view point, they thought it was rich with black magic and so built a school on top of the crown. Over time the school expanded and became an academy and at that the greatest Academy ever known.

Silently, Gruggor looked towards the chamber's entrance, as he heard an irritating knocking on the door, and with a flurry of his wand, the chamber door flew open. He stared with fiery eyes at the still as stone terrified faces before him. Now Gruggor's principle foundation was mortality magic (Egomortalarfos in the wizarding script). This focussed upon something he exuded in every moment of silence, death. Well, technically, rebirth and immortality.

His soul was in the business of death and murder but his head and his heart yearned to find the secret to immortality that the rival black tower had supposedly got its hands on. Yet he was so terrifying, and so high up in the order of wizards, being the head of the orthodox wizarding church, that magic would almost always act in accordance with his desires if the spell was done technically correct, even if they were of non-principle aspects, provided they were not of an advanced level. Gruggor had found this out when he tried to turn into a cat, for human transfiguration was an advanced form of the transformative magic some fellow professors enjoyed, and had instead turned into a mouse which was immediately chased by a homeless cat.

Every reasonable man was frightened of this tyrant. He had, almost to the point of making a tradition, killed his higher-ranking predecessors. He had not, as many other traditions dictated, left anyone behind to mourn for the desist. About half the oldest magical houses were dead because of him. He killed because he could, not because history said he had to. He just didn't like people. Mind you most people persons like only a select group of people, so you might say there was very little difference between him and the average social worker. Yet having magic and an unending will to control the world, brought this dislike to new and more cataclysmic heights.

The last victim of these extreme desires for global domination, was the ex-head mistress of the academy. She was a teacher of mortality and was herself a very devilish individual. Historical records portray her kindlier than she was, for historians dislike the idea of feminine villains preferring to cast them in the role of seductresses or innocent maidens locked in sky high towers. Yet the teacher was evil and not the innocent victim.

Upon one cloudy and stormy day, the headmaster sneaked down to the bakery and managed to fill the teacher's bun with a little too much indigestible sugar. She had already been diagnosed with the hyperactive end of ADHD but the energy stored within these fructose crystals made her so hyper, she threw herself off the tallest tower just for an adrenaline rush. She had been falsely told by the upkeep office, many times before, "we cannot build a roller coaster or 'ride of doom' in this academy, so if you want a thrill, you'll have to…" they added jokily, "…throw yourself off the tower and hope there's a large bouncy castle waiting below."

She took their advice too literally, and dramatically miscalculated the probability of a bouncy castle happening to inflate right below her falling body.

Gruggor then in other indirect means finished off anyone that could so much as call her a friend. This was done before feeling it was safe enough to open up his previous position to his colleges and anyone beyond the walls that might wish for an interview. He then threatened the assembly. He was made headmaster immediately.

So he stood here now, in his well-earned, well bribed and fiendishly gained, chamber. By just being there, and allowing the demonic energy to dance around him, it seemed as if he was building a wall of fear in the beings before him.

What beings, you ask?

Well, the most terrified creature it is possible to be, a job seeker.

There were two candidates for the position before him, and one had to die. He could not bear the thought of having two more people he would have to have polite conversation with, or make small talk at official staff meetings.

As if they were telepathically mind-reading Gruggor's distaste of social situations, they greatly extended their own survival chance by giving absolutely no response to anything the headmaster did or said over the next hour or so. Instead they stood there, are stiff as bone, with even their pupils seemingly pinned into place, feeling very dizzy and light headed by the end of the experience.

Time passed on. Eventually, the two men standing with aching knees, feeling like celery, did not exist as far as Gruggor's mind was aware. Completely ignoring them, he stretched his thin and burned hands out to the desk. His nails were long and grubby and slightly extended as if they had been pulled by a rack every day since he was a boy.

He picked up a huge document. He slammed it onto the nearest duelling board. They winced and Gruggor remembered he had company once more, so he put on a large pair of snufflers to keep the sound of their breathing out.

Gruggor's teeth bared like a lion, he ran his nail down the first page and quickly flicked through the rest of the registry.

His coal black robes engulfed the candlelight as he stared down at the last entry with massive satisfaction. The room was consequently bathed in a faint half-light. An almost sickened shadow of true light. Rising up as the room was illuminated with that deep amber candlelight, he broke into a wide grin.

Here we find Gruggor adopted a tone of speech that defies both the round and pointy eared array of adverbs. The best description which can be said, was that he staired with a complex and dark snarl, something like the growl of a furious wolf which through high pitched crackles started splitting and reforming into twisted merriment. In this horrible voice, he said, "What idiots do we have here, I wonder. Well, well, well, we shall see. You have come and now I shall show you what Mados Mordrė is about. From this point onward you are the devil's spawn, and your identity otherwise shall be annihilated. You are the lost god's slaves to command and so you shall always be!

"Your soul will find no escape beyond these unbreakable academy walls save the ever-open door of death. You shall become quite comfortable with avoiding those doors if you wish to survive the many assassination-attempts you shall find here." Holding up his platinum wand and turning his fierce eyes towards it, in a carrying whisper, he said, "Our lord can enslave, terrorise and destroy."

The sound carried to the gentlemen and they tried desperately to theorise how to decline the interview process, without being given a swift exit from life itself.

Dropping his flashing green eyes, from a black marble draw he slid out a scratched and blood-stained sword. The scraping sound reverberated around the room. Gruggor now pointed to the sword tip. He moved it towards their heads, caressing the flattened blade with almost loving tenderness. As he held the blade to his eye, he whispered, "Now which one to kill?"

The wide grin became even more exaggerated as the two candidates looked mortified at each other, hugged one another as if now was the time to declare how camp they were in the face of mortal peril, and desperately glanced to the door. They shook with fear. One clinging to the other as if this would shield them from the magic of the most powerful wizard ever to exist. Still they said nothing being far too afraid to trigger yet another violent outburst or in any manner displease this horrific power. They kneeled in unison, got up and tried to hurriedly get to the door before more dreaded syllables emanated from their interviewer.

"Sit," was all he said.

They looked desperately at each other and started to try to bang the door down in attempt to flee, till Gruggor whacked them both with a bat from behind and they awoke to the need of following orders.

Sinking, the sofas groaned under the new weight for much of the furniture had not been sat on for years. Gradually Gruggor's mind felt that it was becoming apparent neither had the desirable urge to kill the other. Gruggor always looked for the deadly duel-stage in his previous mortality professors' minds and to not find it was alarming. These two candidates were, as terrifying as it might sound to Gruggor, simply nice people.

Perhaps too optimistically, the candidates timidly relaxed, being very delighted that the sofa was at least not a fatal death trap. The old emotivist Sir Pongo was not so lucky as he was merry enough to become a big enemy of Gruggor, he didn't fit into the militaristic academy Gruggor had envisaged. The candidates wished they could talk, break the eerie silence, but both were far too afraid to say anything.

Twisting his mouth, Gruggor once more said with that unforgettable grimace, "Do not displace our lord through the liking of fruit. Do not."

Gruggor walked over to his desk and pulled out his silver chair. He stared down at its spindly legs, as the silver scraped the marble floor. The legs gradually folded inwards till they were forming a cross shape which most wizards thought as a metaphorical symbol of the grim reaper. Once the scraping sound had gone away, the candidates thought it safe to look up, only to find him advancing till they were an inch apart and felt the gaze of Gruggor hollow out their souls. They winced instinctively and flinched as if hit by an invisible whip. His bright green eyes flared as they pierced the ambitions and wishes that brought both men so far from the world, they once knew.

Burning brightly in both was that eager poisonous fever for success. "Ah, yes," whispered Gruggor. Yet again only talking to himself.

He thought he could see that starved and devouring lion in both.

Dividing the true professors from street magicians was always that high bar in the pain and sacrifice they were willing to injure to see their ambitions flourish. In whom dwelt the greater lion that would slaughter the entire pack to take one bite of meat for itself? That was the only lion Gruggor wanted to employ.

After rampaging through their thoughts and ambitions once more, his eyes dimmed. He then turned round, moved the silver chair closer and like a guest at a delayed theatre production, he sat placid watching them.

Instead of the poisonous bite of a serpent, what came out of the job seekers was but the mutterings of an inner squirrel. Then one foolish individual had started to mutter some garble about why they ought to be given the job. This was the sort of reason Gruggor could never stand human company, for he was only willing to handle so much trash from someone, and he felt it understandable that he currently had a formidable urge to kill.

Had anyone been told to speak? No! Had anyone been given permission to talk when he was so busy thinking? Most definitely not!

So why was there a petty wizard whispering garbled words now?

Why? Asked Gruggor internally, his mind racing for a satisfactory answer to settle his boiling anger. He gave no sign of this internal battle, but still sitting placid, he stared unmoving at the muttering man. Well, probably the frightened fool felt he had to say something, Gruggor noted, just out of desperation to break the intense air.

This made Gruggor even more infuriated, for he considered fear an inexcusable sign of weakness. In total outrage Gruggor banged his fist once more on the duelling mat. Now a torrent of fire leaped forth. The mumbling candidate buried himself under the sofa and laid there quavering.

Gruggor rose from his silver throne.

Once raised to his incredible full stature, he bellowed "silence fools!" Momentarily after he sat down, wearing a wide grin but otherwise acting as if nothing had ever happened, he felt the presence he had so long ago experienced. His friend was watching.

The tranquil peace Gruggor felt descending upon him was short lived. For in that burst of magic, he had noticed an abomination in the physical, coming from the shaking figure under Gruggor's furniture.

In the headmaster's haste to be thorough, and inform the two candidates how he would surely kill either, if they did not show utter perfection and obedience in their new post, he had left his vision somewhat to one side.

It had completely passed his notice that one called Westog, was showing an almost unforgivable and criminal disregard for a vital aspect of life.

Next to religion the highest call of life was fashion.

Fashion was clearly not a word Westog understood.

The only just punishment for such failure of fashion, was surely a trip down to the gallows.

This Westog had come to the greatest academy the mainland had ever known, and dared to be dressed in a muddy garment that was once a filthy rag like the worthless peasants down in the streets wore. He had then spoken when he had not been given permission to speak. He had not bowed when any respectful person would before the majesty of Gruggor's might. Gruggor would give both the interview they had long prepared for of course, they had risked their lives by applying after all. But the scruffy one, was clearly going to be cast out. Him and his rags, as quickly as formality would allow.

Upon the disgusting candidate peering out of the furniture, Gruggor carelessly said, "Go now." Waving his hand carelessly, he spoke as if to the desk, he dismissed them without giving any further sign of recognition.

Assassin defenders then violently shoved the two gentlemen to the nearby armouries, where in Gruggor's ideal world, one candidate would violently kill the other, being understandably desperate to ensure a speedy promotion.

Laughing, a well of hope filled Gruggor's heart.

Imagining an arrow piercing the scruffy ones back, and cleaning his clothes with his blood, Gruggor beamed down at the stack of reports. He had slammed them carelessly on his desk only minutes ago, but now he hugged them affectionately, and with the thought of the scruffy one's tragic end in mind, he joyfully started reviewing both candidates' profiles. Then low and behold, coiling out the dust and dirt and intertwining it with the light rays of candles, came forth lord Ariton, prince of hell. Immediately grabbing the profiles off Gruggor's hands, he blew a hot flammable substance from his gut unto them, and they burst into flames.

But Gruggor began feeling very sleepy, and then drifted off into the realm of dreams. The sphere so very close to the world of hell, where demons could speak night and day.

Then Gruggor's dazed face, dropped in total shock, and he stared in horror at the ashes which now covered his very affluent office. Smoke still wafted around from the visitor's fiery entrance.

Attempting to disguise his dislike of this kind of messy arrival, he put on a fake smile and reached under the cabinet for two glasses. "My lord, what an honour, would you like a glass of sherry to act as a welcoming present for your coming?"

Ariton had liked William a lot, but was not a fan of this Gruggor which William had morphed into. Technically, now that he had fully trained Gruggor, he was Astaroth's pupil. For Astaroth had finished his apprenticeship with Ariton at the same time William was christened as Gruggor, and let loose of Ariton's leash. But he couldn't allow for Astaroth to handle something as delicate as a promotion which might change the fate of the world, Astaroth was a very forceful demon given his domain was overcoming 'will' with 'magic' and drawing his servants unto his purposes with sheer demonic rapture.

Ariton liked more calm-headed demons, those who followed well thought through lines of reason and thought, though of course when it came to those that followed his beloved, well then falling flat on their faces was only right and proper. Lucifer had personally given Ariton the task of helping Gruggor not make a complete fool of himself and avoid dismantling this blessed arrangement of circumstances.

"No sherry for me, my dear Arch-demon," said the demon as he made a chair out of the vacuum and sat down upon it, looking distastefully at all the torture devices and weaponry along the walls.

The term Arch-demon referred to the morph being produced when a Sapiens engaged in regular séances and possession rituals with demons, visiting them often in the dream realm. It produced in all realms a hybrid creature. A demon-man hybrid like the one which was now leisurely drinking before Lucifer's lieutenant.

Such a Hybrid was the inevitable end point of any wizard who took on the full satanic responsibilities of being the spokesperson for all orthodox Wizards around the globe.

Still Ariton thought this being was pitiful. It lacked the spice of life, to put it comically. But still such an end point was necessary for his master's purposes, and at least this gave the Wizard the ability to take enormous strain and deal with floods of magical energy which would kill most mortals.

Then coming out of his deep thought did Ariton say abruptly, "Hire Westog!"

Gruggor spluttered as some of the whisky went down his chin. "But my lord, you can't be serious," stuttered the wizard.

"Oh my dear friend, I assure you that I most certainly am. But I am also very serious that if you cock this one up, then my beloved shall make short work of you or perhaps send a few demonic spirits to do that on his behalf. They say the tortures available to those who challenge the majesty of Lucifer are most rich in suffering. They lie, of course, but there are always worse things than torture that we can bestow upon block heads such as yourself when your instinctive stupidities begin to arise and cloud your reasoning and judgment."

With that, Ariton walked towards the walls and passed straight through, entering back into his home.

Gruggor was completely bewildered but read the heavy document that had materialised during their conversation, unnoticed by Gruggor, but now unmissable given its current title was "Why Christmas has come earlier, my dear disciple." Gruggor hated Christmas.

Growling, he picked up the document, kicked off his shoes and with a glass of Pena Caldera began to read the demonic script. Mercifully, it was devoid of all festive songs.

According to the code-stained pages, it turned out Westog was not some ordinary vagabond but by an unlooked-for stroke of fate, which destiny had brought to Gruggors interviewing process. Apparently, he had been chosen by the horned god (who needed to have more sense of the importance of fashion and the latest women wear and men's suits), to do some nice dirty work which would get him usually thrown in a cell for the criminally insane.

Westog had become the high priest of the holy Great magician in one of the southern king's courts (this place was now overrun with barbarians but it had used to be a great place for magical learning and research). After Westog had reached this incredible post, he left it unconventionally (i.e., with his head still attached). You see, dear reader, most wizards are forced to leave their posts by being forcefully pushed into death's forever waiting arms. Leaving a post by choice, without having needed to receive amputations, was totally unheard of.

Westog was thrown out of the order while still very much alive.

"Curious," whispered Gruggor. Gruggor thought, for why abandon royal vagabond status (an inch away from being acceptable) and drop to street vagabond status (an inch away from being exterminated).

Apparently, the order had considered him gone too far (whatever 'too far' had meant), when he seemingly spontaneously had made a massive attempt to kill but a small and tiny baby. Now, killing babies was simply part of the job description as far as Gruggor thought but what was fascinating to Gruggor was that he had tried to kill the exact same baby. Miraculously this infant had now survived two attempts of murder from the two most feared wizards in the continent.

Gruggor, unlike the bunch of fools that ran around in the barbarian courts, knew exactly why Westog had tried to kill the baby. For this tiny baby would grow to pose the first real threat to the religion of the lost god, designed to test and challenge the forces of darkness. He was baby Christ!

Speaking directly to Gruggor, the horned god had long ago warned of a time of fire, a time when the academy walls would be bashed and thrown down to the grounds, a time were his power would be brought to nothing. Battered by dragons and strong doors torn down by the claws of wolves. Most alarming, this future time was one were Gruggor would be cast from the seat of rule. This vision had appalled Gruggor and he spent the remainder of that dark day in prayer and sacrifice to try to appease the horned god. Hoping against hope the horned god would abate from his wrath and council wizards how to change this terrible fate.

Long ago, in his blackest robe Gruggor had stridden to the temple and begged to his god from dawn to dusk, as a way to detect the Christ and be sure in his deduction. Then, feeling Gruggor's pride was humbled, Lucifer gave in a dream to Gruggor, a secret spell. Upon casting it in his high chamber, did a sickness come upon the entire land of Mados. And all the people of the unfaithful families of those who held pendants and books of God in the realm, died. A whole village was annihilated, but left were only two people. A humble Shepard, who had often been seen preaching the gospel, and his baby son, Christ, the key to Lucifer's rise or fall.

Records had shown that Westog had tried to kill this same boy, a couple of years on, whilst the kid was still of infant age and before it could pose a threat to the kingdom of darkness. He had failed to kill the boy, for Christ was forever protected from Sharir by the presence of God which surrounded him.

Gruggor saggy as he was, realised whomever Lucifer had chosen to be this boy's fateful enemy, needed all the help Gruggor could offer, for only by rallying the boy to the point where he was forced to defend himself and stand upon his own feet would he be suitably strong enough to pose a real threat and test Wizard's metal, and then be crushed victoriously.

Then again, maybe this boy might even have a knack for sorcery, and be persuaded to turn to the dark path. For that he needed a teacher of mortality who could steer the boy along the right lines, and who would be better than one which had embraced the full power of black magic?

He wept, both with joy at this potential present gifted to him, and for the sad fate of fashion, for Westog's rags still filled Gruggor with disgust.

Consolingly, he whipped out a dirty piece of cloth from the chalkboard drawer and drying his eyes said to himself, "First, we enrol the new teacher of mortality, then we send for the boy. Then we use this Westog, Westog keeps a very good eye upon Gallat, and gets him all angry and wanting to rally against wizards. Then we begin some private lessons. And then we see if the boy is for us, in which case off he goes to recover the last of the Septicon, or he makes war upon us all and we show Lucifer that his kingdom on the continent is strong and ready for his ascension, by crushing the boy. I can always fetch the scroll myself if I need to."

Quite why Lucifer would not let Gruggor just steal the last of the seven scrolls and set his master free without having to go through all this Christ malarkey, he couldn't remember. Though he got a faint feeling that he had tried before and failed, but that must have been just some stupid dream, as much as Gruggor had wanted to, Lucifer was very clear he should remain at the Academy and train up this Christ, and that was that. Gruggor like a loyal foot soldier did as he was told, though he was always a little offended and hurt at his Lords apparent lack of self confidence in him.

As the Arch-demon snapped back awake, the wandering people far below heard something that, in Gruggor's joy and hysterical evil laughter, he had just completely missed. While locked in his chamber, a million miles above any other living human, he could not hear the howling of the Dylan. The howl that made all the lords and ladies of the southern lands quaver in fright, and those in the north shed tears of repentance. In the streets people stopped playing their flute and stringed instruments, and stood as sapiens being brought before the moon god.

For in that howl they heard but one thing, the fire that burns but brighter in the dark, the lightning that cleaves through the grey clouds, the sharp edge of the broken silver blade, the ring tone of hope. An ethereal echo of forgotten roaring of the ancient fire. The anti-human fire of the dragon and the wolf.

Unaware of this answering battle cry, Gruggor sighed, feeling the religious joy of second possession fill him. He smiled. One horrible grimace of a smile.

Hoping that Westog had carried out something unspeakable, Gruggor called loudly for the other competitor, and sadly found that a moving head poked around the door, asking, "May I enter?"

"Yes," said Gruggor ethereally. But then he commanded the demonic possession to cease and got back into the business of killing, um, I mean interviewing.

He was now rather irritated feeling like someone had punctured the internal inflating balloon.

The candidate seemed nervous at first, but lifting his shoulders, he started to walk with true dignity. Though his eyes were aligned towards the desk. Dignity was what the headmaster usually sort. This was unfortunately not what Gruggor was hoping for right now. He wanted to see something fun. Something more aggressive.

The candidate was not, for instance, being dragged in by Westog with a sword at his throat. There weren't any wizard bang ups.

Whispering to his snake, he said, "Obviously entertainment is much lacking tonight. Could someone not show some selflessness and brighten my hours of boredom? I would even accept someone almost being a lethal assassin by this point."

Despite the lack of suitable entertainment, the night passed slowly on, like the movement of the second hand on a clock. Soon it would be midnight, and this caused a grin to cover Gruggor's deathly white face. Midnight was the most popular time by far to make a sacrifice to the horned god. In days gone by three in the morning would have been better as its then when the spirits are at their strongest, but most just couldn't be bothered to stay awake that long.

When the candidate had bowed and relaxed himself in a brown armchair and put his hands around the grand sides, Gruggor broke once more into a nasty grin. He lifted his nose into the air and sniffed as if trying to catch some longed-for scent. He then relaxed, and leaned forward, sitting with eager anticipation. He did nothing but wait, and silently sniff and listen, hoping for some sudden gasp of horror to enter into the mind of the man before him. Maybe as Gruggor sat here, the candidate might unsheathe a sword, only to be punctured in the back by some unseen wizard. Eventually Gruggor let out a grunt of disappointment, having realised this man was not in the mood to do anything deadly today. He sagged in the chair.

With a very bored expression, the headmaster finally began what was to be the candidates last ever conversation. "If it be not too challenging for one, so boring a man, perform for me the following. The deadly curse so often named the Arithmetical. Show me this piece of magic by the black master, with as much grace and menace as possible."

The candidate stared in horror at Gruggor, hearing so clearly the voice of an insane man. Gruggor's lip was so bloody it reminded the candidate of veins spilling their juices. It didn't help when the head master took a gulp of wine and let it drop down his chin. After realising, that himself was staring right at

Gruggor, he hurriedly looked away as if in fear of being burned and, grabbing his wand, thrust it straight towards the sky.

Stretching his arms to the night, he opened his mouth wide and bellowed "Oppo—"

"Stop fool!" commanded Gruggor. "We are not trying to blow the academy into ruins. Calmly perform this spell." And now, in an almost hungry expression, added, "Show me you can kill, immediately."

In an alarmed but confident expression the candidate started once more the long incantation, "Opposo—"

Gruggor greatly disliked the man's drawling tones. Snapping another blood-stained sword, he shouted with spit flying out of his mouth, "Silence, silly man. Why are you pointing the wand at Frosh's painting, you are about to destroy a great monument to my personal family. Frosh was my snake's favourite piece of barking food."

After sputtering and wondering what on earth the legendary wizard was playing at, he finally lowered his wand away from Frosh's mussel. Putting his wand away, he squared his shoulders and with difficulty calmly said, "I apologise. Though your room is covered with so many paintings, I can hardly avoid pointing my wand at one of them. You would not like me to point it at you?"

"So of all the paintings in the room, you chose to attempt to break the painting of my pet's. What poor practice you have at courtesy. Without destroying my possessions and, if need be, while destroying those of fellow academics, show me how the spell should be done. Show me you are a true master of wizardry."

Now pointing his wand like some poised dagger, he rested it carefully on top of the tablecloth, not wanting to destroy anyone's belongings. "Opposo... soso..."

The headmaster yawned and shouted, "Are you prepared to perform the spell on a student?"

This question took the candidate by such shock that he stammered and finally ended with saying 'carraito' instead of 'caito'. This was a disaster for the candidate. The spell 'Opposososo-carraito', which had never been tested before, caused a carrot to fly like a sword into the room and begin a fearless combat with the candidate. Inanimate objects as a rule are very fearless, because they are not equipped with survival instincts. The vegetable was finally defeated but only at the cost of the smart clothes being stained with orange paste.

"What kind of rotten trick are you playing at!" shouted the candidate.

"Disgusting!" laughed Mr Gruggor, completely ignoring the candidate's question.

"On a more serious note, I was concerned that you took so long to overcome a single carrot. Carrots are not something most high-level wizards fear. I would be seriously concerned, thus, if my students were taught advanced magic by someone who has nearly been overcome by vegetables. Even the chef has never encountered any such difficulty. Perhaps becoming a cleaner may be more worthy, or something similarly cowardly."

Expecting the candidate to storm out of the room in complete outrage, the headmaster was incredibly surprised when the candidates face made a gradual transit from fury to concern. Then after resting heavily on the chair, the grip on the wand changed from relaxed to that of iron. Concerned frowns then changed to terror.

The candidate appeared to be awakening to some horror lurking in the room.

Gruggor instinctively swung his head around to ensure that one of the many assassins had not invaded their privacy. After concluding that they were indeed secure, and very much alone, the headmaster asked, "I want to know your family history. Have any others aimed to serve the academy?"

"Yes. Both my parents served dutifully as dream assistants and, and…"

"And they what?" snapped the headmaster

The candidate was now running his hands through his brown combed hair. Then the candidate turned and looked past Gruggor at the wall, before bellowing "came to kill."

The black magic guru, Gruggor, made a glance behind him, but there was no one there. Then what if he was talking about the parents? Eagerly he made a quick note of the candidate's most illuminating suggestion.

"You mean that your parents were proud to continue the historic successions of murder. Took pride in the ritualistic killings of this academy."

Gruggor was beginning to feel very impressed by the quality of this candidate and might even give him a seal of Pedro or let him walk away alive. This was a rare exit for someone who entered Gruggor's chamber. However, just as Gruggor was turning from killing instincts towards these unlooked-for acts of humanity, the candidate bellowed, "If my family were here, they would slash you to death. Leave this place, oh foul fiend of the dark pit, and fall to your doom."

With that, he drew a wand. Opened his mouth wide to unleash a spell of dark sorcery. And it was over. Gruggor sat perfectly relaxed.

He was enjoying the theatrical display. His assassin defenders were well trained to deal with much more dangerous persons than a maddened wizard. Seconds after the outburst, the man was wrestled to the ground.

"Send him to the gallows," commanded the Arch-demon dispassionately. "And cut off his head," he added as an afterthought.

The Arch-demon could, of course, tell that the candidate's sudden change from annoyance to pure terror had meant the wizard was not himself, though sadly, a medical discharge was a far too lengthy alternative of dealing with the situation than by use of gelatine. Short executions were much more speedier.

He had no wish to remove this howling man from the world of the living, but simply by living he would be using up more time than Gruggor had. If the struggling wizard had problems with this, he should simply of signed a medical discharge form for poison and cursed minds at the entrance gates far below, in case of such unlikely eventualities. The candidates lack of paperwork was not Gruggor's fault, therefore he could not understand why the wizard seemed so incredibly distraught. Though it would be very wrong to suggest that Gruggor did not enjoy the screaming he so wished to hear.

Concerning Westog though, well 'he's in for a shock', gloated Gruggor. Rubbing his hands, he mercifully decided to let the scruffy one attain his heart's desire, though Gruggor wished to play with his food first and stain its joy.

"Westog, or whatever your name is, come in and let us get this over with. So are your parents in any way related to this academy?" Staring hopelessly at Westog, Gruggor added, "Either answer is likely to act against your application."

"No," quavered the candidate, while he watched his rival being dragged out the office and forced down the winding staircase into the underground dungeons. He heard a cry as the rival was shaking to try to escape.

"Ignore him," said Gruggor. He reached out his hand and drew his wand, with a swish, the rival candidate fell limp and was dragged out of Westog's sight. "Now to a matter of much longer-term importance. Are you sure none of your ancestors has walked in these ancient grounds?"

"No," repeated Westog with a strain, indicating he wanted to get back to what he saw as the very significant problem at hand.

Oblivious to Westog's pain, Gruggor continued, "That is a relief. You're clearly from a poor family and we do not want the academy to be disgraced by your poverty. Your attempts to ruin our reputation would justify a tour of the dungeons. Would you like a short trip to the axeman to finish your experience or prefer to see the execution of your competitor?"

Falling to his knees, Westog begged Gruggor to take him to the gallows if only the other candidate could be spared the horrific punishment. "It was not his fault. It was, was me who, well, I should bear the blame. I spiked his melon juice with magic mushroom powder."

Slowly, Gruggor's face changed from an expression of disgust to one of astonishment. "You mean to say that you cheated. Made him suffer his worst fears so that he would appear mad, and by elimination I would choose you. How did you buy such expensive ingredients?"

"I'm too poor to buy anything of the kind. But I didn't steal, no never steal. I created the concoction with the use of the principles of elemental magic."

"I don't believe you. However, that is completely irrelevant. I clearly misjudged you no matter how you developed or stole those ingredients. An excellent brew and stewed with skill few have ever been gifted with."

Admiration shone from Mr Gruggor's face. "You cheated and did brilliantly. Start your shift of teaching tomorrow at precisely 2:00 pm and make sure you bring decent clothing."

Still weeping over his criminal act, the candidate cried, "But what will become of the other?"

In a heartless laugh, the Arch-demon yelled, "Let him burn. You've got the job you so craved, so just get on with it."

In a loud crack, the servant of Lucifer vanished.

Chapter 9
Soufflés

After returning from the dungeons and gallows, Gruggor's assassin defenders dragged Westog all the way to the edge of the far crescent tower near to the western wing. This tower was built some thousand years ago, being a part of an original complex, and it was covered in marble with statues of the great wizards of the academy who had served, dotted around in hexagonal arrangements. The academy itself had a pale grey covering with vines running through the cracks, and looked like a medieval ruin from the outside. Yet inside, it was opulent.

Hexagons were common arrangements since all practitioners of the satanic art in the continent saw the unholy polygon of the demonic. Within the centre of the unholy polygon, there was a roaring fire which flickered from dawn to dusk eternally. Each wizarding statue in the hexagon had their hands outstretched to the flame as if they were offering something up unto Lucifer.

Burnt offerings were not part of the custom of wizardry these days but Westog would have been quite shocked to see such a reminder of barbaric systems here still, if he was not so distraught and out of his mind.

There were paintings on the wall of wizarding jewels they won in combat, some with a bloody finger or even a whole hand still attached to it, a reminder of the sheer power they wielded and the damage such power could bring. The marble floor had a crossed like pattern which re-emphasised the sharp edges to the massive coulombs which stretched from the base of the seer's spire to the very top of the tower, a sign of the bitterness and coldness of wizardry and the heartless route needed to rise to the very top of the order.

Yet in this grand place, one which emphasised the violent nature of modern wizardry, were palace guards. They were found slouching upon the pillars, looking like they were having the time of their lives. They had their helmets round the wrong way and had breast plates two sizes too big. Their spears seemed to have dull edges and grime covering the handles. Their swords were not kept tight in shiny scabbards, but were hanging loose at a precarious angle and their scabbards were dangling from the loose end of their belt. They looked pretty comical.

Thinking a distraught man in a grubby robe, now screaming, having been dragged by Gruggor's wizards and thrown into a coulomb, was quite a trivial matter, they looked longingly into the distance and outside to the blue sky beyond the clear window, dreaming of an apricot souffle. It was such a nice day and how much they wished to be outside, milking cows like the people below. As a matter of fact, if they had the fate of the world resting upon them, they would consider such concerns to be hardly worth consideration. Some chemistry in their minds caused thoughts of anything of a serious nature, to be obliterated. For it was their waking thought and their night delight, the realm where the egg whites were light and fluffy and the whisk was forever whisking.

They were suddenly woken from their soufflé slumber, when the man made one most heart-wrenching howl which even my chief would be proud of. Then they sank back. Momentarily forgetting that a man had just collapsed yet again and now lay unconscious beside them, they sighed, feeling overworked and exhausted. It was tough work being a guard, and though the headmaster ensured that meals and floor living space were included, some pay would be nice. Some shiny gold, though they didn't want this for wealth you see, they wanted to melt it and put it into a soufflé mould, so they could have a model to gaze upon whenever the need arose.

Yet these two men were not always so lifeless. They had succumbed, as did all who entered into the academy to what was known as the 'soul-sucking' virus. This was an entirely mythical virus, but it describes the very real change in state of an individual's vitality as their soul expired within the walls, and their bodies became more lethargic. People felt like their life was being drained from them, but the promise of power was so great that no one felt this was an important issue to tackle.

Everyone's hopes and dreams vanished into myth and they were left as husks of themselves. The soul-sucking epidemic was devastating.

With only the soufflé to act as a memorial to what was once two formidable men. They still didn't exactly believe in all of Gruggor's warnings, but they had seen enough to make up their own minds about their smallness and insufficient power. Yet a tiny part of them still wanted to escape the walls, or what was beginning to feel more like a prison. Yet this too was squashed by the fact that no one ever did. Or those that did never came back.

So, they buried their last grains of hope with wine and jolly song. Within the academy they lived impossibly long lives and upon their last birthday, at the age of some four hundred years old, they thought of how, though it was very true they had survived far longer than most and never seemed in any obvious peril under the watchful eye of Gruggor, they were yet more pleased to be the great whiskers of the continent.

And now they were too weak to even battle the weakest of the old foes. Now a days they would have been horse meat if they went anywhere even mildly dangerous, so they stayed under the watchful eye of the headmaster, merrily staggering around the corridors and outside the banquet halls.

Gruggor, had taken his safety moto, even further than this in recent times and trying to squash the vaguely true but unhelpful rumours of unexplained disappearances and murders, he assured every new student that they would be perfectly 'safe' under his watchful eye. Many believed him, not that after getting to know him would anyone consider him a safe individual to be around, but who would dare challenge the power of Gruggor. He was a legend. He always said at the welcoming feast, that they had 'nothing to fear for I'm the greatest practitioner of the secrets of the horned god that has ever walked the earth, fear not my fellows in the secret arts'. Contrarily, this invoked so much fear into the professors that they didn't dare correct these assertions, this was extremely effective.

Yet let's not be super-judgy and let us assume Gruggor genuinely felt the academy to be safe, we must not accuse without direct proof of course. Well, if he was genuine, well then, safety is clearly not a word Gruggor understands.

Upon declaring anything about the academy to be 'perfectly safe', corresponding standards of danger were set so high, it is extremely likely that if the guards were to encounter anything 'dangerous' according to Gruggor's standards, then the wisest course of action would be to welcome it with open arms. Just as if being in the centre of a hydrogen bomb is considered 'safe', then the only 'dangerous' explosion must be something relatable to a supernova. If you do meet a supernova, the most worthwhile way to spend one's last few seconds is to sit back and enjoy the view.

In fact, if living within ancient walls was 'safe' and a 'dangerous' enemy force was preparing to assail it, one might as well send them flowers and chocolates and kneel before them as soon as they were in sight.

The guards felt very strongly that they should do this if ever the need arose. Then again, they had lost so much of their former fire in life, that being oppressed by an enemy, would do little spiritual damage and if that enemy liked souffles it might even give some meaning back into their repetitive and dull lives.

They would occasionally hang around passages drinking whisky dreaming of their home being overrun with extremely dangerous barbarians. Or if they had too much to drink, be found shouting at bees and professors alike. This was more funny than scary, for these two gentlemen were the most non intimidating people imaginable. But they also happened to be the most innocent and thoughtful, and the future masters of all things sugary. Jumping with a start, they reawakened to the world around them.

"Getting lost happens all the time, no need to worry. Here now," says the other guard handing Westog a piece of unstained kitchen roll to wipe tears from his face. "It happens all the time! Just make sure you break into every room and you will eventually, at some point, find yours! Everything will be completely fine."

The guard's vague attempts of support did not prevail to cheer Westog up. Yet soon, as their knees started aching and their stomachs rumbling, they wondered upon a much more practical issue. It was almost dinner time and Westog had not moved unless he was attempting to go slower than the pace of a slug. Before the guards could fill their stomachs, they had still to traverse any further distance and venture into some room and get the weeping man onto a bed and out of their care.

Fortunately, the guards didn't have to search far in front of them. There was an unlocked door hanging ajar, right ahead. And what kind of guard would leave a man, while looking as forlorn as a collapsing souffle, abandoned having not yet reached a safe destination. Yet this man was, most uncooperatively, insisting on this odd behaviour of wildly hitting and destroying the ground.

They considered grabbing his limbs, then swinging him and then letting him go as he sailed through the air. Assuming their aim was accurate, he would in very good time be safely on the bed. Of course, he could just walk to bed but there he was, still beating the floor.

Thankfully, in the end, they decided that a slower, but more reliable procedure, might be to drag Westog into the room. Therefore, the guards bent down and grabbed Westog's arms and legs in a firm grip. He then was dragged, as he slid over the ground. He became very well acquainted to the floor and the carpet in the first few seconds of that very first night and got a very sore and runny nose to remember it by.

In the case of the guards, this was the most exciting thing that they had only dreamed of, they had passed beyond the door, into the hallowed room beyond!

Westog crawled into the sheets, pressing the puffy pillow over his even puffier face as he wept. Upon some ungodly hour, he had exhausted himself with sorrow and so fell into a disturbed series of dreams. After a time of dark nightmares, and visions of being dragged away, his thought returned to his old home that he would remember the details of, for last time in many a year to come. He had not forgotten yet though.

No one ever seemed to retain their former memories for long after passing the walls of Mados Mordrė, the place had a way of taking one's thoughts and filling them up with new ones. Finally waking he opened one eye and then squinted up at a figure waving a bottle of wine above his head. Unfortunately, the bottle was the wrong way up and its contents were covering Westog's face.

"Good morning, my miserable friend. Why so sad in the morning? Does the bubbles not burst from thee?" so said one of the now many guards as they staggered across the room. Though Westog did not know this, this was the curly-haired dude named Jasper, who as it happened had very good relations with the Arch-demon, thinking him the iconic villain, and taking great interest to see what destiny had in store for him beyond driving him so totally loopy.

Jasper tried to give Westog a glass of champagne and a full-frontal hug, but Westog just backed away a little uneasily, for this teenage dude was a total stranger unto him.

Westog tried to look out of the window to check if this dude was actually making sense, but there were two giggling girls blocking the view of the world outside. "Morning? But it's pitch black and I've got to get out immediately!" spat out Westog, coming to his senses. His head felt quite sore and his eyes stinging slightly from all those tears that streamed down his face. Clearing them, he now saw the room was being gradually filled by person after person. He couldn't make out any details, but he could see the vague outlines of a massive gathering.

"Of course, it's pitch black, for it's only two in the morning. It is dark most of the morning these days, but no worries, it's party time."

In response, all the guards shouted, "Party time!" Music sounding like growling wolves reverberated around, and the individuals began dancing in some hypnotic rhythmic form.

"But I have no time for parties. I must get out. Don't you know Gruggor is a murderer?"

"Murderer, of course he is, he's such a good killer," shouted someone to which they all replied, "a great one."

Despite Westog's growing sense of alarm, he bravely continued, "He killed the other, and I must get out before he kills me. He's totally mad." This seems to be a universally accepted fact, almost axiomatically true. Everyone knew Gruggor was most definitely utterly mad. It was so obviously true; it was often claimed to be a wizarding baby's first words.

The problem was Gruggor was also incredibly powerful, so everyone responded to these dangerous words by becoming as transfixed statues with mouths sealed shut. Then a frantic muttering broke out, before there was a crack and the door split open.

There was silence.

Then a deep and rasping voice in the black hallway said, "Well, I'm terribly sorry to interrupt this party."

One may wonder what happened in the course of intervening years. I shall but leave a question mark. And leave it to historians to fill in the details.

The trees in the forests kept growing like they always had, their roots digging into earth minding little but the iron content of the soil. It is an eternal comfort that no matter what trauma we find in our day to day lives, the world is uninterested in human suffering. This isn't to say it's not important, this is only to say there are things undamaged beyond it.

Of course, when grief comes along, it feels like the world should stop to mark the passing of a soul, but even ignoring the issue of the living occupants hurtling into space, it is probably fortunate for the emotional health of the soul that it does not.

Chapter 10
Never Eat Lobster Roll

Some ten hilly leagues from the lush flat grounds of the academy, was a royal man facing a whole set of vastly different challenges. These had regrettably sent him down a very wobbly spiral into tea-madness. The non-magical challenges a king like himself was facing, included drinking enough tea to suppress the need for solid foods such as bread and potatoes. Also another troubling facet of his station was the more serious job of battling the uprisers from Mados Mordrė. These uprisers made cleverly disguised assassination attempts upon his royal self, on a weekly basis.

Only last week, for example, had a dog that had been infected by rabies, been released onto the royal court. Thankfully, it was tempted enough not to bite his leg off when he waved a piece of roast duck before the four pawed aggressor, but this was a close call. Not only this, but he was juggling the 'fear of death stress' with the pressure of convincing the public to remain calm and unafraid of the kingdom's terrifying wolven neighbours.

Unfortunately, since extensive deforestation of the northern forest had begun, the kingdom was in some kind of cold war with its furry forest neighbours. Needless to say he was a man who did not have things together and Mados was only just about holding itself together.

He twirled his big brown moustache and pulled it taught like a man might pull string. After many iterative stretches it formed into a tight cone, then remained in that shape for an inconceivably long duration, given that he had forgotten to bring wax with him. With disturbing frequency did similar designs collapse during evening meals, where the waft of the gravy made his facial hair that bit more moist and flexy, such that the moustache dropped into a curly thin parabola. This consequently left many thinking 'how does he not bite his mouth-hair off his face'. The court was often found to be discussing this, appalled with the facial look of their king, when they were not so drunk themselves that moustaches seemed like the best way forward.

The ruler of Mados had bright brown eyes, and pointy eyebrows and looked like an insane scholar crossed with a drunken sailor.

The moustache man drank one large gulp of orange rum and placed it precariously on the side. He staggered backwards as the strength of the alcohol struck him first in the throat and then in his head. This aged man was skinny and so possessed little resistance to the liquor. Thus, his head went slightly cloudy as images of brown syrup and his best-friend, the local donkey, flooded his mind.

Once more, he foolishly took another sip, but this time with the idea being drowning the donkey images out and replacing them with cute cuddly pillows. He particularly wanted to forget that terrible day when the local donkey had trampled all over the birthday cake that the king had specifically made for him, with his favourite flavours of spiced tea and ground pumpkin.

Eventually, the king found sanctuary in the oak barrels, those which were used for the production of oak tea. For he was in the oak tea room, with a desk full of bank balances, a few candles dotted around, and walls covered in even layers of brown paint. It was dark for the window curtains were closed, and the palace was silent for it was late evening, and so the king was trying to relax in this blessed room and forget his tasks. Stress has a curious way of being the most clingy companion ever though.

Now, oak tea is the marvel of the kingdom. It was sold in the barrels to the people of Mados, and since the kingdom's formation has acted as the financial and cultural lifeblood of the realm.

It was often said mockingly by the people of the rival kingdom of Ontock, that Mados was founded upon the delight of drinking hot brews, and the king, Bartibus the barmy, kept it true to its legacy, and not the true spirit of a brave and bold warrior. Though the people of Ontock were a bit out of place to say this, given their adoration of peppermint tea.

But the wolves never quite understood why an outlandish production rate of oak tea, justified the chopping down of their oak tree forest and the annihilation of their homes and sacred groves. In a desperate attempt to appease the hostile creatures of the northern forest, the royal palace offered some extra barrels up to the four pawed border controls. These muscled and fierce wolves lived near the forest and were put there by the chieftain to remind Bartibus that he would not be king of anything but a desolate land for long if he kept messing with the forest.

Now Bartibus offered up these oak barrels, in the name of peace, and as a sacrifice unto the wolven people. Every knight tasked with the daunting trip of delivering these barrels, noted that the border controls never exactly said thank you for the oak, which pissed them off a little given they had to travel some fifteen leagues from the palace just to hand over a stupid barrel. But when the knights went on the journey back to recover the barrel, to see if the sacrifice was accepted, they always stumbled across a dead deer that the wolves had supposedly left out for human cooking. Better yet they always came across such a gift some couple of leagues from the border controls, saving four leagues on the planned round trip.

You know they say you should never question a good thing. Well, I'm sorry to tell you, reader, when dealing with wolves, you really should!

Exactly why they found the carcass slightly far afield from the place the oak barrel sacrifice was laid, was a benevolent enough matter, since it was probably because wolves find it very unhygienic to stay in close proximity to a dying body. Yet the wolven folk's lack of willingness to pay their own personal respects and great humans, to thank them in person, as they would have if the carcass actually been intended as a present of gratitude, should've raised a few alarm bells.

However, sadly, the dead deer was taken by the court as sufficient payment and left at that. It was not considered to be a warning. Dead deer is not a sign of thanks; it's a sign of what kind of damage can be done when a wolf decides you are its prey.

The king clambered out of the oak barrel he had submerged himself in, and walked like a giant ghost towards the mirror. He had sharp bits of oak covering his clothes and one peg like peace stuck onto his nose. This meant he couldn't smell the muck covering his feet or the stench of rotten meat that emanated from his mouth. He had mud splattered on his face like he was trying to camouflage himself in the middle of a swamp. This was sad considering he was a good-looking guy given his age, but he never really took care of himself nor his hygiene.

Yet because of his unusual appearance, he was staring right back at his reflection's terrified eyes.

The reflection looked like the living dead character, from Peter the zombie, crossed with a village farmer. It was a terrifying combination, though most monsters crossed with a farmer would be terrifying, if only because of them carrying a nearby corn cutter. To the mirror he said, "The people, we must tell the people!"

The mirror did not respond; being inanimate, this was not shocking. Yet despite mirrors never responding in recorded history, humans have always found a strange comfort in speaking to mirrors as if the world they see reflected there, is another dimension, and contains real people who hear and fully understand the mutterings of the speaker.

This mine furry self is only pondering, for I cannot fathom all the oddities of the sapiens people, yet their actions clearly demonstrate that in some form, the human mind is convinced there is such a caring world on the other side. Or at the very least this distressed king was.

Mind you, all the men in the kingdom were distressed. But the only more distressed man than Bartibus the barmy, was one of the mayors who was desperately trying to warn the community something terrifying was about to happen. At least something truly of wolfic proportions would ensue, if they continued down the dark and twisted road of consuming so much oak tea. He even ended up feigning his own death to prove this, only to be killed by assassins a few days later. Bartibus then gave these assassins golden medals and power in the rougher cities of the kingdom, for their determination to prove that tea was not the real reason to be afraid, and so give peace to the tea drinker. For they had shown how assassination by fellow humans was the real danger at hand.

Without this tea epidemic, nothing would get done. With it a small number of things got done. I'm not sure that things got done super well. Judging by all the rioting about homes collapsing, the tax system being ridiculous and about pretty much everything else, it got done pretty poorly, but it got done nonetheless.

A duke of the northern realms, Sir Pentafield, had perhaps not helped the king's cause by saying that he could not possibly of signed the 'legalise theft agreement' without the great changes to his mentality made with the aid of the oxygenic drug found naturally in oak tea. Yet that was honestly a small set back when looking at all the things tea had done for the kingdom.

Tea had for instance helped invent the wet digestives and soggy biscuits. Something letters from the rival realm of Ontock, constantly teased Bartibus about.

Bartibus checked he was wearing two pairs of woollen socks, and then looked at his reflection in the mirror for any hint on what to do. With delight he saw his reflection turn towards an oak set of draws, and no, this was not a magic mirror, for it was only mimicking the king's every move. Bartibus then looked back around and nodded wondering if his reflection was still thinking along the same line of thought, and luckily for him the reflection did indeed nod as one with the man.

Within Bartibus' mind, the man on the other side of the mirror must have agreed with the king. Taking this as confirmation that his thinking was correct, he rushed through the draws trying to look for the parchment in which were listed the main reasons for tree destruction, which his advisers had kindly written out for him.

What would he do without his royal advisors? They were the lifeblood of the royal court. Yet, staring down at the tea-stained bent floppy thing, his mind felt even more confused. He attempted to re-read the parchment just to make sure he had read the messages clearly. Upon failing to read it, having been illegitimate for a long time, he got a scribe with a thick Cornish accent (well, an equivalent tone) to read it out for him.

It went something like this:

Reasons to continue annihilating the forest:

1. Trees release oxygen. If we want to limit the risk of being invaded, we must make sure there is not much oxygen to spare. Till people must gasp to breathe, we clearly have too much available air left, and should thus continue extensive deforestation.

2. Trees are very old. We should cut them down since their age makes us feel like we pass away far too speedily. So, it helps the mourning public when we cut down their sacred trees. And helps everyone feel youthful and like they can throw parties even at the age of retirement.

3. Trees take in dangerous excesses of carbon dioxide. Similarly to the overload in oxygen levels, this means that trees make our cities nicer. We should surely not want our cities to be pleasant as this would encourage invaders to take over our otherwise undesirable kingdom.

4. Trees dry up our soil making our land dryer. We need to conserve water to ensure we can continue drinking a large excess of tea and should therefore wipe out the local tree population.

5. If we cut down trees, no cat shall find themselves stuck up at impossibly high heights. We shall be loved by the cat fanatics.

Reasons not to cut them down:

1. Keeping trees alive = Not getting murdered by packs of vicious wolves.

It's five against one, so logically the reasons not to cut down trees are way outmatched by reasons to leave the tree cutting industry alone. He forgot perhaps that quality over quantity is what validates an argument.

The king smiled, feeling comforted enough to continue his deforestation plans. But then he read one of the points again and broke down into tears.

Only the last of the pro cut down tree points made much sense to the drunken king since he liked cats and often dreamed of becoming cat man. However, oxygen and carbon dioxide focussed ones, seemed to imply that the court thought the king, that is to say himself, was governing an unenviable kingdom which was too undesirable to attract invasion. Or at least an undesirable atmosphere. He made a quick note on his hand, with an angry face emoji just to remind himself how angry he was with this.

Later after retiring to his dormitory, he opened the cage of his crow and using some tea inked substances from his bedside desk, wrote a letter which he handed to her before she sped out the window. It was the greatest mistake of his life. He had just sent an official document asking the nearest pillaging and invading community to help prove that his kingdom was worth invasion. But this was the kind of man he was, determined to prove his worth no matter the cost to his people.

But back to the present and the barrel room, he almost nodded as he thought to himself, *The wolves are not a match for Barbarian steel*; surely the impeccable prince Rupert and his knights would make short work of them. "Yes," he said to himself, jerking back awake, "there were small mumblings about how the wolves were rising, and the barbarians might even be trying to make a deal with them to surmount a massive attack, but what did that matter? Surely not. It was only theory after all."

The king smiled. He was so lucky to have these Cornish and Devenish scribes and advisors. It was long ago when they had all been led by a man in a cloak, who seemed so eager to help out the court by offering some talent he had found when scouting. Yes, this was a little strange, and given how highly convenient this was and how it came the day after many a royal servant had been found poisoned at the last banquets supper, most would question it.

Bartibus did not like questioning. He just liked being comfortable, unafraid and totally chilled. He was clearly boldly confident and mightily impressed with how well trained the knights of the realm were. Particularly how they soothed his worries when that wolf fanatic everyone kept referring to as the Dylan came to try to talk sense in him. It seemed very concerned for Bartibus' own safety if things continued the way they were. He kept mentioning grave tales of how many even within his own community, were turning to the aggressive whispering of some elders who wished to see all tree destroyers eaten to death or cooked like steak upon a massive bonfire.

Apparently, the Dylan was falling out of favour these days and his message of 'peace, harmony and love for living beings' was making him more an outcast than a hero. Bartibus felt sorry for this furry soul, but his advisors made very clear that anyone who wants 'peace, harmony and love' to flow freely between all peoples, was clearly in cuckoo land. They also whispered to him in private about how the wolf only wanted to darken his days with misery and woe.

Sadly, backing them was scripture. For it was clear to anyone who has read 'The Book of Homosapien Dominion' that the horned god (or Lucifer to you and me) had wanted humanity to exist as overlords and masters of physical creation.

In the doctrines and human scripture that Bartibus had clung to since childhood, it clearly stated that the horned god long ago gave Jim and Clive, the right to name all the animals present and cut down as much of the forest as they liked. They then began the righteous campaign of tree destruction that would be valiantly continued by their ancestors, to build themselves a nice mansion and a gorgeous treehouse on the side adorned with lilies and roses. And after their fall did Lucifer kindly provide them with some polished weights to look all manly and all that, to boot.

Even Bartibus, who never went to high school and could just about recount the numbers from one to ten, knew that!

Supposedly, there was also a female given they would need to procreate, but hey, if the frail sapiens form before the fall was designed to be immortal, and death was waiting its telephone call to come in and mess with creation, why insist that only females could give birth and were a necessary component in creating a baby? Maybe men could procreate with other men then, and perhaps even a little after till the biological effects of their decent became significant? I mean, if pre-fall earth was a paradise, surely it would also be a paradise for gays and lesbians.

Bartibus thought about this kind of thing a lot. He liked anatomy and actually had literal skeletons in his closet.

Now, Dylan tried to bring up that all are equal under God's eyes, and there was now no male nor female, boy or girl, or furless and furry. But Cornish people apparently don't like this talk and his advisors backed Bartibus' resistance, and love of tea, every single step of the way!

So Dylan often plodded away feeling rather dejected, and like perhaps this entire mission of global unification, was impossible, even for him. Though the furry one, decided to keep a good eye upon those advising the king, they seemed to have something shifty about them and their smiles were always a little too rehearsed.

Bartibus turned unto his Cornish comrade, Jim, and said unto him, "Where upon this sunny day was the prince? Riding gallantly through the meadow fields? Laughing as he chopped off the head of an orcish foe?"

Josh, named honourably the first Josh of all Sapiens people, beamed back, and without saying a word just scribbled a few things on his paper notebook, like taking over duty from some kind of Gregory, the ancient angels whose job it was to keep eternal tabs on their charge, so the one had always an up-to-date catalogue. Omniscience implied God didn't actually need such a detailed recording, but we all know how fun it can be to go through Argos Catalogues looking for the latest DIY, so supposedly the one felt similar with regards to flicking through the thoughts and actions of his beloved creation.

As for Rupert, he was not engaging in any combat for the glory of the kingdom, but was walking forlornly on the stone ground, sulking almost, for the short spear fights throughout the late afternoon had left him with an aching arm and one very sore leg due to a miss angled cylindrical piece of wood, with a pointy metal shaft. The memory of the romance filled morning felt like a memory from another human, with another life.

Sweat poured from his brow and he felt like smashing the wood against his knees into shards. Meanwhile, while the prince was caught up deep within his own mind, thinking how useless training was for the randomness and pure pot luck of real combat, some slight and well-armed individual in slippers rushed by, careful to remain quiet and unseen.

The king, very oblivious to this truth, sank down in a tea barrel for an early nap preferring the bed of tea leaves to the royal mattresses.

Things were getting rather exciting in the king's barrel as a maid had found it a good place to hide and appear upon this Valentine's Day. Neither were quite prepared for the following outburst of activity though.

A man with two missing front teeth leapt out of one casket and whipped out a massive blade. He then realised he couldn't see all that well, it was evening and it was getting pretty dark with only candle light to make out the faint outline of caskets, time must have just moved very fast within the barrel. In self-defence he jumped away and stared around before correcting the blur by picking up a pair of dusty glasses one of the king's waiters must have accidently dropped. He had been sure, to see the king before though during the time in which he had slowly arisen from the deep depths of the casket, the king had either gone invisible or had hidden surprisingly well. Just as he was thinking, *I can't be bothered to look in all these barrels! I don't like tea*, the king arose, albeit covered in lipstick.

Upon seeing the king, and then the crown on top of the occupant's head, the man jumped away, feeling lacking in bravery. He was not an inexperienced assassin but was on the contrary experienced enough to be nervous about attacking a king, since most southerly bandit tribe leaders always elected a sort of barbarian king who was super fierce and knew how to shout and beat his chest, and assumably the same would be true about northern kings.

Still, this assassin was overestimating Bartibus' combative abilities. Perhaps more dangerously though, he was underestimating his own abilities to retreat, or more so his abilities in navigating in almost pitch-black darkness. He wacked his boot on one of the caskets and let out a massive howl. He then surveyed the area, stood his ground, and walked casually forward gradually regaining courage.

He was just about to strike the king down as the king was cowering before his blade, when wishing to do the whole thing properly, he abandoned his first attempt and he sunk back into one massive barrel ready to make a grand and terrifying entrance which would go down in history forever. Thus with an evil laugh, he then rose out and lunged.

Despite the assassin's many setbacks, this still could have been the end of the king. However, when taking the time to pick up night vision goggles, fit into a barrel, get back up, and all that jazz, he did give the king plenty of time to scream.

Screaming was a well-practiced talent which had kept many in the royal court alive far longer than their lack of self-defence might have made likely. In truth screaming was so useful that the first week in any Madosian knight's training, was learning how to give a blood curdling scream. No knight was ever knighted in the realm, without becoming a proficient expert at the art. It was taken very seriously and there was even an oral exam at the end of the knight's training, though the knight's master board, had to keep changing the expert examiner every year, as the screaming could be very hard to cope with.

The assassin may have noticed Bartibus' favourite Pier scream, one which always drew people towards him like a flock of sheep to a shepherd, if the assassin was not also profoundly deaf and way too busy laughing with triumphant joy.

The assassin thought he had finally put the king in an inescapable position, until a blade slid clean from his back, and ripped through his coat. The assassin stared down at the slit through his favourite chilly weather wear and then to the king as if asking for some explanation. He clearly was from the realms where polite etiquette was followed and no one ever stabbed an armed man from the back, or lowered themselves to an unfair and undignified move.

The expression of confusion and inquisition remained on the dying assassin long after his death.

As exciting as this was, the king had not yet managed to avoid the peril of the evil spirits which lay unchecked, within the oak barrels. Or at least he saw them as spirits, not believing that any mortal man would dare attack his highness, not due to his royalty, but since this would damage the most tea infused body ever known to exist. Everyone must surely bow in the deepest part of their hearts to the 'tea angel', as he often said to himself when looking at the mirror and thinking how magnificent he was. Pride and tea were inseparable in Bartibus' mind.

Upon the ending of the king's screams, another assassin arose to finish the work. However, her first action was to check that her fellow criminal was indeed dead, and upon finding him just about breathing though with a lot of pain and rasping, she walked over to the oak desk which the king used during oak tea meetings, and used the king's walking staff to finish her fellow off.

You see, she must have been from another rival group plotting to take over the crown (keep with me here, I know there are quite a lot of treasonous peoples, the kingdom just had like a gazillion enemies). She could have been from many a faction, being that Mados had no real friends beyond its borders and everyone saw the king as weak and deluded, and thus the kingdom as a soft spot for the beginning of global domination. This is why villains were typically found wearing their black capes, and staring evilly down upon a miniature set of the kingdom, till their cat comes wandering in, and then they start trying to prove they have the cutest and baddest cat in town.

Now villains are always scared of good guys winning the day, but they are even more terrified of another villain winning the day instead of them. Evil is in this way remarkably selfish and self-destructive to its own ambitions. I mean like whatever you think of evil, its damn ineffective in this way. No wonder only fools think any good will come out of it.

Well the deaf female assassin was given just about enough time to consider this, though she was a busy lady so immediately went on to her main task. After dispatching her rival, she turned upon the king.

He gulped.

By the way, this is not what one should do in mortal peril. Few will ever hear you if you only gulp. The number of decibels assigned to it is pretty low.

Still this was about all the king felt able to do, all that screaming had made his throat sore.

Luckily by this time, some royal guards had ventured into the room and made short work of the female.

King Bartibus looked around at the dead bodies. He bowed his head and pondered and asked the mirror, "What is the world coming to? I mean, females being trained in assassin guilds, doesn't anyone know only males are criminals. Next we will have feminine demons." The guards looked at each other and despite having caught many would-be female killers, nodded in agreement. Sexism was, you see, sadly tolerated in Mados.

For surely if it is sexist to say a woman can't be as good as a man, it is also sexist to say women can't be as bad as men. Therefore, this tale is very sexist, not that there aren't many strong female characters who shall appear into the absurd story here spoken of, nor that there aren't many very important heroines, but there are very few evil ladies.

For those feminine dark minds among you, who harbour evil and devilish plans and are sires of the late Maleficent, I do apologise for this. Please do not strike me down with your evil powers, for I am but a humble furball trying to paint a picture of the tragic history of Mados. I'm not saying any of this is an accurate portrayal of how things should be. I'm all for that all-out evil lady who has global dominion, buts that's just not this story.

King Bartibus laughed confidently, putting his hands on his hips, like he had single-handedly overcome all the peril that had at unawares fallen before him. He then took off his wrinkled black shirt which had a picture of a teapot painted onto it, and pulled up his baggy brown trousers. He then began dressing in the female assassin's clothing, since he liked to dress out in drag and thought now was the time to celebrate.

The guards didn't know what to do. They were waiting for orders from this drag queen tea king but might never get them or worst be ordered to join in this cabree performance.

King Bartibus went to the stove as if nothing happened and lit it with a box of extra short matches, after nearly burning his fingers off, he made everyone tea and posed at various moments to impress upon all present the beauty of his new outfit, regally lifting his heal to show his new shiny high heels.

All was as it should be in the king's mind.

To end here would be wonderful, though to leave Westog in the nightmare situation of being at the most dangerous academy in the world, the king madly plotting how to commit treason and the soufflé guards perfecting their next masterpiece. This would be an abuse of my role as a novelist. Still if you like a good old digestive with a cup of Sussex tea, and want to think up a happy ending, now would be a good time to stop.

If not, then on with the show!

Bartibus' son, Prince Rupert, had spent his morning being a really big romantic. He had tried to woo a woman, something he had done many a time, but this time had got two for the price of one since both the lady in question and her friend found him totally irresistible. But sadly this afternoon had him bruised and battered and he was quite moody, valentine's day was short when you were a prince carrying the weight of the kingdom, and your father's iniquity, upon your shoulders.

As far as his father's tea campaign was concerned, well he thought it was a total waste of time. He was not the tea type you see, he preferred coffee due to its nice wake-up chemical composition. Latté was not a thing though, so those of you who do not like the most intense expresso's ought not to accept an invitation to a coffee bean festival, held during summertime in the courtyards of the royal palace. He was young, in his early twenties, and had longish brown hair, broad shoulders, an incredibly merry face and really looked the part.

Rupert was strolling along the corridor, feeling boosted by his morning successes, and the oncoming moment. He had waited so long for the time when the king would pronounce a magnificent quest for the prince to prove his valour and necessary prowess for the crown. And the day was today, a day that would forever be remembered.

126

It was remembered but not for these reasons.

Nevertheless, an internal battle broke out in Rupert's mind. *But what if his father had gotten side-tracked with that ridiculous tea and deforestation business? It had been pretty much the only thing he had talked about all month? But surely the king couldn't forget today, I mean it's my biggest moment, even Bartibus must consider it above all other matters of state. Yes, I shall receive my right to passage today!*

Rupert had heard the screaming in the oak barrel room as he descended, and this seemed exactly like the usual joyful outburst the king would make, when finding an inspiration for his son's new quest. Doubtlessly he had spent many hours in darkness, meditating unto the horned god for inspiration, as he knelt before his treasured oak barrels.

And Rupert knew that his father would remember his son was nearly twenty-four, so the king had his kid's future on his mind. Surely he must have been thinking about it all, at least somewhat. So he put doubt aside and stepped confidently into the dark room, waiting for his future to unfold.

The guards saw a tall figure blocking the doorway, and so quickly lit one of the barrels to make a bonfire as to see this imposing dude better. There went a thousand silver coins of oak, but no one complained, yes, the king would have gone berserk but he was snoring.

What the guards were not expecting to see was their prince there, he almost never visited the tea sector of the palace. He almost acted as if the tea industry did not exist.

What the prince was not expecting was to find multiple dead people, a father fallen asleep on an oak barrel and two guards chopping down neighbouring ones. Then he looked between the dead bodies and the guards and he realised something. The king had just been nearly killed during his mediation exercises. No doubt the assassins were sent from the barbarian community or that pesky king in that silly rival kingdom of Ontock. He was livid. They had ruined his perfect moment.

A sword went high into the air and met another steel weapon. Before the occupant of the first said "oh, hi" and the occupant of the second said "what", a second female assassin was slain.

Then his knight, the second in command of the knights of Mados, Sir Hamfield, came proudly walking in before looking around at everyone in great confusion. He said, "Ah, hi boss. Sorry, I seem to be slightly late and much seems to have happened in so short a time." He was meant to stay at the prince's side all the time when the prince wondered the palace, with all the assassination attempts I'm guessing you can see why, but sadly the second in command had spent dramatically longer in the toilet than he had expected—that lobster roll really gave him some dire issues.

The prince was not impressed with the lack of military devotion his second in command showed. How was he meant to be seen as a respectable prince when his second in command left him upon a fearsome outbreak of assassin fighting, he did not know.

Nor did Rupert like being called 'boss', as he had made clear many times, so he said a little rudely, "I'm the prince, remember! Not Boss! Well, I am but never call me boss again."

"Oh yeah, sorry I forgot, man," said Sir Hamfield. While the third in command, named Sir Soffty, wacked Sir Hamfield around the head for his continued informality. You do not call a superior 'man'.

It was a good thing that the room was so messy and unexpectedly covered in oak. The destruction distracted the prince long enough for Hamfield to look at Rupert a little too long without being wacked yet again. He thought Rupert was a totally handsome man, with a cute puppy like expression. And did I mention lovely ears.

Hamfield stood there like the rest of the world was non-existent. He seemed to be hanging on to the prince's every word (or even moments between words) as if it was a wonderful symphonic movement that he simply had to be in the front row to hear.

Eventually, the prince did get his head accustomed to the mess and found Hamfield looking at him rather oddly. The prince then looked around for oncoming assigns, undoubtedly putting the puppy like demeanour down to the knight's admiration. Hamfield thought wistfully of the prince's unbeatable vigilance. The prince for one would not be attacked unawares.

The prince studied Hamfield carefully. Hamfield had grown up in the outskirts of the country, a foreign sounding word to the prince, no other knight had grown up in rural places, among cattle. Undoubtedly his second's informality was due to a shallow upbringing where he had not learned the correct etiquette for speaking to royalty. Sir Hamfield could be pretty brutal when it came to battling the wolves, but he needed to work on his conversation skills.

The prince then did something he never did, except when he wanted to look brave, he stabbed the last assassin in the gut and cleaned the blade with his shirt. As he did the full benefits of his time in the gym were shown and he smiled, a smile that Hamfield thought was an angelic smile, and one which made Hamfield speechless.

The king broke the silence.

"So, what happened here." He looked sternly at the guards and the knight as if they were solely responsible for all the mess, and he had not in any way contributed to spilled oak and need for the assassin's untimely deaths. King he was, but a messy man, this was a thought he could not fathom to think.

One of the guards looked at the other, clearly putting the blame on someone else. This someone else, was staring at the prince. The prince looked defiantly at the guard and then the king stared angrily at the mirror. The reflection stared angrily back at him. This went on for a while.

The king then broke the silence once more, but this time with a piece of gobbledegook. "Sense any de shar voo?" Don't ask me what it means, I really have no idea.

There was once more a continued cacophony of silence, save everybody, including the knight and Prince Rupert, chose someone else to stare at.

"So, what happened here?" the king asked, feeling very irritated. He was desperately hoping someone else would take all the blame, but no one manned up. And the staring began once more.

"So, what happened here!" shouted the king. He stamped his feet on the ground, apparently trying to appear angry. He hopped from the pain, slipped and hurt his back.

"Owwwwww," cried the king.

The king started rubbing his back against an oak barrel to try to ease off the pain. Like he was a briar trying to get the itch off by rubbing a prickly bush.

Prince Rupert and the two guards evacuated the room, leaving the king to his strange ways. The king looked at the dead bodies surrounding him and cried.

Prince Rupert stopped walking and started storming away, feeling like the king was acting like a toddler. He was so embarrassed to be related to his tea-obsessed dad.

Prince Rupert flung open his door and sat fuming on his bed. His mind was far from the realms of the living and in some dystopian future where he was riding chariots and being glorified for the wonderful and cool knight he was. A world where he wasn't thought of as the son of Bartibus the barmy.

Then he went to sleep, resting under his thick duvet covers.

Chapter 11
No Sex Tonight

Eventually, there was the sound of faint knocking on his door. And in his pyjamas, Prince Rupert rose out of bed, half still asleep, and grabbed the round knob, taking a couple of moments for his mind to rise from the foggy landscape of the world of dreams. Yawning, he asked, "Who is it?"

The man who stood outside, simply said, "It's me. The poor street magician from yesterday." He made a quick flourish of flowers appear with his wand. By wand I mean a thin twig, made in the volcanoes of the earth and imbued by many a demonic spell. Though puppies often think of it as a play toy and munch it down quite happily.

As Rupert opened his mouth, he moved his arm gesturing to the inside of the bedroom, saying, "Lead on. You are alone, right?"

"Yes," answered the magician, being quiet enough not to wake anyone up who might be within close quarters.

The young lad walked into the room ready to lead the prince to heights he had never reached. The guy knew the prince, and knew from all the gossip that he liked getting all ruffled up. Particularly given the stories which had often floated around the peasant folk concerning the royal family. Many of them were concerning how Rupert, disguised as a sea explorer, often went to the local tavern and asked the ladies if they wanted the stiff one. They generally sighed, gasped and fainted, and this had put him off from drinking for a while. He liked getting a response but liked his interests to have some back bone. Though he could still be found on occasion drinking vodka around the palace, to show he was still the manly man he wanted to be.

There were a few moments silence as the prince sat in the most masculine stance he could fathom, looking regal and ready for company.

The young lad clearly was not very experienced, and kind of walked around slightly aimlessly, not wanting to get the night started but still sort of wanting to, all at the same time. Humans in this sense are very indecisive which has often puzzled many fur balls such as myself, who think the excitement of one of the most intimate human experiences ought to leave little time for waddling. But then wolves have very busy lives I suppose and time was something the two humans had a lot of before them, for the night was young.

The prince walked over to the young lad, flexing his massive muscles. He liked showing them off and judging from the transfixed eyes of the lad, it had its intended effect. Rupert pushed the door fully shut and then turned and gave the lad a kiss on the cheek.

Rupert went over to the table and pulled out a bottle of dim prarv. This was a common royal cocktail in this continent and was loved primarily for its illegally high alcohol content.

The visitor lifted his brown hood and revealed a well sculpted white face. His eyebrows were particularly fetching.

Rupert offered him a well filled goblet and sat beside him humming to the horned god. He was praying tonight would be one for the books, and everything looked pretty promising so far.

"So ah, what kind of things do you like?" asked the visitor.

The prince smiled at him like a beaming ray. And didn't give much of an answer but just shrugged as if to say, "Well, I like about anything, and by the way, my Prince, you might want to know, my name's Jeff."

The breaking open of one's heart is one of those frequent miracles requiring nothing but love and attachment. Some describe it as feeling the appearance of many butterflies in the stomach. This anomaly is strictly allowed by Heisenberg's uncertainty principle, but which has yet the probability to make it close enough to a miracle, a physically impossible event, for it to be called a miracle.

Yet this Heisenberg uncertainty, goes deeper than feeling, for it captures, on the whole, the main difference between a theoretician and an experimentalist. Experimentalists care deeply about what will happen, or how one can put up the warming field of romantic intrigue with a practical chance of success, while theoreticians focus on proving what concatenation of physical principles will allow any desired romance to occur, no matter how low the probability and unrealistic the likelihood of its occurrence.

Rupert was a theoretician by nature, and therefore had hope that offering a drink and a smile as well as putting an arm around the shoulder, would create an extremely unlikely quantum romance field, which by some odd concatenation of physical principles, would lead to a night full of perfumed romance.

The magician showed off his talent and made a rose appear in the cocktail. He had a thing for romantic flowers, since his parents were both florists, or used to be before they had been forced to go bankrupt when the taxes increased greatly to pay for the wolf-border control, and much of the smaller and start-up companies met oblivion.

Perhaps the prince could see the sadness upon the magician's face. He put a hand on his shoulder and said, "That's sweet." The prince found the tentativeness of the magician very attractive. It showed him he cared deeply, and wasn't the kind of guy to just have a moment of fun and then leave, he wanted this night to be special.

It was all going perfectly till the rose began to wilt.

The prince was looking horrified at the wilting leaves and pondered if this was a divine doom prophecy, some omen signifying that the horned god was not approving of their time together. Rupert would have got his Tarot cards out to check whether this was a subtle message from up above, but the magician placed a gentle kiss on the prince's check. A battle arose inside of him.

The tiny little men representing his conscious was now carrying pitchforks and making a remake of the battle of Troy.

Thus, the eight hundred seconds that followed was a curious mixture of love and horror, much like the pseudo love zombie movies portray.

The music started playing in the magician's head, some romantic ballad with the occasional long note of a cello or brassy brass. Love of something filled the air. Botany was all the prince could think of, some strange combination of snogging this magician and being turned into a wilting rose.

Finally, Rupert's heart broke open, they started making out and then the prince fell into a deep sleep, at peace in the magician's arms. Before Rupert let him go and he sunk onto the bed. He was exhausted from the day, which had been like an emotional bungee jumping exercise, and he didn't land in a very knightly position. It looked like he had collapsed after having taken a very drunken night out. The magician placed a glass of vodka in the prince's hand in case he woke up and made sure his head was resting comfortably on the pillow.

He lay for a while with the sleeping prince, not wanting to disturb him and being too shy to ruffle the prince's feathers to put it politely.

The visitor felt bad for leaving the prince in his slumbers, he kind of liked the guy but wanted a bit of time to get to know him better. All this intimacy was just too soon. Besides, he hadn't even told the prince his full name, which for your purposes you might want to know is Jeff Brookly, just so that I am not forced to obliquely refer to him as 'the visitor', which would have unfortunate connotations with horror movies. Jeff was the most innocent, most kind hearted magician ever and actually would have done well to of lived in the white tower down south if he knew there was such a place. But anyways, back to Jeff's romance.

Jeff got up from the cosy bed, and pulled out a wooden chair from under the desk and began to start to read.

The book was one of the princes, and was a standard piece of literature in Mados, though this copy had a few pieces of graffiti over its pages.

He coughed politely into his fist. The prince stirred but then went back to sleep and so the magician began in a broad voice, like stilton spread roughly across a cracker, to read.

"In the beginning, far, far away." He slammed down the book in annoyance, this was not the book he was looking for, it was for kidlings. The library of the prince was full of far more well-spoken literature.

The prince didn't awake, but grumbled something about water, roses and eventually dicks. This kept the magician entertained for a while till a soppy expression came over the prince and he fell right into a silent sleep once more.

Jeff would have gone over to him but needed a little space to let his emotions cool, he didn't want to keep the prince up all night when Rupert had so much work to do tomorrow, or wake him from his slumbers were he could be free of the heavy burden of his enormous responsibilities.

Finally, finding a chapter written in a much older and dustier book, with the more rustic version he was used to, he got ready. Then saying unto the Prince, some dirty mumbo jumbo, he coughed twice and began again.

He was now imagining how it would be when he awoke and the magicians sneaked down to the kitchen and brought Rupert some breakfast before having to swing heroically from the window and run from the castle, the prince being so taken by his Aladdin-like skills.

Then he decided to whisper the story and stop dreaming, so it would look a little less weird if the prince was to suddenly awake seeking some personal attention.

"In the beginning, uncounted times before the overhanging forests, previous to the first twitch of the tail or howl to the moonlight, the gods made the world of mud and clay. From metal and the salts of the earth did they make life and dicks."

The magician read the line again and realised the prince's mutterings must be interfering with his reading, blast that prince, or as his internal thought might well say, blast that awesome and totally heroic man for messing with my head.

But this is what I guess romance does, so the magician only blushing a little, just read on. Still thinking time upon time how totally awesome the prince was as much as he pretended to be a little less soft hearted.

"In the begging, life took in its dawning two mighty forms, wolves and fiery dragons.

Soon after, the gods formed from the carbon soot of volcanoes and the gasses of the upper atmosphere, the birds and squirrels and all minor life of the woods and heavens.

The gods themselves were a mysterious folk. Supposedly they had a beginning, a pre-time before time, but of this we cannot say. Partly because this concept only exists in mathematics, secondly because being godly ancient only requires a spatially lengthy bearded, and any beard made before time would be a beard before space, and so all relativity studies would suggest, it to be a hyper beard. Hyper beards were often considered a necessary characteristic of a godly ancient being, though the question of their existence is heavily debated by many modern-day fashion theologists."

He thought out loud that 'the gods are as incomprehensible as they are old and grumpy.' The prince let out a little 'ow yeah', probably thinking along different lines but the irony of his response at such a perfect time made the guy laugh. He then carried on.

Originally, when they were young and vigorous their task was to enlighten and advance the civilisations of the world. Therefore, the gods made a great council far in the south [or north depending upon which priest you speak to]. This was a blessed area held between the most southerly [or northerly] mountains. The gods love of heights has forever had all but the toughest mountaineers questioning their sanity. This is a major objection made by many unbelievers, for greatest of all is the eternally convoluted discussions of why the gods would choose such a lofty and perilous point to drink a few mugs of tea and have a long chat.

Let us hope the rocks were comfy; otherwise, the needle-sharp peaks would have caused many medical practitioners to be in large demand, after such a lengthy talk was over.

Gods debating is no quiet thing. It is more like a group of charging dragons, without the fangs, claws and tails of flame but with a few dozen trumpets being blown using their massive lungs. Although there was no great care between these four beings, they did eventually come to an agreement based firmly on dispassionate truth and upon unbiased bias.

Yet on seeing the fruits of each other's labour, as beards grew longer and longer, they did come to a fond liking of one another. The female god even began to grow a moustache, a wonder that many jokes has not allowed anyone to forget lightly.

Dragons and wolves alike became great friends and companions. In some exceptional cases, even neighbours. The dragons were ok with this arrangement, till the cubs started messing up their treasure hoards. The wolves managed quite well with the arrangement till the kittling's started hatching and within a few months started burning down their wooden huts.

Only Sir Triffon the tragic ever managed a lifelong neighborship with a winged family, and spent much of his later years living on a bed of treasure when the oldest sibling had accidently set fire to his bed.

From tree and river to mountains, the wolves howled long into the night as the air broke through the trees. Glancing up the ancient wolves would see dragons thunder by.

Eventually, the gods blessed both races with super uber offspring with a red mark going down their central forehead. These were the priests, in charge of the bonfire and solar flames.

The wolven priests made mighty pyramids of oak and sapling branches and lit them so their magical light filled half the world and left the other half in shadow.

The draconic priests trapped energy from the sun in their long wings and flung it downwards so that beams fell sharply upon all worms or creatures of prey, and the eagles and hawks had a feast.

Priests gained many magical powers aside, and it is said, these have all but faded away though their magic fortifies the cities of men for these were once the congregational areas of the religious orders of old.

Migrating the ancient peoples spread steadily across the north and south, west and east. The wolves made a particularly strong stand in the south, while dragons went to the bays of the east and enjoyed the company of near-shore birds. There was one naughty flock of seagulls that loved dragons so much, they sat on their backs and use them as free transport. The seagulls would often wail in their screechy voices, 'ah, this is so relaxing', while the dragons would roar in their more volcanic tones 'we are not flying steeds'. Thus we get the myth of Pegasus, the flying horse.

This same family of seagulls was told by the gods in a dream to respect the elder race, their rightfully kings and rulers. Thus the same group that began the human idea of magical horses, formed a small 'anti-god' group which protested heavily against the gods' holy decision to make the dragons the rulers and kings. They didn't dare protest openly against the gods, but took to pooping on top of the draconic priests' snouts every time they began to talk. Thus, respect for the great dragons of old became diminished. Eventually, after the draconic priests had long gone into hiding (perhaps partly to escape from the poop), the seagulls took to stealing human cheese and ham sandwiches instead, as many a seaside human could tell you.

In the passages of time much was forgotten that should have been remembered, and much was remembered that would wish to be forgotten. And there was peace, but a dark kind of peace, one which is like the pause between the lighting of a bomb and its explosion were a bright party changes into a bloody nightmare within an incremental moment in time.

The gods were needed less and less to walk visibly in the world and so became more and more myth as the people became more dependent on their own devices, and less on the divine guidance and power of the gods.

Eventually feeling like some time off was warranted, the divine made a mainland far from their charges and the poop dropping birds of old. This became the island of Sussex. A place that was to be their home.

For the gods to rest it was sundered very far from the content that they made long ago and far out of reach of any existing civilisation.

The gods put a few pieces of aubergine on their heavily bagged eyes and took a breather from their world and went into the unphysical form of spirit. After the first ages mentioned previous, it has always been so, that the gods would seldom be visible in our lands or sit with us at our tables. In the spirit world the gods dwelt, for there they were immutable and indestructible but it is said in the physical form of matter, they are weaker, subject to change and injury and even perhaps mortality.

On those rare occasions where they did tread far beyond their island, they came in great wolven or draconic forms, much mightier than the humble bodily frames of the created people, but more gentle than a young kitten.

After many eons, the youngest god (at least by nature and maturity levels, if not time) grew tired of being tired.

The old do not get this, for being naturally tired, they view active life as rear excitations of an underlying natural way of living consisting of bed and onion soup.

The young however see all aged things and way of being as boring and a waste of time.

Thus, the youngest god began to become unrestful and a spiritual buzz started going around the island as he ascended into semi-conscious awareness, and began even then, to teach the ancient races secrets none but the divine should know. Forbidden knowledge the wise call it and being wise they know it not. The wolves and dragons made books upon books to record their dreams, but when read and moreover understood by the priests, dread fell upon them and they demanded that all such books should be locked up and buried far underground.

They put them in a black basalt cave, were only the hissing of sea could be heard through the small crack into the outside world. Guards were set their and bound books in metal chains. They then sealed the mountainous stacks in massive concrete slabs. The dripping of water was all that could be heard but even that seemed an eerier thing in the green light that it reflected from the glowing pile of forbidden knowledge.

The priests felt strongly like the books should be burned but fear, the number one weapon of the enemy stopped them, for never did they dare disrespect a god.

But then the fourth woke right up, and things got worse, much, much worse.

He was irritated by the buzzing he had heard when he was focussing on dreaming about a nice peaceful and quiet meadow, perhaps with a couple of chickens to keep him company.

The other gods were meant to look after the youthful god, but no, like usual they couldn't keep that youngling under control and were leaving the work to him, simply because he actually could be bothered to do something. He left them all and began to plot a new evil, to mess up all the gods work and get back upon the youngling for making the buzzing noise and the other gods for yet once again leaving the disciplinary duties up to him. He invented pain.

Suddenly, the buzz around the island was accompanied with the buzzing of the cries of the gods' charges. But the clamorous unison could not awake the older gods, for their age, they had gone but slightly deaf. It fully awoke the youngling though. So he got up, left the group and began to design dark plans to really mess things up and get the oldies back on their feet.

Plus, he felt like the other gods just didn't really care for him or get his youthful and inventive ideas, they were too set in their ways. So he wanted to truly make the sleeping brethren pay for their negligence and take his first steps into youthful arrogance. A pit many youthful souls fall into.

So, he called forth the elements and it is said that the moon and the sun stood still, and then he plonked right back for a finishing nap while his monster creation bloomed in the snowy mountains of the north. As they passed through a forest, they broke trees, hunted birds and brought chaos to a tranquil realm. They went from outsiders to barbaric invaders, and conquers of the land. They were little in militant power but great in number, and like many ants attacking a lion, cut away at the people.

The sleeping gods heard the crying of the ancient people and woke. They guessed, that the youngling knew that he would be blamed under the charge of youthful stupidity, so they took no chances and responded immediately. Storming over to the first, they shouted, "What have you done!"

He said, "Nothing!"

They shoved a hearing horn into his ear and blasted, "You hear the cries of the kings of the trees and sky. Do you not hear their weeping? What is wrong with you, man!"

The god said, "I did nothing."

"You call that nothing?" fired up the female god. She waved her hand around to indicate the buzzing and fractures and pixelated bits of screams and cries swirling in the air.

"No, that's something, but that something has in its creation nothing from me. Not my mind, nor hands nor heart had any working in this deed." He stomped and pretended to look like his honour had been wounded by unfounded accusation.

"Oh okay," said the two gods. They didn't really believe him, they just wanted to get back to sleep.

They felt that this was far too much effort, and did not want to start a long disciplinary process until they were triply rested from their labour.

Upon reading of being triply rested the magician yawned and took a large swig of the cocktail. He thought of cuddling up to Rupert before going to sleep himself. But he didn't want to wake the prince up, he needed to rest, the burden of the kingdom and training of the knights must weigh heavily upon the prince in his waking hours. As the magician was thinking this, he went off to sleep.

There was a plonk while both were asleep as the prince fell to the ground, the glass smashing but both were so peacefully asleep that neither were disturbed.

When the sun arose and morning came, the prince's hand servant came wandering in ready to give the prince a really posh version of royal porridge. This is simply to say that the golden syrup, oats and milk were ridiculously expensive and the cream was more like clotted cream.

However, upon seeing the prince apparently thrown out of his bed and a glass smashed upon the floor, the servant gasped and dropped the porridge. In horror he ran out. Or at least he tried to run out, for sadly he screamed. The guards upon hearing the scream, supposedly coming from the prince as some assassin attacked him, had silently moved to behind the door. As still as stone, as quick as a leopard, they were ready to burst upon the assassin.

To be totally fair, the king had been nearly assassinated by three assassinators the day before in the oak barrel room, so the over-the-top reaction is understandable. Expecting the prince to be locking himself in his safety vault within his wardrobe, for protection, they were ready to stick the spear to whatever horror was fleeing the palace, after being repelled by the well-practiced Madosian scream.

Thus, the servant met a swift death and the waking magician woke to the sight of two spear men puncturing a high-ranking servant, he could only shout "Treason, the prince is under attack, treason!"

The guards looked confusingly at each other. "Treason?" They pointed the spears at the visitor, questioningly, as if he was an enemy spy who had just accidently let slip that he was withholding a very secret plot to kill the prince and king and the entire royal family. Perhaps a third assassin who had slipped passed their guard in the darkness of the barrel room that evening not so long ago.

They said none of this but walked boldly up to him and said, "Look here, young man, only guards and knights get to say treason round here. So, you'll leave that phrase to us thank you very much."

"Treason!" shouted one of the guards, enjoying the sensation of exercising his special right.

"What treason?" asked his partner in confusion.

"Well, whatever treason this visitor has been shouting about, that treason, of course!"

"You mean we don't know."

"Well, it's treason, isn't it, it doesn't matter that we don't know what type. That's just getting all pedantic here."

The visitor, still rather dazed, said, "Look here, gentlemen, I don't know what treason—"

"Treason!" said one of the guards.

The other guard shouted, "No one but us is allowed to say Treason!"

The visitor stared blankly up, before asking, "What's wrong with saying treason?"

The prince tried to get up but clearly was recovering from a hangover caused by the pretty intense cocktail, and he just collided with a large chair and fell over, knocking himself unconscious but thankfully avoiding the broken glass.

One of the guards gasped and said, "Treason! The prince has been poisoned!"

"There's no treason…" shouted the visitor, getting quite irritated.

On and on this went! Eventually, the more aged and tired of the guards considered why this back and forth had gone on too long and when he would get his mid-morning nap! Yet why the visitor was so interested in talking about treason, and they weren't just dealing with him here and there, as well as how easy it would have been for him to poison the prince during his sleep, well no one knew.

In a flat tone, one of the aged said, "So you wanted to get caught for plotting treason? Well at least you're an honest criminal. But I need some sleep and this is getting boring."

The other guard stopped looking dazed at the prince who was just regaining consciousness so his mind could continue its experience of this confusing nightmare. Finally, the guard shook his head and turned to his companion asking,

"Oh my dear, I am sorry. I forgot. Well, what treason are we shouting about this time?"

"For heaven's sake, please get your head out of the clouds. We stopped the first treason attempt yesterday. This is the second—"

"The second coming! Where are the carol singers, I must inform them?"

The guard looked around excitedly as if expecting to see shining people of the end walking out of thin air, and the great garble to fill the atmosphere. Instead he saw a bird chirping on the top of his helmet, he wept with sadness, he had long been part of those doomsday groups and was sorely disappointed that the end of the world was not the immediate crisis at hand.

Then he heard a voice, but it was an all too familiar voice. His fellow guard, his comrade in chivalry.

"No, not the second coming! The second plot to kill the king and the prince, the plot which comes after plot number one."

The weeping guard pulled himself together and said, "Which is?"

"I don't know! For heaven's sake, that's why I'm trying to find out if you would just let me interrogate our suspect. That's why we are still here you see, I'm trying to force the information out of him, or am waiting for the visitor to tell us of his own free will! Have you learned anything?"

He let out one large gasp of breath, it was hard work being his apprentice's tutor, for his apprentice was at times annoyingly slow to catch onto the situation at hand.

Taking out his frustration upon the magician, he stared accusingly at him, as if it was his fault, they were all wasting so much time. The porridge was getting very cold by now.

The magician took in a deep breath and said, "Well, look, you don't need to worry. I'm not going to hurt anyone. I'm a friendly guy, you see. Just a street magician. My granddad was thrown out of the academy of Mados before my dad was born and now were just kind of homeless, then the prince, well he invited me to come to the palace under dark. He said he would pay me if we well you know, though to be honest he's such an amazing guy I would probably do it for free if it weren't for the fact that I need the funds. Got to pay for college and my mums pretty ill."

One thing you should never do is say that the prince was inviting you to the palace, and then say you're getting paid for questionable services. If news got out that the king's son was occasionally paying poor people on the streets, basically like prostitutes, then Rupert's image would be ruined. So the guards did the only thing they could do to protect the prince's reputation, they cut the young lad's head before he could say anything to anyone.

Hostile guards are generally not the most well calmed individuals so you must forgive them, they were only trying to do their job. But like all efforts, there are some rewards and failures, such as a few accidents like killing an innocent servant and murdering the prince's lover, it was part and parcel of taking on such impossible tasks like protecting the entire royal court. Their enemies did after all, outnumber them, ten to one.

The prince woke a few hours later, when the bodies, broken glass and blood had all been thrown into the furnace and any sign of violence was removed from the room. He would never find out what happened to the young man, or to his servant, he assumed they just weren't interested in seeing him anymore which hurt his ego big time.

Rupert spent a lot of time giving himself pep talk in the following week, reassuring himself that he was a magnet for decent blokes.

But here he could have made great use of knowing the human self is much like a compass, we can only see clearly what road to take after taking the wrong one because a mistake isn't just something to learn from, its building that south pole so when you want to go north, you'll know exactly where that is. His lack of romantic activity on one night only helped spur him on to be more manly and attractive in the future, thus increasing his chances of finding the 'one for him' if such a person existed.

Chapter 12
Horse Meat

As could be seen with Rupert's wild hairdo, eventually he got so annoyed at all the generals and even some of the Madosian knights, comparing him to his father, that he was determined to give himself a quest to prove them all wrong. And prove to himself how totally irresistible he was, and how much of a fearsome knight the kingdom had. So he decided to go, find himself a dragon, and kill it swiftly, like the great St George had done, who happened to be his distant cousin.

This sounded lovely and indeed there were many wild dragons in the known north, that did not belong to the Sahara lands or the mountainous end of the known regions. There might even be thousands of dragons residing further up north than anyone had ventured, for the known continent was covered by ice at both ends, yet the temperature and oxygen levels dropped so sharply in the frozen north that only a small segment of it was plotted and how long it went on for was anyone's guess.

Now, Rupert could have put himself down in fame by being the Scot of the continent, venturing further than any other explorer, but his heart was in sword combat not trudging through an endless slice of ice.

His other reason for taking some time off from the palace, was that he didn't always get on with those Cornish advisors. Furthermore he didn't like Cornish pasties, they were too peppery and didn't have enough chilli chicken. Anyone who defended them, just wasn't his cup of coffee.

Cornish and Devonish meat never intrigued him, he liked more exotic food, the tarts of Ontock, the stews of the Barbarian tribes down south and the soufflés of Mados Mordrè were the kind of thing that ignited his passion. Had he actually met the soufflé guards he would have got on with them greatly. Yet he was unlike them, a brilliant knight and a master in both swordplay and hammer throwing. Yet, a brilliant romantic.

And yes, as I said long ago, he was Alpha!

Yet among the Cornish advisors misplaced culinary loyalty, they had mentioned that there was a dragon which was taking people's sheep, and terrorising the locals and was now moving onto the barbarian lands to wreak havoc. And there was this rather odd dude by the name Ariton, a strange name I know, but anyway in an awfully realistic dream this dude did speak to him of the glorious applause he would receive when he brought back the dragon's head.

Ariton was pretty scarily obsessed with the idea and Rupert regularly had to tell him to just 'chill' because Ariton's desire to help was almost psychotic at times, and Ariton had this weird sneer. In the dream there was a lot of flames but Rupert liked the overall point if not the style.

He loved how all the people would come to think he was so cool, if they would have a statue of him heroically slaying the beast in every house. In short Rupert was persuaded by Ariton's ideas if not his charm.

Rupert therefore gallantly went forth to prepare, at this early hour just before sunrise, in the knightly quarter of his dormitory, for his manly mission. Now this place was usually covered in roses and such for romance but was now full of knives and other knightly things, given valentine's day was well and truly over. He did so with a spring, with his favourite hit Disney song, *I can go the distance* from *Hercules* running through his mind. Since a child he had dreamed of being like this son of Zeus, and had paintings of Hercules, or 'the Herculean' as he was known unto the land of Mados, covering the dormitory walls.

Around the shelves at the back of the room, he also had many rings, and one favourite one that the magician, Jeff, had left behind doubtlessly as a present unto him, perhaps he had even spent the last of his mother's savings on it to offer it up as a proposal ring. Jeff was poor and couldn't have otherwise paid for this but then the black market had many valentines' bargains.

The ring was a series of silver threads twisted together, to form a circle, with a spiral of dragon made of enamel running along its length. He kissed it and prayed that his magician might wonder return, for despite all his hurt at Jeff so abruptly abandoning him and the lies he sometimes told himself that he didn't need another man in his life, he remembered Jeff fondly. In fact it was the first romance driven by more than feelings, and the first time he had felt true romantic love. Rupert then slid it upon his finger.

After doing a few press ups and lifting his weights, a few times to build up his strength, Rupert went forth to face his adventure confidently, feeling like today was the day everything would change. He would become the unlocked for star of the world!

His new servant, who for some mysterious reason had replaced his perfectly good one which had mysteriously vanished, pushed him right back into the room complaining how Rupert was always doing silly things that made no sense to anyone, but gave him some polished armour and also a new sword from the smithy. Rupert liked the weight of it and tossed it up and down in the air till it made a dent in the wooden mattress, and Rupert's servant thought perhaps the prince had done enough sword playing for the day, and was more than happy to let the prince put himself in mortal danger. Consequently, the servant allowed the prince to leave with no threats of alerting the entire kingdom to his desertion.

Rupert went forth, but not outside yet, for he had to take a nip into the bathroom near the palace dancing chambers, in order to make sure his hair was all shampooed correctly. When he had given it enough time to dry, he walked bravely down the castle steps, his fully armoured suit making him very obvious. The king looking on from the balcony was thinking how his son was surely going forth to crush the wolves and waved a cupped hand to say goodbye, in a manner which came to be known in Mados as 'the queen's wave', for it was first developed by Bartibus' mother who got her idea from wafting fumes of chemicals towards her nostrils when trying to brew the perfect poisons.

Upon reaching the final floor, Rupert decided all this armour was cumbersome and not needed for so manly a knight of his proficiency, so he just threw them to the nearest waiter who was already trying to juggle some five plates. A smash could be heard behind him but soon he was on his horse, Sir Boltimor, and was riding off into the start of a new glorious day.

The Dylan knew well of Ariton's plot, for father had sent word by a few weird prophetic dreams which had to include a few 'thine' and 'thou' because he was so medieval! I mean seriously, Dylan was going to have to take his father to one of the clubs the knights put on one of these days, or perhaps get him to try out some of the land's salty beer. That would wake him up to the new world sharp.

So Dylan went to the one person which just might be insane enough to try to convince the prince to turn away from a chance of glory, and this person was Sir Hamfield. Upon the wolf pointing to stashes of paintings the knight had secretly made concerning Rupert, and then pointing onto a few dragon statues, finally Hamfield understood the wolf's gestures and howling speech.

Hamfield bent his face into his hands and grabbing tightly unto his 'I love Rupert' cover, which they sold in secret team Rupert fan clubs, Hamfield in a muffled tone said "what does my prince think he's doing? Going on such a perilous quest without his knight by his side, really, what was he thinking? What will he do if he gets captured without me?"

Now whatever Prince Rupert was going to do, he would do with or without Hamfield there, but let us not underestimate how love has a fascinating ability to skew with one's reality. Anyway Hamfield was somehow sure that his presence was crucial to the success or failure of the prince's insane mission. So he ran from his dormitories, knocking over plates and pushing butlers off stair cases whenever they passed his progress to the courtyard. He confidently knocked aside anything that might cause even a second's delay.

Nothing could come between Hamfield and his prince!

Well, nothing apart from destiny, but we'll get to that later.

"Stop that intruder!" shouted a few of Hamfield's own knights on morning watch, from across the balcony, as they thought this man must be running from justice judging by how he was causing more hazards in the court than a dozen assassins might. They didn't have their glasses on, so to be honest this was fair doss.

Hamfield, ignoring the commotion, pushed a butler right into the wall as he flung open the gates and ran towards his mighty steed. A donkey, named Freddie.

Freddie looked at Hamfield in some sleepy state, thinking about how it was hoping to just do some sunbathing by the feeding bowls today.

"Ride my deer Freddie, ride!"

Freddie trotted off, walking about one and a half times the speed of an old lady, but Hamfield beamed at the onlooking crowd, not realising they were staring at him because in his haste to save his prince, he was wearing nothing but underwear and a tight top saying 'Roses are red, violets are blue, but man, sometimes do I need a poo'.

Anyway, Rupert who was covering more distance than Hamfield was ever likely to, at this rate, laughed at the wind, feeling free, and like he didn't have a care in the world but that one goal, killing that dragon.

Boltimor neighed as he sped through the country and woods. Now wolves usually dislike human travellers but there was an off and on truce around the 'valley of passage', a paved path made some couple of hundred years ago when there was an explosion of emergency food deliveries to the kingdom, after a heat wave had decimated the crops of Mados and the entire Northern realm for that matter. It led through the forest and allowed merchants to travel into the Barbarian land of the south of the continent.

This took him literally months, and many an adventure he had, but if we are going to talk about all of them, we would be here till your hair fell off and your bones crumbled into dust. And even then, we would still have much more to say when the trumpet of Gabriel sounds and the forces of heaven wage war upon the damned.

Needless to say, Rupert just about made it out and travelled for a few weeks onwards with a smug sense of invulnerability, not realising the dangerous part of the quest was yet to begin.

A giant lizard by the name of Thompson nearly ate Rupert and his steed whole, but after wafting some garlic cloves near its nostrils it quickly slid away. However, as Rupert's horse was leading them both to safety (well away from the giant lizard anyway), Rupert was whacked around the head with a club. A group of barbarians then took his horse and galloped away with it, having much experience at working with unyielding steeds. Plus Baltimore was tempted after a while with the offer to have fresh bundles of hay to eat every single day. As soon as the barbarians got to their secret place, they cut the horse's head off and sent it to the king of Mados, to fake a capture of Rupert and demand payment before they set him free.

Fortunately, the horse's head got stolen in transit by another barbarian tribe before it reached its intended destination, so Bartibus was saved from the prospect of having so much stress heaped on top of him, that it might well have killed him.

You might think all this was a little extreme, but that's the cut-throat and dagger life the tribal barbarian groups lived out. For it was difficult to survive, particularly in the wild south, were there were hundreds upon hundreds of vicious and nasty creatures and worst of all, the black tower, which struck fear into the hearts of all Barbarians.

Well anyways, Thompson eventually found Rupert stranded in the wild, unconscious on the cracked dirty ground, without a steed to protect him. Thompson felt sorry for Rupert and was against eating helpless prey, it was beneath him. So it just slid off, feeling hungry, and would long after remember the day he almost ate a prince.

When Rupert awoke with his head feeling very sore, he realised his steed was gone. After losing his horse, he trudged through the broken-up ground, and ventured into a mud pit. (It was a very large mud pit and Rupert could not be bothered to go round its edges.)

Almost reaching the evil oxen of the black flame, which laid upon the other side, he went right through the centre of the pit, concealed by two swamp bushes. After being met by a luciferin devil, he splattered out of the mud pit with the sound of the dirty liquid gurgling behind him. Hearing the loud growl of some monstrous wolf nearby, he dived into the bushes for cover. Stumbling across some deer carcasses, he bashed down the stalks and with his annoying shouts, he awoke a more ancient evil and promptly got himself captured by another barbarian tribe.

(I know, reader, there were a lot of wild barbarians, but to be fair, the prince was like gold to people who sought to make a ransom out of him. Princes don't exactly make it an everyday thing to go unaided onto the Barbarian south so the wild peoples had to be opportunistic, and my minimalistic approach to the prince's adventures might not be satisfying but going into detailed description would be greatly ink-heavy. Not to mention too much of his story is dark, and I do not like spending over long on the horrors of the world when there is so much joy to consider.)

So let us just say this, through a series of very unfortunate events, involving capture and escape, Rupert made it through many tens of leagues on foot. Rupert grew a very long beard, but managed to shave it off using makeshift crocodile teeth scissor found near a local pond. Perhaps my furry self shall make a new work concerning this one day, but for our purposes the overall details are not integral to the grand plot my research uncovers concerning the history that thou is reading.

And as destiny would have it, at the corner of the savage south, did he find a lovely thing, a sign of civilised society. Destiny sat on his stool, smoking his cigar in his business jacket, feeling he was doing a brilliant job.

Rupert in great joy went in to dine at the bar and brothel of 'the pub of Bob'. He put his two feet on the rickety wooden table and with a swig of blackcurrant beer, said unto a fine young lady, "You do look good, my darling. Fancy a meal with me? I am a prince, you know, and I'm like so cool; I even got naughty with a wizard a while back, you know, and he was so inspired by my charm he hid because he couldn't get over how good I was bed." He then winked at them.

She seemed genuinely interested and Rupert would have shown off his sword too, till this suitcase guy who worked there grabbed her arm and led her sternly away. Perhaps it was because she was pregnant and the guy was just overprotective. I mean, back where Rupert came from, it wasn't unusual for a pregnant woman to sleep with a few knights, particularly if one of those dashing guys in armour was himself.

He looked around at some ladies who were pondering how best to ask him out, like not for work but pleasure, as could be seen from their nervous but excited faces. None of them stepped forward until he went to the bar and ordered some bottles of wine. They flocked to him. They loved playing with his hair, and he loved telling them of his adventures.

Rupert felt like such a cool dude tonight. And when he went to bed, he did so with a happy heart and not a few invitations to dinner the next evening.

Now this is a pub you shall hear plenty of when I get round to that little detail, but for now let us just say the owner was in much debt and Ariton's offer of giving him a ton of cash if he let the dragon know exactly why she would enjoy the company of the prince, let the dragon kidnap Rupert from his bed.

When the Rupert awoke, he was in a cave, covered with basalt rocks. And above was a samba dancing dragon by the name of Madam Crumbler. Or Mount Crumbler, if you wanted to get fancy.

The cave's magic washed over Rupert and he felt the irresistible urge to join in with her ground-shaking dance moves.

So, my dear reader, we have covered much so far. The wolf lands, the northern wizards, the soufflé bakers and the secret admirer of Prince Rupert. Despite the prince being well hidden from any secret admirers for the present, which might help some of them get their minds off Prince Rupert and onto more mundane things, like taking up a hobby or enjoying the single life. These are all important facts, some more relevant to the deep truths humanity retells a thousand times over; others just the events of life. But they are all important in one way or another.

Part 2

Chapter 13
Miffty's Master

The scouts from the Academy of Mados Mordrė were unceasingly on the lookout for young and talented spell-casters. Now, the term 'conjurer' refers to any being that can consciously or instinctively make use of its magic, the term 'spell-casters' refers to individuals who are under the magical age of maturity, yet display an ability to grab on and make use of their internal magic.

The scouts, named in the wizardic script as 'scythan', desired secretly to build an army to set Lucifer free from his prison, and so hoped to bring as many 'powerful' spell-casters as possible unto the academy of Mados Mordrė. Once at the great academy, they were put under the personal training of Westog, Gruggor's second in command and vice-principal of the institute. It was then Westog's sacred task, once the contract with magic was sealed, to initiate them into the army of Lucifer as senior members of the orthodox wizarding church.

Expanding the hand of Lucifer over the world as it were.

Yet none of scythan men or women, had managed to convince this young farming boy to join their ranks, for he had no interest in harnessing the power of magic within him. Instead he just wished to follow its will, and be as a servant unto magic itself, like a Jedi might the force, and not use it selfishly to for fill his own urges and dreams. This was a peaceful view that would have made him a perfect candidate for the white tower, but the boy was a little too young to recruit. And his philosophy made him incompatible with the doctrines of the orthodox wizarding church, who respected magic to a degree, but thought of it, at least thought of the principle foundation, as a tool to be wielded and used.

But the High Necromantic Order were interested in him for reasons far beyond this, for they believed they had finally located the Christ like figure, who would prove to be the master head of their war against the peoples of God and both the black and white towers.

How the boy got lured into the academy, given the many factions desiring this boy's induction into the wizarding order, is thus a tale worth telling. Though this rendition may well have a degree of artistic license.

The boy was farming, like he did every day, and the sheep were grazing upon the hilltop in the Grand Valley of Grode were Grode pie had famously originated. He licked his lips, and tried to gnaw on a piece of grass to appease his hunger, he spat it out immediately since judging by the taste, his cattle had seemed to use the wet patch as a peeing ground for the day. Owls hooted on the tree tops nearby and flew around, skirting the borders between the corn fields and the forest of Leviathan, where the devil's servants often went to practice their nightly rituals.

He had always wanted to have a peek through the trees, and would often be found skirting around the borders before his father's heavy hands were laid upon his shoulder, preventing him from venturing forth. For the world was a scary place, but this just made the boy want to explore it all the more.

Now the boy's name given unto him by his dad was Gallatarnin in full, or just Gallat in short. It meant 'he that brings from death's door' for he had often been found doing impressive works of healing upon wounded animals, that were inexplicable to his fellow farmers. He at one point brought a sheep who was bleeding profusely back from the brink of death, even though it only had a cup full of blood running through its entire body. This made him weak in the knees and very light headed, but the sheep was eternally grateful to him and from that day on always did as Gallat's sheep wolf, Miffty, told her to do.

Gallat was a teenage lad and had bright green eyes, dark brown hair which hung just above his eye line, and thanks to both his and his father's upbringing on the borders of the Sahar, a grand Buddhist capital, he had very dark skin. He wore a modest brown shirt on most days and wore a tight pair of slightly pink trousers. He also always had a grey hooded fleece in case the winter grew particularly chilly. His father was known as the master shepherd and he had been tending the flocks around Grode hill, for a decade or so.

Gallat's father was well respected and loved, though tended not to speak of Gallat's childhood or birth, save mentioning some strange folk all dressed in black hoods who seemed to float upon the earth, and then he would grow silent, and say no more. As for speech concerning Gallat's mother, well it was almost as if Gallat didn't have one. Gallat just supposed his mother must have died in childbirth.

Miffty, now tired of hoarding duties, just sat glumly at her master's feet, thinking how much she was looking forward to that steak that the master shepherd was probably frying for her right now. Convention had it that human food was given to humans, and the scraps and leftovers to her; she liked to think it was the other way around. She also disliked her master's love of origami, given that paper was for ripping to shreds, not construction, though all manmade constructions were also rightly a challenge for obliteration by the strength and cunning of the four-pawed.

There was a squeak as the gate of the pen opened and the robe holding it in place fell away. Her master probably just thought it was the wind, and the gate was so far it was impossible by sight to validate or disprove her master's theory, but unlike human noses which seemed an unnecessary facial appendage, her nose was actually fit for purpose and could make out the creature and paint a picture of it.

The man that came through the gate seemed at first a shadowy figure but then as Miffty focussed, she could just about make out the red cape with sea blue ribbons along its front and sides, and the gold Asian symbol of Lucifer in central view. The figure had a bronze mask which glowed slightly, and there were only slits through which the man might perceive his surroundings, she was sure she had seen this figure before in the edges of her memory, yet couldn't figure out when.

By some delicate magic, for destiny and magic in this were united and working as one, the figure's cape and the mask seemed to evaporate away, and there was left an old, old man, in fact so old, he should not be alive by any natural laws. He had long fingernails and black eyes, he seemed like the image of death but as he moved forward his image shifted and he became a middle-aged kindly dude, with light brown hair, a plump belly and a jovial attitude. Though his eyes still had his true self, almost like they were dancing in the fires of damnation.

Her master would run away, and he definitely did jump far upon seeing the transformation even considering the limitation of his eyes, but something within his blood recognised this man. Blood bonds are something poorly understood for they relate to a kind of magic one would not think could exist. Most certainly it was not a form of magic that could be controlled or understood and the teachings of the wizard's didn't cover it in any degree. Yet the figure, who truly was Westog in disguise, felt a surge of hatred which he concealed well upon seeing the kid that escaped his potent mortality magic and survived not even a scare.

155

"So my boy. This is your domain of grass and sheep?" asked the man, a little oddly.

Westog's face then turned pitch black and he waved his hands dramatically around. Whilst turning upon the spot said unto Gallat, "Where sheep and cattle fall and kneel and beg for mercy!"

Gallat shuttled backwards, getting away from this gaping hole in the air.

It then shifted back to normal, and Gallat felt once more the fuzzy and warm feeling of familiarity which silenced his nerves. The figure smiled apologetically and just said, "You know, I do get a bit excited, my dear boy, when speaking over domains, do forgive me, so your domain is thus?"

He offered the boy his walking stick, which felt a lot heavier than it had moments ago, almost like it was pure gold.

Wind curled in the air as the figure confirmed to himself, ignoring for a moment the boy and whispering, "Yes, I do believe it is the lord of sheep and cattle should have more than a wooden stick to mark thine post."

"Myself does guess." Gallat shrugged, feeling like this was a rather unusual way to put, *I admire your herding skills*.

"Well, I've come because I can offer you something much better, much richer, much more rewarding of your talents."

"You mean, like a sheep wolf competition? Me and Miffty have been training hard this summer, and we were hoping she might get scouted by one of the village elders."

Miffty cuddled up to her master's leg.

"How sweet," said the man, forcing the words out of his mouth. "But no, no, no, my dear child. Absolutely not. I'm here to offer you power that will make sheep wolf competitions look like toddler play. I'm here to offer you a personal invitation to the academy of Mados Mordrė."

"Ummmm, but I like farming. Are there many sheep there?"

Laughing, Westog said, "The flock is many but those of the ram are few in number yet even the least of us outrank the greatest of the flock in power."

And with that he was gone.

"Buddy," whimpered Miffty, now looking up at Gallat with her big eyes. "We really shouldn't go there, you know the people of Mados Mordrė don't like wolves like me, they think we're just lesser beasts, and you can't abandon your farm here. We need you, your father needs you, and I need you."

"Don't worry, Miffty," said Gallat. "I'm not going. No way hozay!"

Miffty bounced up and down, she would not let a shape-shifting homo sapiens take her beloved master away from her.

Gallat strolled home with Miffty by his side, and if he only had night vision goggles and could see miles of miles away, he would have seen a gagged man fighting a gathering of hooded figures in the clearing, being dragged into a steel bar prison, and much might have been different. Or if Miffty was not so focussed upon her joy that she did not see a shadow that filled the painted window of the house of the master shepherd.

For when Gallat was about to open the door, a fatherly figure answered, that looked and smelled like Gallat's father and as far as anyone could tell was, for the moment.

He had a kettle bubbling away and some scones on the table.

"How was your farming today?"

"It was good, dad, and Miffty rounded up all the sheep in record time, I think she's ready for the village fair prized championships, dad, I really think she is."

Miffty gave Gallat a quick lick and pretended to herd a flock of invisible sheep into the side of the wall, doing all kinds of four-pawed acrobatics.

"Miffty is a fine wolf. But what about you, my son? Where are you heading?"

"Ummm, I'm heading to sheepy greatness?" He thought this a rather strange question for his dad to ask, he knew that Gallat's chief ambition was to see Miffty happy and achieve her potential, he didn't really want anything else and had no what you might call personal goals in mind beyond being a good and kind hearted guy.

"Son, Miffty is important yes but you'll be eighteen soon, you're coming of age. Now is the time to start to consider your future, perhaps going to college or even—"

"Even what, dad? Come on, you know I love Miffty and if she's happy then I'm happy too; I don't need to go to college and I don't need to learn to read or do algebra or any of that stuff. I like my life as a shepherd, dad, I really do."

"Well, what I need from you is to achieve your potential. And look son, I didn't want to tell you this but when your father died, he wrote you this letter."

The shepherd drew out an envelope entitled "for my son, when he comes of age."

"I know this is a little early, and I wanted to talk about all this properly when your birthday comes but now—"

157

"Now what, dad?" Tears began falling down Gallat's face. "Or should I even call you, Dad? What do you mean my father died, I thought you, I thought you…"

He couldn't get his words out, the day was turning into some twisted dream. He was begging to feel like he had been lied to all his life and everything he had known about his identity was a lie. Some people think the shock of finding out your parents may not actually be your parents is nothing but a realisation that you do not share the same blood line, but having been an adopted wolf from quite a young pup, I can say that the shock goes deeper.

For you find out that the heritage and history of a family that you thought was your family was in fact an illusion, and that you have a whole other heritage and history which has been kept from you. It's not so much the shock of realising you're not genetically quiet who you thought you were, it's the shock of realising that you're a person of two worlds and one of those worlds has been hidden under your nose your entire life.

You feel like you've been kept from the truth more so than been told an untruth. But this was all too much for Gallat to explain at the present. He just stuttered and wept and felt so confused and lost.

His father came to sit next to him. "Look my son, perhaps now is a little too early—"

"No, I want to read it," said the son, still sniffling every now and again.

He then carefully prised open the envelope and began to try to read but was illiterate so Miffty, who had to read books upon sheep law to be eligible for intellectual village fair competitions, read for her beloved master.

Dear son,

You have been kept from the knowledge of me not because I am ashamed, nor upset nor displeased with your existence. It is simply because I feel like you could have a better life far from my halls. Though you have heard of me, and I have always kept a careful and watchful eye upon you from afar, and it has been my greatest sorrow that I have not had the pleasure to be the father you deserve, but my beloved left me and at the time I was a poor traveller and unable to care for you properly.

The life of a wizard is a dangerous and complex affair, and I never wanted to throw you in till you were old enough to take the burden of the calling from your blood. My name is Gruggor the great, headmaster of the academy of Mados Mordrè, and your very proud father.

Your adopter, a lovely man of kind and genuine heart, loves your dearly and has played with you often when you were a little baby, and I trust that he will bring you up as if you are his own. But when you are of age, if you wish to embrace the magic and destiny of our line that is within your blood, come and find me. You have a great destiny my boy, for you shall be named none other than Christ, the challenger of the black flame. And long have the prophets been awaiting your entrance in the magical world.

Yours lovingly,
Gruggor the great

At the end Miffty just cried, then looked up at her master and jumped onto his lap.

"I know like you really want to find out the truth, but your truth is here, in this farm, with me."

Gallat huffed and buried his face in his hands, partly to hide the tears, partly to try to have some privacy. He loved his father and his wolf, but this was all too much to take in and he needed to be alone. But Miffty needed to hear him say, he wouldn't go, that he would stay with her forever, but he wasn't sure if he could do that anymore. *I mean, would it be so wrong to take just a few years away, I could always come here for holidays, I mean I could come back every weekend*, he thought.

In reality, he wanted to get away from his supposed father for keeping this from him for all those years, at least take a couple of weeks away and he had to find out who he was, what he was and sort out this mass of confused emotion welling inside of him.

"Miffty I love, and I'll come back on weekends I promise. But I need to find out what all this means and what all this makes me."

Miffty bowed her head and said, "I know. Just write to me every week, won't you?"

"I'll write to you every day."

Miffty jumped on top of Gallat and gave him a massive neck hug before realising she was strangling him and so loosened her grip a little.

She jumped off and ran over to get Gallat's golden walking stick, though holding it between her teeth proved an impossible challenge so she just dragged it along the ground.

The master shepherd packed the bags and made sure Gallat had enough food, water and maps for the ride. He also lent his son his finest stallion to carry him off.

When Gallat was poised firmly upon the saddle, his father said to him, "Go, my son, and may all the gods be with you."

The son then said, "Look after the wolf, my father, for you are my father, though now I have two, you are still as much a father as you ever have been, for the presence of another does not detract from your kindness or parenthood."

The wolf shouted, "And bring me back some steak!"

And with that Gallat was off. Soon he was out of sight and the sun began to rise.

Then a firm hand grabbed Miffty by the back and smoke started swirling around it and the changing shape of the master shepherd, till it resembled the same dark figure that Miffty had smelled coming towards them that very night.

"Your master is running into a trap, my dear wolfy, and you'll never see him again!"

She whined and then tried to get up but as she did she was kicked hard in the stomach and wheezed in pain.

"You liar!" she screamed as she tried to bite at the figure.

"Oh my dear wolf. I am the best liar of them all. I am the chief servant of the divine, I am Westog, head of the Scythian order, and my master, Gruggor, wants to boy! And as for the true father, that stupid master shepherd…well, he is heading right to the gallows and shall be hanged and cut into many pieces and given unto my beasts, before Gallat ever arrives. Or perhaps I shall lock him away and keep him close to his son, but just out of reach.

"He can see the destruction and mutation of his child's soul, a beautiful torture, you might agree. And Gallat shall see Gruggor as the loving father figure he shall pretend to be, till Gruggor either morphs him into an image model of an orthodox Luciferian. And I shall dance with glee when Gruggor, him and me rule the orthodox church together. Else I shall dispose of your master. And as for that letter, well that was the most beautiful bit of forgery ever. But it is nice to see you again, Miffty, I remember when you were but a pup and was hiding in a set of draws as I tried to kill your master, but never mind, perhaps I still shall one day"

With that, Miffy was struck dumb and whacked with a massive plate that shattered upon impact, she fell unconscious and was thrown into a cage, with her siblings, sundered from her beloved master.

Chapter 14
The Banjo Rock Star

Transiting from farm life unto the wizarding world is a leap in which one can hardly assume anything to be unalterable. Gallat's head was spinning with a swirl of ideas concerning how wizards frustrated the common laws of nature, there were so many things he had wanted to learn. His head filled with the idea of sparkles and bubbling potions.

He had been thinking of this all through the carriage trip, a long journey lasting some two months, were there was little to do but eat stale digestives, the generally accepted continental snack, and consider how he could formulate the new wonders he might see in an essay for Miffty.

Eventually, he did reach the academy but naturally forgot all about writing. He opened his mouth wide at the astonishing displays of magic around him, with students practising in the lush grass. And rising high was a massive academy, dull and grey and the most awesome gothic architecture ever.

Gallat almost jumped for fright when the two soufflé guards appeared instantaneously at the gates to welcome him.

"Good morning, my dear fellow," said one of the guard's heads, showing a warm and genuine smile. Though he could do little else, for the rest of him had yet to materialise. Magic was once more playing its games for the guards did not specialise in invisibility, indeed invisibility was one of those magical tricks not found in any principle foundation, and so becoming invisible and then visible was always a game of luck.

The other guard, whose hands were now beginning to take shape, smiled even more at Gallat's look of utter horror. And offered him a mug of coffee.

Gallat unfortunately accepted the brew, not having read its contents written on the label stuck the mug. Feeling suddenly very hyper, he bounced into the academy. The guards had added a few herbal ingredients to the traditional brew, these being necessary to boost the darkened mind that one often suffers from living under the shadow of the academic authorities. To a farm boy though this boast was nothing but a piece of shimmering heaven.

This happened rather literally as Gallat's vision began to break up thanks to the hallucinogenic drugs.

Waltzing into the academy did the dancing boy welcome his new life. Within the walls of Mados Mordré was more magic than in any other orthodox wizarding organisation. For here by the powers of Lucifer would magic not only reliably aid the practitioner in their principal foundation but elementary magic of other forms could be called upon reliably. And the high density of magic users, and life force within the walls, amplified each wizard's magic so that each was an unrivalled skilled wizard. It was a place of power and ancient learning, were old magic ran deep and many secrets were long kept, that should never have been known.

Skipping through the corridors he grabbed people's parchments and flung them into the air.

He practically glided past the professors who all stared at this unprecedented display of joy which left a trail of parchment in its wake. Bouncing across into the nooks and crannies of ancient learning, he waved carefree at the concuportion class, who smiled back waving at him. Some thought he was funny, others wonderful, some just thought he was mad. Knowing him well, most would think he's all three.

An entire army of rusty speared guards were running behind trying to keep up. He did not mind the clattering of their armour or wheezes of pain, for he was free, a delocalised spirit.

His joyous mood had rung alarm bells in all security personal, for merriment among the students was incredibly suspicious. Within the academy, for any but the most proficient emotivist, it was almost a non-entity.

They found this display almost alarming as Gruggor's outbursts of fury, but those they had at least had time to get used to and within the militaristic nature of the school, shouting was kind of fitting the moto.

In the farm boy's dizzy mind, he remained completely oblivious to this alarm and began forgetting the strange welcome he had got only a few moments ago. He was sure it was two men he had met, or maybe two ghosts or who cared, it was becoming fuzzier by the second. He was dazzled by the magical spells whizzing by left and right. He was to become a wizard. He felt so proud! And serve under the most powerful wizard the world had even seen, Gruggor the great! None other than his hereditary father.

If only his mother could see him now. Beaming he looked around so confident that they would be mightily impressed. He supposed anyway. He did not know of course, for his mother along with most of his relatives died in that horrible pestilence when he was only a baby.

A tear ran down his face at the thought of his dead mother, he didn't know why it upset him so much. He barely knew her. But there was a part of him, nonetheless, that wanted nothing more than to see his lost family. Lost to him before he could even speak or utter anything but a cry of farewell.

He shrugged off the sadness and the herbal brew quickly dispelled the last drops of sorrow. The present was so bright and vibrant after all.

Not realising how happy he was becoming, he broke out into a run and kept dashing along until he came across a man speaking to the moon. He froze. Looking up at the night sky which seemed to be hovering below the ceiling, he watched the moon he thought he knew so well, answering the inquisitions of a hooded figure below. The guards were panting as Gallat stared at what he had always known to be nothing more than the sheep's sleeping lantern. He had never seen it talk! Tentatively, Gallat squealed "hello", staring up into the night sky. He wondered if the moon would notice him.

The moon gave no response.

Instead, the hooded figure turned and saw this farm boy staring upwards.

"Hey bud, you look a little lonely there by yourself." The shadowy man moved forwards, though he kept a covered face, till lifting his hood he slowly walked over to shake Gallat's hand. His serious demeanour then suddenly changed and he burst out into a wide grin. He looked almost like a seventeen-year-old, a little perky and youthful, but so dude-like.

"Sweet molasses, you look good, mate; my name is Donkark. I'm an advanced practitioner of the magic of mortality, and you must be Gallat, I've been waiting for you. You're lucky we're not in lessons else I would have to bark at you like a dog, its unfortunately the way things are done here as Gruggor likes to keep things formal." Looking at the guards, they nodded in confirmation, still panting from their burst of action.

Then Gallat said attentively, "Hi Donkark, yeah, I'm Gallat."

"How good to meet you, buddy. You've got so much to learn here. Good souls can thrive within these walls, and I will tell you about the place."

Donkark shook his hair and created a glowing orb which pulsed radiating a gentle light over his black wand. He shook his hair once more, as it fell below his shoulders.

At the sight of the black wand magic, the guards backed away. Like moths in an anti-light field.

The two wizards strode out of the grand hall. Proud to be students within the legendary walls of Mados Mordrė.

Without Gallat saying another word, Donkark showed Gallat around the duelling areas, theoretical libraries and wizarding supply rooms. Explaining as much as he could about the workings of magic and spells, in that little time, in which there was barely any time for Gallat to ask anything.

He did not mind, though he followed little of what was said, he was glad at least to find someone to whom he could act normally with. Country humans, of which there where a few sprinkled around, for instance were sort of the same, even if a more bonkers version of those older generations, that looked after livestock.

Exhausted, Donkark and the newbie crashed on two vacant chairs in some vanadium and grand silver almost temple like room. It had images of the lost god displayed everywhere. Of course, no one quite knew how to depict this power, for this mythical being has never in living memory taken a visible form.

Gallat could make out a small silver candle, which lit up when Donkark stared at it. It made a bright violet flame. With the new light of the candle illuminating the empty space, he gasped for he had never seen a place so magnificently decorated.

"Impressive, right?" commented Donkark.

"Um...yeah," responded Gallat, wishing he had something more impressive to say.

"Cool, man," said Donkark saving the newbie from any further embarrassment. He reached under the chair and from nothing pulled out an army cap and a banjo. He put the army cap on, did a solute and then started playing one quirky arpeggio. He swung his long hair in an almost Rockstar imitation. Closing his eyes, he sighed and added in a chilled-out tone "cool man, cool!"

With eyes at first wide open but then drearily shutting and opening, Donkark satisfactorily added, "I know you'll be very happy here, and as for Gruggor, well, he's positively desperate to see you," said Donkark very merrily. "He's an amazing Wizard, has a few minor angry outbursts, but who cares." Donkark gave a small giggle.

In an almost reverential tone, he added, "You know, he's such a pioneering wonder."

Recovering from the incredible shock, Gallat hastily asked, "But I don't get it. Why's he so excited? It's not like I'm important, I've spent all my life in the country doing nothing worthy of note. Why's he so interested now?

"Coming out of almost worshipful silence, Donkark bluntly went, "Uh, what ya say, didn't catch ya there, buddy?"

Gallat simply repeated himself, though now sounding like a starved man asking for food.

Donkark tossed his thick bushy hair once more. "Oh fair, man. Fair," added Donkark playing a few Rock motifs. "Cool man. Cool. Ya know of Wizard auras?"

"Um…" mumbled Gallat a second time, feeling like a total stranger to this alien world.

Perhaps understanding Gallat's nervousness, Donkark patted the nervous figure on the shoulder. He then drew his wand, gave it a casual swish, and made a pint of vodka appear. He drank a good portion of it and then gave the half full glass to the newbie. Now gazing around him he bobbed his head up and down saying "yeah man." With one final swagger, he sat down.

"Well man, ya know, it's rather cool. They, wizard auras, travel like the wind. It's the air along which magic can be conducted. Kind of like an expanding cloud of ionised gas, you know plasma and the like, carrying an electric current. Though" rushed on Donkark almost inflating "I have never seen him so delighted as he was when he picked up on yours'. He stared with gooey eyes almost in awe of Gallat"

Gallat looked blankly into Donkark's pupils till he suddenly got the point of what Donkark had been telling him. Almost jumping to his feet but dropping halfway up as his feet gave way, Gallat burst, "Gruggor the great! Wants to see me. Well, I thought he might, but I don't know if he'll approve." Gallat sat back in his chair looking up into the night in wonder. Even in his wildest dreams, he had not expected to be noticed by such an acclaimed wizard so quickly.

"Yeah. Soon as you got within a mile, Gruggor was charging to his office with an almost manic smile, shouting very clearly, 'Ah Gallat. Finally. He shall join us'!" Beaming at Gallat's clear merriment, he added, "One hell of an aura you must have, mate." Donkark flicked up his head and his hair spun all around before settling in a messy confusion. Eventually, Donkark just sat waiting for the newbie to say something.

"Bu-u-u-t-t..." stammered Gallat. "I...um...I don't know what to say, though perhaps I should tell you something. But I don't know how to put it."

"Well, I do, buddy. You're tired, exhausted and almost certainly going to be something of a favourite around here. If Gruggor picked you out of the pack, mark me, you're someone that's going to go far, very, very far."

"Donkark, you don't get it, I really want to be the amazing pupil I know he thinks I'll become, but I'm scared of failing, I'm scared of being a disappointment. I've never done anything great before but look after sheep, and my friend Miffty isn't beside me anymore and I..." A few tears spilled down his cheek, he couldn't hold onto this amount of emotional confusion for any longer and there was something in Donkark's calming presence that just made Gallat want to tell him everything.

"Oh, mark me, man," said Donkark, putting an arm around his new buddy's shoulder, "there's something important about ya, even if ya don't know, and the profs will pull it out from your sheepy past. You're on the fast track to marvellous stuff. You're goanna achieve some great things. You're gonna be the best student this place has ever known. Miffty goanna be proud." Swinging his head from side to side he played a famous rock number. As he dug the tune, he hummed the tune too, before the confused face of the newbie caught his attention once more. "Man listens to the beat."

"Um..." said Gallat after listening to the musical interlude but just imagining his old life, and the sounds of those bagpipes in the highland farm lands.

Many musicians would not like to be interrupted by meaningless sounds. This was not Donkark who after doing a dramatic dive to the floor joined in with Gallatarnin. Still wanting to be a bit cool though he went for the mildly more sophisticated "hum..."

Eventually, the newbie stopped humming so the budding rockstar stopped h-oo-u-ming. Gallat then said, "Uh well, it's been, uh a busy day."

Now taking a vigorous head swing Donkark's hair flew around.

Gallat took a sip of the harsh drink and spat out the vodka. Donkark kindly took the glass from Gallat's hand and downed the rest of the drink. He stood up like a dog called suddenly to attention and threw the glass sky high into the cabinet. With a slight wobble he dropped back onto his chair. The rock dude did a little more h-oo-u-ming and then, "Hmm. Cool Dude. Busy. Yeah man. Cool. Had a busy day, Dude," concluded Donkark before putting away the banjo and swinging his banjo-themed bracelet around his hand.

"Um…" for the final time uttered Gallat.

This time, Donkark did not accompany Gallat's questioning sounds, with rock star vocals, as Donkark was starting to feel tired himself. Giddily, he stood up and kindly said, "Now though, sleep. Sleep well, my wonderful wizard."

With one more kindly smile, Donkark haphazardly walked off. And feeling so incredibly joyous, Gallat felt like he was flying as he wondered all the way to a nice warm bed in a lovely grand room. Oblivious to the sign indicating the proper owner of this tiny segment of the enormous castle (which luckily was indeed Gallat) he fell fast asleep. The smile on his face told of his very optimistic thoughts about the coming dawn.

Gallatarnin woke up in his warm comfy bed and his ears were no longer ringing with the noisy banjo sounds. His head had stopped hurting from the dizzy sensation it had achieved after drinking the vodka.

He yawned and got grudgingly up. He made the decision to spend the day exploring his new local area. But then with a large bang, Donkark appeared right outside the doorway. Gallat spun around in fright and the clay mug almost smashed into a billion shards. Then Donkark leant on the door and once more gave a super pompous flick of his hair.

Gallat couldn't see him clearly before but now the pitch-black hair and red dye caught his imagination. But before he had time to admire Donkark's hairstyle, Donkark bent down and seemed to mime opening some massive cabinet. From it he pulled out his very solid and loud banjo and played a few 'wake up' motifs. After strumming a few chords, he waved his wand and the banjo vanished as if it was no longer there.

"Man. It's breakfast. Um, breakfast…ya get me…like breaky breakfast?"

"Yeah, I get ya," said Gallat, slightly hesitant.

"Cool buddy. So let's bound along and with the fiery fuel bounce to the great heights of our great professors. Come buddy, come."

"Ah" said Gallat as Donkark stood there, beaming at him.

"Yes dude, ya go ah, what ya say, becky breakfast."

"Becky breakfast!" shouted Gallat.

Donkark ran towards Gallat and then gave him one huge hug. And then raced away being so positively overjoyed to find a friend.

Gallat hung behind for a second but then with one sigh of exasperation he dropped his mug and as it smashed on the silver floor, he shut the door, only just remembered to walk quickly back in and grab the nearest keys he hoped were his. He locked the door and dashed away.

He then raced down the stairs and just saw a trail of jet-black hair swish around the corner. Using this 'locate the hair' strategy, Gallat eventually made it to his seat with his heart thumping away. His forehead was sweaty, and he felt overheated. There where fire places every in the academy, but maybe the professors just wanted to impress upon the students the sensation of hell fire. Gruggor probably thought it was good for their souls.

Breakfast consisted of porgies, bacon, sausages and all manner of things. They ate in a massive hall, on modest wooden benches. The outer benches, upon which students were sat, all bonded together so that they formed a hexagon, a traditional shape in the working of magic. Then a circular ring at the centre of the hexagon was composed of many decorative chairs on which the professors sat drinking cocktails and eating fruit salad. At the centre of the circle was a gigantic statue of the horned god, the bringer of light or the lost god as he is commonly known.

Then Gruggor stood up halfway through the full morning dine, and raising his goblet shouted 'hail the prince of darkness'. A dark shadow seemed to flicker in his eyes. Yet his words sounded so profound, so full of adoration that Lucifer in the black pits of hell, smiled. His beloved creation was calling unto him.

Gallat was full of wonder. And he felt Ariton's warmth flood his heart. So, on that fateful day did Gallat's concerns and fear fade, for at that moment he felt truly and totally loved, which was what he was looking for in the first place. He felt like he was somewhere he might one day be able to call home.

Gruggor, after his solute to Lucifer, took a gulp of wine and made a prayer to Baphlotos, and his red wine shone with a ruby glow. Smiling he sat down. He planned this night to make a special celebration unto his lord for being so bountiful as to bring this boy unto his grasp, so together they might break the seal within the cave. But Gruggor's concepts of celebrations were those of a bar man, who decides the amount of lager, he is consuming to be too manly, and so looks through his wife's wardrobe to find frilly dresses and bras to fit himself out with. Following the sunset when everything is dark and all others are deep asleep, he then presents himself as the drag queen he is inside unto his secret dancing group.

Such was Gruggor's nightly activity, for though he had no wife, he had many second-hand corsets. And there was a special amber one, with a rosé bar, he wanted to make use of tonight. Most of the professors thought Gruggor's secret nightly activities to be dark occult practices, probably involving human sacrifice, but they were mistaken, although the thought of Gruggor doing drag dancing is perhaps more horrifying than any occult ritual could be.

As for Gallat, well the drink made him forget all about his shepherd past and Miffty never received a letter from her beloved master.

Chapter 15
Chicken and Bacon Soup

Jasper was now heading north with his hood covering his curly hair and his shepherds stick making holes in the wet mud. He loved seeing the wolf cubs play in the forest but today he had business up north in the academy of Mados Mordrė, for he was himself one of the first conjurers to ever walk the planet and would always be welcomed at a wizard's gathering, even if not liked to be seen there.

Gruggor particularly was displeased to see Jasper at such events due to Jasper's buoyant soul, which exuded life, and Gruggor's natural distaste for life which comes when considering death on a professional platform. And Jasper's continual attempts at flirting were maddeningly dismal to say the least. But Jasper had to be there for this secret meeting, for being a part of Gruggor's closest circle by way of charm and successful flirting (at least according to Jasper), he knew it was time to be discussing Christ's part to play in the great overture that destiny had designed.

Now Christ's existence was a complex thing. Demons loved him, some black sorcerers liked him, yet others thought he should be dead. For he resembled both the rebellious attitude that defined Lucifer's fall from heaven, and yet rejected sin by virtue of his nature being always to challenge the orthodox churches actions if not their preaching. And rebellion and sin are too often tied like a knot, for most theologians were often to be found saying that something is wrong because it falls into the category of rebellion against God and is therefore sinful, or saying it is sinful and therefore to be discouraged for it is rebellious against God.

Yet Christ embodied rebellion attitudes, and the desire to question all establishment, but was made to hold the firm belief that sin was to be discouraged. This was something that many found disconcerting to say the very least.

Now all this is naturally dependent upon your perspective of god (be that God or Lucifer), given that if sin is described as anything destructive, then the most destructive relationship one could probably have with god is to not be rebellious in some small fashion, for this would surely prevent any real growth and begin to encourage seeing god as some kind of overlord. Being a teenager once upon a time, I can confirm that a time of disobedience is critical to the growth of such a bond, although one may well grow into an understanding of the reasoning and validity of the rules and beliefs of his father, and so come to respect him more fully in time.

So, with the confusion, how should one look at Christ? Should he be sung as a hero of Lucifer, or as a preacher of the ways of God, or just thrown out of society as a radical. Or even be executed? All these thoughts went through Gruggor's mind as he built a pile of twigs and lit them ablaze with some magical fire liquid he had stolen from the potions master supply room. Jasper was calmly walking towards the black series of turrets and towers but none could see him, for it was pitch black.

Now, darkness is something the religious are even more squeamish about than rebelliousness. For it is a concept rejected wholeheartedly by the Christian church, whom see anything showing any sign of spiritual blackness as a sign of doom or destruction. Admittedly Gruggor disliked this philosophy given that he spent most of his life as a Nocturnal animal.

Though he thought unto himself that *Anyone who does this creates an internal battle between their light and dark sides and adopts a yin and yang philosophy which simply results in someone being slightly self-destructive or self-loathing. Not good at all!* Jasper would have agreed though he didn't really get the 'self-destructive' part, for everything around him seemed to be conducive to growth and life.

But in respect of the moral peace, one can have once one learns to dance with one's inner darkness, let us judge Jasper not too harshly. The chanting of worshipers was thinking along similar lines of thought concerning the inner darkness, as they bent before the altar dressed only in long thick black cloaks. They were gathering in secret at this late hour, for they, the High Necromantic order, wished to discuss how to utilise the new chess piece that had entered the cosmological battle between Lucifer and God.

They wished to discuss about Christ. Or at least all did save a priest who was feeling very peckish, but we will come to this in a bit. And a curly dude who was throwing paper balls into the blazing furnace at the centre, which spat out sparks of flame which came to life as small little cartoons of pixies, before disappearing into the night sky. Jasper clapped and cheered as a couple of the animation pixies began arm wrestling with one another, now being close enough for everyone to notice him with mixed reactions. Jasper was also trying hard to get the Arch-demon to join in with jubilations, but Gruggor was just sitting there muttering fancy words with his hands raised unto his god, it was so transcendently evil that destiny would never stop gloating about this perfect picture.

Jasper looked onto Gruggor's facial shadowy outline, not quite being able to make it out fully in the midnight blackness and with mock seriousness, told him, "Make sure you deal with that Gallat, can't have a hero winning the day, but maybe you can bring him round to your way of thinking if it suits you. Unless of course, he's too dangerous a risk to take."

With that, Jasper picked up his shepherd's stick and just walked off, to have a chat with destiny and make sure he attended destiny's press conferences which would surely be entitled: "Gallat and Gruggor, the innocent sheep farmer life takes a turn for the worst, go to the next page for more details."

The Arch-demon barely acknowledged him but just waved him away, till a Shepherd's staff was at his throat like it was a spear poised for a deadly blow. It was as if Jasper had just vanished and reappeared within an instant, something that should be totally impossible and must have been a trick of the light. I mean imagine the number of plot holes destiny would have to tie together if people could just reaper in one place and appear in another, no man could ever do that, be he an eternally eighteen-year-old or even an evil tyrant.

Blast it, even Christ himself could never do that. But anyway that wasn't Gruggor's priority right now given the staff has formed into a blade. And the blade was digging in just enough for a drop of blood to form at the knife's tip, as Jasper said, "…and you better make up your mind, old man, I'm not to be tested, and I want a significant update in the story soon else I shall pulverise your head down to a thick paste and spread it over my morning crumpet. And Gruggor…"

"Yes," said the Arch-demon solemnly as if the conversation was killing him, which indeed most conversations with people did in his eyes, but that's for another story.

"I really do think destiny's got some love matching to do, and if you ever wonder, well needless to say, you do know where to find me if you get lonely upon Halloween and want to be naughty. You know I bet your something of a sweet heart inside." Jasper beamed at Gruggor and then skipped off with a couple of dogs bounding after him. Dropping his knife on the ground as he went, not even caring about arming himself if Gruggor was going to make a surprise attack. How very rude.

Everyone was silent. No one had ever seen the head of the Necromantic Order so humiliated before, and Gruggor never felt so much like angering some mountain dragons and letting them just burn down to entire civilised world there and then. Still, once the shock was over, Gruggor coughed a few times and as if nothing at all had happened, the gatherings agenda was made doubly clear as Gruggor, newly humiliated head of the Necromantic order, read aloud in a deep and carrying voice, "We are here my most feared brethren. And now we are all united, we must decide whether to kill the Christ like figure, or teach him advanced magic.

"If we kill him before he could become a puppet head unto the wizards of the white tower who are loyal unto God and consistently oppose the work of Mados Mordrė, that might prove a wise tactical manoeuvre. But if we take the risk of teaching the Christ magic in the hopes of turning him to our cause and using his position that destiny had given unto him, to demoralise the resistance and spur wizards around the globe to crush the white tower, that might too be prudent."

Westog leaned into Gruggor and pulling his black robe sharply told him, "It is hoped by many, that the Christ might itself be a prodigy in the foundation of magic it mastered. And I have taught him my lord, and have made him the core concern of the Scythan order, and he scares even me with his raw potential. This would make him all the more might a spear head for our advancement and our preparing of the lands for our master's return. Then we could with great ease bring forth global domination!"

The hooded figures laughed and the Arch-demon spread out his hands, his black robe rolling back, and fire fell from the stars and danced around him. Everyone was silent as if squirming like a rat trying to escape a mice's claws. Gruggor held forth the knife that Jasper had dropped, and he smiled with glee as it flared and stretched out into the staff of the Caduceus. The symbol of the Arch-demon's power. With it Gruggor smote the ground and fire danced around them as demons could be seen running like smoke under the ground for the briefest of moments before the crack shut and the magic of Michael broke the small thread Gruggor had made between the realms.

Everyone looked on in shock for never before had a wizard done anything to challenge the magic of an immortal. And never before had someone made a dent in it, even if only for the most minute increment in time and space. Now it was less like Michael's magic became imperfect, and more like the connection which still existed, the crack if you like, widened a little, before snapping back to its normal size. Still this was a most spectacular satanic miracle.

Gruggor, with sweat pouring from his forehead, turned to Westog and said with clenched teeth, in a sickeningly sinister tone, "But he shall never be the prodigy I am!" As if there was any question, given that Gruggor had just done the most impressive magical feets since Michael's charm.

Everyone around the campfire was silent, too afraid to move. But then Gruggor just dropped his forehead, hiding it with his cloak's hood and relaxed a little, thinking he had made his point perfectly clear, and began singing worship songs unto Lucifer his lord.

The Necromantic order, sang in a Gregorian chant into the night. The key shifted into minor overtones. As they sang did a demon possess Gruggor, drawing life from Gruggor's tentacles of dark magic, and put in Gruggor's heart a darker design, revealing how glorious it would be if he used this evening's power within the Luna cycle, not to pull his apprentice into depths of hellish magic previously known, but to take from him his life and bear it forth as a gift, where he would gain many gifts and riches, and cakes.

After every song the gathering marched around the fire, saluting the spirits they were worshiping. The words they used were something like snake language, again not that snakes are actually evil, but humans being bipeds have always found the wriggling motion of snakes slightly mystical. It ought to be said here there is nothing evil about crawling on one's belly and humans can do it, though they tend to get a bit of a burn on the stomach and find the dirt discomforting.

What was evilly sinister about the process was the drawing of magic out of the dripping of blood from the members hands. It fell into a basin, to mirror the falling of angelic blood unto the earth of old. For tonight they would require it for an astral-obliterators curse, one which was designed to kill an individual's soul, but leave them intact in the body so as to not arise suspicion of murder. The blank and emotionless life the individual would then be forced to live would be worse than death.

Blood-spells were common in the secret gatherings of wizards though it was usually not attributed to dealing with death magic, for it was usually a sign of desperation, self-hatred and something to encourage sympathy and more a cry for help. On occasion, for some individuals, the motive behind cutting lies in the fact that it is destructive to the body to cut. And the release of some chemicals does give a degree of pleasure to relieve the sense of hate one is internally holding within.

The immune system would have cried at the sudden influx of bacteria but at the time, they were all crying salty tears which may had inadvertently cleaned the wound. For bacteria do not like salt.

One of them had long brown hair and rose his face into the night. "Oh…ooh…[snarling]…Oh…[snake stuff]…wow."

His hair was very impressive but the other members were clearly impressed with his snarling and snake speech because they clapped every time he ended. One of the gathering had drifted to sleep, but it was hard to see if that was because he was extremely tired or was fainting from loss of blood. Neither was much concern, as losing enough blood to lose consciousness would only help lead the individual to the blackened gates of hell. Which was were all of them hoped to go.

Some are afraid of burning flames, but they forget that there are compensations. One of these was melting marshmallows, a sugary image of the afterlife which greatly appealed to all but one of the collective gatherings.

The dislike of marshmallow hell, emanated like a tidal wave from a diabetic who disliked sugar almost as much as he disliked angels, but was on such good correspondence with the devil that he believed if the flames of hell didn't harm the prince of darkness, then the prince of darkness would not let the flames harm him.

This is not entirely barbaric, since immunity to spiritual fire may well be possible for blessed (or should I say damned) souls.

Scientists had been unable to determine the exact properties of astral fire on astral bodies, as they have yet to attain anything about the astral world at all. Thus, what happens after death is like asking when you will wake up tomorrow, to which the correct response is 'I cannot know.' By the time you are aware you've awoken, you've awoken for a long time. It's like asking when you go to sleep, you can only remember the last time you remember being awake.

There are many questions that cannot be answered by the very people that want to answer the question, whilst those who don't need to be told the answer often already know it. Those that are dead probably do know what it is like being dead, but I'm sure they would have liked to know this before dying, and I doubt knowledge of the state of their existence is helpful to the experience itself.

For take a moment to consider thine self. If thine was in a state of torment and was burning, would someone telling thee this, make thy life any easier? Would thine not probably spend eternity trying to convince oneself that there is no such thing as eternity and thy pain would end abruptly?

Of course, you can't literally have flames going on for eternity in any absolute sense, because thanks to relativity all time itself is relative. And there's no such thing as a definitive 'eternity'. You see from the perspective of say a particle on the event horizon of the black hole, that moment is in itself eternal. So literally an eternity is equivalent to no time passing at all, in which the flames of hell would only be an instantaneous if eternal event. At least until the hawking radiation over time causes the black hole to evaporate away.

Assuming though that hell is not located at the event horizon of a black hole, eternity shall feel like a very, very long time. But it is so long there are probably philosophers that argue it is a meaningless concept. Therefore eternity isn't a thing, so eternal flames of hell are not a thing either. Nor is an eternal heaven for that matter.

We also must note that god creates flaming furnaces in the hearts of stars, so hell would only be mimicking the great work of the creator.

Gruggor did not believe in hell in any literal sense, since taking it literally creates all the metaphysical complications discussed, rather he saw it as a state of existence where the soul is trapped in perpetual spiritual darkness. This was quite contrary to most of his peers, who saw hell as having some pseudo-physical form, but Gruggor was always the revolutionary in theoretical magic.

Hell was in his view better than being in heaven, a place of perpetual spiritual light, for at least in hell one could get a good night's sleep.

Gruggor coughed twice and the rest of the circle turned to see him. They had been looking at tinder and seeing if any of their favourite candidates had swiped them. Gruggor's cough though did awaken them to the dangers of allowing their minds to transgress to dating, whilst in the presence of the extremist who had killed some of his ex-wives for simply not staying on task and daring to ask for such insignificant things like 'a kiss' or sex.

Many believed Gruggor had in fact never so much as made out, they were correct in a sense, though William the wanderer was quiet the woman's man and Gruggor's early years as the new figure head of the kingdom of darkness, was

177

something he didn't exactly take in his stride all the time. Those were sad times for him, but many would then have said he was at least outside the black hole event horizon which marked the boundaries of salvation, but now had long fallen and there was no getting out.

Of course, if one does lend credence to such an event horizon, then this is saying that God has limits and there are places where he and his mercy cannot reach, and where the bonds are indestructible. This would surely mean that the one, would no longer be all-powerful, and in fact would be outstripped in power by his arch enemy, sin. So such people arguably do not believe that the one is who he said he is, the all, and it would surely be a stretch for those people to call the one, a god, and a total lie to call it almighty. Forgive my ramblings here, I am simply trying to fathom the leaders of the religious order of the one who claim Gruggor is beyond repentance but yet profess the all power and limitlessness of their lord.

But Gruggor was not concerned with this, be it an irreversible truth or not, for the moment he was bound to the kingdom of the light bringer, and this was exactly how he liked it. So he opened up his arms, and said unto his gathering, "We are gathered here today at midnight."

Swinging the amulet of Lucifer which he had taken out of his robe, he began a chant to Belial.

"At midnight? I thought we met at midnight when all the modelling wizards came out to play? Does midnight last longer than a moment in time? Or have we entered the event horizon of a black hole on this black night?"

"Fine! I was going for a more atmospheric effect but if you insist, we meet here my dark comrades at this blackened moment of 10 seconds past midnight."

"No, no, no, this won't do," said the most aged member at the circle. He had a long silvery beard and was a lovely old man, who had risen to the rank of a high priest by a few stabbings and medieval techniques in his much earlier days.

The others looked wearily at his knife belt but before he felt the urge to feel the movement of the steel in his wrinkly hands, Gruggor coughed loudly again.

"Fine! We are most dark comrades." The fire roared in response and a gratifying look of fear passed the circle. "Now we are gathered at this dark of the dark moments, of 1 full minuet cycle after the blackened hour, the sacred of the unsanctified midnight time. We shall invoke the power of—"

"Soup."

Everyone turned and stared at the old man.

"What!" said Gruggor indignantly.

"Soup," repeated the old man. He was now stretching his nobly legs towards the fire so his hair was singed and his crooked teeth reflected the fire upon their yellowy brown surface.

"We can't summon the power of soup, high priest, with all due…" said Gruggor, feeling very annoyed with this old man. It was a shame this old rascal was more powerful than him, else Gruggor would turn him into a marshmallow as punishment for wasting his time and delaying the moment were the ceremony would be over and he could take a bite of his next marshmallow.

The old man like a lightning bolt moved and before anyone could do anything a sharp point was in contact with the surface of Gruggor's neck.

"Now listen here, silly wizard," said the priest as Gruggor spluttered and his hand waved wildly in the air trying to grab oxygen. "I like soup! So if I say we shall summon soup then soup we shall summon. Now be a good boy and don't disrespect an old and helpless man."

The priest let go of Gruggor's neck and he spluttered on the floor before finally shouting "Fine! Fine!" Gruggor silently thought this priest was anything but defenceless, he couldn't even be sure if he was old or was using an enchantment, he sure didn't seem to be old judging by the priest's strong grip around his throat. Yet Gruggor began again, moving his neck only a little till it felt less sore and being sure to keep the magical knife that Jasper had dropped, under his robes well wrapped up. He was ready for a surprise attack this time.

Raising his hands to the sky, he chanted, "We shall invoke the power of soup."

Tears filled the priest's eyes, he was so longing for soup in this cold night.

Gruggor was crying, he was going to do so much evil but now all that would be done tonight was worshipping edible liquids as they called upon the vegetable fumes of boiled soup.

"BACON SOUP!" shouted the old man. He had a very loud and cocky voice.

"Bacon?" Gruggor asked. He preferred garlic and lamb soup.

"YES, BACON SOUP!" shouted the high priest. "We shall invoke the power of bacon soup. The saltiness of the bacon shall give rise to the power of—"

"My stomach," finished the old man.

It was now becoming clear the high priest had only gotten out of bed so they could do a series of rituals to worship his unending stomach, and love of old man food.

This was not what Gruggor was going for, given a very, very important student had just entered their midst and Gruggor desperately wanted to see him crush the rebellion or be dead.

Luckily for Gallat, the high priest loved bacon soup so there was no incarnations of death to chop him to bits as he slept. Gallat woke up the next morning very, very well, with only the dangers of living in a magical academy to face. The priest however found upon nodding off that a knife in the digestive system really does mess with the experience of midnight soup.

Gruggor went back to his chamber and closed the curtains. He thought in bitterness about how he had not achieved any of his goals since becoming headmaster, he wasn't used to having to wait. He had sent assassins, two of the three, to kill king Bartibus the barmy, but word reached him a while ago that one sent by that blasted king in Ontock had to mess up his plan and killed his best swordsmen.

Then there was the boy, he was here but every time Gruggor tried to invoke the powers of darkness to turn the boy to evil something went wrong, like there was some kind of unseen force working against Gruggor. Perhaps he needed to just be patient with the boy. But what if Triffon's prophecies concerning Christ were right, and he really would become more powerful a wizard than he.

Gruggor would not stand for a rival to his position. Yet, he was getting over worked, Christ was not going to be better than him, for his own station as Arch-demon assured him of this. And hey, as for taking control of the kingdom of Mados, well Triffon might be able to send a message to the king if she could just be persuaded to leave these walls.

Gruggor went to bed that night, having decided the next morning to send a raven complementing his spies in king Bartibus' courts. For Judging by how they had managed to get the king into thinking his kingdom was undesirable and so manipulate him into believing he needed to get it approved by making it the spot for a barbarian invasion, he felt like the kingdom would soon be crumbling. The royal court would not dare stand up to Gruggor's power with the destruction of a barbarian invasion to add to his bargaining guns. The main city of Mados might already be destroyed by the barbarians for him, when Triffon arrived to deliver a message to the desperate people, in need of wiser and much more powerful leadership in the difficult years ahead.

Lucifer was not overjoyed in the realms of his hell and cried that he could not ascend to world above yet, and even more angry that some guardian demon had even suggested that Gruggor kill the boy when he would need to harness both Gruggor's and Gallat's powers if he was to break free. He needed them both! Gruggor seemed currently poised to begin destroying the only hope the world ever had for igniting the people to rebellion and accept Lucifer, prince of darkness, as their one true and rightful lord. Looking over the archives which the demonic scribes had kept, it appeared Astaroth might have his own agenda and even desire mutiny.

Lucifer in his fiery furnaces brought to the attention of the council of Hella, with all the chieftains of the underworld, what he had dug up concerning a traitorous demon. Kneeling before him was his lieutenant and those who were in charge of various rebellious offices, ready to serve their lord as seemed fit, but a servitude based upon mutual agreement and respect, and a servitude were disagreement and conflict was much welcomed at times. Lucifer wore a crown of golden laurels and held in his hands the sceptre of archaic knowledge. The amber light of the fire gave as it were a perfect spot light upon his shining face and fully relaxed wings, large enough for him to fly faster than any messenger of god.

"My lord and master, where is thine will concerning us, for looking upon you, I cannot verily see it?" said Amaymon. He was in charge of the angelic order of rebirth, for his professional countenance was always concerned with allowing one to emerge from crisis unharmed and undamaged.

He was the polar opposite of what most might consider demonic, and though was by no means benevolent, to call him evil would be to call a snake such, simply because it has venomous fangs. Lucifer pierced into his mind and was glad. For in his mind did Lucifer perceive love and kindness. Lucifer then looked around, at the hearts of many before him, and noticed how the words were not associated with Astaroth's heart, but how Ashtaroth felt land emergence.

Myrmo, who was in charge of finding answers to the most difficult of difficult questions, answered with surprising abruptness, "The banishment of a traitor."

Lucifer's boyfriend pushed through the throng and walked up to his beloved. "My friend, if anyone here is of mine's kind and means thee or thy kingdom harm, do not hesitate to say and I shall remove this traitor as a doctor may remove a virus."

Lucifer looked lovingly down at him but said, "My friend, did I not rebel in the name of free will. For I do not rule hell nor the kingdom above by asking for complete devotion, nay, I rule for I am greater than all that would cause discontent and can deal with the thrills of rebellion that shall surely come under my leadership when I champion the very freedom this rebellion illustrates. I shall not be a god of contradictions, my friend."

His boyfriend looked forth at his lord with total wonder, for never had he seen him more in his element than when he was talking about freedom, and to believe in it at such great cost as to allow his throne to be jeopardised, that made the king of the fallen all more admirable. He kissed lucifer on the cheek and Lucifer blushed. His wings turned slightly red, this didn't help him look mightily kingly, particularly given he was very nervous among large crowds though he had learned to hide it well.

Lucifer's beloved said unto him, "I thank you for your acceptance of freedom of action and will, my lord. Yet I see that you would have me do something, though you fear a little for I shall not be at your side while I am away. But you are at your most powerful in this realm my lord, were as I am very much torn between both the world of men and of my fellow kind. This visit to help circumvent the plans of Gruggor may well serve me and our friendship greatly.

"And I shall discover the full purposes of this traitor through my observations in the world above. And yes, I know of Michael's magic and I cannot go into the physical world with even half my being. But I shall go there nonetheless, with as much as I can muster through the small portal in the Black moor of the world above. The guardian hounds were sufficiently dealt with upon Jorge's ascent into the abyss as well you remember.

"Thus, some small fragment of me has a good chance of making it out unharmed. I shall be vulnerable though and much lacking in power for I shall be ripped from myself by the passage. Yet I am strong enough to injure this, for the strength of my love for you shall keep the ripped essence of me from falling into disrepair. What say you, my prince?"

"Oh angel of the silver moon, Ariton. Who forever protects those who are challenged and most of all your beloved, in whom you delight. I love thee dearly but if it is your will to go, then go with my satanic blessing. For you are as the sun is to the earth and as the bonfire is to the flame, you are what gives me life."

Ariton hugged Lucifer and they had one most emotional farewell, before Ariton left and Lucifer departed tearfully from the council. He went into his dormitory, locked his silver door and sank to hide under his rose red covers. He desired to bury his sorrow. Lucifer had never before been so alone as he felt now, as his boyfriend was no longer at his side, and it made him a more fragile angel.

But Ariton went straight to the Academy of Mados Mordrė and there came in the form of a youngish pupil undertaking an advanced apprenticeship. He eventually found out the full extent of Astaroth's betrayal and how Astaroth had been altering the course of magic beyond the instructions initially dished out by Lucifer. So he went instead to the royal court of King Bartibus.

All the current knights there could swear of having known for over long, despite his arrival into this world only moments before. There he began to plot how to take over the Academy with the motley crew before him, and would have rallied the troops under his banner at once had he not been distracted by the many new experiences that existence within the physical world upon this age offered. They had even invented cupcakes! The best invention since the fiery sauna lakes which new damned souls enjoyed as part of their welcome package.

Chapter 16
Groovy Daggers

After returning from his search unsuccessfully, Hamfield had told the king immediately that Rupert seemed to be making an attempt to prove his valour very rashly and without anyone's championship. You might have expected Hamfield to cry, and he did. You might have expected him to cuddle all statues of the prince he had locked in his private stash when he returned to his dormitories in the king's place, and he did.

But another thing he did, which is to his credit, is pull himself out of the sadness that the emptiness that Rupert's absence was creating. Of course he believed Rupert could handle a dragon on his own and perhaps even the dragon would just gladly lay itself by his feet. And Hamfield didn't yet know of the capture by Madam Crumbler, as even the Dylan, was still unaware as to why the prince was taking so long, but that's probably for the best of the kingdom.

Being the lieutenant of Prince Rupert, Hamfield had a madly busy schedule and had increased his hours significantly so he had no time to consider his friend.

Hamfield during this period of loneliness, never had time to introduce himself with his full name when meeting new knights, so he just named himself Hammy. In fact upon Rupert's eventual return, which we will come to later in the tale, when addressing anyone but his beloved prince, he just referred to himself as such thinking it was noble to be related to the components of a nice ham and cheese sandwiches offered at royal banquets. Hammy's chief responsibility whilst the prince was gone though was to uphold his title as captain of the groovy dagger squad.

He liked having a hearty breakfast given the long hours of workouts and chivalrous chivalries a knight of his calibre was expected to do.

What he was not expecting was one or two cupcakes to be delivered to him as he thought this was a plot to make him fat. This is a hysterical hypothesis as the allowed calorie count for a professional knight was so high he could have had cake for breakfast, lunch and dinner and not put on a milligram. In fact giving him a cake had less of an effect upon his mass than the relativistic mass he gained due to time dilation when riding his horse. And for those of you who are not into relativity, well that's a tiny correction. If this were not the case, then tournaments would be a far more mathematical challenge than they ever were in practice.

Still Hammy had brought a bottle of anti-fatteneen with him, that dissolved all the butter and converted it into pure water. His now very soggy tasteless cupcakes were sent back to the kitchen to be steamed and mixed with custard before given as food for his father, who was already on the larger end of the spectrum. Steamed puddings were one of the kingdom's well-known skills, mainly because the winters were very chilly and everyone outside of the academy walls had not invented soup to warm up their stomachs. Exactly how they had not invented soup, one of the most basic boiled food dishes necessary for living in such a chilly climate, during the long winter months, is a wonder.

The people of the local town were poor but, in their huts, had fur coats, pots and pans and sleeping beds as was needed. The people had picnics in the few summer months when the weather was pleasant and long evenings in each other's houses in the dark nights of the year. They spoke in a language known as 'Maddic' which was like Welsh but a little more rustic and Germanic. His family was most talented in linguistics and spoke draconic, angelic, demonic and apricot. They also spoke to rats, but they kept this quiet.

Or at least now they had to speak apricotic given that the whole world was in a state of crisis, and encouraging fruit awareness by championing every aspect of apricotic existences, might be able to save their livelihoods and love of fruits from Gruggor.

Speaking apricotic was seen as a primary need in the Ontocian court, they looked down upon the tea obsessed Madockians, given that it did nothing to prevent the growth of Gruggor's hand over the continent. The court had even set up the 'fruit society' and to keep the 'fruit society' club going, given the 'no-fruit' wizarding society was cutting off its present members at a very high rate, they opened it up to the poor people who were at risk of dying from pneumonia upon the streets, such that even being assassinated seemed a blessing. A high enough rate was attained such that recruiting was totally immoral, but necessary, if the kingdom of Ontock was to preserve its fruity cuisine.

Hammy was always furious that in the land of Ontock, that ridiculous prince, had mimicked his idea of dancing knights but rejoiced that they had not yet mastered the tango or had prince Rupert's soft hair on their side of the battlefield.

Yet the secrets of the smooth apricot surface were something that many a Ontockian high ranking priest had pondered. What an apricot would say, if it could speak, is one of the most puzzling questions up there with Schrodinger's cat and the reason behind the madness of king Bartibus. One successful theory that was becoming eerily popular was the 'don't eat me' hypothesis that conjectured all apricots would make an effort to save their flesh. The suicidal therapy squad though did not like the 'don't eat me' theory as all brave apricots should have the freedom to say, "I want to die."

To willingly sacrifice yourself at the fruit stand is totally okay.

This controversial viewpoint known as the 'suicidal apricot theory' actually saved many of the fruit societies members from being murdered since all its supporters were encouraged to go round market stalls dressed as apricots, selling leaflets whilst shouting, "I want to die."

The job of taking out one of the members was made somewhat hard when the victim, said just before death hit them like a bullet, 'I want to die', since most wizards do have the moral decency not to kill a suicidal member of society but offer them help and therapy. You might say but Gruggor would never do that, and you would be correct, but he and most dark wizards are not typical of wizards as a whole. And most wizards, particularly young ones, take pity on suicidal friends in need, dressed during the blistering heat of the summer months, as apricots.

Not a few wizards actually took pity on their suicidal non-magical brethren and took them away to a place where they would hopefully be happier and learn a kindlier magical way of life. Thus, by actually standing up for 'suicidal apricot theory', a very profruit movement, they ended up saving their own necks and became integrated into the very vitamin deprived magical community. They found there one hero they could all rally around, one that wore apricots on her headdress, Miss Triffon of the academy of Mados Mordrè. Though they were too scared to tell her this as they did not want to endanger her life, particularly around the 'no fruit eating' extremist professor Gruggor. Thus, they had Miss Triffon fan clubs in secret under the dim light of a few candles.

This goes far off track though of our main topic here, but hopefully gives a glimpse of just how barmy the people of Ontock and Mados were. Anyway, back to Hammy. Hammy, was now doing some pirouettes for the pre-pre balance exercises he had planned. For today before he began the pre-prep for the pre-prep of horse riding, a skill that required impeccable balance, he had a lot of work to do! There were lots of Pre's in his schedule since he liked doing things really rigorously. Then there was a knock on the door and the prince opened it.

"Yes," said the Hammy rather impatiently. Hammy hurried past Humphry who looked like he had been about to say something but was not given much opportunity due to the incredibly buzzy lifestyle of Hammy. Humphry had liked his captain for some time but telling him this was like trying to catch a fish in water. Every time he was about to say something, the words slipped away. Humphry felt a little crushed but given that this was what it was, he put on a brave smile and followed the captain into training.

Today they were practising their group dance off. This was a very important part of the Madosian knight's discipline, given that the difference between a peasant savagely killing his foes and a knight doing the same was according to Hammy, a matter of style. The knights didn't just fight, they danced like they were clubbing or moved as some cheer leading team to an invisible baseball match, while the cheerleading squad met the lethal blades of their enemies. They went into battle bravely, almost sacrificing themselves for their imaginary baseball team.

The dancing style had some disadvantages and advantages, the biggest one of all is at least if one was to die one could do so doing a couple summersaults or a split and be marked down as the grooviest man to fall in battle. The second main advantage was that you knew where all your comrades were and after getting a good feel for everyone's own unique dance flavour, join swords with anyone in need of back up very effectively.

The disadvantage however was that you would very really move off rhythm so off rhythmic attacks were very hard to fend off, and most incoming enemies do not come in with rhythm in mind. Thus, though they were very good swordsmen, they were touch and go on the battlefield and victories were rarely attained without one or two unnecessary injures. They became known in legend as the groovy daggers.

Hammy didn't like the mixed results of victory but loved dancing more than life, so was willing to take a risk. Yet all the writing concerning the knight's death toll and his rivalry with prince Rupert meant he felt like it was time to do something revolutionary. He was going to introduce freestyle. And thus, the revolution began.

"Two hands up and down, like this!" shouted Humphry, looking at Hammy for approval given that Humphry was trying to impress Hammy with his confidence and leadership skills. As well as choreography talent. The knights knew exactly what arms up had meant but forgot to draw their swords at the same time, so it only took about two days, with breaks between, for them to make free style a combat art. Some fourteen dances were needed to achieve this.

At the end of the two days, Humphry (a close friend of Hammy) dropped to the floor and thought to himself *way too much freestyle*. If the styles were as varied in combat as they were in practice, then the knights will have chopped each other to pieces. Somehow the Hammy had to figure out how to allow each knight to do their own freestyle dances without one knight stabbing another through the breastplate. He needed to get the royal choreographer's help.

On the third day, the training continued.

"Two hands down!" Some people responded by staring, others putting both arms halfway down, some putting one down. This was not going very well. This problem continued to the end of the third day. If there was an infinite number of ways to do the very same move, everyone seemed to be taking one out of the bag and no two took the same as if they were purposefully trying to avoid similarity which is not the common method for synchronistic techniques.

Wolven wolves were not the worst things that are imaginable, the dancing knights were.

At the end of the arguidos session when everyone's limbs had become like wooden staves, and their ability to move diminished to a standard far lower than that of the most immobile broken robot, Humphry finally waved goodbye and went into the royal court. He walked in with a slight frown. He was not feeling all that delighted by the bandits of men that had attempted to attack them in training, only to laugh at the non-synonymy of the moves.

Hammy threw his sword onto his armchair in the castle and sat moodily on the bed. By moodily one might think he was down; he was not, he was so far down that the very word down was a step upwards. He was so moody he even ate all his lettuce without a complaint or noticing it.

Then he flicked open his chess set and won the game almost immediately. This is to say he threw the chess set away knocking the king off his position as soon as he had set up his pieces and tried to focus on the game. Hammy concluded that in life as well as chess, the best game winning tactic is this "not try to succeed" route.

Meanwhile, Casper, the prince of Ontock was flicking through Hammy's stylised routine magazine which he had pillaged from a Mados marketplace and was feeling weak at the knees.

If Casper was to overcome the knights of Prince Rupert, then he and his knights were goanna have to crack down on their free style hard. And how much he wanted to see prince Rupert dead, ever since Rupert had taken captive his pet dog as a punishment for one small attempt at aiding a Barbarian battalion which had nearly invaded the capital of Mados. Casper would have attacked Mados much sooner, but sadly there was the river, Thyme, between them.

This had posed a massive challenge for centuries since swimming through its lengths meant that by the time you reached the other side, assuming with all your armour and weaponry you did reach the other side, you would be too exhausted to fight one battle let alone take out an entire kingdom in a gruelling campaign.

Yes, there was a small strip of land by which the continents were connected, but this was like a bottle neck, so warfare there was strategically very difficult for the offensive army. Plus the bottleneck was bordering with the Catalonian dragon population, which didn't encourage optimism, dragons could be violent creatures and loved eating horse as a mid-afternoon snack. This kind of thing might make cavalier charges difficult.

Yet the Ontocians this time around had a secret weapon, a trojan horse you might say. And they named it a BFV, or buoyant floating vessel, the first of its kind to be seen within the cotenant. You and I might call it a boat. It was the beginning of the end of the watery division line, which had for so long kept the kingdoms at peace.

How great would it be to unleash this new technology upon the world, it would completely change the nature of warfare. So to test it out Casper over the next few weeks brought together a group of well-trained sailors and scuba divers, not wishing to be too picky about the exact profession for they all worked in the sea in some capacity. Marching to a mini BFV, in fact the first functioning BFV prototype he brought into reality, his motley crew headed to the sandy edges of the Thyme near to the point whence the river split into two dams.

A surf instructor came jogging along, with sea turtle images blowing in his trunks and sunscreen covering his dark skin in a way that made it look like he had white spots, whilst the last members of the voyage were getting onto the prototypes creaky deck. Maybe he was going for a tiger like look with his fierce eyes as he charged towards the crew? But anyway he waved a flag he must have got from the shop to try to draw their attention, but was too slow as the ship began sailing away and soon the man was a mere speck upon the distance from the viewpoint of the lucky sailors.

Now, Casper had a girlfriend who had simply refused to let him go all by himself, as she stayed at home baking cupcakes and making it ready for a massive welcome home party when he returned from the first ever raid that make use of aquatic transport vessels, such as this baby.

Casper's lady also didn't like the way he spent more time on his ship than in their bed, and would often talk about the ship in a very fond manner, even going so far to talk about it as a living being by giving it a gender pronoun, 'she' or sometimes 'my darling'. Anyway, they were on the deck having a nice bottle of rosé when a storm started brewing and the ship began struggling.

Many on board believed the bad weather was due to having a woman on board, which is a ridiculous sailor myth, but anyway most of them believed it given the female was as stormy as the weather above most of the time, so there had to be a connection. Therefore when Rupert and his lady were kissing and all, and lightning was flashing around them, and sailors were with buckets tipping water out of the deck so the vessel didn't go under, a sailor with blond curly hair hoisted the lady upon his shoulders, and threw her overboard.

Destiny was so surprised at this that he indeed asked the north wind to chill a little and the cloud spirits to clear up the sky, so he could see things better from his perch on his high tower over which he could see all events occurring in the realms. His perch was named Hlidskialf by the Norse men which once lived in the cotenant. And there he hung his head, as his good friend Jasper was snogging Casper just after committing murder, not that murder really registered in the eighteen-year-old's mind.

Casper at first was taken aback, but soon joined in with passion, holding Jasper's face tightly in case he broke away too soon. Casper liked experimenting you see, and his girlfriend was just getting too annoying to have on board. Also Casper liked the athletic build of the guy and his witty personality, and brilliant sense of humour and thought this eighteen-year-old murderer was just the right guy for him. So the raid soon turned into a romantic date out at sea, with a few random sailors enjoying playing with the dolphins and enjoying freshly caught salmon every day.

When they got back to the Ontockian shore (having completely forgotten all about Mados for the time being), they said their goodbyes; Jasper admitted to being a bit of a naughty guy when it came to romance, for he was already having a relationship with Triffon and was hoping to start one with Gruggor soon.

Casper just beamed thinking how skilled this dude was at getting the best out of polyamory whilst being in a series of supposedly monogamous relationships, it was super impressive. How Casper admired him. So they parted on good terms, and Jasper promised to spend the next summer with Casper and make up some good story to his other lover over why he had to be away for the summer break.

Chapter 17
Heroes of the Age

Relativistic four vectors, are the strangest construction known, a very real aspect to the universe and yet totally insane. Well, that is how four vectors work upon Minkowski space. It is like upon adding a step on a ladder, you find the ladder is a few steps shorter than before you added the step. It's insanity in scientific code.

The earth-shattering fact that time and space are in reality both the same thing, and interchangeable depending on reference frames, makes common sense vanish but replaces it for the gifted with 'the extra sense'. This madness is how fortune tellers read your fortune or at least how those with tariff cards, read them.

John Jovolty, a most adept seer, once commented unto the astrology club, "Corporal beings must try hard not to think too much about their temporal existence, else they would start measuring the length of the dining table in the ages of the earth, and distances upon maps by the gaps between the beats of the drum."

Josh Gorgostone, of the white tower, put it more rashly, "Upon considering temporality and its true nature in relation to geometry, the mind must accept a true study of time shall lead to but one ultimate destination, madness or eternal confusion." As you may gather, the white tower disliked fortune telling for they like the wolven folk were firm believers in the importance of living and not seeing what is to come.

This did not however stop a few hard-hearted professors within orthodox wizarding groups from diving into this study. They were called pholos professors, coming from the Latin phrase 'philos' which loosely translates as knowledge. Travellers of the left-hand path would rightly associate them with novitiates of lucifer. And perhaps the more indulgent, and light-hearted with that of the more traditional aspects of the bountiful horned god.

The other branches of magic were morphic, emotive studies and mortality studies. These were all valid studies of the mysterious forces beyond the scientific laws of nature. Emotivists had begun to develop a 'love' philosophy which was anything but satanic. Gruggor smacked tables to rubble and burned with anger when hearing about them, he would have left them with a missing limb, save for the odd fact that Gruggor never seemed to be able to get away with torturing these individuals and was beginning to fear the existence of the 'love-focused deity' himself.

One of these rebels against traditional belief was Professor Triffon. And her much more intelligent and socially adept adopting mother, Miss Roseton.

Triffon was adopted and never met her birth mother but grew up healthy and well under the watchful eye of Miss Roseton. However, unlike her adopting mother, she had little luck with men and insisted upon wandering around with apricot stands attached to her gigantic Caribbean hat.

She sat, looking dreamingly at a glass ball. Yes, it was a glass ball, just a glass ball and nothing more than a glass ball.

It went bright and started glowing when she lifted her eyes. Her hair shone, and she looked for a second, almost beautiful even behind all those bangles. She was covered in necklaces, so many it was a surprise she could breathe and her dress was a foot too small, so her bright green socks could be seen.

She had makeup, a lot of makeup, around her face and very white teeth. In truth she often cleaned them before, after and during dinner.

Her eyes were old. Her skin was very young, at least as far as the two fingertips of showing flesh could demonstrate. Her nails were black. Black hole-ish black.

Her voice was ethereal but slightly girlish and her hat was, well, very obviously laden with apricots.

"Ah, oh my day, my students shall soon arrive, and I have not had buttered toast." She flung her hand into the air as if being on the verge of fainting, she kicked off her very high heels as she felt she towered over the average fourteen-year-old enough that the extra height was unneeded.

Jasper forgot to buy butter you see, instead of the hated 'healthy' flora, a tasteless and almost inedible spread. Jasper, a wonderful dude, but forgetting the importance of many things, including butter, jam and good quality cooked yeast, sometimes got on Miss Triffon's bad side.

"Scon and scone," she muttered.

Those brought up in Devon, would likely have very qualified opinions on the correct phrasing, but for the sake of argument let us assume Triffon new the right pronunciation and if she was wrong, well she was not of this world, so it's hard to say that we can apply our vocabulary to hers.

She hopped, yes hopped to her desk. She took out her feathered pen and wrote in orange writing (literally, orange-flavoured ink with a few added orange zest scrapings) a very fruity letter to her lover, insisting he went to dairy school.

Before she could seal it with banana squelching, there was a large nock on the door. The class had arrived.

She lit a few dozen scented candles, and the smell of cinnamon filled the air.

She lit the fire in the large room, she squirted some rose into the air.

It smelt rather pleasant, albeit a boiling room, till black soot filled the air and her pet dragon made a few burps.

She made a vacuous spell near the door mat, to pull the newbies in before they felt so overwhelmed by her magnificent appearance, they decided to run and shout 'she's mad'.

Then she flung the door open and a band of teenage coughers were whisked off their feet and being sucked in, ventured forcefully into the mystic's room.

After whacking into desks and chairs on their flight forwards, they, with some effort, hobbled onto stools to sit on and as the mist cleared noted nearby tables with glass balls sitting on heavily embroidered stands.

They would have walked out, but the door was blocked by a fanged dragon.

"So, we are here…we are here. And so, we shall begin, for dreams are dreams and dreamers but dreamers, as they say in Dundee,", she beamed at them all.

They all stared blankly back. Apart from Donkark who nodded recognising her catchphrase and suggestion of a deep, deep secret, for Dundee was a deeply magical place for the mystics, and any sentence with a mention of it was full of foretelling power. Repetition was also something that marked out a true mystic, from the phony fraudulent people, for repetition made those that heard it more likely to act upon it, and so cause the very thing that they had been told would come to pass, to come to pass.

She pointed out of the window in the approximate direction of Dundee, and said, "They scowled back, but a few loved me."

She seemed to be getting her one attentive very confused, for he noted that if they were going to go on that trajectory, they would end up on the land of Barnsley, ruled by the barbican chieftain 'Mr Corporal' who would steal their drinks, snacks and clothes. They would then all be chased by his dogs, totally naked, till they either broke their ankles from jumping between the knotted roots of the aged trees or be struck in the head by the gigantic acorns that were originally designed as a defence against invasion, but now just stood there being an annoying hazard and resulting in a few broken skulls.

Technically, Triffon was only one degree off, but one degree off when talking about such large distances as Triffon was, results in dramatically different end points.

Swishing her hair and turning on the spot to bore into the bewildered eyes of Gallat, she said, "So apricots…apricots." She paused and no one said anything. Gallat went into a full-on slumber, the gentle tone of her drawling voice and the scent of the room was perfect for meditation, perfect for stimulating naps.

When Gallat's head hit the table and Donkark decided to take a nap beside his new friend, feeling that he could take a nap without being found upon, he went to sleep and began snoring. Soon all the class was asleep but Triffon went on as if talking about something remote, at the edges of human comprehension.

"We are here to see the eternal mysteries of the ever-flowing river of the special four components of the four forces, of four positions, of… As Drude said in the dreamer's parchment, the dreams are dreamers. And pumpkins are pumpkins. Dreamers see…like the seeing of the eagle…far off…off into the darkened night…off into the mountaintops…is the time we see, that we see, as we now look and as we stare, looking we shall see."

Gallat then woke up to the smell of burned cloves, a very potent smell, as Triffon's long speech continued steadily and stubbornly on. After a while he was struggling to keep his flickering eyes wide open and failing, but every time he was about to nod off, a new wave of burned garlic would hit him and he would reawaken.

She then brought her voice up two octaves and everyone was brought back to wide awakened states. Her pupils dilated and she seemed like she was on the edge of a precipice, about to plunge into the grey water below. Shouting forth, she said: "So we now command our eyes for as you see your ball! so the ball shall look to you and you shall guide it to the fields of the future, the lambs are waiting for our inner mind to perceive there oncoming footfalls. We shall slaughter them all! So we go thither!"

She said the last brief cry with such gusto, her eyes seemed to burn as she pointed right at the ceiling. It was a common symptom of her insanity, a result of the soul-sucking epidemic which seemed always to effect foreseers. The traditional sickness which drained the soul as with the guards, though it exaggerated its effect with those whom could see into the future, seemed to drain them of sanity, drawing perhaps upon the confusion the study of relativity does generate.

Her former love before Jasper, a guy named Geroldon, had helped diminish the rate of this maddening sickness, but when Gruggor rose to power, he had vanished mysteriously. Later she found Geroldon's head on the black market, when she had been looking for a pair of sexy-jinxed tights.

She then had collapsed on the floor and went into seizure as the shock had allowed the madness sickness to suddenly start to grow at an alarming rate and the pain this unexpected attack put on her soul almost killed her astral form. When she was taken to the wizarding medics, and returned back to the academy, she was never the same again. She had covered the ceiling with broken hearts in Geroldon's honour.

This was a mistake given that upon pointing at the ceiling, she then bent to her knees and started crying at the thought of her previous boyfriend, who the headmaster had long ago decapitated.

Crying as you may be gathering was common, but this was one of the first times Gallat had seen a grown woman cry. This is because in his isolated farmhouse, where he had grown up, crying was only a public thing when a woman was giving birth.

The farm boy had not known the crying cries of the womanly women of the city lands, or how much a decapitated boyfriend could plague a survivor's mind.

Yet she rose with her long blond hair sagging behind her neck, and her balance a little wobbly due to the prosecco she had gulped down to quell her sorrow.

She staggered towards Gallat's desk and flung both her hands into the air. In a screeching wail she said, "Oh may the flocks make even steps tonight, for the odd ones are cursed. Heed the warnings of the inner mind class, heed their warnings for dreamers are dreamers yet pumpkins are pumpkins." She flung around and smashed a few glass balls. She waddled back and forth, in a line, in the centre of the room. There, there was a very large glass ball awaiting her vision. She ignored it. It exploded in anger.

Instead of continuing to teach or check if the students now with glass gashes on their face and hands were okay, she smashed a few more glass balls and then after shoving a table against a student's desk, collapsed on a padded sofa. She yawned. The dragon roared in unison and let out a cough and farted, a very spicy fart filled with flammable gas. The gas diffused forth, hit the candlelight and fire broke out.

When all the screaming students had evacuated the tower, and the smoke in the classroom was blocking all air, clean air stopped becoming a free commodity. Coughing, Triffon crawled towards the door and instead of taking a breath of fresh air, she locked it. She flung her arms wide with her sagging dress weighing her down and her many bangles orientated at all conceivable angles. Her glasses were covered in water and dragon fire particles.

She pseudo-said and pseudo-coughed into the air, "No, I shall not prevail to the need of my young, I shall stay in this solace place; oh holy, holy god of the love-group wiggly wiggins, I shall stay in this place. You shall not tempt me with your offer of open air and freedom from suffocation."

Thankfully, a few faithful students returned to save her from her suicidal concept of resisting all 'temptation'.

When the word 'faithful' is used, its highly dependent upon what is meant by the word. Triffon seemed mad, and trapped in a fire hazard. Thus 'returning faithfully' would here mean, making sure their professor wasn't suffocating to death. Given I would do that for my least favourite professor, 'faithful' is perhaps not the right word. Maybe a few humane students would be a better grouping term.

Donkark and Gallat naturally fitted into this category, as well as a couple of young ladies named 'Amanda' and 'Pontziana'. These were Italian and so would have opened bottles of white wine and spoken about their quest to find the most perfect pasta sauce, after escape, till a Frenchmen of the name sir Gorge joined them and began a long discussion on the ideal bounce back feel of the beget.

Given Triffon had locked the door, which they found out after trying to kick it open a zillion times, the Italians and Frenchmen went in via a trap door and soon Gallat and Donkark came in through the drainage pipes. Sadly both escape routes were blocked when a banner from the ceiling broke the drainage pipe so it curved in on itself and flames engulfed the trap door and sent debris falling down the passageway. In alarm, and beginning to feel the heat burn the hairs of their skin, they wondered what they were going to do. Had they been anything but heroes for the professor they would have tried to save their own skin and left Triffon to her fate.

Donkark however walked straight to Triffon and punched her hard in the stomach. He was hoping that this move might force Triffon's lungs back in action and knock out any harmful smoke that she had breathed in.

This saved her life but also gave her indigestion. It's an interesting property of memories, they remember everything but not necessarily equally, so that indigestion forever became a barrier whereas Triffon very soon forgot the 'saving life' aspect of interrupting the stomach's hard work.

This ought to be modified a bit, for Triffon, unlike you (I hope) was being saved by fate, people or magical skill from death on a day-to-day basis. Triffon was therefore not overwhelmed by Donkark's generosity. It wasn't exactly an unusual gesture of kindness for a student to save her life.

Pontziana, seeing Triffon's annoyance, punched the coughing Donkark in the stomach for causing the professors first moments of free breathing to be shadowed by a scowl. Donkark was saved from suffocation from the smoke, but was irritated at his punch friendly buddies. So he punched the young ladies in turn, not being able to work out who had hit him.

The now saved from suffocation team noticed Gallat was crawling towards the window, in a desperate attempt to open it and get some air. But they knew what to do. They knew how to react to highly breath heavy environments, so they gave him one massive punch in the stomach to save his life. It worked (and hurt a lot to).

This is how Gallat's first introduction to magical fortune telling ended in a more or less benevolent punching match.

His vision went blurry for a second, but as no one could see perfectly in the blackened room, this made him only a little worse sighted than his fellow students of magic.

"Shall we make the smoke vanish?" coughed Triffon.

They stared at her, like she was a perplexing individual who had just revealed something they wish she had said before they all punched the newbie in the stomach.

The newbie for his matter just was thankful the punching had come to a close.

She waved her wand and nothing. Absolutely nothing happened, it was like they were stuck where nothing ever happened or changed, apart from dying of course.

They would have evacuated the door, apart from the fact that to exit the chamber required a spell which Triffon alone new and was unable to say with any clarity.

"Gagga-goo-gaga," she sputtered as she tried to take a few gulps of water to sore her dry throat.

"Gagga-googigow-gaggagaragar" was something like the combined imitation of the students as they attempted to repeat her magical phrases loudly.

Finally, they gave up trying to interpret Triffon's gargling and made a run for the windows.

Triffon however flung herself ahead of the glass, clearly thinking the need for clean fresh air to be a weakness, not a necessity for human life.

She would have protested if anyone thought they had the right to leave the academy, or let anything in from the outside world, seeing it as a failing of being an all-sufficient leader of the magical community. No one else held this view, but Gruggor for one was not going to dissuade her.

Gruggor was so fond of the idea of no one, for any reason, ever, ever leaving the premises, that he had appointed her a new position, called 'mistress of the academy', for a while, till the many times students that fled from her 'never leave' sermons, gave him the impression she was not right for the job.

Pontziana screamed, "Why don't we throw her out the window! Else we are all going to die."

Donkark turned to her like he couldn't believe she could say such a thing. Thus a second bout of punching matches broke out.

Gallat would have been safe, apart from the fact that he tried to shove the window open and instead just received a punch in the face from Donkark for taking so long to do anything.

Triffon then kicked Gallat in the stomach for daring to try to let in some outside oxygen, and he wheezed on the ground for a minute.

They were all very panicky.

Finally, Donkark realised that he was, after all, a very advanced student. So, he raised his wand and did the magic Triffon could not. The air became clear and he begged Triffon's apologies for 'outsmarting the teacher'.

Begging to be forgiven by reiterating one's crime, either goes very well and results in huge sympathy or goes awfully and results in cursing and some hitting home of one's wrongdoing.

Triffon was a good lady though, and forgiving thankfully but still had not forgiven being punched so used her futurometry arts and the undamaged crystal ball to show to the full-of himself rocky dude, that a mysterious figure would one day come into his heart who would teach him that there was far more to magic than waving one's hand, doing a few spells, and such insignificant things as saving everyone from suffocation and certain death.

You might have realised the French dude is mentioned little here. This is because upon seeing the extent of the devastation, and being unable to wrench open the door, he had decided it safer to turn into a baguette. Baguettes do not need to breathe you see.

However, baguettes are, well baguettes, and as incapable of turning themselves back into wizards as my carrot is at speaking to me.

Thus, the Frenchmen has forever remained a well-cared for member of the bakery section.

Sadly, he is getting increasingly stale and fragile, and the phrase 'looks like he could fall to pieces any second' describes him perfectly.

No one has ever managed to get him back to him, as no one save himself knew exactly who he was. Only he knew the real him, so at best his best buddy could say bring 99% of him back but that would be like bringing back half your best friend, a truly unnatural thing to do and emotionally difficult to live with.

We have left our ventures alone, and so must divert our discussion of inanimate-animate transformations to later chapters or books in long forgotten stacks of the documents of Mados Mordrė.

Anyway, Donkark managed to curse the door open (now he was not suffocating magic seemed a lot easier) and changed his attire the moment he got out of that door. What self-respecting wizard would walk around with flecks of black everywhere and clothes reeking of a burning smell?

His new outfit was a bright red T-shirt, and woollen mittens. He had a pair of genes and looked very much like the kind of guy you see modelling, apart from the fact he didn't pose, he stood still and flung his hands wide open as if to say 'I'm amazing'. (Gallat kind of agreed, not that he would ever say this out loud.)

The girls sighed and Gallat suddenly found the stress of his first day in magical fortune telling training a very distant thought of little significance.

Here we see some of the many challenges facing human behaviour biologists. As well as defending exactly what a 'model' in our current modern age looks like, they also have to correctly interpret the many possible meanings of 'flinging one's arms wide', which as we have seen recently can mean a thousand things.

To block an incoming bunch of outsider oxygen molecules, to give a warm hug and showing off in an egocentric manner are all many reasons to open one's arms as if preparing for flight. Dragons however often misunderstand this and assume humans regularly attempt to prepare for flight but have wilted too soon so their feathers are no longer with them.

We have of course mentioned dragons, a bit. However here it seems that a dragon chapter is needed to balance out the professors, aristocracy and other humanity focussed groups. Hopefully fellow writers will note this and expand the amount of non-human fiction, which is a somewhat lacking genre given the many, many species of highly real and mythical animals to select from.

And given the fact that dragons are cool, and intelligent, and just awesome.

Chapter 18
The Exodus of Mados Mordrė

As destiny would have it, overhead soared a desert dragon from the Sahara lands, where the legendary Stepny of the deep Buddhist order had once meditated.

In honour of her, many centuries ago, there had been significant migration of the northern mountain dragons to this blisteringly hot region. There they breed with the local desert dragons, and formed cross breeds which sadly were still referred to as classical desert Dragons, even though the technically accurate name was rather different, yet unlike Tolkien I do not wish to bombard you with a massive avalanche of law, so I'll leave the crossbred details a little out for this story.

Thankfully, their own Hhai Sharir had prevented the new folk's scales from falling off which could easily happen when the filament under the scales connecting the hard shell-like smooth surface, to the flesh, curled in on itself. There it would harden and lose all its stickiness. This always happened when they stay exposed to magical fire for too long as had sadly been proven in times previously where wizards used to burn dragon's alive for daring to attack their precious establishments.

Even the usually benign white tower had been known to do this for they saw crossbred dragons as being associated with evil, and focussed too heavily upon their mythical background and not upon the morality of the dragon's actions themselves, as if it was a crime to simply exist as a cross bread. White towers were puritans.

The mountain-cum-desert dragons evolved very quickly, for such was their magic, to the climate and soon grew small pores between clusters of scales to let the air through so they didn't overheat or feel faint. The dragons also developed very keen night and infrared vision which could prove extremely useful when hunting at night for there wasn't really much wood to make torches or wax to make candles out in the wilderness.

However, they did lose a lot of their strength and replaced it with stealth. Their claws also diminished in size and the spike at the end of their tail become non-existent. Also they had learned to swim in deep water, for the edge of the desert laid very close to the oceans were salty water sprayed forever upon the sand at the border of the known world. These genes they passed onto their offspring as well as the traditional desert dragon genetics.

Exactly why a dragon had travelled so far north, to the academy, was something of a mystery unless the pooping had got really bad or the seagulls upon their heads, had got dire, and it was desperate to escape the falling sludge, plus why was there one dragon? Dragons despite their size usually travelled abroad in large number to show strength in number and to further the awesomeness of their passing, in case any wizards thought them easy prey.

Jasper ran onto the top of the tower and called over the winds, "My dear dragon, I'm Jasper and am honoured to meet you, would you like to come down from the sky and have a chat. I have good communications with the wizards of the kingdom, and can assure you safety upon my hand."

He then held his hand to his heart to make clear he meant the oath very literally, a part of the gesture-based language that dragons and humans have long enjoyed between each other.

The dragon knew Jasper, in that this wanderer was pretty much known to all dragons as the only guy which didn't inherently mistrust them. So he gently came down, dropped a piece of brown parchment and then rapidly flew away again into the midst of the atmosphere, and under cloud cover, to get back safely home.

The parchment had the golden seal of the lamb upon it, for as much as Jasper hid it, he was still willing to commune with God, despite having clear leanings elsewhere. He read the document and it said without any description, "Get Triffon, Gallat and Sir Courtney out of there immediately!"

Now, immediately has lots of different meanings depending upon whom you ask. To some it means that very instant, to others just long enough away to have a quick brush of one's teeth and put on shoes, and to others, well, it means whenever you feel like it so long as it's in the near future. Plus Jasper wanted to survive, so wasn't going to openly kidnap three wizards (sir Courtney being a professor within the academy), particularly when Gallat was of enormous interest to Gruggor and he would most certainly notice this one's absence.

Mind you, Gruggor would probably notice Triffon's absence to due to the lack of bangles and apricots lying around the tower tops of the academy. Though Sir Courtney could probably be kidnapped and no one would notice. This may sound harsh, but it is not my job as a journalist to be humane, in fact it is my job to be brutally honest and direct with you. Then again Courtney was more the research guy and at Mados Mordrė, this was not considered very practical or important. His skills would probably be better put to the black tower, but anyway, we are diverting here.

So burning the letter in the lit chandelier as he was passing down the windy steps to reach the bottom which was so long down, a man could die falling that distance even if released from rest at the top and just dropped like a ball, and this wasn't just theory, this had actually been proven many a time. Gruggor once wrote a whole academic paper on 'the wonders of dying by speedy descent'.

Yet when Jasper reached the bottom, he set to work with surprising agility for he felt the power of God aiding every movement.

He raced along the corridors, crossed the ice bridge and banged loudly unto Gruggor's door.

"Yes, come in," said Gruggor as if he was expecting another one of those annoying journalists who liked firing really intrusive questions at him about his wealth, his academy and his past dead dogs.

"Well, Arch-demon, I have been thinking of how to deal with that ridiculous royal family of Bartibus, and how to seize control of the kingdom." He picked up an orange to demonstrate this and crushed it, unfortunately he squirted some of the citric acid juices into his eye and had to rub the tears that fell from his face upon his recently dry-cleaned sky-blue shirt.

His eyes now red and soar, he still tried to pull a smile. The result was semi-successful, though he was clearly still experiencing retina stinging, which is not the most pleasurable of sensations known unto man.

Gruggor looked on with remote distaste for this foolery and said, "Why are you troubling me with this, I already have the keys to the kingdom in my hand. My secret spies have infiltrated the royal court as scribes and advisors, and have rebutted the attempts of the Dylan to convince the king of anything but their council. He is known to be in the process of drawing up a treaty to present to the representatives of a Barbarian clan from the wild south and the wolves from the forest kingdom, with the intent of finding a suitable way they can invade Mados. So then, the king may say unto all that doubted that his kingdom was desirable, that Mados is so bountiful that both barbarians and wolves wish to invade and plunder it."

Jasper was taken a little back in shock at the flattering sneakiness of this Arch-demon. But quickly Jasper regained his footing on his mission, and said unto Gruggor, "This is a marvellous idea but the process will be slow, and even with the royal family abolished you'll still have to deal with the invaders before you yourself can take over the kingdom and claim it as your own, as part of your quest for the global domination of the orthodox wizarding church. We could however take a more subtle manoeuvre.

"Keep the advisors suggesting invasion if you will, but we can use the populaces lack of confidence in their king to our advantage. For if we send in someone to say, take a more governing role, then the people will turn to them gladly in these troubling times. They will steer the way for the future. And someone with sufficient power, such as a wizarding professor might well gain more reverence than the king, for Sharir is a powerful political weapon when its leverage is used correctly."

"I like your idea," said Gruggor. He then thought hard of what professor he could spare, given that having most of them present was helpful as the less life force around, the less Sharir would be available within the Academy, for Sharir goes were life force ventures. So he said to Jasper, exactly what Jasper wanted to hear, "I shall personally convince Triffon to come to Mados, and her appearance shall be so majestic that many will think she's a god, thanks to my wonderful designs. And it would then be my pleasure to open her advocated position up to some new candidates and have go at interrogating them, I dare say if it's as anything as amazing as the one where Westog's competitor was sent down to the gallows, I shall be mightily impressed."

Gruggor, not wishing to end with references to melancholy memories, then said something even more extreme, partly because it was true, partly because he wanted to inspire some fear in this individual and disliked the way the usual talk of death didn't seem to impact Jasper in anyway. It was as if death to him was an inconsequential event.

So with as much terror as he could conjure in his voice, Gruggor said, "And I shall kill Sir Courtney too, for I think he might well be onto us, and quite frankly I can't deal with him. My spies seem to indicate he's actually been in league with the desert dragons, would you believe it, and has been praying unto God to send one of them to carry him away, as if dragons ever liked acting as steeds for mere Sapiens."

Jasper just shrugged and shook his head, feeling not frightened in the slightest, but intellectually aware that not everything was going exactly to plan. God had very clearly asked for all three wizards to be saved. And he would have spoken about Gallat, and asked if he could leave the grounds but standing face to face with Gruggor he knew the answer would be no. Besides, in this current eerier, saving one out of three lives was staggeringly impressive statistics.

So Jasper went away feeling very proud of himself. And Courtney, well Courtney by that time had already fled the academy and was out on the run. He knew Gallat was Christ and the Septicon had to be protected by the Northern Dragons at all costs, and he suspected an even more terrifying third fact which shook his bones to the core.

But as for the sight of a dragon, well that had scared enough wizards that it acted as the last little push they needed to run away, for they were greatly afraid of being burned alive. So Mados Mordrė had quite the exodus that day.

Chapter 19
Excavated by Dragons

In the cold northern mountains lived two dragons to battle the most evil forces in creation. Now who were these fearsome creatures, they were but immature dragons. They knew though as yet little to nothing of the grand cosmological war, or evil wizards in black or white towers, but they did know the meaning and immeasurable value of friendship.

"My tail's on fire," shouted Amanda as her tail swiped side to side trying to flap the flames away. She looked at stone-cold Rupert. This was the dragon Rupert, not the prince Rupert, though they were both very fierce in battle. She was clearly telling this Rupert, "This is not at all amusing and if you do this ever again, I shall burn your ears off." Rupert was cool with this, he liked being threatened to have his ears nearly being burned, it was the kind of threat that illustrated a close partnership between the two.

Rupert responded to this kindly by grabbing a massive bucket of icy water and throwing its contents over Amanda. She now looked fuming. Her long web-like wings were extended as far as they could, a clear signal of "watch it, big boy."

Rupert was undeterred, knowing that Amanda was more putting on a show than actually that put off, he just went back to chasing the bird around the garden. Like a cat. Dragons are in fact very cat like when not burning down villages.

Amanda smiled a little. It was not within dragon culture to smile but she loved reading human magazines so had learned to imitate their facial expressions with her very different facial muscles. Her amber eyes lighting up. She couldn't help it, it was pretty sweet seeing Rupert swerve and try to grab the little creature.

Finally, the bird dropped exhausted to the ground. Snow dropped from its wings as it tried to ruffle its feathers, in a feeble attempt to get back up.

Amanda however picked it up, being careful to keep it from the edges of her sharp claws, and she carried it to the water bowl. She was the world's biggest naturalist.

It chirped thankfully, fluttered a few times. Then it promptly hopped onto the edge and took a few sips. Ruffling its feathers, it had a quick hop around.

It then gave another couple of chirps of thanks. Released its feathery wings from its side. Finally, it had a quick bath before soaring into the air.

Rupert watched it fly away, with his eagle like eyes, faintly shining purple with a black slit where humans may have had the pupil. He let out a sigh when it had flown beyond sight and looked across to Amanda questioningly, as if saying "what we gonna do now?"

They had known each other for years so she understood perfectly that look, she was the one to come up with the plans, being the clever one, after all. Rupert was more into sports and jumping around. Amanda liked playing board games. Well the usual kinda light-hearted set piece games anyway, were mischief or a bit of more adventurous ideas were concerned, well, that was Rupert's kind of thing.

Rolling her eyes at Rupert, she told him clearly, "Well, since it's my turn again to make some plans." She tried to say this like an exasperated squashed orange. She actually sounded pretty enthusiastic. Rupert gave a swish of a tail knowing they were going to have a brilliant time together whatever she came up with, and she usually came up with the best plans ever.

He had a bit of a grin on his face, that told her, he knew perfectly well she was enjoying thinking through the thousands of activities on option.

Rupert waited patiently, his ears occasionally flicking from side to side in anticipation for the new chapter of a few fun filled hours to begin.

"Well..." said Amanda hesitantly.

Rupert looked at her slightly eager, now starting to wag his tail and perking up his pointed ears. "Yeah," he said, trying to read her face for clues.

With a face that masked Amanda's great happiness, which to Rupert was a transparent layer never hindering the sight of Amanda's clear bubbling enthusiasm, she said "Well we could take a good explore in that nearby mountain." She lifted her left front paw and pointed the reflective curved claws towards the mountain. With a very well-practiced professional tone, and after a few seconds of very serious observational analysis, she said, "If the slope is about say, 4rad from the northern star, we could take about, um, give me a sec, ah, two hours to get to the peak. That's if we swoop directly over there and start at the bottom anyway.

"I mean, I'm reasonably confident we could get the full round about journey done before teatime. I could have misjudged temperature gradient or the number of updrafts from the wind curl, but I'm in the right ballpark providing my trigonometric skills are anything as good as I hope they are."

Don't worry if you don't understand most of this, it's just dragon mumbo jumbo.

When they landed upon the white precipitates, an avalanche covered the higher landscape. The snow went five feet down when they pressed their massive dragon paws into it. The weight and force of landing turned the compressed ice into water, and it ran straight down the mountainside, giving a few struggling snow plants hydration.

Rupert looked around. "Snow, snow and yeah, more snow. That pretty much sums up where we are."

Amanda sniffed the snow very carefully and grazed through it with her claw.

Rupert looked…concerned.

"Amanda, why are you sniffing snow? And you know, we really should be getting back, we've both been gone long enough for one of our tutors to come running, the flight took longer than we both had anticipated."

Amanda didn't respond. Then she took a deep breath and said, "I think someone's been buried here. I can smell the odour."

Given the mountain was at least four times as tall as Everest, and was totally impossible for humans to climb or scale (due to the lack of oxygen available at those altitudes), a man being packed under at this altitude either meant he had befriended the dragons in life or used magic to get himself all the way there. Humans and dragons barely ever got on, and as for using magic, who would want their last resting place to be a deserted high up mountain with no grave to signify their passing?

But sure enough, a face, then a stomach then a pair of legs and arms became apparent. Soon Amanda had cleared off the last layer of snow off the man, and it quickly could be deduced that the guy was neither a dragon-buddy nor a common magician. He seemed to be dressed in woollen clothing and carrying a crooked wooden stick like a shepherded, save he had a thin layer of wolf drawl running along his cheek. Clearly this was a last goodbye from a faithful hound.

Amanda hugged the corpse.

This may seem odd at first glance, but she was in fact simply being a splendidly caring dragon.

In her heart she wanted to give the man a good hug, given it was the last hug he was probably going to receive. He was there, away from civilization and had ended up being in that long permanent sleep, till the end of time in this the almost eternally isolated, resting place.

She laid the man down and started to cry. A soft humming came out of her, as she hummed a song to give the desist a safe passage into the afterlife.

Yet as a wave of tears fell upon the ice-cold human, something incredible happened.

He woke up.

However as soon as he had been unfreezed by the warmth of the dragon and the dragon's warm watery tears, pneumonia went in for a rematch. The altitude was too high and the wind whipped like an invisible showering of ice. It howled like a wolf, though the chattering breaking out from the human as his teeth ground together made it sound as if he was a squirrel eating a nut.

Given these extreme heights, it is not a surprise that pneumonia tends to go for it very quickly, so the unawares have little time to deflect its killer blow. It acts like an assassinator carrying a sharp dagger, all too quick to attack but all too hard to deflect.

Rupert had no idea what was going on as the human's hands started shaking and his teeth jittering, but Amanda, knowing something about the limited adaptive temperature properties of human beings, immediately wrapped him up in her wings and gave him a hug.

He stayed protected by her warmth. However, his stomach, now eager to be heard, took the hug as its cue to start telling the brain it needed sustenance. It rumbled and the man tried hard to think of anything but lamb stew, and in fact only thought of a hundred things to have with lamb stew which made him even more ready for a full meal.

He finally realised he could not do anything about this, and so started singing a song about lamb. Amanda liked it so much that she joined in. So it was that 'Lamb and gravy' was the first human song ever to be sung to a dragon.

Amanda was unique in that she didn't associate this man's flesh with the lamb and blood with the gravy but unlike her kindred, saw humanity as a precious people.

Amanda in this light-hearted spirit of friendship, therefore, sang along with 'Lamb gravy'. The first dragon-human duet was born, and many have followed since, but none so high above the clouds.

To humanity, it may seem obscured by anthropocentric tendencies, but all life does not consider human life important or even sacred. However, a dragon thinking humans' matter, is like me celebrating the birthday of a local ant. Not celebrating such an event does not mean I'm necessarily a bad person, but if I considered all life very important, and put it all on an equal pedestal, the amount of mourning would be too painful to show such broad love to all living things.

The birds below heard the odd combination of tones and musical melodies and thought it revolutionary.

Since then, some birds have attempted to sing along to the calling songs of humans. Bats have gone a step further and decided to beat our best altos by going into the ultrasound range. But much of the acoustic talents of flying creatures would not be present at the current time, if it was not for that first inspirational dragon-human duo.

Amanda was a natural-born soprano. Her mother, Pammanda, sang in the 'jewellers choir' and she had gotten Amanda involved in as many choirs as she could. Amanda could also play the trombone but she rarely used it because dragon-sized trombones produced a loud bass sound which drowned out almost all the violin section even if that violin section was being played halfway across the content.

Rupert meanwhile preferred card games for a bit of a relax. He knew them all and was incredible at cheating in half of them.

He also regularly used sleight of hand to impress the girls with his magical talents. Here we use magical in the way a secular non-magical member of a bank might, that is to say pure illusion and trickery. Yet magicians are meant to be the most honest people in the world since they tell you they are going to fool you right before they do it. Rupert however was anything but honest.

Still he was a good kid, well behaved when he wanted to be and great at navigating the catacombs of his home and jumping unawares at much older dragons passing by. He meant well and was liked a lot by pretty much everyone.

Apart from Sally, who always envied the colour of his nostrils.

The human was eventually taken back to the dragon's home. He entered into a massive cave like interior, fit with the most modern utilities of the age, wooden torches and firelight.

The torches went a little black around the outside but most of the base was a bright shiny brown, the kind of shiny brown that only exists in a magical dragon kingdom.

The floor was very dry and full of rubidium crystals which explains the rarity of human visitation, for as any radiologists should know, rubidium is radioactive.

The man, now almost back to a survival temperature, did not know this, but enjoyed the weird glow like there were a thousand luminescent worms under the rock's clean surfaces.

A smell of boiled parsnip came through the open tunnels and the sound of dragons discussing herbs began to break the silence.

The fumes of oregano seemed to be a heavy favourite of the dragon kingdom.

Rupert looked towards his father, Sir Wensledale, and said, "Hey, old man. We have a two-legged visitor who recently has been unpacked out of a gigantic refrigerator. But I taught Amanda how to catch a couple of birds and she was a very fast—"

"Yes. Yes son. Now going back to the first point, the most important point, the man who's been refrigerated. Who and exactly what is he?"

Many of Rupert's peers seemed dumbfounded at the question, they never had heard of a refrigerated man before. Still they could sense that father and son where not on the same page about bringing back a human to their home. . They looked between Rupert and Sir Wensledale as if they were watching an invisible game of table tennis played by the father and son's minds.

Then a thin and croaky voice, one Madam Parsley, said, "This young man has brought forth a…a human."

Silence then reverberated around the cave, with such intensity, it almost became sound.

The Wensledale roared and fire belched from his nostrils and destroyed the scene of the dragon feast above him. Tatters of it fell flaming to the ground.

Dragons, as a rule, did not like humans.

Particularly not human men.

Chapter 20
The Biggest Homo Sapienists in the Galaxy

Dragons infected hatred of men from generation unto generation. The wide variety of extinction and other unforgiving crimes within draconic law, homo sapiens had committed, is truly off the chart.

Dozens of leaders and senior dragons gathered around this survivor of the avalanche, for they had rather rudely been woken by a dropping bomb of snow, from a neighbouring mountain, and wanted to watch the man get eaten., plus they were all imagining human jam covered on sugary bread.

The oldest of the elders felt the man's aura and instinctive protective feelings flared up within them, and they were almost salivating at the thought of the man's destruction. Few of them knew exactly why but millennia of dealing with the orthodox wizards of the northern realms, meant they grew an inbuilt hatred of the wizarding aura all powerful practitioners of Sharir radiate.

The man stood so still, one might think he was still buried in ice, even though he felt like wobbly jelly inside. His face was also deathly white and he made a great deal of effort not to look like a piece of living meat which had foolishly been captured and then carried to a cave full of gigantic predators with the power to breathe fire and crush him like an ant, but this is exactly how he felt.

Amanda being very compassionate gave him a little nudge on the shoulder and put her head at his feet. This was a clear sign of welcome and the best way the dragons had of communicating 'be not afraid' without doing childish things like playing with wool or rolling around on the floor. The last couple of methods proved very effective but felt very degrading to the dragons involved. The dragons had previously also tried hugging humans, but few humans felt comfortable with being raised twenty feet into the air then nearly crushed before being put neatly back on the ground like a doll, plus the humans involved found this very damaging to their macho image. Those who went to the gym and did lots of push offs to prove just how manly they were often ended up having nervous breakdowns.

Thankfully, the prisoner seemed to know something about dragon practice and sat next to the dragon's head, crossing his legs in an act of serenity and peace.

Then Sir Wensledale began to act as chairman over this meeting. "So, my dear dragons, my son and his female friend has seen fit to bring this…man…before our presence."

Madam Parsley commented, "A man. No man is ever welcome here, the knights are nothing but dragon killers and St George is nothing but a murderer."

Every dragon roared in agreement. The man's hair stood up in fright.

"Thank you, thank you, Madam Parsley. We all know the history of St George. However, as my son has seen fit to bring this human here, I doubt he means us any harm, I hope so anyway, else Rupert shall not be attending the party next week."

"But father" complained Rupert.

"No debate son, if this man is like any other men, then you shall miss the party and all the dancing and cake and shall not be allowed to go to any other party for the next month."

"But daddy…"

"Not now, son!"

"But…"

"No! That is final. Now to discuss the fate of our prisoner…um…I mean our guest."

"To the animal pit!" shouted Madam Parsley. All the other dragons roared once more in unison. The man was begging to desperately think of how to escape without being noticed, it was such a shame his gear and invisibility fleece had been left on the mountain side.

Amanda lifted up her head and roared. Everyone went silent.

"I found this poor young man frozen in the ice and you want to throw him in with our hungry cattle, what are you thinking?"

"We are thinking…" began Sir Wensledale with forced calm, "that if we don't kill this would-be knight—"

"I am no knight, but an outcast forced to survive on the outskirts like you and your people!" shouted the man.

There was a brief moment of silence.

"Anyway," Sir Wensledale continued, "we must deal with this outcast would-be knight."

"I am not a knight nor ever have been nor ever shall be! I'm a wizard for heaven's sake. You know." He raised his hands in the air and swirled them mimicking the typically techniques of spell casting. Every dragon took a few steps back in horror, every dragon apart from Amanda who nudged the human on the shoulder as if to say 'please continue'.

The human took a few deep breaths and then said, "Please, you must listen to me. I've been travelling for weeks till a large avalanche drowned me in snow not that long ago, a tumble of ice and snow doubtlessly caused by that traitor Sir Gruggor. He has not only risen to the highest position of authority among the wizarding counsel but has our only hope of ever over throwing the tyrant right in his lap, in the very grounds of Mados to be more exact. We must rescue our one hope else the poor boy will meet a fate worse than his parents, or he will be twisted to Gruggor's evil schemes and become an unstoppable demonic force."

The elder dragons looked around at each other experiencing for the first time in hundreds of years the feeling of dread pass through them.

"Gruggor you say?" asked Wensledale feeling a shiver of pure hatred course through his body at the sound of the name.

"Gruggor?" asked Madam Parsley. She scratched her chin with scholarly thought, analysing the name like it was a distant and slightly distasteful part of some exotic peace of dragon history. "Gruggor has taken under his wing the blasphemous child, the child that shall be the standard and spearhead of the great revolution?"

"Most regrettably," nodded the human solemnly, "either that or he has just taken under his tutelage the child that shall bring eternal darkness upon us all."

Or die, thought Amanda with a tear running down her cheek, she did not know this boy but the idea of anyone dying under the hands of Gruggor was enough to make her want to fly away and weep. Still she pulled herself together and tried to look hopeful and full of determined resilience for the sake of this small human.

Madam Parsley made a complete U-turn and her eyes lit up with rage. "Are we, the mightiest of winged predators, to be tricked by this weak wizard and driven out of hiding by such fibs. Really, what chance is there that the boy is indeed who this wizard claims him to be, in fact, what evidence is there that this boy exists at all and this man here is nothing but a spy sent by the traitor to convince us to show ourselves and leave the protection of our hidey holes."

"I'm not lying," pleaded the man, "you must…"

The avalanche man looked around pleadingly and Amanda felt like she wanted to defend him but how did she know he was on their side? She thought him a friend but how could she be totally sure? She had only just met the guy.

"We must, is not something that you have the right to say, human," said Sir Wensledale sternly.

Amanda pleaded, "But what if he's telling the truth?"

Sir Wensledale looked down at her sympathetically as if talking to a young child who needed the direction and guidance of her elders to survive in this treacherous world. This made her feel very much like she was being treated like a kid, which in all fairness she was. "My dear Amanda, if he is telling the truth then I and I alone shall bear the blame being the leader of this gathering. However, the chance of this child actually being the one this wizard speaks of is like the chance of finding a banana tree in the middle of the desert, or a bowl being randomly reassembled by a passing hurricane."

"Or a man surviving an avalanche," muttered the wizard. However, the dragon went on as if nothing was said.

"We cannot know if this main is truthful, a spy or simply mistaken but one thing is for certain, Gruggor has many spies and has tried many times to force us out from hiding. We also know that even the most adept wizards can mistake a member of the living for being the bearer of a destiny mentioned in prophecies when in the end their lives end up indicating that this is not so. Plus, not all prophecies are known to be true anyway for the future has many mysteries and confounds even the most talented of the crystal gazers."

"Then what shall we do with the man?" asked Amanda, looking over at Madam Parsley's angry facial expression.

"I say eat him," suggested Madam Parsley though this time not every other elder dragon roared in unison and quite a lot looked confused, even a little fearful. The wizard cried out in fear and then, exhausted and dehydrated and famished as he was, felt very dizzy and let out a beautiful sigh before he collapsed on the floor.

Sir Wensledale looked down in displeasure; it was rude to take a nap in the middle of a meeting. 'We shall keep our prisoner…um, I mean guest…as a hostage of war and send our greatest warrior, Sir Thunderbolt, to the castle of

King Bartibus to make a deal. The deal shall be this; we will offer up our prisoner of war to him so the king may use his knowledge and magical skills be they given freely or by use of torture, to fight off the raids from the city of Mados Mordrè and Gruggor's minions. Yet we shall do this on one condition.

"This condition is that he sends a scout party to ambush Triffon from her high tower and bring her to us to confirm or deny the allegations of the man before us. She is weak, has little to no magic and probably thinks the ambush is just a highly excited bunch of tourists bringing her along on holiday. If the condition isn't met, then we shall kill our magical prisoner and Mados will lose the only lead it will ever likely get in how to defend itself from the powers of Mados."

Every dragon apart from Amanda cheered in unison including Rupert who felt like he was going to be allowed to go to that party after all, he felt very manly doing his roar, but he closed his mouth suddenly when he caught Amanda glaring at him. For all dragons due to visits of the wolven folk, who they bonded with long ago due to their love of bonfire, had often told them of the weakness in the grand plan of Gruggor, Triffon, who shall be a seer revealing all the truth and perhaps even telling them how to snuff out the ridiculous conjuring folk.

Rupert tried hard to look displeased at the fate of the prisoner of war, this sort of worked and Amanda gave him a quick nose to nose sniff showing that she was at least impressed by Rupert's musky scent before flying off deeper into the cave complex with the prisoner on her back and Rupert's dad gliding right in front of her.

Chapter 21
Destiny Ruins the Day

The next day, Rupert arose from his dragon-sized bed and went to the pool to bathe. He made sure his wings were nice and glistening and the diamonds upon his scales were clean and pretty. For today was a day to impress and Rupert definitely looked the part. Although Rupert was by no means a model, he knew how to go all out to impress a female dragon and made sure he was covered in that musk Amanda had seemed to find pleasant a day ago. Yet again this could just be because he smelled so much better than humans, particularly that individual they had rescued but he hoped this was not the case, he had spent like two gold coins on the musk after all.

Rupert was rather fond of Amanda and he knew that she was just mad about perfecting the perfect flambé. He would often spot her practising again and again in the kitchen as he sneaked down there in the middle of the night to grab some tasty food. The secret to this, Rupert thought, was to tip the alcohol in just before the spirit of blazing hot fire issued from the dragon's mouth. You see thanks to dragon physiology the need for stoves and gas-lit flames was minimal and only the stubborn traditionalists insisted on buying these out-physio-ed kits.

Amanda had a different secret however; you see to really get the perfect flambé it is necessary to pour the alcohol directly into the path of the blazing hot fire. Yet this must be timed perfectly as if the alcohol is poured too late in the process, then the pan will burn or combust and if it's added in too early then the alcohol has a slightly burned flavour from being exposed to the heat for too long.

The culinary experts among you might find the idea of breathing over food to ignite the cooking process as very unhygienic however this couldn't be further from the truth, since only the one specific bacterium had the audacity to outstrip death in the dragon's heat with all other microbes becoming lifeless ashes very quickly. This bacterium was called the taxotornophead.

The taxotornophead survived not just thanks to its ice cold exterior but also survived due to the magical shield around it. It was developed by the statistical council of wizards after they realised that claiming to kill all bacteria by fire-breath would lead to a never-ending investigation for impossible claims. Thus, they picked out the name of the soon to be magically protected survivor from the hat. This was considered a very diplomatic way to do it and it avoided the dragon-speciests from showing their hidden agenda by condemning the lords of the air to injure a newly magically defenced resurgence of the Bombom microbe which had nearly devastated the dragon population previously.

Anyway, it was coming to the first day of the flambé challenge and Rupert was looming his bright green eyes over the pre-flambé assortment which rested on the table next to his new and bright bronze pot. It was his pride and joy and he was delighted when Amanda took notice of it, However, Rupert was very displeased when Amanda took more time admiring the pot than his extra-sharp claws or newly decorated breastplate of diamonds. He swore not to throw the pan in the bin where it would meet many predecessors who had come to a similar fate, as this pan was very expensive, and he had saved up an entire year of hard labour earnings to be able to purchase it.

By hard labour, a dragon tended to mean pouncing on a few sheep and carrying them to the fashion experts to make nice dragon coats out of their fur. This was the equivalent effort of a human taking a few ants home and making use of the leaf that they had spent so long carrying but let's politely ignore this else this entire story will find itself at the end of the dragon's fire.

Still Rupert desperately wanted to impress Amanda with his stunning physique and so flung open his paws to fully bring to the forefront those impressive claws, she just whacked him round the head with her tail and moved off to see how the other rivals were doing with the flambé challenge.

Amanda watched with fascination as the other contestants added their diced onion to the pan, the different colours of onion was incredible. Some were green, somewhere pink, some red, some purple and others a nightly shade of black. Amanda noticed all this but destiny watched closer, for he liked to play with fire and he was begging to feel everything was going a little too smoothly for his liking.

Rupert's tail dragged as his mind seemed to sink into the bronze metal of his cooking pot and he puffed out a large ashy cloud feeling pretty disappointed. He stood there for a few minutes till he saw out the corner of his eye Amanda patting another dragon on the back for their hard work and very shiny pot. Yes, this was not as difficult as when Amanda had been gazing at the competitor with total delight but still he felt like he had a point to prove.

Then fires started erupting around him and he knew the time was at hand. He lifted the bottle high into the air and let loose the flame as the alcohol spilled down, the timing was perfect and it lit up like a stream of fire in the air, cooking before it ever reached the pan. Rupert felt so proud and puffed up with himself, that was until he noticed his aim was very much aria. The stream of flame did not fall into the pan but hit the floor with a splash.

Transfixed in horror, Rupert looked on as this stream turned into a puddle which grew and then split into smaller streams, covering the floor in a thin carpet of flame. The other dragons around him ran away in horror so as not to get their legs flambéed. They ran into other dragons knocking over their pans till soon there was carpets of flame spreading everywhere and every dragon was pouncing from one shrinking spot to another for dear life as they tried to escape to the front doors.

Luckily, most of the judges were sitting in high seats to as survey all the competitors with ease but they were now like cats stuck at the top of a flaming tree unable to get down. Still at least they would have time to pray to their gods and repent of all sin before reaching a very fiery end.

Although dragons are resistant to almost all fire, there scales, armour, jewellery and own brand of natural magic cannot protect them from the fire of their kindred.

The screams did wake Rupert from his transfixed state and he joined in the chorus providing a nice tenor to the wailing song of death. He did not feel cool, not like the cool dude he meant to be one bit.

Only Amanda did not lose her head. She hit upon one very important fact everyone else had seemingly forgotten, she was a dragon. Dragons can fly.

She spread her wings and soured around the sealing and much like humans who forget that they wear glasses despite literally having them resting on their scalp, all the other dragons remembered that they had wings and soared into the air and laughed at the flames below.

The oldest judge named sir Pan looked down at the flames below, he had not felt like moving so soon after lunch and would not be like those cowardly dragons who ran from flame like scaly wags who deserted the sinking ship. He felt proud of the room's ancient history and had such a strong connection to flambéing and dragon flame barbeques, that he felt it would be sacrilege to let the room burn without him. If the room was to burn down, he would bravely burn down with it.

Looking to the cowardly dragons gliding above him, he cried, "Oh ye of little faith and timid hearts, ye that would forsake this room in its dire hour, see now that I Sir Pan do stand alone in faithful friendship with the stony walls. Thus, I alone oh ye of little faith and timid hearts, shall live forever in the halls of my godly friends and shall be blessed beyond any worldly heart. See now I shall not be damned as you shall be or sent to the depths of Tartarus as you all shall, dragons of little faith. Where is your manhood? Where is your fiery desire to be as one with the stone, men of weak knees and stubble beard…" He shook his paws in the air in fury.

The flames were now nearly halfway up the highchairs and the melting stone released disgusting gasses which made the dragons cough and sneeze, but the oldest judge went on and on till Amanda swooped down and saved him from his 'eternal blessing'.

Pan writhed and shouted at her, "Unhand me this instant, young lady, you are disgracing my honour. Let me go, you willingly wimble." Yet she carried the judge out of danger through a large hole which marked the place where the entrance once stood. The other dragons followed her with much cheering and delight. There was much to be grateful for, mainly that no one had died or been badly injured, but Pan had to be wrestled to the ground when he tried to make a quick getaway into the flaming building.

While the wrestling and paw grappling was going on, Amanda took Rupert to one side.

"So," she said with a sigh, "you caused this fiery incident."

Rupert mumbled to the ground, "You saw me."

"Yes," she said simply as if they were just chatting about whether it was going to rain or not that day.

"I'm a—" began Rupert, feeling really shitty, till Amanda interjected.

"You're an amazing flambèist, I watched, those flames hit the alcohol bang on time and cooked it through at just the right temperature, I couldn't smell any burning from your bench and the flame was just the right colour. You're fantastic, maybe just work a little on your aim next time, but apart from that…"

She kissed him.

This left Rupert feeling stunned. He barely moved. He almost forgot that he had nearly burned everyone to a crisp. He puffed up his chest and did a merry dance.

Amanda began to dance with him and they were the happiest dragons alive, despite the burning building in the distance, the mass of dragons pinning Sir Pan to the ground and the thunderous shouting of Sir Pan over the roar of the flames "what are you dancing about oh ye of small hearts and feeble stature. The great building is burning, and we are not burning with it, we are all going to be in grave danger when the gods release their anger onto us."

And indeed the gods would, for war was coming, and it would soon engulf all sentient life. And would pay the currency of pain to all living beings with conscience, as it would devour souls.

Chapter 22
An Unexpected Ascension to Godhood

Prince Rupert had valiantly dashed away some moons ago, with his steed Boltimor, to prove his knightly bones as has been told. He had longed to put away the churning doubts of his people who mocked him, and viewed him only as the son of Bartibus the barmy. Yet he was captured by Madam Crumbler, and was long held captive at her mercy.

Kneeling on the ground, now he was building a castle of stones, virtually the only possible intellectual activity to be done in his mental condition, when stuck in a cave with a dragon. Dragons were not the destructive reptilians, that their reputation describes. They actually had long understood the concept of building as it was necessary within their life spans to look closely at architecture designs so they could learn how to build their own homes. Although on accusation they would indeed use this knowledge to burn buildings down in the most effective manner.

In addition to architectural classes, they had ones on dragon aerobics, dragon history, dragon lore, dragon combat and dragon hoarding. Many had got it wrong in thinking dragons liked treasure, you see, they were more the kind of creature that collected treasure for more prideful purposes and impressing their fellows in accordance with what their society demanded of them. For the dragon, the greatest act of strength was to burn down a village in a staggeringly impressive feat of effectiveness, and something their culture delighted in, even though each individual dragon often just wanted a peaceful life after their formative more energetic youth.

Dragons also had an unwritten rule which had almost become etched into their society, to allow some survivors out of the burning buildings through some secret trap door. It was often thought, wrongly, that dragons were unaware of these get outs, but they thought it only decent to allow humans who kept their heads on during a dragon attack to live another day. If only to spread the word about exactly how terrifying the attack was, and increase the dragon's reputation.

The samba dancing dragon had eventually told prince Rupert about her former days of glory when she had been known as Mountain Crumbler, and had scared away the northern king Sir Domfon, till he ran screaming and left the dragon with the very treasure she had come for, the king's Weetabix.

If he had not had Weetabix that day, or poured steaming milk and honey into his bowl, the fate of his kingdom would have been very different and the blasted wizards up in the north would be far less of a political power. As it was the wizards had held sway over the kingdom for a long enough time before a governor was appointed, to really start getting their foot in the local governing bodies.

Mount Crumbler was a serious threat though and the northern cities needed the wizards even if it didn't want them.

They felt it almost evil to allow wizards to be in charge, and it definitely opened the door to a lot of evil, but the ironic thing about evil is that it is evil that sometimes allows you to live another day in order to do good. Had they, for example, got a monk to face the dragon. The monk would not last a second.

Some people are willing to die for what they believe in and the purposes of good, but at least for those that want to wake up the next morning, leaving wizards out of the picture was an unthinkable thing.

Mount Crumbler's history aside, this aged lady dragon had inadvertently by her potent magic drove the king's son mad. She had, you see, created a field of 'dragoness dancing' by her sheer will to be a dance tutor and so turned the cave into a trap upon which all thought of anything but dragon dancing left the unfortunate prince's head.

It was then that a band knights lead by Sir Peturbarer, of the royal cavaliers made a rescue attempt. Expecting to see the prince fending off this dragon and making every effort to escape, they were unprepared for the prince to begin a samba session and take Peturbarer through his paces. When not even the point of a sword would convince him to go with them, all the knights gathered in a tight circle and punched the prince very hard in the head. He fainted. The dragon roared. They ran for their lives though a few were found doing a few pirouettes and groovy moves which they had not intended to do when planning the rescue mission.

His father meanwhile was up in the tallest tower, in the middle of many upper-class individuals, crying an astonishingly large number of tears. So much in fact, he should be added to the Guinness book of records.

Then he burst into the grand universal Guinness book of records, by belching out an aquatic pool of salty water when his son came bursting in.

The prince was dressed in a tight tunic and long brown trousers. He walked right up to the king's right-hand side like a robot would move if it knew the pain of arthritis. This deterred the usual female fans in the caught from leaning in for a kiss. Then he reached over and from the gathering, grabbed one of his ex-girlfriends. He kissed her, nothing but a peck on the hand, but this was what she had been trying to get for many a moon. Upon the lady taking a swig of ice-cold tea to stay upright and conscious, so much was the shock of this prince kissing her once more, the prince began swaying his hips, doing lightning dances and really giving it all he had.

There was silence. The prince's crusher, our dear Sir Hamfield, looked on in great pain.

Yet the prince seemed to be dancing to his own invisible band and conducted the last trumpet heavy replay of the motif. He beamed around and did the last move to prove his point, to prove how awesome he was.

His father opened his mouth in horror. He was looking more worried than he had been since he was attacked by a group of converging tourists, when after wrapping himself tightly in the nearest curtain, he heard with a gnashing of teeth that they were upset by the abundance of only half-filled swimming pools. They were not deep enough for instance to go scuba diving. After the king's lawyer, who had just plucked up the courage to emerge from under the coffee table, ended up pointing out that it was the driest year on record, they were still angry.

Not till an expert on swimming pool law was summoned from the courts were the band of frustrated humans finally appeased by the irrefutable argument that the cracked tiles on the bottom of a fully filled swimming pool were not worth the bother of underwater observation. So they all stared mournfully at one of the only filled pools, feeling its sense of pain at the knowledge of its complete lack of worthiness.

For humans have always had a particularly strong ability to empathise with that which truly has no emotions, while humans empathising with fellow humans with emotion has been proved by history to be somewhat harder.

Amway, Sir Hamfield and the deputy, Sir Potty, who, like almost every knight, had a big heart for the prince, walked forwards to ask the prince if he needed some wine to relax and feel less pressured to demonstrate his dancing skills before the knights. You see, they were under the impression that this outburst was due to a lack of human contact for a long time and the extreme nerves that must come from reintegrating into normal society.

The king was very old and given the sudden drop in action, fell asleep. If he had stayed awake, he would have noted that Sir Hamfield was not letting good behaviour get in the way of his emotions, when Sir Hamfield pounced on Sir Potty and tackled him to the ground. The prince stood there beaming, till Sir Hamfield rose victorious albeit with a few scratches and a bleeding lip. As for Potty, well he was out of service for a long time and decided eventually to go to the training academy of the Barbarian leader, as to keep a good distance from Rupert, so he might not allow his feelings to overcome his dignity ever again.

Yanking Hamfield up, the prince asked, "Are you okay, Hamfield?"

"Are you okay, prince?" said Hamfield rather awkwardly.

"I am swell, my young dude, swell," said Hamfield's crush.

The knight was taken aback by being addressed so fondly. He had often imagined the prince and him spending time together by the pools of the mountain dragons, and the sensation of feeling the prince's smooth hair, wash over his skin. As Hamfield was daydreaming, Rupert said unto him "Call me darling, no need for silly names such as prince here. You are my prince, my dear Hammy." Those eyes that beheld him were surely the moon light focussed in to a perfect diamond which danced in the silver light of the night. How they would rap arms around each other and glide into bliss, like a swan through the lake, before resting under soft and warm pillows.

Slowly, a dazed expression swam over Hamfield, he went something like 'ah' and he just smiled. The prince beamed back thinking this was but a revival of cave man speech. Then the knight fainted.

There was now two people technically asleep. Hamfield may have suffered a heart attack due to the pure outshining of love, but as God judges the virtue of the heart not its capacity, this is a sure way to enter heaven. So naturally the prince was unaffected by the fainting of one of his most reliable knights and felt the kingdom could not possibly be in better hands then those of the valiant men before him. As for the other sleeping person, well old men are prone to random sleep spurts.

One of the knights was wearing his breastplate the wrong way around, two of the nights seemed to feel only one of their legs needed protection and some of them were wearing a dozen knives as if they had fifteen pairs of invisible hands with which to wield all of them. Two further knights were hiccupping having drank too much lemonade and four very out of shape individuals were looking like eagles and were seeking the nearest custard puff.

Any enemy, and I mean any enemy, would surely be able to annihilate them all.

This was until Triffon appeared behind them and pushed them to the ground as she walked past. She tried to run away from their rusty spears but she tripped over her dress and was grabbed from behind and held firm. The guards then met with horrifying awareness, the enemy that they truly could overcome. And this was such an earth-shattering event that the god of incapability, and yes, the king's people had one, did something he was incapable of doing. It was there, literally there, before them. You see, a being of incapability by all logic should be incapable of doing anything, even existing, for such a god is the embodiment of incapableness.

Yet here was an incarnation of a totally incapable being actually doing something, existing and appearing before them. It was a miracle. In times long gone there was much debate about the validity of a god of incapableness being worshipped, but the believers proclaimed loudly that they did not in fact believe in such a god, for a god that is incapable of anything must surely be incapable of all states, even existence. Thus, a true believer in the incapable god, believed not in it. Which made worship of such an entity entirely logical for they were in fact worshiping nothing. And nothing is known to exist, unless you take account of quantum mechanics which we shall not do here. Incapable guardians as the god's followers were known as, were the epitome of religious atheists.

Triffon's arrival was the proof that they were indeed valid in their belief in worshiping the god of incapableness, apart from the fact that now they were no longer atheistic theists but just common theists as their god had shown itself to them in such a way that no one could deny it exists. The shaken worshipers of the god of incapableness were further blest by her appearance making themselves and all the incapable worshipers very capable in defending their king against their god and for filling their knightly duties so much so, that their god had actually for the first time ever made them feel capable.

And the knights liked feeling capable particularly now that though they could not only boast to be able to defeat another knight, but they could also boast about being able to defeat a god, and so the knights dropped to their knees in adoration of this woman, a divine creator of their new found ego.

Never has the lack of ability in a knight, when met with a truly terrifyingly incapable force, been known to lift the knight to heights that even the most capable of capable mortals could have never since or after achieve. You see this is why Triffon was born said the profits, so that by her incapableness might she be risen to glory shared only by the all father who is indeed capable of all things.

A few apricots dropped from her overladen straw hat. The squelching that followed became a rounded sound in the royal court. After a few weeks it became so ingrained into people's thinking that they would often bow before the confused fruit dropping butler under the impression that the butler was actually Triffon in disguise making a secret inspection of her palace.

She stood up straight, albeit at a slight angle to add an extra 'weird' effect when speaking to the listeners, before she flung her hands wide. Bracelets dangled and her aged cape snapped down the middle. She took a bite or two of the fruit on top of her headdress. Then she said, "Gruggor has declared war on this kingdom, doon, doll, no doom. Yes, doom shall before you all."

With that, she was just about to vanish, and ensure the safety of her head, when the knights dropped to their knees once more and begged, "Oh lady who makes the gods come into being, help us in our peril. Be our shining lady!"

She clumsily bowed nearly falling to her feet while the knights watched her upper half apparently swim upon invisible water, while the mid-section rotated like a gyroscope. She was praised for her athletic ability. When she finally regained balance, she said, "Finally, my talents are appreciated. I shall stay here with my friends. Here my life and powers will not be put to shame or shunned by those who fail to see the depth of my true skill."

She shouted, "I shall stay!" And with that Gruggor smashed his crystal in his higher tower, for Triffon, of all the witches he had ever known, had surprised him. She had in fact totally outwitted him. She was not dead or despatched unsuspiciously by the knights so far from the academy that no one could possibly blame him, she was not thrown in the dungeons and removed out of the way, she was welcomed and treated like some divine lady. The only way he could get rid of her now was to declare full out war with the kingdom of Bartibus and though he did not fear the knights themselves, if the wolves ever got involved then he would be in serious trouble.

There was a loud crack over head as thunder roared about professor Gruggor's office. It was electrically prickly and made enough nitrogen oxides to make Gruggor's two applicants for a recently opened position, have cardiac arrest.

Gruggor stomped around, feeling angrier than angry. It was like a sort of buzz you get after eating a bar of chocolate, having already had a chocolate sponge dessert. Or like the feeling of waking up in the night, shivering and naked and then going outside into a February evening.

Gruggor stopped processing his anger at this point and thought what it would be like to venture out into the chilly air with only underwear on, it would be an…experience. Perhaps he would get some of his students to look into it, but right now he had more urgent matters at hand.

The door kept shaking from the knocking, yes wizarding doors do indeed knock themselves whenever a wizard with an intent to enter approaches. He ignored this focussing on how incredibly angry he was at Triffon.

Then there was another knock.

In the devil's name, come in!

The man dressed in a black robe slid through the door. His eyes dark, and full of malice.

"Triffon has betrayed us headmaster."

"I know," said Gruggor solemnly.

The atmosphere was ruined by Gruggor's pet snake eating away at the man's cloak and the tug of war that ensued, but determinedly the headmaster stared at the wall of the room as if building up some unthinkable magical curse to destroy Triffon.

Gruggor's thoughts was now turning to whether his snake needed more milk or if the milk she should be provided with ought to be the more manly full fat kind. He verbalised nothing of this, wishing to keep up his villainous reputation.

"So Triffon," said the man, now lifting his hood to reveal Jasper's pale face.

"Triffon," said the headmaster. Now looking lovingly at that springy, curly hair which was distinctive to Jasper.

There was another pause, a key step in the dramatic tension that was building up.

Another knock, and an advert guy barged in taking advantage of the slow momentous build up.

He waved four wands, did a prance, introduced the latest 'best' wand which was so good that it might actually have been a noticeable improvement to the last one, and then left. I'm supposing he quickly gathered that now was not the time for wand advertisements.

"Triffon," said Jasper deeply now staring oddly into Gruggor's eyes with a deep evil.

"Triffon," repeated Gruggor. Though now there was something of a more affectionate tone to it.

After multiple phrasing of the traitorous witch, they ended up so greatly in unholy thought that their heads were literally in contact, then their mouths and soon, well, more.

All was turning out very fairy tale like until in one make out manoeuvre, Gruggor stepped upon the glass of the smashed seeing ball. Pain went straight up his leg and Jasper tried to kiss it better. Unfortunately this caused more bleeding and Jaspers lips to undergo a few cuts.

Next thing both new, they were in a hospital and would be unable to find or kill Triffon for quite some time. This was a fortunate turn of events given that if they were on the move then this story would end very briefly but their departure from mobility gave the time needed for the wolves, dragons and humans to rally their strengths and together fight to overcome the domain of the lost god. And also this pause in evil gave Triffon the slightest chance of evading the clunking heavy shoes of death.

Chapter 23
Apricots

There is one experience that never ceases to spring up upon the unexpected traveller, and that is of the heart falling in love.

Falling in love mirrors in many ways that of becoming the best of friends, though the former tends to tug at the heart strings far further than one would expect the bow of romantic friendship to. Or at least that is what one would always assume apart from night clubs were love is such a random and spontaneous thing it is anyone's guess if the two very close friends will make out or not, after drinking a few shots.

However, the two friends will most likely find themselves miles apart at the end of the night, or perhaps arise the next morning and wonder 'where am I?' as they smell the hot fumes of coffee coming out of kitchens they had never used or seen before.

Love is not something knights tend to show much of though. Yet, whereas most knights of Mados wear stern expressions, Prince Rupert was kneeling down as tears fell from his eyes. When broken by love the soul faces a cross road to either pin down the broken part of the heart as a cat might a mouse and force it under the sea of other thoughts, or to for a while live with a beating heart broken where the shards are often felt to be grating against one another.

The advantage though of a broken heart is that within the fictitious heat of the stone against stone is produced a spark of life, a fiery light to kick start a revolutionary change and sudden lights which kick previous processes into action and so allow one to develop and become far more than one was before. Yet underpinning love, despite its ups and downs, is a gentle warmth you see, which has loud orchestras playing above it.

"I shall never see my love again," whimpered Triffon who could just imagine now the thought of Jasper crying in her high tower with his hands outstretched to her. But Triffon felt like she had to now be a strong woman to hold her tattered heart together, for her love's sake at least.

So, she went over to her curtain and tossed it aside shouting into the new day, "I am coming for you, my love."

The only complication was that the dancing prince had seemingly taken an interest to her delightful personality and magnificent form. She had continuingly rebutted his attempts to offer her flowers and did not like it when Rupert did pose with a grin at her door. She didn't like the prince, not his odd samba dancing nor his shows of manly fighting nor his boastful tales of how he had single-handedly defeated twenty of the dragons most fearsome warriors before being trapped by a stupendously powerful dragon.

Besides, she knew Rupert's version of events was a stretch from the truth, and she had some of the finest knights in the realm correcting his story on a daily basis. Why Rupert could not just fall in love with the knight that was clearly quite obsessed with him, she didn't know.

The prince had no appreciation for the finer things in life, no ability at card reading or crystal gazing and couldn't even make an apricot crumble, I mean really what had happened to the great gentlemen's men had used to be?

As she turned around, she saw Rupert standing there at her office door as he did whenever he had a free period. His hand rested smugly on his sword hilt and he said, "Do you want to go for a walk? I know the fields are absolutely charming at this time of the year."

"No," said Triffon abruptly who had found a hardness and strength to her personality since being separated from Jasper that she had not known existed within her before.

"But my love…"

"Your love! What the hell are you saying, apricotless man?" Apricotless was the biggest insult she could think to give.

"I'm sorry my lov…lovely goddess. I step out of place only because I am dazzled by your godly headdress. It is most fetching."

Never before in the history of the entire world had anyone called Triffon's headdress 'fetching' but then each man to his own.

"I do think it rather becomes me, don't you?" asked Triffon, giving a weak attempt at a smile that looked more like a grimace.

"Yes absolutely, it is sword crushingly—"

"Please enough of these sword-based adjectives, I am a lady of peace not a warfare-loving knight, and you would do well to remember it."

"Yes, my goddess," said the prince, looking a little upset.

This was just the right moment for the obsessed master knight to entire thought Triffon, thank the heavens he was around to get in the way of the prince's continual attempts at romance, a subject even most twelve-year-old boys would be more adept in.

"Um…ah…wow," muttered Hamfield as he began talking to his secret crush, this continued till he managed to pull himself together. "My prince."

"Yes, yes what is it now?" asked Rupert kicking the ground.

"Well, it's the barbarians, there having a meeting with your father about how to take over the city, and the chieftain of the wolves is there to say that if the deforestation doesn't stop then they will personally invade it even if the Barbarian plan fails."

"My dad!" shouted Rupert angrily. "He doesn't know what he's doing half the time."

"Sure. But he booked the secret room and I had a sneak peek through the not-so-secret window to check your father wasn't going along with the plan to make his city look more attractive and worthy of invasion, but it turns out he is going along with it. And the wolf, it'll bite your dad's head off if you don't come soon."

"Why is the wolf almost as angry at my father as I am?" asked Rupert testily, thinking how he had managed to get Triffon to accept a compliment and felt he was surely onto a winning streak or would have been had not the knight had to come running to tell him of his father's madness.

"Because the king keeps going on about the importance of oak tea," sighed the knight.

"Damn it," said Rupert banging his hand on Triffon's desk.

He turned much more calmly towards Triffon and said, "My dear goddess, I am sorry to inform you that I must depart from your company, my father needs my wisdom to guide him through this tricky meeting without his head being torn off. I shall return soon lady, once my father has been locked in his dormitories for his own protection and my peace of mind."

She nodded, spilling more apricots from her headdress. "Take as long as you need, prince, as long as you need." In her head she prayed to the gods that he might take a very, very long time indeed or perhaps be ambushed by the Barbarians and taken hostage.

Happily, oblivious to these thoughts, Rupert bent down and scooped up the apricots and carried them as if one was carrying the sacred apples that legend had said kept the Norse gods alive, he walked off regally from the office.

Triffon though not being a fan of the prince did appreciate that he didn't just step all over the sacred apricots, something the king's knights were learning not to do. She was a god and when she gave bountiful fruit, she expected it to be treated with the highest respect.

Rupert stormed into the bargaining room, his hair waving wildly in the wind coming from the open window, and his sword swaying at his side. "Father, what the hell is going on here?"

The king leapt up in shock and nearly wacked his foot on the table, unfortunately his kneecap collided with it and he dropped to the ground howling with pain. As is wolf custom, the other wolves joined in and howled in unison. Everyone else clasped their hands over their ears till the howling stopped. Eventually, it did stop.

The king rose steadily to his feet, gripping the chair with dear life so he didn't crumple once more.

"My dear son," he said, now sitting down calmly. "These are four of the members of the four-pawed defence guild." They waved a paw in a gesture of welcome. Then the king turned towards the group of men analysing the teaspoon and tea mug as if it was the finest pieces of craftsmanship they had ever seen. "And these are the barbarians," he added. They made monkey noises in a sign of good will and to make it clear that Rupert was not the alpha of the group.

The wolves had nicely groomed fur and polished claws with impressive golden armour over their muscular bodies whilst the Barbarians looked like cavemen who had barely showered or washed for months and only wore patches of cloths round their privates. The wolves didn't seem to mind the poorly dressed barbarians but were looking at the king with a mixture of annoyance and hatred whilst the Barbarians were too interested in trying to bend the spoon with one hand to be interested in royal company.

Rupert sat next to a barbarian who started trying to sniff Rupert's hair and comb it with a greasy fork. He quickly moved to a space near the much more well-behaved wolf and got out a piece of dried chicken from his hair.

The wolf didn't sniff him or comb his hair but stared at him with those intense eyes as if saying 'don't get on the wrong side of me, human', and Rupert actually felt pretty intimidated, which was unusual given his confidence in his own abilities.

The biggest and oldest wolf present began to inform Rupert upon the discussion so far. "Your Father, King Bartibus the tree destroyer, has decided to prove his kingdom as being worth invasion by enlisting the help of the Barbarian army. They wish to invade and kill, plunder and dance with the hopeless maidens and people of the town as they run around burning your villages and farm markets. However, we are not happy with this plan."

Rupert made an inward sigh as he thought at least the wolves were not barmy or blood thirsty invaders. Yet he wished this too soon.

"You see," said the wolf now leaning towards prince Rupert with his upper body covering half the table, "we do not like Barbarians any more than you civilised people since you both have a reckless attitude towards nature and all that lives in the forest and uses the forest as a home. We therefore will slit the throat of your king if and when he signs any such invasion agreement with the Barbarians or does jeopardise the future of my people in anyway. We want the barbarians, humans and wizards all gone from our land and this cotenant at once else we shall slaughter every tree destroyer without mercy or compassion in our furry hearts."

Humphry gulped. "But the…the deer carcases, they were—"

"They were warnings, not gifts as it appears your silly king has led you and all the people of this kingdom to believe. If we see one more oak barrel near our borders, we shall not hesitate to attack."

This shocked Rupert and triggered one of his newest involuntary reactions to social pressure, he got up and did the waltz with an invisible partner, feeling his cheeks turn red as he realised how stupid he must look.

"The prince mocks us!" shouted the wolf, feeling enraged.

The king suddenly spurted out, "Um, my son has recently been held hostage by a dancing dragon and now feels the need to show off his motor skills by demonstrating his new talent to all, but particularly to the most esteemed guests such as your furry selves."

"Father!" shouted the prince as he was grabbed from behind by one of the barbarian ladies and led very forcefully into a stompy dance.

"This is an outrage!" shouted the wolf, not feeling very much like believing the king's ridiculous lies to get the wolves off his son's back; I mean dancing dragons, who's heard of them?

"Please, you must listen to me," cried the prince as he was flung into the air in a very acrobatic moment in the Barbarian dancing routine.

"Ahhhhhh," was the ensuing sound.

"My legs," cried Rupert.

"Stop this nonsense at once," exploded the wolf now punching the tabletop, fangs bared.

"Everyone calm down!" cried the king.

"Father, please help me," cried the son as he was propelled into a tango routine thanks to his dancing instinct.

"Yes baby, do the tango, my young lad, dance!" boomed the Barbarian now kicking him in the shins as she failed to aim her leg movements accurately. He felt the many bruises begin to form.

The other barbarians started singing together in a traditional northern version of a tango inspired rhyme, in the old language which held many similarities to French. "Oum bar derouge sholdey Oum, bar de bar," they sang. This has too rude a translation for me to write down so let's not worry too much about exactly what the barbarians were saying about the prince.

The wolves howled with anger and jumped to attack. They aimed for the dancing lady in an attempt to get the prince alone and unaided, and then punish him for his foolery. The other barbarians drew their clubs and started whacking the wolves round their heads. One wolf was struck upon the forehead between his pointy ears, he tiptoed lifelessly for a while and then dropped to the ground, his lifelong partner, now enraged, bit and scratched at the Barbarians.

The king hid under the table thinking that his son, being a well-trained knight, could deal with this all by himself.

"Father!" cried Prince Rupert as he was dragged away to safety by the dancing lady. The king was crawling like a toddler towards the nearest exit.

The king stopped, looked around and began in a solemn tone, "Ow my son, my wonderful boy. I see, now that you have a fight on your hands, you are gratefully sacrificing yourself to give your father time to escape. I thank you."

"No!" cried the son as he was forced towards the large doors.

The king shouted as he was nearly through the other door, "Oh my son, in the name of peace, I give this dancing lady my blessing to marry you. She clearly has taken an interest. Now your father must say goodbye and wishes you many a happy day while the dancing lady claims you as her husband if she is willing to forgo harming me or the court for your impotence upon the incoming barbarian invasion." The women were beaming at the king with delight, and Rupert was staring at him with total horror in his eyes.

"But father—"

"I cannot, my son, keep you here whilst you have angered the wolves and the barbarians, if I keep you under my roof then it shall be bloodshed for all. Though I go with a heavy heart, your heart must be offered up to this charming lady in the name of peace, and my life."

"But father—"

"See you sometime, my son, though my spirit shall forever be with you."

With that, the king was through the door and the dancing lady whacked the prince around his head and he was taken away by the barbarians to be her future husband.

The wolves gave up biting and clawing at the barbarians when they left the room and decided to nip down to the kitchens to get an ice pack for the injured wolf. There were occasional screams and shouts of 'who let the dog loose oh oh oh oh' as they charged into the downstairs room. Eventually an icepack was found, and the wolves returned to their injured fellow. He tentatively lifted his paw and counted how many digits he had, few there were five, the barbarians had not cut off any.

The wolves left soon afterwards feeling that they would get their revenge soon. They also felt that charging round the palace announcing their presence would just make their enemy on their guard. Their evil plan was to wait for the barbarians to invade the place then once the palace and Barbarian forces were defeated by the ensuing conflict, they would charge in and in one sweep, annihilate them all. Then give their claws a well needed manicure after.

The king meanwhile was so shaken up, any plans he had before coming to the meeting were completely thrown out of his mind and he quickly thought of what excuses he could make to explain his son's absence without making it look like he was kidnapped by Barbarians under the king's very nose, and worse that the king had allowed this and sanctified marriage. At least if the Barbarians liked Rupert that much then they would spare Rupert's father, himself, from any death or torture they invoked upon the others of his kingdom when they came to invade.

Still he thought he should inform Triffon of the disappearance of Rupert right away, she would surely be devastated by the loss of someone who she had become very close to. At least she spent more time with the prince than anyone else, so the King was assuming they were close and no female had said no to the prince's advances before. Surely Triffon would right now be thinking of how impressive his son was, and the king had to tell her how hard he fought against the dragons that corned him and turned him to ash and how he, the king, slew the beast that vaporised his son in one awesome moment of revenge.

He knocked loudly at Triffon's door. He usually had to use a map to remember who stayed in what room, when you have over two thousand servants and five hundred guests it can get pretty confusing, but Triffon's room was easily identifiable by the wafting smell of burned cinnamon coming through the crack in the door.

She stepped out, bangles bangling and apricots oscillating. She smiled and giggled girlishly. "Ow my dear man, you look so, so tired."

"No, no, my dear lady," said the king, shaking his head vehemently.

"Ow you're so sweet, come in."

She now looked slightly mad and not like someone who he wanted to hang around with any more than he had to. The girlish facade was gone and there was now something much darker lurking in her eyes.

"Ow um…no I don't."

And then two bulky knights forced him into the room, locked the door behind him and guarded the entrance. He should have made a rendition of the Pier scream, but this time just looked frantically around for an oak barrel to hide in.

"I am a seer, my dear man," Triffon stated matter-of-factly, as if by this point anyone in the royal court had not known given her bangles and Tarot cards, and love of a see-through spherical objects which reminded her of her prised prophetic glass balls. Often she would be found waving her hands over the fish bowl that Sir Softy had recently placed in the centre of the dining table, in the banquet hall. Let us just say dinners were an unusual event full of mystic mumbo jumbo.

The king nodded to make clear he totally accepted this statement and had no sceptical thought upon the business of fortune tellers.

"Yes, you're a seer alright, now about my son…he's…ah…dead," he muttered quietly, being careful not to make eye contact with anyone in the room, as if this would make his efforts at creating an alternate truth all the more convincing.

"Well, that is interesting about your son," she said softly. "Your son has just been forced away by a band of barbarians, I saw him being wrestled away through the courtyard, through my window."

"Ow...um"

The king was beginning to feel his face go a cherry red.

"What I wonder," she said with inquisition leaking from every word as if she could not restrain her curiosity, now she was leaning towards the king, "is why you want me to believe your son is dead and why he's been forcibly led out of this palace by a band of ferocious individuals which you let in for a private meeting."

"I ah..."

"Well, it does look a little fishy to me." Turning her head a little, she asked, "Doesn't it, Sir Hamfield?" The knight, forcing back the desire to cut off the traitorous king's head there and then, nodded with a confidence that radiated conviction in everything Triffon said.

"Well, it is mine and Hamfield's belief," whispered Triffon so quietly that it made the sound of a vacuum like that of a rock concert, "well, we believe that you are killing your first in line so you can have your second son became the first in line."

"But I don't have a second—"

A faint fire danced in Triffon's eyes as she continued cutting the king's babble short. "Well, did you know that the whore you slept with a few days ago...she tells me she is pregnant. The whore who is more commonly known by the title as the princess of Ontock. The same woman that has sadly been thrown off deck by that Casper as rumour has it. For as Jasper hath told me long ago, that when he went out with the prince on a sailing mission did the prince get so irritated that he gagged her, tied a stone to her and then in rage shoved her into the storming sea below, and then she got eaten by sharks.

"But I am curious if you by any chance were conspiring with the enemy ere this tragic event, trying to remove Rupert out of the picture and have your second born become first in line in one foul swoop. Perhaps you thought peace between the two rival kingdoms, would come when the son of a king of Mados and a future Queen of Ontock was born."

"No, no, no. I hate that rival kingdom and that awful princess, well, I only slept with her because I thought she was hot! I mean, it was only like once, and mine advisors had said that you know, the royalty of Ontock have too tiny dicks and too strong an inbuilt phobia of vagina to ever make a child. Now I guess I did go in with enthusiasm but hey, I had a banana peel over my private organ. And everyone knows I like bananas" Now I know, reader, this is most uncomfortable to read, and not the most grammatically fluent, and it's rather distressing to write, but well, that's the words the king said, so that's what mine furry paw must convey to you.

"What do you think?" asked Triffon, turning to sir Hamfield.

"I think this traitorous fool is lying and should be thrown into the dungeons and then executed."

"What a good point," beamed Triffon. "Guards, take this fool from my sight!"

"You cannot do this!" screamed the king as he tried in a futile attempt to wrestle two of his knights as they grabbed his shoulders.

"Well yes, I can actually."

"But I'm king."

"But I'm afraid, my dear man, I am a god! I am divine! My word is law! As it is in heaven so shall it be upon the earth."

With that the king was taken away to be locked in his own dungeons, imprisoned in his own kingdom.

Sir Hamfield bent down towards Triffon, bowing to pledge his word before the new holy queen, and he asked, "My dear lady, my crush has been kidnapped by a bunch of violent and dirty people from a clearly uncultured and poor land. Please let me rescue my prince and return him to my arms…um, I mean to the palace's safe walls."

Triffon beamed at him and said with a tone of total control and superiority, "Yes my dear servant, go thence and save our prince. May the blessing of the squelching apricot be forever before you. And I shall be watching you my dear knight, for call upon your lady if you are ever in need of assistance, and Triffon shall surely provide."

"As you so kindly say, my goddess," said the knight, bowing a little before saluting her. With that, he hurried off to save his secret love from a terrible fate.

With the king and the prince finally out of the way, Triffon felt like she could finally get this kingdom back on track, and out of the dregs it had been in. Without the prince's constant attempts to get her attention, she could now focus on the only man in her life that ever meant anything, the noble Jasper. Thus, began the catastrophic rule of the apricot obsessed lady. The beginnings of an apparently benign dictatorship.

Yet if Hamfield had but waited a moment, he would have seen a shadowy stick like figure, some seven-feet tall, come out of the shadows. And to this entity did Triffon say 'my lord, I have abolished the establishment of Mados' royal court for the king has been retired of his duties, and the prince is nowhere to steer the land. I have done thee a great service, and I beseech that thee help me lead and in time bring to naught this kingdom, son of Ariton, and lieutenant of the black tower. All is going as thine has foreseen it."

Meanwhile, the knight was most looking forward to having some quality time with Rupert, particularly given he now had a lot of time to constantly mention, on his travels, how Rupert would have to be heroically saved by him.

Chapter 24
Willy Wonka's Gift

Rare as it was in the hospital wing of Mados Mordrė, there were two sleeping people with one being Gruggor and the other not in imminent threat of death. To find one's self in serious pain and not being attacked by a band of ruthless wizards trying to take your place was a blessed event that was all too rare in the academies culture with wizards trying to ascend both to higher levels of academia and those of the orthodox wizarding church.

Jasper stretched and then winced, he still had lots of cuts on his legs and though most of them had turned into scars, a few of them were still very red and soar, oozing with puss for magical glass inflamed the oxytocins within the blood and brought out a magical goo, which had wonderful transformative properties and helped dissolve the glass.

Jasper drank a glass of ice-cold water on the side, and then turned to look over at the beautiful Gruggor by his side. Jasper thought he looked perfect being so peaceful, image of an angel. Dark evil maniacs were simply Jasper's type it had appeared.

Somehow Jasper managed to look away and roll out of bed.

He crashed onto the floor and alerted the nurse by swearing very loudly.

A nurse made dressed in thin white garments rushed over and told him off for trying to get out of bed.

"Bad, bad, bad wizard," said the nurse, now whacking him around the head with a magical newspaper which was titled 'How to keep your patients happy'. She clearly needed a re-read.

"For God's sake, woman. Stop that," slapping her head he growled in annoyance.

"Only if you promise not to be such a silly boy again."

"I am not a boy!" shouted Jasper. He did not appreciate being treated like a kid when he had been eighteen for countless millennia.

"Oh, my dear little one, now, now, there is no need to get all shouty with me. You need your naps to help your growing bones…" Pushing him onto the bed, she resettled him while pulling the perfumed covers over him.

That was enough for Jasper who took out his wand, waved it and caused glue to seal the nurse's mouth shut. She seemed to be trying to say something like "bad, bad boy" but Jasper just flicked his wand and she flew into the locker which locked shut with a massive slam.

Gruggor stirred and looked blearily at Jasper. "What are you doing?"

"Um well, she was treating me like a boy." Jasper looked down at floor red-faced.

"Who exactly is she?"

"The nurse that is now making strange sounds in the locker."

"You mean, she's not trying to enrol as a mime artist?"

"Ow come on! Now is not the time for witty comedy"

"Only joking."

Gruggor tried to move but like Jasper he couldn't do much without wincing so flopped back onto the bed looking up at the star covered ceiling.

"Oh my dear Jasper. What are we going to do about Triffon?"

"Well, I don't quite know. All I know is that Triffon is in some far-off land, being exalted to godhood by a bunch of idiots who have never even heard the voice of the lost god before and will doubtlessly be even now teaching the king and his ridiculous son how to make apricot tarts. Well, I suppose things could be worse."

"Worse? We're stuck here in a hospital, being outwitted by the dumbest witch in history, and you think things could be worse?"

"Well, we are not being attacked by werewolves for one thing or dragons or any other of our many enemies?"

"Well…no," admitted Gruggor. Still he was hardly thinking that this pause in being nearly killed was a welcomed repose given how Triffon's arrival had seemingly gone so awry and her strange apricot phrases scared even Gruggor at times.

"Perhaps a slice of cake would make things better?" suggested Jasper, who knew that Gruggor in his previous life as William the wanderer loved sponge cakes.

"Well, I'm not sure if we can have cake given my teeth are rotting like mad," snarled Gruggor.

"Oh you're such a boor, my darling," muttered Jasper. He then went on with more plot schemes, dancing in Jasper's wild mind, to try to brighten Gruggor's day. "Well, if I'm such a boor than how come even when asleep did I send visions that almost convinced Gallat to join the trip up to the northern mountains to kill those dragons."

"You did!"

"Yes, till one of our wizards went rogue and into the mountain territory to warn them before we launched our attack, anyway."

"Oh, how fabulous, may the lost god have mercy upon us both."

"But headmaster, don't you see!"

Gruggor snarled, then let out a little whimper as tears filled his eyes from the pain of bearing his broken teeth.

"What I see," he began to say, breathing heavily, "is a wizard who escaped us, another rebel wizard who has been welcomed by our enemy, and the boy of prophecy who has thanks to my injuries not been exposed to my poisonous teaching or promises of power. In short what I see is our failings!"

"But headmaster—"

"There shall be no buts! I am awake, I am alive and ready to serve the lost god however I can even in my currently injured state."

"But dear—"

"No buts today! Today we shall only say yes to the power of our god as shall the boy. I need to see him immediately and begin his private lessons. He has much to learn and very little time to learn it!"

"Yes headmaster," said Jasper sadly, feeling like despite how admiral Gruggor's passion for serving the lost god was, he was missing out on the nicer things of life, an evening just with the two of them for instance.

Jasper left the hospital feeling very heavy hearted and went to find Gallat.

It was now a couple of months since Triffon's disastrous lesson and Gallat was doing extremely well. He sometimes got confused and ended up doing something different to what he had intended but that was the same for all young wizards.

Jasper found Gallat having a practiced duel with Donkark and seeing the displays of power between them both was incredible, but it was clear Donkark had the mastery. Donkark lacked the imagination and charisma of Gallat but Donkark was still the most skilful wizard apart from Jasper and the headmaster.

Gallat had found his speciality was time-based knowledge, and so much of his spells took the form of visions and bringing to light past events to put Donkark off his balance and guard, whilst Donkark adopted a much more aggressive fighting style being a master in the making of mortality magic and armies of skeletons rushed at Gallat at Donkark's command.

Jasper raised his wand and the skeletons started laughing and giggling. Donkark and Gallat were confused for a moment till their eyes settled upon Jasper, and Jasper adopted his usual fake act of incompetence and foolishness by jumping in and hugging the skeletal warriors.

He then tripped off the duelling mat and landed flat on the floor. He beamed widely.

Then he gestured at Gallat to come with him and Donkark felt a little upset, they had been having a lot of fun together. Still Donkark waved goodbye, played a few banjo chords and then jogged back to the dinner hall to have some nice steak and black pudding pie.

Jasper took Gallat's arm and they vanished reappearing in the hospital right in front of Gruggor the great.

"You are welcome here," said Gruggor, gingerly taking his hand out of his pillow to shake that off Gallat.

"You know Jasper?" asked the headmaster.

"Certainly," said Gallat. "He's my emotivist teacher and well, he and Triffon are kinda inseparable, I used to be in her classes to till the substitute arrived."

"Oh indeed," said Gruggor coldly. He didn't like substitutes as they rarely were very committed teachers. Letting the thoughts pass, Gruggor waved his hand dispassionately towards Jasper and Jasper disappeared from the room.

"Now we are alone and without the listening ears of passers-by, I would like to tell you secrets."

"What secrets?" asked Gallat innocently.

"Oh, some very powerful secrets, my young lad, very powerful indeed."

Gallat beamed but then frowned a little, asking, "Headmaster, has someone attacked you, you look awful?"

Gruggor let out a cold laugh.

"I look awful, do I? Well, I've been worse, child, much, much worse. Still, I will recover my full strength soon and then we shall, well, seal your fate."

Gruggor moved his hands towards some peppermints that some students had placed at his bedside table. He chewed a small bean, enjoying the upper-class flavour profile. Gallat did similar but didn't like the new flavour, he thought it too medicinal.

"My dear young lad, please sit down," requested the headmaster. The student sat attentively on the bed wanting to impress the headmaster in their first lesson, but being afraid he might fail.

With that, Gruggor began, "So where is your favourite constellation, my boy and what does the group of stars mean to you?"

"Well, I quite like the farmer, the one hardly anyone knows about but I like farming." He looked over at his teacher as if to ask that talking about such non-magical things as agriculture was okay.

"I like the farmer too. You know, before I was a wizard, I was a farmer. Life was simple and straightforward, I do miss it from time to time but then there is always a cost to the wizarding life. We've both lost much already."

"Yeah," said Gallat. "When I was younger, well a baby really, I lost my mother to a terrible plague."

"That must have been painful, my young boy, I really am sorry that you had to endure such pain at so young an age." A tear dropped down his cheek, he really felt for the loss of this boy. He couldn't connect with most wealthy young wizards, or stiff academics but this ex-farmer reminded him of himself when he was younger.

"Well, we can't dwell upon the past when the future looks so determinedly ahead. It is frustrating sometimes, but time waits for no man or wizard for that matter."

"Not even for Gruggor the great?" asked Gallat jokingly.

"Not even for this old man," responded Gruggor. He looked at his thin burned hands and said, "I don't have that long left in this world, Gallat, and I have been searching for my equal to lead the academy into a new golden age, for a long time."

"That must be pretty challenging," said Gallat, thinking how few wizards would fit the requirement of being Gruggor's equal.

"And I think I've found my perfect replacement," said Gruggor, smiling his wicked smile.

Gallat was looking attentively towards the chocolate buns which some other student had put by the headmaster's bedside before returning to the conversation. He felt like the soufflé guards when put in front of some new delicatessen.

"A replacement, you say?" looking right back at Gruggor.

Gruggor looked back. "I would like you to be my replacement; with a little training, you could be my equal."

Gallat jumped up in shock. "You mean, you want me, me to—"

"Inherit the academy upon my death," suggested Gruggor.

"Wow, thanks," was all Gallat could say. This was a little overwhelming and he hadn't really let the thought sink in fully yet. It took him many weeks to process it. Over the next few weeks did Gallat train with Gruggor hard, and he flourished like a flower witnessing the coming of its first spring.

Chapter 25
The Great Conjurer

Being captured by dragons is usually thought of as an honour, at least it is more well thought of than being captured by Barbarians, a group of bandits who eternally dress as babies. Dragon capture makes one the upper class of the imprisoned society. Though being forcefully carried by a pair of younglings and then held prisoner in the mountains in order to be either killed or traded as a slave to king Bartibus was not ideal at all.

Sir Thunderbolt had recently been sent on dispatch and was now on his way to tell the king of an escapee wizard's existence and enlist the initial stages of the bargain. The prisoner really hoped Triffon was still alive and not killed by the headmaster else he himself would be of no use and would be executed. Then again Triffon had a very unique ability to stay alive so was probably still safely sitting in her high tower at Mados Mordrė, staring dreamily into her crystal balls.

The crows had not had enough time yet to fly to the mountains, so information had not reached him yet of the power move of the kingdom, nor Triffon's succession to Godhood.

He had made pretty good friends with Amanda and had regular visits from her. The manner in which he was held captive, was being held by a cord attached to the rugged wall, in a large semi-spherical cave with rough rocks sticking out of a pool at the centre. Fortunately there was some colour present unlike the dungeons of most human design, for it was bright green in places thanks to the crystals spread around and there was a slab of rock that he used as his bed.

The pool was not the kind of cave man styled engineering which he was used to drinking out of back home, yet it was the only source of fresh water available. On the upside, it was very refreshing and cold, but then again it did come from the mountain range, so this was not a surprise. It still took some getting used to though, he had grown up with the much more murky muddy water available at Mados.

Amanda flew in, rested her large paws on the stones, beating her wings slowly up and down so as to create a cold draft to make the prisoner feel less humid. She then curled up her wings and began asking how things were going.

"So, you ah, like it here?"

"Well, there's lots of rocks," said the wizard, with forced merriment, though she could tell he was poorly nourished and longing for a mattress and blanket to sleep upon. So, she stabbed a few fishes in the pond with her claws. She quickly cooked them in her flame and then tossed them over to the man. He gratefully gulped them down. She offered her wing as a pillow for some rest but the man seemed to prefer just leaning against the wall, still being suspicious of all dragons given the welcome he had by the majority of the northern mountain dragons.

"Ah mate, these are perfect!"

"Well, I am a very proficient cook, in fact I'm a flambé master and one day I want to be a cook just like my grandad."

She beamed at the wizard, which was an overwhelmingly human gesture for a dragon to make and let's just say it didn't suit her kind very well though it did show she was happy, which made the prisoner happy, so it did brighten his mood.

"A chef, hey," said the wizard.

"Yeah," she beamed again. Clearly, she had learned how to show human facial expressions from a textbook and this looked oddly forced and very unnatural, still she was in principle doing everything perfectly.

"A dragon chef," mused the wizard. He had heard of many strange things but never one as strange as that.

"The best chef ever!" roared the dragon, or at least that's what the human assumed the dragon meant.

"I like that. Amanda the dragon chef of the north."

"Roooooaaaaar." Fire, as red as the blood of sapiens, came forth from the dragon.

He went up to her and stroked her chin. She sneezed and then rolled on her back in a classic sign of "it's time to play with me."

Once play time was over, the wizard asked, "Do you remember why I'm here?"

She nodded.

"Well, if the other dragons don't listen to me and we don't save the boy then things are going to get very ugly for everyone, even the dragons can't hide in secret forever."

She puffed out smoke as if saying "yes I know but what can I do?"

She heard coming along another dragon. She lifted her wing and the human crawled under it in case it was a malevolent dragon that was on approach, or worse a benevolent one which wished to adopt her new friend as some kind of pet.

It wasn't anything less than the totally benevolent "cool guy of the mountain" that emerged out of the darkness, even if he, like most of his kindred, was a little suspicious of humans. It was Amanda's friend, well, I guess you could say boyfriend, since they were sort of dating now. Though Amanda did dislike Rupert's superiority complex when it came to wizards, as far as Amanda thought both dragons and wizards were equal.

"Amanda," cried Rupert with joy. He'd been looking for her all morning. He had hoped they could go sledging together early on when the sun was newly risen, and the snow was still mostly solid.

"Hey Rupert. It's awesome to see you. Me and my friend were just having a chat."

"Your friend...do you mean the...the human?"

"Yes," she said whacking her tail so hard a wave of water passed right over her back and onto Rupert's head. "And he's my friend, Rupert, so please stop calling him 'the human' and call him by his true name, the..."

"The Courtney," said a muffled voice from under Amanda's wing.

"The Courtney," repeated Amanda confidently.

"So, Mr Courtney," said Rupert puffing out his chest, "shall I chop thee into pieces of fresh meat or barbeque your skin?"

The wizard sprang from under the wing, his anger overcoming his fear.

"I am Sir Courtney. The Courtney the cuddly! I am not to be intimidated by an underage dragon!"

Rupert began to puff out smoke and would have incinerated the wizard had not Amanda snatched the man in her claws and flown away, leaving Rupert to spend the next few hours in solitude.

This sucks! thought Rupert. He didn't get Amanda's obsession for this human and didn't like it when it had to come so soon after their first dance together, just a dragon's luck that Amanda had to find this wizard under the ice that day. Sure Rupert had heard of a pompous man named Sir Gruggor and his evil schemes but he was just a man, nothing to be scared of, he couldn't get why the dragons didn't just fly over to Mados and burn the kingdom down, then execute this human for spreading fear and concern over nothing.

He kicked over a few boulders till his father Sir Wensledale glided down to the prisoner's room to meet him. He had heard Amanda's shouting and thought he should come to investigate; he knew his son could be rash and may have upset Amanda a little.

His father began speaking in a low comforting voice, careful to show his concern without making it sound like he was criticising Amanda for her kindness to the human. "My son," he said, patting him on the head, "I know Amanda is a little one might say strange. At least she makes unusual attachments to beasts…um, I mean men, but these are early days my son. She will grow out of it. Now maybe come back later this evening when her pet…um, human will be tired enough for a nap and you and her can have some quality time between yourselves."

Rupert slouched off, feeling very down.

"My poor son," said Sir Wensledale as he watched Rupert go down some dark tunnel.

Meanwhile, Amanda and the prisoner had made it to a mountain retreat where Sir Courtney had first been excavated from under the snow.

To ensure the prisoner didn't escape, there were two draconic guards either side of the mountain. The draconic guards were like smaller versions of dragons which wielded metallic electrical pikes, and though not being capable of fire breathing did release a sleeping agent into the bloodstream of any victim they bit.

She had brought the wizard here to practice magic duelling since she believed it to be an inevitable event that one day the dragons would have to face the wizards of Mados Mordrè, and she wanted some tutelage and practice. She wasn't going to let the opportunity this prisoner brought pass away. In secret she had gathered quite the dragon crowd on this mountain top, including her two cousins Miss Kate and Miss Scoom as well as her sister, Miss Cathryn.

Spells bounced back and forth, flame to and fro and though not much was learned, the wizard did find out a spell to block the heat of dragon flame if not the soot and gasses, and the dragons found out that their claws could block the balls of light which transmitted the magic from the wand to the opponent.

After this all of the dragons save Amanda left so that their absence would not be noticed upon, but Amanda decided to stay to have a chat about the deeper secrets of magic and exactly what made this boy of prophecy that the wizard had come to tell them of, so powerful.

She sat like a cat might with two front paws and then the lower back paws resting in the snow, but she leaned her neck down and in a quiet whisper asked, "So what exactly makes the boy of prophecy so special?"

The wizard grinned and looked right into her eyes. "That, my young dragon, is a secret. But as you are to one day face Gruggor, or at least as your people shall, it is important because it is a secret that will become known by your people, though even most wizards at Mados Mordrė are unaware of it."

"Unaware of the boy?" asked Amanda.

"No, not the boy, everyone knows that Gruggor has found a favourite pupil. But hardly anyone knows why the boy is so valuable. Westog might but even he, well, I'm not sure," answered the wizard.

"Then tell me, master of magic, what is it that makes the boy such a valuable student?"

"Well, dragon, what I'm about to say describes the foundation of magic and wizardry. Promise me that you shall share this with no other save one to act as a sidekick to help overcome the powers of Mados. This should not be shared amongst many."

"I swear on the paw, only me and…um, my boyfriend shall know of this, he'll love being my sidekick, yeah."

"Well then, dragon, I shall open the foundation of wizardry to your inspection."

"So um…my ah, dude, as thy earth-bound people say. Where does magic come from?"

"Well, my dear, this is much debated, there are so many both political and moral viewpoints that influence the answer. My personal belief is that it is simply another fundamental force within the universe, much like gravity, electromagnetism and all the rest. The only difference between them and it, and the reason it seems magical, is that it acts not according to the properties of objects themselves such as charge or mass or anything else, but according to the life force of things. It is the force whose potential generates life-energy. It is the force from which all life itself comes."

"And well, are all men as you are and not scaly or beautiful as I am. Where forth comes your magic, for only dragons have a strong connection to life force itself, or so my father told me, less he is prejudice."

"He is right, my dear dragon. But chieftain of the angels, Sir Michael, came down from the heavens and gave us a tool to connect with it. Can you guess its name?"

"Umm…a stubbly bearded."

"No, my dear dragon, guess a little harder."

She thought hard about what her teachers taught her about human anatomy. "A fully erect dick?" she posited.

"No, no, no, my dear dragon. Females you see in our species do not have such bodily objects and so if it was dependent upon such an organ, then it would generate sexism which even the feminist movement would be unable to end. It is the wand my dear dragon, the wand, which connects the wizard to the life force."

Rain began to poor heavily down as the wizard unveiled the secrets of his fellows and the foundation of the super natural powers of his people, or at least those secrets based upon traditional magic, for the wild magic of the dragons and beasts of the world are a different thing altogether, far more instinctual and far less learned. Yet human magic could be studied and intellectually understood so the wizard began instructing the dragon on the mechanisms by which it worked. He then came to the limitations of magic, in which the boy of prophecy came to view.

"There are five main foundations of magic. Within the archaic form of wizardry, we have the first couple of closely related foundations, **emotiavartos** (emotive studies) and **egonounos** (linguistic studies). Then we progress to the more middle mire of magic where morality is on a much darker terrain, and these are governed by the foundations of **egomtranfornos** (transformative studies) and **egosphilos** (knowledge studies).

"Lastly, we have a most demonically associated magic, **egomortalarfos** (mortality studies). It is commonly believed that only fallen angels and those eternally damned do practice this, and that it is outlawed in the heavenly realms, but I see it as a necessary part of all magic for death and life are aspects that affect us all on a very deep level, and impact everything we do and the way we see the world.

"Beginning with the lighter forms of magic, we have emotive and linguistic aspects of the art. These are considered to belong to the 'light-band' of magic, for they are in character young and without any perceivable sense of ill will. At least the magic seems so, and they are commonly mastered by wizards who have large hearts and a great desire to make a positive improvement upon the world, not for selfish reasons but for true altruism.

"Emotiavartos includes studying all aspects of emotion. Principally how to create, control and manipulate it using primarily potions but also some enchantments. This is considered the lightest of the arts, since emotive studies encourages empathy, and empathy leads to compassion. Compassion shall always lead to a purity within the heart and soul.

"Secondly, there is linguistic studies, which is my speciality. It has some darker connotations due to the application being sometimes for Satan inspired rituals and definitely that is something I do join in with enthusiasm, but it is also a branch that leads to light and enlightenment associated with the counter-ego of the prince of darkness, known as lucifer. Thus it unites common beliefs concerning the prince, and so leads to contentment and inner peace.

"Within it is included runic magic, ancient languages such as Hebrew, the grammar of magic and magical communications. Hence why I am so adept at chatting to dragons and other magical creatures. Though this power might seem for the translator only, having a basis of the underlying grammar of magic gives one a lot of power over more wordy spells and means a wizard is gifted with a large array of moderately powerful attacks and defence spells.

"Though by the nature of this magic, only spoken word can be used and silent spells as well as potions in this field are not possible, it is very useful when combatting anything but a war-mage wizard.

"With regards to transformative studies, again potions cannot be used to perform such enchantments but both silent and spoken spells can. Transformation varies from transforming one's self, and inanimate objects though it is said that one cannot easily transform one living life form into another living form. Though the reasons for this are unclear to me for it is a very complex bit of theory that I am not privy to, being not a transformative master.

"But as well as the basics and deeper insights into the nature of magic that comes from attaining such mastery, there is a more obscure branch of magic known as energy transfer, which can also be harnessed by the wizard. Energy transfer allows one to move energy from one place to another and more importantly transform it from one type of energy to another. Thus, though no known spell can create light, an expert on transformative studies could use energy transfer to utilise their internal body heat and turn it into electromagnetic energy.

"Knowledge studies concerns telling the future and reading the past, and is a fine balance between studying the mathematics and geometry of spacetime, and gazing longingly into crystal balls. It grants the user little magic in the way of combat, and is not what you wish for if you are going for lightning flashes, blazing solar flares or other dramatic displays of power. It is not surprising therefore that Gruggor has difficulty and somewhat of a dislike for it. But even he admits that it is remarkably useful in the hands of a wizarding councillor.

"One can use this branch of magic to see into the past, far off events of the present and even the future, as well as predicting destinies and creating prophecies. It can allow you with some accuracy to determine the possible arrangements of your enemy's troops and observe their meeting sessions through temporal portals, hidden in plain sight. It can tell you enough to allow you to win a battle with just one soldier, even if the enemy has a million.

"We had long hoped that the dislike Gruggor has for knowledge magic, might mean he could be defeated if we could gather our seers together and use their magic to deduce the weak points in Gruggor's plan for global domination, and discover weak decisions currently being made on his part so that we might take advantage of them. But sadly this will not be so. For the boy of the prophecy does unfortunately have proficiency in this exact art.

"This is made clear in his prophetic fits, for this foundation of magic is slightly involuntary and sometimes one might find one's self having unexpected visions that break up dreams or come suddenly upon one while awake. One can also use this magic to reveal deeper secrets of spells and underlying magic known as base magic. Base magic is much more potent than normal magic but is thought to be similar in many ways to the wild magic dragons carry.

"Sometimes dragonic magic is thus colloquially referred to as base magic, and this may not be acceptable to most scholars, but I think the power dragons carry might well be exactly the underlying magic wizarding scholars speak of. This is thus why your dragonic elders train so hard to become experts in this, and why an elder's fire is in fact impossible to fend off using wizarding spells.

"Lastly, there is mortality magic. This is the quickest route to the darker sides and many a mighty wizard including our enemy Gruggor is proficient with this area of study. Mortality magic covers death magic, life magic, birth magic and most interesting of all resurrection magic. Resurrection magic is seen by many as a despicable corruption of magic and most that openly practise it are either only accepted due to the influence of Gruggor in the magical world or are shunned out of civilised society."

"You mean, the barbarians practise resurrection magic!" cried Amanda in horror. Dragons heavily despised such things given that the naturalness of death was a major part of their teachings and something even the young were encouraged to accept. Playing around with death was a sickening to the natural order of things.

The wizard laughed. "No, no, no, my dear. Not every uncivilised creature or man or dragon for that matter is a dark enchanter, I just mean that those wizards that are, well they are usually shunned or worse become part of our enemy's army."

"Oh, cool, go on," said Amanda feeling a little embarrassed.

"The boy of the prophecy is special. The Arch-demon is convinced this is because he is Christ. He may or may not be, but this is not what worries me. I'm greatly concerned that he might actually be the great conjurer. Assuming this to be true, he can master all forms of magic with total control. Every other official wizard, well strictly every other magic user when they come of age, can only master one of the five foundations of magic, as any magic from any of the other foundations would lead to an internal battle.

"It would be so severe it might tear the universe apart and most certainly would spell the end of the wizard in question. There are those who refuse to choose a certain practice and leave the order, they are known as druids, and they can wheel all forms of magic just as adolescent students can, but they are a master in none. A jack in all trades you might say. They tend to be shunned from normal society and live in isolated bands in the wilderness and wild places of the world.

"Yet the capacity of the boy to master all foundations, makes him the most versatile, most magically capable being ever, some would even say he's more of a god than a human once his full potential is unwrapped. With him on our side we might be able to take out Gruggor, without him we are doomed and if he joined Gruggor and seeks total power over the world then we are all worse than dead. In the legends of my people this boy is called the 'Great Conjurer' and we have been waiting for him for a very, very long time.

"However, he can only harness this ability once he has taken part in the unificanous ritual, to release his power, and for that Gruggor needs a scroll hidden here in the caves of the mountain dragons. The last of scrolls. The others were taken by a traitorous dragon some thousand years ago though the council here likes to keep this all very hushed up, it makes human traitors look far more the enemy and your people all the more righteous, if the truth is not known.

"Gruggor may not suspect the full power of his new pupil yet, but it won't be long before he finds out."

"I must warn my friends!" shouted Amanda. She was about to fly off till she felt the small human's hand upon her wing, and stayed ground locked as he said, "If you share this tale, your life shall be in jeopardy, for know that there are those who shall defend hidden secrets with their life in the name of retaining your people's honour."

Amanda was so shocked she didn't move, she had never imagined that a dragon might harm another. But then she had never known anything of truth, and she was beginning to think that she would much rather just lie in bed and pretend reality was a bad dream. Yet for the survival of her people, she had to listen, she had to learn and she had to become wiser, though wisdom was a heavy burden to bear.

When it became clear that Amanda was not going to take flight, the human continued though now in an even more solemn and depressing tone than before.

"And ah…the lost god everyone keeps mentioning?" asked Amanda hesitantly.

"That's just superstition of the non-magical folk of the Northern realms' said the wizard. It comes from a fairy-tale were the non-magical questioning mind, tries to explain why some creatures have certain kinds of magic. There is no lost god, no found god and no god at all, and I unlike Gruggor do not insist upon invoking non-existent entities when conducting a grand spell, and mine work fine.

"Angels, my dear, are different, for they are just magic beings whose bodies exist entirely in the magical dimension, and have no form in our worlds, and yet save in this are very much like us. You know you shouldn't believe everything you hear my young dragon, particularly if it involves being fearful of a god."

"But didn't you say the great conjurer could be like a god?" asked Amanda.

"Like a god but not a god. It is not possible to become a god through magic though many claim it, for even magic has its boundaries and a god, by definition, must have none."

"Then there are no gods," agreed Amanda resting her head on the human's lap. She was a firm believer in the perspective that said everyone had a boundary.

The human stroked her ears. She made a soft hum of appreciation.

"And if we cannot get the boy to our safe haven?" asked Amanda.

"Then there is no hope," said the wizard softly.

"Unless, well, unless we break our connection to magic and permanently seal the door between us and the angelic guardians who watch over us from the passage way. But that my friend is a worse fate than death, for who are we without magic?"

Amanda didn't answer, the thought of existing without magic was as horrifying to her as it would be to imagine existing without a soul, existing without a self. She closed her eyes and went to sleep.

Gods would just make life complicated, thought the wizard. Everybody needs limits, gods would be so overkill.

The wizard looked up into the midday sun and went to sleep. When he awoke, he was back in his semi-circular prison and Amanda was nowhere to be seen. Thus began the first tutorship of magic between wizard and dragon. And an unexpected friendship bloomed, whilst the dark storm that set it in motion covered the sky. Back in the academy, Gallat, under the teachings of Gruggor, learned many a forbidden thing.

Part 3

Chapter 26
The Closed Contour of Our Tale

Dear reader, I would like to break away from the discussion of my world's events and passage through time to thank you all for staying with me thus far, and pat yourself heartily on the back for continuing with this tragic tale. For it is as hard to write about the horrors of reality, as it is to read of them.

Yet having been faced with lots of wolf jargon, weird and terribly performed sexy-ish romance and a gallon full of trivial information about magical cases of madness, you shall no doubt be wondering why so long a tale. Specifically you may ask, why, when all that has really come to pass is everyone is unable to do anything but dance in the weird moves of politics, religion and magic which have so sadly defined our world ever after Michael's bit of Angelic magic.

Well, I think it is a marvel that the cotenant remains void of enemy raids, given the insanity of the people governing it, and it must be commented that at least everything is pretty much, just about, in tacked and functioning. Mind you, this is exactly how mine furry self doth feel about my life most of the time, things are just about holding together, and I'm at the helm completely overwhelmed and struggling to know reason from balminess. But that's a story left for soap operas and other depressing media which is not conducive to the factual work of a generalist, who seeks only the truth of the world and does not dwell upon the emotional state of things for too long (for the sake of one's sanity).

One might suppose, there has been little global change or change that the shadow would consider as significant thus far, after the battle of Ichor.

Yet a tale is not worth a claw if it does not have at its centre, the self-centredness and obsessive obliviousness of love. For love takes account not of grand trajectories, not of kings being imprisoned or handing over their children to barbarian women, nor to the plight of imprisoned humans being held as war criminals. It takes notice of only itself.

And the story of love has flowered tremendously within the heart of our dear Sir Hamfield. For a story is, in my humble furry opinion, not about simply getting from one point A, to another point B, but about the shape and form of the journey that one takes to traverse the great gap. In short, it's about the transformation along the path, and the nature of the path itself.

For the more mathematically inclined, one might say that it is not about the result of the integral around the closed contour itself, for this would make story writing nothing but a piece of computation, but about the nature of the parameterised curve that leads to the closed contour. Or for the more seafaring types, it is not about how you get from one island to another, but the nature of the sea that journey lays upon.

We must mark our hearts upon this, the quest of Sir Hamfield to recover his beloved prince Rupert from the hands of a Barbarian woman. It was and will always be totally the kind of obsessed love story that makes a traditional fantasy a classical version of the great tragedies of old. All other plots and narratives are but subsidiary to this, the quest for love.

Sir Hamfield could only begin to see this, for the fact that every known collective of people were preparing to attack and take control of his beloved homeland was as nothing in his mind to the importance of the mission before him, of all the balminess in this tale, this is probably the worst.

But upon injuring the elements for a while, the heart does indeed question things. By the time Sir Hamfield realised his more merciful demotion in rank within the eyes of the public, he was soaking wet and hurriedly moving into a large ramshackle bar with benches of oak lined in front of dusty shelves where a man was pouring an old gentleman's Stergers beer. He was called 'the owner'. No one knew his true name, or even his species, given that his parentage was a mystery.

The owner seemed slightly elfish, so most guest he must have elves in his close relations but there was the complexity that he was born with only four fingers, and elves always have five digits. He was wearing a brown jacket, that wrapped around his large belly. He was pretty tall, but so was Sir Hamfield, so this didn't affect their chats. Mind you his son, named simply 'the owner's son' or when people were feeling sympathetic to him, 'Bob', was dressed in a dirty shirt and shorts.

He was the owner's adopted son, given that the owner had always wanted a son but could never find a lady who would want to have a son with him. The owner's son, whom I shall call bob, was one of those which were descended from the line of the original people of the Barking Bishops. The athletic build of the people had clearly descended down into him, and he spent most of his days moving heavy crates and barrels in and out of the bar. He was the perfect person, to become an unlikely hero and go gallivanting with the knight on the perilous mission to find prince Rupert and free him from the Barbarians.

However, there was one big complication, his girlfriend, whom I shall name Jacklin, was four weeks pregnant. Bob often dreamed of going on adventures, but he loved his girlfriend more and wanted to be there for the birth of their child.

The barn in which the bar was situated, smelled like mud, and dusty enough to be classed as unhygienic even without the flies that were buzzing around. It was very down to earth, rugged and exactly what a forlorn knight of Mados was looking for.

Hamfield ate the bread that had been served with his iron brew and went up to the bar to have a chat with the owner about getting a room for the night. And he made doubly sure to make clear he was staying here for the bar and normal hospitality, not to interact with the women who pretended to be interested in his looks but actually just wanted his cash.

Whilst he was there, he ordered a large glass of purple pushinger beer. It smelled like sour grapes. It tasted like rotten strawberries. It looked like boiled cabbage. But just as Sir Hamfield was getting into the room price bargaining traditional in the outer reaches of Mados, bob dropped a dozen plates and the owner rushed over to swear and sweep.

By this time Hamfield had grown a beard since it was a month since he had been tracking the prince, and beard cutters as they were known in Mados, are not very common things to be found in the wild. Often Hamfield would chance upon a coin and use it for needed nourishment, since he was spending most of his money on accommodation. Being a knight up till now, no landlord would allow him to degrade himself by buying any but the best and most expensive room on arrival. Every bar owner in Mados knew how wealthy the knights were.

However, it appeared in this far off place, near to the borders of the southern edge of Mados, knights were not nearly as respected as they were further north. When the owner returned, he offered the knight a cheap room which judging by the reviews on the crumpled review book, was nice and rigid with the windows half smashed and the floorboards so squeaky, one could not get a good night's sleep upon the floor. There was also a bed, but in the tradition of the borders of

Mados, near to the barbarian realms, men were looked down upon for relaying on soft fabric to ease their strong backs. They believed in the philosophy of physical pain building the spirit.

It was about two more days ride to the border, and if he had a good night sleep, Hamfield, going under the pretend name of Druesberry, felt certain that he could get there in good time and finally start interrogating some of the barbarians who lived on the other side of that border.

Hamfield ordered another drink, then another, till he felt jolly enough to sing for no apparent reason. He burst out with the classic 'Oh ye of little tea dippers'. The aged crowd joined in, making a lovely discordant tune. Flagons and wooden mugs banged upon the benches as he rose up and danced upon the bench tops. Litres of beer and wine were knocked aside by his dancing feet, and yet more alcohol was ordered to speed the night along. The owner hurried, weaving in and out of the singing crowd, to clean up the spillages before reappearing like magic before the jolly customers to fill another flagon.

Everyone clapped each other on the back and began to wobble in and out of balance. Soon people were dropping on top of one another. The owner was doing a game of avoiding the raining customers. All shirts were wet and soggy, and they all shared their wretchedness with their fellows.

Meanwhile, the king was hungrily chomping away at some mouldy and tough bread. It was dry white carbohydrates, and there was a mug of basil soup next to it which the guards had seemingly used as a toilet considering the smell emanating from it. It was damp in his cellar and the skeleton lying upon the bench adjacent to him didn't lift his spirits.

As for Gruggor, he felt very content, he was instructing Gallat in the first axioms of mortality magic. You may well wonder why he was teaching him such things given that he didn't have access to the mountain dragon spells, and thus the boy could not be the man to free Lucifer from his confines, as of yet. Well Gruggor still wanted to give the impression of caring for the boy whilst he was still a student and had not proclaimed demonic allegiance or bounded his power to his specialty in a ceremony known as 'the knighting of the conjurer's mastery'.

Plus, even though the boy could barely do any of what was being taught yet, for a lot of it required mastery, the headmaster thought he might as well give the boy a heads up and a lot of homework, so he knew all his stuff once the time came upon him to utilise it. Gallat was doing extremely well, in the course of their first few lessons, he had become well acquainted with four of the five fundamental laws of mortality magic.

These four were that of strawberry infusion, the rights of the dead, the rights of the living dead, and the rights of the dying. The rights were of the utmost importance as they provided the circuit upon which all mortality magic could flow, and a misunderstanding could lead to the circuit overloading or producing an undesirable effect. 'Death burnout' was the common use for the magical equivalent of mortality's magic metaphysical circuit going up in flames, and this often resulted in short bursts of death magic being fired sporadically from the magician, like the way an on and off alternating current would generate electromagnetic waves.

Bursts of death magic were well, the most lethal weapon ever and no one had ever thought of a way to stop it, as there is no metaphysical equivalent to put out the overloading mortality magic. Controlled death burn out would therefore be an unbeatable weapon, and it was this that was Gruggor's current research topic. As for strawberry infusion, well it was well known that strawberry milkshakes helped fuel a mortality magician's life source.

Over in the Barbarian south, the soon to be wife of Prince Rupert was sowing her dress which had been passed down from mother to daughter for generations. It was assumed that at some point it had been stolen from a bridal shop, but looking at its dirty silk fabric and holes, it would not be something that could be redeemed or handed back. The barbarians thought the tattered nature of the dress allowed for their own self to be more visible and therefore lead to a more honest ceremony, where the guy really knew what he was getting himself into.

Besides, individuals before 'the knighting of the conjurer's mastery' are more flexible, less strong willed and attached to their principal magic, thus easier to teach in many ways. Yet Gruggor never forgot who he was teaching, or what the great conjurer in time could do.

Such was the content at this point in time. Therefore, one can say humanity was a very mixed affair, but on the verge of being melted into ice cream. The Barbarians, wizards and wolves were just deciding the fine details of what chocolate flakes to sprinkle upon it. The Ontockians working out how to splatter it when it first showed signs of dripping off the cone.

While we are at this, ice cream in the liquifying stage, we might as well give the continent a name. No one in Mados or Ontock or the wolven or barbarian kingdoms had ever developed a name for it, given that it was all that there was, at least as far as anyone knew. Giving it a name would be like calling our universe, the universe of 'George' just so we can distinguish it from other possibly non-existent universes. It was silly.

When has any Buddhist mentioned becoming in unison with the cosmic George? But given the fact that we now know that the landmass was only a part of all that was in the world, we could name it without being thought of as silly. Thus, the continent shall be named henceforth, x. X can be anything you like, as this is the wonder of algebra, so metaphysically I have assigned all possible names to the continent, meaning no one can complain, hopefully.

Well fine, I guess being a writer I should be more creative, I shall call this continent, Sharlger, which in the language of my people means 'the furry land' or 'the land of the wolf'. Given that it has always belonged to the wolves and humans are just visitors which have stuck up temporary residence.

Chapter 27
Let Us Pray for Bob

Please, most warmly welcomed reader, be patient with me here, for my furry self, being generally much more along the gay end of the LGBT+ wolf spectrum, finds it is hard to picture the flares of anger and passion that must pass between two straight lovers when one is found to be cheating.

Bob stormed into the musty room as soon as all the guests were asleep and in the lounge, spilled drinks and bottles of beer had been sorted. He thought it was odd that the light was off given his girlfriend didn't usually sleep early and her active baby had been making sleep even worse. As Bob went upstairs and approached the heavy wooden door, he could hear muffled groaning and sighs. He thought for a moment she might be preparing for some fun tonight, given that getting into the more sexual areas of romance had been harder and she was less easily turned on since that fateful day when the pregnancy test gave a clear answer.

That is to say one of the Mados Mordrė doctors had been visiting to deal with some affairs of the king, and had been about to bang her for some fun and an illegitimate heir to stir up some intrigue in the neighbourhood, before he felt the living life force of another inside of her and cried for his misfortune, sobbing, "You have a baby already!"

Upon this faithful night though, things were different as a visitor hadn't just gone suddenly into a mode of sexual pleasure, it was clear that bob's girlfriend and this other man clearly loved each other. The way he was caressing her (insert the description of whatever heterosexuals get up to here).

She was gazing into his eyes…oh man, I suck at this. Anyway, they did love each other, I know I'm pretty crap at explaining this, but you've got to take my word here.

Bob stormed over, the man who was making out with a girl turned just in time, then he was forcefully pushed off the bed and banged his head against the side of a cabinet on his way down. Now almost concussed, he said, "What the hell are you doing, man!"

To this Bob said irritatingly, "I am Bob! And you better leave this lady alone, she and I have been in a relationship for a long time, and I'm way better in and out of bed then you could dream of. I'm a sex god!"

The women then cried, "Darling, Jorge, please get this insanely—"

"Insanely sexy?" asked Bob who had found time to wink as he blocked a second punch from Jorge and managed to kick him hard in the groin.

Jorge rolled on top of Bob to begin a punching rave and was just about to proclaim how manly a man must be to be called Jorge, and how unfortunate a fate a romantic guy named bob must have, when there were heels coming up the stairs.

Bob knocked Jorge out before his gang of girls could take Bob away from his beloved. He then cried, "Oh my darling, I shall not let anyone take thine from me." Then he heard the girl speak once more, but this time it was a different sound all together, she shimmered and an apricot dropped from the girl's head dress.

Bob stared in shock, he turned to his side and looked up and couldn't believe what he saw. There at the door was his real girlfriend who had come surely to investigate why her boyfriend was confessing his love to someone else, and thus abandoning both her and her baby.

Bob let the apricot women's waste go and rose weak kneed to confront his fuming girlfriend who was so over the top with rage she might as well of become a dragon.

"Darling…I uh…I…"

"Felt like running away from your responsibilities as a future husband and father?"

"No, I would love to be a father; I mean…"

"Well, you never wanted to be a father before, you were always going on about how poor you would be at looking after the child, how you hated the baby's wailing and how—"

"But my darling, I do want to be a father, ever since we've found out you were pregnant the desire has been growing on me. Yes, I still have reservations but I love you and want what's best for you and our family's future."

Bob went over to his girlfriend and touched her belly. "You see, my darling, there is the seed of our future growing. I would not throw it aside." He attempted to hug his girlfriend, though she tried valiantly to wrestle him off.

The guy who had been making out with the apricot lady in the form of bob's girlfriend, just looked very confused before walking up to this shape shifter and despite the recent events, start making out with her. The apricot lady appreciated this, and returned with enthusiasm.

Bob's girlfriend shoved Bob's hand off of her body and spat in his general direction. "I thought you were amazing, I thought you were my most awesome of awesomest friends, I thought you could be my beloved but you through that away to have sex with a, with a, whore. I mean I saw you catch some of the prostitutes' eyes as they drank all their drinks and pulled up their tights but I thought you would be faithful, I though, I thought…"

Bob half sobbed, "But my lady, I don't know what, I can't understand what's—"

Bob's girlfriend then just threw into the mix as if the emotional tension in the room wasn't sufficient enough to cause a volcanic eruption, "That's why I went and had a baby with another dude. I knew you didn't want to be faithful with me, and all those excuses about not wanting a baby. I thought if I got pregnant, then you, thinking you were the father, might feel more obliged to pay me attention and take our relationship more seriously!"

Tears spilled from her eyes. She knelt down and wept.

Bob tried to get to her but the apricot women got between them and knelt down beside Bob's girlfriend. Mind you, this might be for the best given Bob was a little angry and might have just shouted at his beloved, or just simply told her he understood. He didn't know what to do. He didn't know how to feel. She was carrying someone else's baby. She had slept with another dude. She thought him inadequate. Mind you he was beginning to think himself inadequate by this point.

Meanwhile, Triffon said to Bob's girlfriend, "My dear female. You are truly a wonderful specimen of your species, like the rising flowers of spring. But cry not, for your boyfriend has only fallen for the most fetching whore in the land."

She kind of roared and screamed with an emotion and pain beyond human description, took off her heels and threw them at bob. His nose was broken in two places and with that bob's girlfriend turned away and thumped down the stairs, never to be heard of in the bar again. It is said that one day she became so distraught she drowned herself in a pond, but let's not focus upon that. Did I not worn you there would be many killings at the start of this heart-breaking history?

The apricot woman called into the dark cottage, "Sir Hamfield. I have found your companion and set him free from his bondage and responsibilities. He may now be easier to hire upon this adventure of yours. And remember to take these supplies, it might help you." She threw him a bag of ropes and apricots which had previously been concealed under the bed and which she must have brought with her.

Hamfield doubled over in shock, his metal armour clinking and his eyes full of sleep powder, as the expression goes.

"Triffon, is that you? What are you doing here?"

"I have been keeping an eye on you, my young lad, I know you needed a sidekick and this boy seemed the right balance of wackiness and ale-knowledge for this mission."

Bob was hardly comprehending what all this was about but was about to protest that he had a distraught girl friend to see to and that this Triffon was one evil woman when shadows came up the wall, and the sounds of men speaking of sinister things could be heard.

Bob's last memory of this sequence of events was hearing Triffon say 'Gruggor's men', whoever they were, and then like magic the room was gone, Triffon was nowhere to be seen and Bob and Sir Hamfield were alone in a place with rolling hills almost in the middle of nowhere.

Then Sir Hamfield just said, "So, on we go with our perilous adventure," and he trudged on, feeling he didn't need to explain to any man who was capable of attracting the attention of Triffon, the importance of following her will and joining a knight on a heroic quest.

Bob just stood there before running after Sir Hamfield and crying out for all the birds and badgers to hear, "What the hell have you done and where is my girlfriend!"

As for the man who was making out with Triffon only moments ago, well, he wasn't so lucky since Triffon had deemed his bed skills were not close enough to Jasper's to warrant being saved.

The black-robed band of Gruggor's men surrounded him and pointed their thin wands at various points of his body. He felt very self-conscious given that he was wearing nothing but underwear and had been caught red handed making out with "the hottest prostitute in town."

A tall man stepped forward, lifted his hood and asked, "Has my dear wife been helping our valiant knight. Well, I'll need to bring you in for questioning, we can't have our knights quest fulfilled now, can we?"

The man was chained up and carried away, supposedly tortured, but as he gave no useful information, records of his torture were never made. Thus as to his fate, well let's just hope it was better than the eventual fate of Bob's girlfriend.

Bob did not like carrying suitcases and pouring flagons but was content with the availability of free beers and living in the same accommodation as his girlfriend.

Bob did not like the practicality of the adventure he was forced to go on. Of course he could just completely leave the knight to his mission and begin wandering in some random direction, but given that Bob had no idea where he was and new of the hostile barbarians and wolves which may be lurking behind one of the hills, he really had no choice but to follow his companion. His companion seemed so much more confident in the wilderness and more to the point, had a sword.

Hurriedly he caught up with the knight who had travelled on so fast, it was hard to believe he had not accessed a wormhole when Bob had bent down to remove a stone that had managed to find its way into his shoe.

"So you ah, you know this place?" asked Bob. His blond hair dancing in the air, but his feet trudging so forcibly up and down that his waving hair seemed to be as if attached to another person. Then sweat began to form, and he felt its cool sting as he hurriedly went up and down the hills that seemed to pass before them in every direction. In a daze bob eventually made it to a river which seemed to cut down between the sides of the hills.

Bob felt a lot happier now he was in the middle of a valley and thus could at least identify to some degree where he was, since there was now thankfully a clearly defined middle road as opposed to a seemingly endless lattice of high hills and deep groves. By this time Bob had completely forgotten about the question but Sir Hamfield answered with a very direct response "I have no idea, I'm pretty sure we are totally lost, we are both going to die most likely, but good to meet you."

Now reader, you may well think that here the romantic confusion and interplay was too complicated and likened to a farce. Well, it was quiet a surprising turn out of events for me to when I had first sniffed out the whole

271

story, but then I also did a bit of digging on other promiscuous activities of Triffon and found out that a similar set of unfortunate events happened to another couple, but in this instance the couple was lesbian and quiet forgetting the need of a man in the reproduction process, and so each member was still shocked to find that their partner's baby was not theirs.

Yes, this was in the wild south where sex education is completely non-existent, but even for me, who puts ink to paper to record some very odd truths, this story was a little too weird to tell. So I shall save that treat, for another time, and perhaps another tale.

Though what is relevant to this tale, which Triffon had no time to gloat upon as she ran away from assassins, is to say that Triffon's 'help', of course, wasn't real help given she had cunningly handed over cursed possessions, cursed to bring bad luck which on this kind of adventure meant cursed to attract the desire of Barbarians.

No one really thought to check given that Hamfield had total faith in Triffon, but she had played her cards well, and was not going to allow Hamfield to succeed at bringing back Prince Rupert, if there's anything she could do about it!

Chapter 28
Dissolution of life

Gallatarnin found the month since he and Gruggor had talked in the hospital wing like scaling an unseen mountain. It wasn't that he found the magic itself difficult, though it was taxing. It wasn't even the theory that was beyond him, though he stayed up many a night bashing the stacks of contemporary books against the wall. The nemesis in the closet, as it were, was the moral challenge and dangerously immoral drive associated with a lot of the advanced magic he was being exposed to. Mortality magic in particular.

Particularly since Gruggor went into that weird-like state, where he claimed to be the dragon Jorge and wanted Gallat to end his torment. Apparently, Gallat's ability to snap the headmaster out of this by getting him to drink a bottle of whisky, and then remain unharmed when the liquor went into flames as Gruggor breathed fire, meant he was the great conjurer or something. Whatever that meant! Still, Gruggor was so excited and rewarded Gallat for being such a 'prodigious' wizard by giving him a whole stack of booklets on ancient magical ceremonies to read.

Indeed, all forms of magical law taught within the confines of the academy, felt slightly twisted, like they were working with a strand of a sickly magic which just didn't want to cooperate. Sometimes it felt like it was coiling away as if it was its greatest desire to hide, and recover from some unseen injury. As if someone was leading it down a crevice, one where even magic usually never walked. Yet Gallatarnin being knew to magic had nothing to compare this with so just guessed this was how all magic worked. Yet this couldn't be further from the truth.

At least within the academy, magic seemed to particularly excise this right to coil away, when it came to dealing with life and death. Only a real desire for the magic application was strong enough to swerve the magic along the desired course.

In truth, the origins of this sickness were more associated with the meddling of the magic, which Astaroth long ago had carried out upon orders from the prince of darkness. He constructed an abstract magical landscape, and therein were as chords and cliffs, so magic's natural flow became redirected to this set path, and upon the magical tied did many a wizard's magic flow, which was led through with all magic to the throne of the morning star and then back out into the academy walls and was released to resume its usual path from there, before it was caught in the current once more.

This magical landscape has been there since the first strings in the shadow realm of nature, for Lucifer's order was given when Gruggor had taken over as headmaster and Lucifer had placed thereby the horned god at the centre of power in the land. This isn't to say magic had to follow this landscape-imposed flow, but it just meant there was now a bias towards doing so, never before or since has there been any such thing. For magic was made to be free, unyielding and encourage creation to take its own path (except for when it got together with destiny and decided to do all it could to make widows, prince's and cursed people have the most challenging life imaginable).

Most wizards remained unaware of such bias, again having not seen enough magic outside of the halls to really compare things to. Yes, there was the odd one or two wizards who came to take positions from the outside, but they very quickly succumbed to the madness that slowly took over all who dwelt with the walls. Besides the shadow was forever a sneaky thing, always sort of there but sort of not, for the dragon scrolls had not yet been returned entirely to the cave to free the prince of darkness from his imprisonment in the realm of hell.

This luckily kept him from wreaking havoc upon the physical plain of existence, but it also made him far more elusive. His taint is hard to find lest you bathe the entire academy in light. No one was about to start doing that or summoning holy angels to do a little moral cleaning given Gruggor would crush them down before they began.

Everything there was bent with bias, to the will of Lucifer. Some call this hypnosis, others call this forced will and others simply the folly of things to fall before a fallen's feet. Yet there are those, and among them many fury companions who would argue that this 'twisting of the will' is a necessary bi-product of the sheer awesomeness and power that radiates so profoundly from the prince of darkness. If one is trapped in a trance, then it is a trance of glory which one is held captive in.

Much like many Christians might say it is impossible to leave god's kingdom after entering it, due the sheer awesomeness of God and the wondrous love that he bestows upon his people, so it was with those who followed Lucifer and beheld his wonderous presence. Personally I am torn. For I do not like bias but being like a leaf in comparison to the great powers within this world, it is hard for me to say what is true. And all practitioners of the academy were warned of the almost irresistible pull of the demonic world, once they had stepped over the spiritual barrier and accepting this allowed them to begin their work in their humble lives.

Equally, his magnificence could simply be an illusion which Lucifer does present unto the beholden. Yet one thing all knew who forsook in the baptism of fire, it was strong.

Lucifer had every wizard within the walls linking right up with the spirit of himself, to practise the bent magic was to ally the soul with this dark power. This was a dangerous thing to do, and had many dark consequences, but even here magic was tentative to play life and death.

Gruggor strode around his office with the cabinet nearby and his desk still scratched up by his nails. The sofa was still not boogy-trapped and Gallat was treated as a guest, something few ever were. "Sit," said Gruggor, waving his hand gently in the general direction of the room comforts.

The walls were lined with paintings like before, but unlike paintings of cats and previous headmasters which had adorned it for so many years, now there were paintings of various spells. They were moving like cartoons, for though the figures within them were not alive, the pixels of paint were enchanted to move in accordance with the real life like thing they were depicting. It was a clever branch of transformative magic, which Gruggor being a mortalist was not very proficient at, but Miss Toffton had spent a couple of weeks doing for him.

Behind the window, the stars moved and the rain fell heavily.

The candles were lit to dispel the twilight darkness in the room, but an eerie glow made it even more mystical. The chiming of the windmills outside the window added to this, and the hissing of the snake as it glided around only made the hamsters in the cage a little on edge so they ran a little faster in their wheels. Feeling like they were going at fast as the wind, yet always remaining exactly where they began.

Gruggor was wearing a black cloak with a pointy hood and wore black pointy shoes.

Gallat was wearing a grey cloak but around his head was a gold headband showing his rank as head boy.

"You have shown yourself suitable to your new position as prefect of the house of the bull, my boy."

"Thank you, my father," said Gallat, bowing a little in respect. His prefect badge clearly twinkling under the candle light. It was odd having his dad also being the head of the academy, and his main teacher, but it was the way of things and meant he had complete access to the 'sinistrartum' section of the wizarding library, which contained in depth everything about resurrection magic and immortality studies, something only master wizards were usually allowed to view. Gallat sat down on the couch and drank some of the oak tea which had been on the coffee table top.

"Magic has a limit, my boy. What is that limit?"

"Ahhh…the number of magical rubies in the wand?"

"Nay, nay, my boy. For that is simply the strength of one's connection to the magic. Not the limiting strength of the magic itself. The limit is one's imagination. For each conjurer as you well know, by now, can only be proficient at one of the four foundations of magic, and so though one's natural magical ability and the strength of one's connection to it does come into play, what is far more of a limiting factor is how creative you can be with the magic you have.

"Obviously, there are some things that are specific to one foundation, for example resurrection is specific to mortality, but there are many actions and concepts that overlap. Thus the more creative you are, the more able you are to do things which at first seem outside of your special discipline. While you are a student this shall affect you less for your magic is not bound per say to just one discipline but for most students who go on to attach their soul to just one branch later on, this becomes of the utmost importance. And your knighting ceremony, my boy, is not that long away."

"So ummm, I need to start painting and going to art class to get my imagination all fired up once more?"

"Nay, my boy, nay. It is just worth considering as we begin going down the deeper parts of magic, and I shall expect you to apply them in my class with ingenuity and creativity. But first I want to teach you something of the utmost importance. What it is to kill."

Gallat's face went pale. He had been stretching himself to do darker and darker things and it had begun to put a strain upon his golden heart, but killing, this was not what he had come to the Academy to learn.

"With all due respect, father, I wish you a good night." And with that he got up and was just pushing the door open when Gruggor flicked his wand and it slammed shut.

He tucked his wand away and said to his new student, "I shall not teach thee to kill people, I am only suggesting that you learn the foundations of what it is to kill, even if just a flower, so you might understand what it is to live better."

Gallat hesitated for a moment looking between the sofa and the door, but then thought to himself that he had seen plants die before, why he had even slaughtered farm animals for food before. What did a flower matter? And his father had shown him so much love and compassion, surely he meant well.

So he gradually sat down. Gruggor smiled and then from his robes, Gruggor pulled out a bright lily and placed it in a jar of cold water which was upon his desk. He looked like a scientist at this currently very alive organism, a miracle of God, and he handed it over to Gallat to hold and view up-close.

"See the life, my dear boy. Life comes in three forms, astral life, biological life and finally the essence of life, magic. The details are not important to us, for they are all valid states of 'being alive' and all exist together within us. For the purposes of complete killing the distinction is irrelevant, for to murder in a wizarding sense is to do more than kill the physical, it's to kill all three.

"To kill biology is simple, for one can just extract water or leach away all its nutrients. To kill the astral self is a little harder, but this can be done with sufficient will power and jujitsu, or whatever martial art form the youth are into these days. But to kill the magic in someone, which is very much them and interconnected with the magic that flows through the universe and gives it life, that is where true wizardry must come in.

"One cannot make it vanish, for the conservation of magical energy is as fundamental as the conservation of physical energy. But one can strip it of all that makes it a part of the individual and release it into the universe as pure magic, with only the will and self of the cosmic magic around us. Therefore everything about it that made it part of that individual is gone, it is much like stripping away the colours from a canvas in order to leave it completely blank. The canvas is still there, but as to what it once was showing, there is no clue."

"So, to kill is primarily a task of removing someone's identity?"

"Yes," responded Gruggor as if he was being asked why birds fly. He didn't seem distressed about the idea of erasing someone from the cosmos. Indeed destressing Gruggor on moral dilemmas is like trying to surprise a physicist after they have accepted the reality of absurd phenomena like quantum tunnelling.

Buddhists would be horrified at the idea of killing identity, for this would be like taking a soul that had achieved Nirvana and then taking away everything that made it, it, so it just became some generic spiritual thing with nothing to identify it as part of the colourful and wonderful self it once was. Yet Gruggor, did not like Buddhist theology. He liked theology more along the lines "you go against me: you die"—nice and simple.

And Gallat had to master this philosophy if he, like a good foot soldier, was going to take over the kingdoms and crush any resistance under his feet.

"So you are going to erase the 'self' of the lily?" asked Gallat, wondering what the hell an astral self looked like.

He lifted up the glass to show Gruggor, but it was quite heavy so he slipped a bit of the water down his cloak as he tried to hold it up, and quickly returned the glass to his lap.

Watching the water drip away, Gruggor imagined draining the flower of any of its magical identity. He smiled, feeling incredibly at peace with the dying world.

Then he turned to his student and said, "No. I shall not. You shall kill the lily."

Gallat felt so overwhelmed at this. He wasn't proficient in mortality, and this was the first time outside of knowledge studies where he was actually asked to perform some spell, and not just write a long boring essay upon the theory behind it, or make some silly imitation of it using the limited knowledge magic he had learned this far.

Here was a chance to prove himself to his father. But he really didn't like all this dark talk. Still his need for approval, and to exceed his humble upbringing overtook his sense of right and wrong.

He lifted his wand and said whilst observing the lily, "Father, I do not know the chant."

"Oh, pardon me, my boy" said the headmaster, who had been so wrapped up in the idea of murder, even if it was just murdering a lily, that he had completely forgotten what chant to use. Chants were vital as they were the command line, if you like, telling the internal and external magic what to do. Without it one could do the right wand movement, visualise ones will and have all the talent in the world, but nothing would actually happen.

The wand movement part of it was to etch one's initials on the magic, usually just writing in air the vowels of the magical chant in the wizardic script, followed by one's initials, so when the command line was done, the magic would know from what source to go from. The final trajectory of the magic was determined by the final swish of the wand. The magic would then move at the fastest possible speed allowed within the sphere of reality in which it was cast.

Which in the physical realm was the speed of light, in the astral form the speed of life's last breath, in the hellish realm the speed of rising anger and in the heavenly realms the speed of love. In fact in heaven it was infinite in speed and so angelic cause and effect were instantaneous. This allowed the angels to react instantaneously to events around them and was one of the reasons the first battle was so intense and cosmically awesome.

Gruggor thought for a moment, given that he wanted to make sure if Gallat misfired it wouldn't mean say the snake's death, and so thought carefully to make sure he pulled from the recesses of his memory the chant for killing floral things specifically, or more technically photosynthetic things so technically it might kill some photosynthetic bacteria nearby to and mean the office was this bit more hygienic.

"Grugg Kap," stated the wizard.

Then Gallat placed the heavy glass on the ground. Made the incantation and wand movement and was thrown into the astral plane. There was the plant but now it was ten times taller and with a much thicker stalk, and like in the tv series, the day of the triffids, began advancing upon Gallat.

For the first few seconds, he ran around the white space of the unfilled astral plane like a mad man. Then he pulled himself together, reminding himself that he was a man and men are brave in the face of floral terror.

At least men are till they are knocked head first by the plant and then it begins to wrap around them like a viper.

Hurriedly, Gallat thought about all the advice he had ever been given about astral combat. Gruggor's remark on jujitsu would not help him now the plant had tightly bound his hands and legs. But maybe he could let out his prime weapon, his singing. So he belted out, *I've got to break free* by Queen, and the plant stopped tightening and slid off.

Then it rose to its full height and staring down its victim it was about to smash Gallat unconscious till it started wailing, reaching near ultrasonic pitches. Gallat covered his ears till the volume died down enough to make the wailing humanly bearable, supposedly Gruggor was bashing it in the biological realm and this was like a mirror image of the physical events within the astral realm. Mirror images of events which occur within another sphere, are like the pull of the tide on one side of the world generating a tide upon the other, but this was a terrifying tide. Full of anguish and pain.

And since the realms were not totally separate, the plant could still feel its physical pain somewhat in this realm. Either the plant had actually been strangling him and he was in need of immediate help in the physical realm, or the sounds of *I've got to break free* had driven Gruggor to sudden action, but in either case, Gallat was glad his father was around to stick up for him.

With a renewal of fatherly love, Gallat charged the plant and did some super cool jujitsu moves till its stem broke and it fell to the ground, dead.

Immediately after this, his magic swept him up and brought him to a world he had never seen before. It was dazzling in colour, and had streams of glistening water flowing by. He was on an island surrounded by water and the coloured vapour that arose from them condensed upon the island's palm trees. A cat came by and tasted it, apparently it approved for it reached out its paw and bent the palm tree down so its fellow kittens could taste the water droplets.

Above him were young cuddly things that occasionally belched and let out a flame or two. Gallat's soul could hardly believe his eyes, but he knew that these things were dragons. He had only seen them in fairy tale books before but to see them in real life, he felt like he had discovered another knew wonderful myth come true and wanted so bad to sit and play with them. But then a figure came round the corner and it seemed old, but rather friendly, so Gallat sat down on the edge of the island with this dude and watched the world go by.

Being a wizard it is not suppressing he felt at home in the magical sphere of reality, but he hadn't expected it to be so innocent, so unlike the aura of magic which swam through the academy.

"My dear boy. I am glad you are here, though I question whether you have come for the reasons you think you have. For I am the magical self of the lily, and I saw before when you, or rather the astral you, were killing my atrial self. You did so more out of self-defence I noticed, for I know that you spent a lot of time running and not killing, and was merciful to a flower even though that mercy risked your own life.

"Thankfully, my temperament, is calmness and peace, for I am magic, not matter and do not cling to life in the same way. I know myself well, for each day I take in light and produce flowers. But you, the wizard, seem always so agitated since we met and Gruggor dropped me into the glass."

"I just want to learn how to kill and you're just a lily, why are you so serious, man?" said Gallat, a little shaky and confused. Why were they talking about peace, why did he even bothered to engage, when all he had to do was throw that old man into the river circling this island? It's not like the old man could get him back afterwards, I mean everything would be totally forgotten. Gallat didn't know how he knew this, he just did. Gallat remembered reading about something like these rivers in Greek myth, the five rivers of Hades, were one of them, named Lethe would course the individual that fell into its grasp to forget all things. Why was this man so calm?

"I don't fear oblivion, my friend. For there is no pain there. If there is nothing which is remembered then there is no pain to feel over what one has lost, for one does not remember ever having had it. But I do fear what will happen to you if you carry through with this action of 'magic' as you call it."

"But you're just a flower. I've killed many of you before, I've even killed lambs for their meat and cut chickens heads off to make chicken soup. You're just a lily, what harm can killing one lily do to me."

"You have never killed before though. Not really killed, have you!" His eyes burned with violet flame as the idea of total oblivion danced within his mind.

"Umm, yes, I'm pretty sure I have."

"No, no," chuckled the man. "You have only killed biologically, that is not real death, everything in the biological realm decays to give way to new life. It is the way of things. But to kill beyond that is dangerous. But in killing my astral self you have already put your soul's salvation upon the lines, to go further than that would tilt you beyond return like crossing the event horizon of a black hole."

"But you're a flower. For heaven's sake, why don't I just push you in right now, old man?" He was about to but something stopped him, he didn't feel right about this. Why not just let the old man go? I mean he had almost killed the flower, why take it any further, it felt disgusting to do more?

"You see, life, my boy, is a precious thing. It does not matter whether I am a plant, an animal, a wizard or an angel, all life is sacred. It comes from the one.

281

And to take it and wash all that makes it the life it once was, is to make an act of defiance against the one and purposely go against his law. For by doing this you are not just killing, you are annihilating. And though the one could restore me, he could not do so with your soul less you repent. For in doing what you have come here to do, and if you were to go through with it, then your soul would be cracked and you shall be cast out of sanctity and land flat first into the realm of the shadow and there suffer a torment of forsakenness, where no light or life shall reach you.

"And as for me, well, I'm old and ready to be reunited within the one, be it me whose being reunited or the blank canvas of magic you have come here to cause into existence. It bothers me a little."

"You sound almost in need of counselling, old man. I cannot kill you, buddy, you have suffered enough by the sounds of your dismal talk, and keeping to biological destruction feeds my agricultural spirit enough."

The man laughed and patted the boy on the shoulder. "My dear lad, it has been great chatting to you, just heed my warning." But before the man could get out of sight, Gallat grabbed his arm and held it tight, while looking like a ghost into the waters below. He seemed almost possessed, as if he were beholding the waters as a new man who had only just noticed the power that they offered.

Silently, he said as if unto himself, "I understand, old man. But you are old, and you forget I am young, and I seek not the approval of the one but of my father, Gruggor the great! And thou shall feel the power that under his tutelage is building within my veins." And with that, he hurled the old man into the river and woke with a start in the physical world. Gallat noticed his father beaming at him, and despite the change in his spirit, the crack he had felt within him seemed to briefly heal. He felt so valued, the brokenness that entered his soul that day was worth the price.

Gallat let out a cold laugh, and Gruggor joined in, as Gallat revelled in the new power he had gained. But even as he did so, he felt a sense of lifelessness, a sense of total emptiness dropping onto him. Shrugging it aside, he smiled at Gruggor and clapped him on the back before saying, "Thanks father."

"No worries, my son."

Gallat wondered forth from the office all the way to the dorm with a sense of glory and regality. His shadow flickered in the night time. He turned around the corridor and saw his best buddy passing by, none other than Donkark, a delightful chap who desired one day to become a rock star. Though Donkark noted that Gallat seemed a little disturbed, like he had been speaking to a ghost. Gallat's eyes were as hard as stone and it looked like he was at the edge of a cliff, about to break. Such was the moral and emotional war battling fiercely within every aspect of Gallat's being.

Donkark went hurriedly over to his best friend and said, "Hey Bud. You want to chat? I've made some cupcakes for us both to have at the concert tonight."

Gallat just pushed him aside and sped into his dormitory.

Donkark stood knocking outside, he could of course just teleport but that seemed like a massive invasion of privacy in a time where Gallat was clearly very upset.

"Gallat, please let me come in, I've realised lately you seem a little disturbed. Are thine okay, bud? I know your sessions with Gruggor has been intense, the magic is surprisingly advanced to be taught for one so young. Am worried about it taking some toll upon you?"

Gallat ignored Donkark, he was beginning to feel very ill from the thoughts of that old man drowning within the river. Swiping his wand, he made a vacuum similar to that which Triffon had produced, so not even the sizzle of the candles could be heard outside.

But Donkark was a master at wizardry so simply did a removal spell but stayed outside so as not to disturb Gallat. And being the loyal friend he was, slept by the door, so that Gallat would always have a friend nearby, even if he knew it not. Many say the one is like this, a being there, yet keeping his distance. A loving but necessarily passive god.

Eventually, Gallat did come out in his pyjamas looking like he had packed recently and couldn't sleep, and he just cried. Such sorrow is hard to put across in this tale. For what it is like to engage with the power Satan's malice and destructive potential, and be bathed in his burning light so one does feel worthy and as if you have achieved some great things, and then look into one's mirror and see ones dying face as the chains bend you to your knees?

What is it to delight in his corrupting darkness when languishing in such a broken state as to walk freezing in the rundown ally ways of unknown streets, and to think in what manner one might further glorify one's lord through inflicting harm upon your flesh and rejoice with the demonic chorus over the destruction of the body that God has made?

What is a man who desire's helplessly to learn more of the life-sucking realm, to fall further into its embrace to quell one's sense of pain, to be as an addict who is taking heroin and knows its horrible effects but can't stop himself and screams at the wall for release even as he plunges the needle into his skin?

Well, it is what Gallat and many acolytes of satanic thinking have come to know. Well do I remember it, for I was like an addict, not to sin, but to vulnerabilities and insecurities that Satan there sank his jaws into.

Those who are fortunate enough not to have descended to Gruggor's own very twisted brand of devil worship, what pain you may ask is this? Well it is: To watch helplessly as morsel-by-morsel Satan savours your unseen agony, as you wish you could yell for hope but feel too cast down in the pit to even raise one's voice as a sense of numbness and emotional violence overcomes you.

You feel too betrayed or beaten to even attempt to whisper of your state so you go forth in the physical realm like a robot pretending all is well. So you can't yell, you can't scream for help though your mouth is opened wide night upon night, like some expansive moor. You can only beat ground as you wish you could reach out to anyone anywhere.

As your mind is cast to the nightmarish realm of horrors you have injured were cuts still bleed gallons of spiritual desire to fight, and there you curl up like a baby, sobbing and shaking, begging for it all to end. Wanting above all to die or cease to be and feel to the dementor's kiss. Then the voices start and the realm to the supernatural opens as spirits mess with your head and heart continuingly, playing with you as if you were a rag doll.

To be filled with anguish and hate and speak daily to them ministering, taken to such a level it pervades everything in your field of vision, when all you do is solely out of trying to find acceptance, peace and security, is a pain and a horrible sense of self-loathing until the noose is tightened around the neck, and the overhanging branch of a tree sounds like blissful escape. The total emptiness and meaninglessness of everything is profound, as ones stands one jump away from death and total oblivion awaits thee.

How much does then one's soul sing in agony, now totally under the dominion of its pain, awaiting to glorify Satan for offering deliverance from the exact torture chamber one has believed he was the grand architect in making.

Chapter 29
The Dylan

Autumn made its face visible, the border land forest clearing was a range of orangey-red leaves. Around them was a wolven chieftain. There was Timly the terrible, Clein the clever and Tomson the tailed. Oh, dear reader, let us not forget the wolven high-chief, who presided over all furry paws who lived among the forests, threw out the continent. His name was Greg the gorgeous.

Paws were thumping upon the muddy ground and songs were sung loudly into the night. It was not quiet marshmallow time yet, but the kids, including my humble self, had a stick in our mouths ready to enjoy the taste of roasted sugar goo, and we occasionally prodded our parent's shoulder with their slightly spiky end to ensure they did not forget. To be fair our parents had fur, I would suggest than any human child reading this avoids trying this out.

Greg with glossy fur began the preceding, looking lovingly at the middle-aged ladies on the front row. "Let us lay aside all our differences and berberines. Let us unite under the banner of hate. For all our anger should surely be directed towards the furless tree destroyers, who decimate our homes. Who destroy our livelihoods. Whom is willing to kill us all. Shall we not below forth 'hear the people sing'?"

Clein began the chant but mutterings came forth. And as among their ranks, came the Dylan.

His people snarled in dislike. I and many of my buddies tried to reach our hero, to warn him, for a trap had been laid to rid this radical speaker from our ranks. Yet we were young then and could do little but try to catch his eye and wag our tail fast enough so that he might sniff out the treacherous air that swam around him.

Some allies of the wolven folk walked through the trees. They grabbed Dylan and knocked him out with their clubs. They then led the God wolf away.

Miffty was clawing at her cage. She tried again and again to poke her snout through, and managed half way before having to jump back onto the behind bars to let it get loose once more. The condition she was living in were terrible, there were scarcely any place to poop and she only had a water bowl to drink from and eat from, for they just threw the mouldy bread in the bowl and let it fall apart.

She cried day and night, missing her master and her old farm life very much. The room she seemed to be trapped in was a barn compartment, full of hay, mice and other things such as rodents. All of them seemed too savvy to approach her paws, but even if they had, she wouldn't have made use of her hunting skills for there was no honour in hunting whilst being held in a cage. Wolves were meant to run free!

One very burly man came forth out of the darkness and approached the candle just inside the wolf's vision. He seemed to be carrying a crate. He whacked Miffty's bars with a metal rod and she backed into the prison. He laughed, slamming the barn door shut as he exited into the night.

The black cloth slid off, as a paw from the inside pulled it down. And there was none other than the mighty Dylan. His fur coat looked dirty and his teeth a little unclean, but he was all the more magnificent in his humility to injure such a form.

The Dylan howled in an ascending song, at Miffty, a clear sign of welcome. She had little energy to do much more but liked to see a fellow wolfling smile. He then placed a paw unto the cage door and Miffty mirrored, the greeting ritual now complete.

But then the Dylan closed his eyes and began snoring and Miffty wondered if having a super powerful neighbour by her side, God himself only a few feet away, would really be worth the long nights ahead.

Gruggor came in with a red candle which he placed upon a metal lectern standing at one side of the barn and placing a sacrificial knife at the other side.

He then turned to the Dylan and said, "My dear buddy, how long I have been waiting for you. You know, I shall take great joy in killing you and proving how the servants of Lucifer have been given powers beyond yours to fathom."

The God wolf just looked pitifully at Gruggor and said, "Oh William, well I remember you, when you walked as a spice merchant, happy and gladly making curries for the poor and homeless people of the land. How adventurous your spirit was then, how full of life. Yet now you claim power, well if what you have now is power, then I would call it loss and a detraction, not a wonder."

Gruggor just laughed and got so close to the cage his nose poked through, "Oh God, how pitiful your form. Yes, I was once happy in my ignorance but now the Lord has given me much. I have wealth, power, authority, influence and—"

"And have lost yourself. And if a man has not himself, what does he own?"

Gruggor just banged the cage with his fist. "Don't play word games with me, wolf, I am the mighty Gruggor, the mightiest of all warriors and servants of Satan. I am Arch-demon. And I will not be taught moral ethics but a lame wolf. Your humility makes you weak God, for in such a form you are well within my grasp. And I shall take control of the world by killing Christ and anointing him with your blood, and in a ritual which your fallen angel hath long ago devised, I shall eat Gruggor's flesh and become even stronger so that none may ever challenge my mastery of Sharir again!

"And I know your fur might be tough, but since the first Arch-demon there is a special gift that Lucifer has given unto us ere his imprisonment. Well might you recognise it God. For it is the blade of Lucifer, Ammut, in its Greek form."

The God wolf looked startled for a moment remembering the wailing and pain that weapon had caused, but then just chuckled as he said, "Oh my dear William, how little thine doth understand. Thou hast thought thyself mighty but fails to take account of draconic knowledge thanks to your arrogance. And you think killing him is the end goal, and will give you want you want. You have no idea what is at foot do you?"

"Oh, I do know exactly what's happening," answered Gruggor as he held his caduceus high and said, "Hail, Astaroth, new king of hell and god of the earth!"

With that, the caduceus whacked the wolf's head clean off. It fell lifeless to the floor as Miffty wailed, and the spirit of God went straight to the depths of hell and into Lucifer's clutches.

Chapter 30
The Hungry Barbarian

Magic possesses a personality so vast that the human mind rarely may comprehend it. Thus it perceives its personality as a superposition of many, almost like it has some extreme form of PDD, a personality dissociation disorder. There is apparent 'good magic' and 'bad magic' and I may well in this tale speak in a manner that makes it sound like there are two magics continuingly at war with one another, though in reality there is only one, and the connection between the apparent two is something I leave open to your analysis of the tale, for it is not in mine rights to tell you what to or not to believe, only to record and let thine mind perceive its own reality in what is written.

Some have even said that one aspect of magic is elevated to godhood whilst the other side is cast in the fires of hell, like some step-slave unto the prince of darkness. This may well be true, I do not know. Yet to claim that magic is either good or bad requires a moral lens too big and wide for human use. Only the gods and other ancient sentients may claim to understand magic in a holistic enough sense to talk about whether it was good or bad, but right now Sir Hamfield thought it would be very useful and didn't give a damn about its morality.

They had been roaming the countryside for days, seeing many daffodils and other things including worms and bunny rabbits, but had no clue where they were going or if the barbarian group that had taken the prince, even lived in this particular strip of the Barbarian wild. The wild which made up most of the cotenant. The advantage though of trying to find a needle in a haystack, is you always could be one hay twig away, so there are many psychological tricks one can play on oneself to stay positive. The disadvantage is that you could be an unimaginable amount of hay twigs distant from the treasure you seek, particularly when the treasure itself is moving in some unknown trajectory.

The sun was setting and it seemed lovely to be out here in the country with the strips of orange and yellow cast out before them. Bobs nostrils opened wide as he smelled the bay leaf casserole that the knight had prepared. It contained some stewed pork they had made after Hamfield, exhausted and hungry, began brutally stabbing a pig and doing some rough buttery using his sword, before Bob finished cleaning out the horse stables. Bob had then been on the lookout. Bob did not like the squeals but he liked far more the idea of his stomach being filled (or for the more mathematically inclined, the modulus of the food was greater than the squeal modulus).

They had now travelled some ten miles from the bar in which Triffon had appeared onto Hamfield and gave them their well needed supplies. They had met a few barbarians including the barking bishops but not anyone who seemed to be educated enough to hold a conversation without trying to smash holes in the ground or kidnap the travellers to sell them as slaves.

There were some really witty and clever barbarians a way down south, with the Druids who the knight thought to be merely lesser magicians and joining them was the Horologists, those Druids who had a particular knack for seeing and knowledge studies. Yet the knight believed Horologists were just experts at sleeping with a different person every night, even when married, and this was unfortunate given he had very strong views about adultery, and excised it worse than a hardened catholic.

Mainly, his strong view held that it should be celebrated and they should be worshiped as champions of free love. If truth be told, he believed everyone should aspire to be the best horologist they could possibly be. And he totally could see where astronomers came in, given a good ass could make all the difference in the world.

Thankfully, Hamfield's love of Prince Rupert had kept him on the straight and narrow ever since he was a mere seventeen-year-old, but between fifteen and seventeen he really kicked things off with more guys than could fit in a tree house. He didn't boast of it now a days though, as when I say kicked things off, I mean created a big bang full of passion yet never could keep the fire going.

Bob, chomping his way through a large bit of meat in the stew, said unto Hamfield, "I love the smell of slow cooked pork."

Hamfield hugged him to express his gratitude for being given his first foody complement by any soul outside of the royal palace. He said, "I love the smell of bay leaf to. And cooked pork. And all the delouses that are so hard to come by in this grassy realm. But I love my prince a pie full more."

Bob nodded understandably but commented, "I love mine ex a gigantic tart full more."

Hamfield said, "None could love more than I love mine prince. Some may come asymptotically close but my prince is the embodiment of romantic love, he is as Eros come manifest from the ancient Greek myth."

"Man, that sounds deep," said Bob. He wanted to argue, to say his ex had been so much more awesome, but he couldn't find a way to say it that didn't pale in comparison to the knight's gift at poetry.

"Yeah," said Sir Hamfield.

Bob then said, as if this would help in any way, "I love my girlfriend more than cooked pork and your prince combined."

Hamfield thought drearily of the prince and said unintentionally out loud, "I love your pork." The image of Rupert faded and he decided to try his companions stew bowl to distract him from the bay leaf which seemed to look too much like Rupert's smile.

Hamfield was of course talking about his beloved prince when the pronoun 'your' was applied, but since English has failed to identify a grammatical distinction with only having one kind of 'your' available to choose from, Bob began thinking that Hamfield might be talking about him. To be fair, Bob was feeling very lonely, a little geographically and otherwise disoriented, and hadn't ruffled in his feathers for a good while now.

Bob blushed. He wondered what it would be like to try another's pork. Hamfield noticed the blushing but put it down to the hot stew warming his buddy up, particularly given that summer days down here could be chilly.

Bob said unto Hamfield, "I like thee pork."

Hamfield looked down at his cloggy casserole and said, "Yes, I have great pork." He longed for better pork though and something of that must have shone upon his face.

"Thy pork would be as heaven under the new dawn. Could I taste it? The mere thought makes me feel all warm and gooey inside, like a chocolate steamed pudding," said Bob softly.

Hamfield looked at Bob sternly, as if Bob was now taking the mick of his impromptu pork dish, and said, "Of course, you can taste my pork, I didn't spend like three hours by the fire just twirling my fingers and not getting it all prepared whilst thy self looked for bay leaves, did I?"

"And your pork is prepared now," asked Bob, feeling like a lump was forming in his throat. He had always had private fantasies about getting things on with a knight, it seemed so gallant and adventurous to him, even though he was straight, the fantasy never specified a woman, he just always assumed it would be a female knight under all that gear.

"Well, I think it's quite tender," said Sir Hamfield. He prodded the pork with his hands.

"Then I would like to taste it," said Bob, his eyes looking pleadingly into Hamfield's.

He was just about to try to "taste it", which thankfully looked like he was just going to plunge his whole head into the casserole bowl, when a massive Barbarian came to the rescue with a club in one hand and a gigantic hound dog by his feet. He roared shouting, "I shall have thine pork!" He was very big, angry and seemingly hungry so Sir Hamfield was tempted to give it to him, but as if this was the cue, the hound dog jumped out from behind and knocked the casserole bowl out of Hamfield's hand.

"I want thy pork!" shouted the man, once more, his thick hands clearly showing this was a guy you did not wish to mess with. Or perhaps it could have been the hound that had spoken, Hamfield was too busy covering his head to see and after finding out dragons actually existed and could keep his prince captive, he was willing to believe anything.

"You shall not try Hamfield's pork!" shouted Bob as he charged the barbarian. The dog leaped upon bob and bit him hard in the calf, so he could still support his weight slightly upon the damaged leg but could hardly summon a tackle or full-on combat with the dog's master.

Hamfield was just about to get some bandages out of his bag when the Barbarian came between him and his supplies. Hamfield noted with a sinking feeling that his sword had gone. They were going to be sold for slaves for sure!

"You can have my pork, just leave my poor companion alone. Please!"

"I shall have thine pork indeed and shall enjoy it, it has been a long time since I have had such a delouses in my mouth." The man lumbered forwards.

"Oh I shall take both of yours." Laughed the barbarian. His furry shorts blowing as the wind rustled to mark the final stages of the sun's descent below the horizon. Sadly, the barbarian didn't seem chilly and just continued beating his chest in a sign of victory.

"Bob. Let him take mine pork, and leave it at that. For if you anger him and he takes yours too, then I shall die of starvation, as might you, but much more importantly, I might die. I cannot allow mine life to end knowing I had to opportunity to take upon your pork. Good pork is so hard to come by in these realms."

All Bob could do was cry, he felt so flattered and full of pain all at once. He had no idea that the Knight desired his pork so much that to be robbed of it, might bring him to the brink of death. This was one of those times when compliments are highly unhelpful in team work despite clear boasts in moral, for Bob was now completely lost in thought and doing nothing about the situation at hand.

Thumping the ground till it began to splinter, the Barbarian drew out a sharp hunting knife, and Bob fainted as he said weakly "heaven help us."

When he came to, he noticed that the man was tying up his companion to the wheels of the cart. He seemed so smug and had a massive wicked grin upon his face. From all the wear and tear and bits of wood missing and being scratched within an inch of its life, this seemed the main vehicle the Barbarian used to get around this country side. Supposedly his dog was the one who pulled it, like some kind of slave labour but right now he didn't have time to think about animal ethics for he needed to make sure Hamfield had not been emasculated in a horrible way.

"Have they taken your pork?" asked Bob crying as he knelt known next to the knight.

"Yes, my friend, they have taken mine pork," Hamfield cried thinking how futile their mission was and how hopeless the fate of Rupert would be. Bob cried with him, but for very different reasons.

"Do not weep, my friend, for I have some pork left that you might like."

"Really?" asked Bob, as darkness was settling around them and the last ember of light was going behind the horizon. Yet Bob's face lit up.

Hamfield grabbed Bob's shoulder tightly and said, trying to speak through the head pain, "Yes, and I wanted to give it to you but…"

"But what, my knight?" asked Bob, now holding the knight's head between his two hands, to make sure he could look at him right in his eyes.

"But that shall be mine!" laughed the Barbarian who was actually much less Barbaric than you might think and simply wanted to kidnap Hamfield in order to find the secret recipe he had used for his pork dish. Perfectly normal etiquette for the outer regions of the cotenant.

"No!" wailed Bob, and he tried desperately to unravel the chords holding the knight in the cart but then it jerked forwards and Bob was thrown off as the cart road away across the hills. But Hamfield could not articulate much of a response, for he was feeling very concuss.

The cart was soon out of sight and Bob felt now like he had lost a companion for a second time. At least now he was all alone there could not be a third. Though humans are a strange folk for despite hating the feeling of a second loss, he kind of challenged destiny but claiming next time he would do better, and so sped off (or really hobbled off given the pain of his injury) into the distance following the clearly defined cart tracks in the grass.

And as he followed, he noted a strange object must have fallen from the cart. It was made of some smooth material he had never known before, and when he pressed a spongy thing, a light shone forth. He hugged it, thinking that Lucifer the king of light must have sent this onto him in his hour of need. He called it 'the shining stick'. You and I might call it a torch. A bygone tech from a long-forgotten age.

Chapter 31
Summoning Satan

The ceremony was set and there were red and velvet candles lining the hallway. Overhead was an imposing arch and hanging from it did chandeliers shine. The scent of burned carcasses filled the room and bathed it in the gentle amber light of the five pentagonal flames. These sources of heat and light were lit at the beginning of all rituals. They directly called upon the power of Lucifer and summoned something of his infecting essence into the physical plane.

Thanks to Michael's magic he could only appear in the physical realm after fracturing his self, and even then only injure the pain for the span of a few agonising minutes. For an offering of gratitude, a lamb lay gagged and chained upon the satanic altar. Now I'm not saying that Satanic altars usually have living sacrifices, this is a myth which predates to days of old were pagan practices were ripe and human sacrifice common. Although it should be noted that even in this day, did God command the Israelites to sacrifice specific animals onto him, as the book of Leviticus goes into immense detail upon.

So, there is nothing truly satanic about a blood sacrifice, and usually it would be a sign of an impaired mind and not a follower unto Lucifer's will, to do so. Yet this was a Luciferian practice in the halls of Mados Mordrė, which were extreme to say the least, and they were trying to summon Satan himself into the physical world in so much as could possibly be done.

They were all dressed in ceremonial robes, traditionally those which had violent flames coming from the bottom, and had a pointy black hood at the top. They wore silver masks and had a small slit too small to be seen unless looking right up close, to allow them to breath and for the chanting sounds to come forth. They sang in ancient Hebrew, rolling sound on sound as if they were creating an acoustic musical wave that dispersed among the chamber, rolled into walls, and then gilded back. Two among the seven within the order had mastery over

Egonounos, and as they sang did the letters appear in the air as golden lights suspended in mid-air. The louder they sang the brighter the letters were.

It read for those who could read it, Shin-Tet-Nun, the Hebrew word for Satan and arguably the most dark for it related well to the view of him as thief and destroyer. They focused heavily upon these aspects, and not others, for it was conducive to the atmosphere they had made though contacting Lucifer by lighter means was equally valid, but to coax him in with the offering of a living lamb meant that a happy theme would be jarring and interfere with their magic instead of strengthening and deepening it.

Then the sliding door, made of a lattice of long interlocking planks of iron, swung open and into the mist stepped Gallat. The smoke began to hit him and trying not to cough or make any sound, he walked forwards with a Scythian blade in hand. The path to the altar was long, and the limestone statues of Lucifer in various stages of victorious combat, made him feel enclosed upon. Like he was moving to the inner horizon of a black hole, where all possible trajectories led on in this Satanic procedure.

For once one begins dancing with the devil, one continues, for if one breaks free on a sudden note, then Lucifer takes it as disrespectful and of the utmost faithlessness, and he will punish such accordingly. As Gallat moved forwards, the chanting changed into a recognisable scripture reading from the book of the goat. The verse of the Fallen Star. And it went like this:

Never before or since has there been a cosmic episode so violent and full of anguish. Oh morning star, how you have fallen from upon high, how do I weep for your sorrow. For thine sorrow is the sorrow of all free people upon the earth and the unending chorus of your demonic realm.

How your light does awaken the soul and its darkness give birth to truth and understanding. Oh, lord of the morning.

Thou who walks among the lambs and makes of us but wolves, lovingly independent and yet companionate and gentle.

Hail, Lucifer, Light bringer, mine greatest joy and the demon at the pits of my despair.

At last, Christ reached the bleating of the Lamb and the Arch-demon arose from the gathering, now breaking the circle of bowed wizards which had formed around the soon to be christened wizard. He drew out his dagger, and in one go, plunged it into the Lamb. It whined, as its juice like under grapefruit dripped from the altar and filled the golden skulled cup that the Arch-demon had placed before the falling liquor. The Arch-demon smiled at his pupil and said unto him, "Drink so that you shall become as a master of Wizardry and partake in the feast of our Lord, the god of the earth."

Gallat drank and fought the gag reflex, and instead looked unto the lamb entrails and placed them in a separate chalice. Then he and Gruggor walked forth onto a rectangular slab of cold stone, and bowed down their faces. The chanting behind them grew louder and a light pervaded the room. It took form as a mere mist, but from it could be heard the gentle and warm tone of the beloved god, Lucifer, son of the morning.

"We meet at last, Christ. My heart is glad at your decision to join us and I am honoured to witness the fulfilment of your oath. Together we shall achieve great things, as great as the miracles of the servants of God but more terrible than even the entirety of God's ensuing anger could devise."

"I am honoured, my lord. Fill me with thine blackness and let us journey into the abyss of madness as agents of darkness, in thine corrupting sight."

"Then come, Christ. Come!"

And Christ fell into a weary dream. As his dream-self awoke did he beheld Lucifer in a banquet hall, with hanging baskets of grapes around the orchard and two freshly made baguettes laid before them. Lucifer smiled pleasantly and said onto Gallat, so you shall take up mine call and walk under my banner?

"Yes, my Lord. I shall."

Lucifer laughed gently and patted Christ on the back. "Really, my friend, there are no needs for formality in this realm. In the physical realm I am a little more, unreachable you might say, but here in this realm we may be ourselves for I am at my full power and not a mere spectre of myself. Though I wish I could bathe in the pools of your rivers as I had long ago, or chat with your scholars looking high into the stars.

"And I shall do all that with you, Gallat, and give you a family and all you had ever wanted, I just need that last little thing, the seventh scroll of the Septicon. Without the whole pack, well that's like trying to play a crystal beast deck with the Mammoth missing."

Christ looked at him a little confused but took the courage to drink some white grape juice.

"Oh my dear friend, I forget, you do not do ancient history in the Academy. Well, I suppose the Arch-demon is quite busy filling all your heads with other kinds of info, but seriously, that dude needs to lighten up a little. Remember more of his old days as William the spice merchant. But now he's all grumpy and serious, personally I blame his guardian demon, I'm telling you that dude takes existence way to seriously! I mean, what's the point of being an evil maniac like me if you can't laugh stuff off once in a while."

Of course, Lucifer was joking about the evil maniac part, but he did it to get his point across.

His tunic nice and neat and his eyes as bright blue as ever. His skin didn't really need sunscreen given the melatonin levels was decently high enough to deal with the Mediterranean like weather, but he flicked his hands to make some appear, and dabbed some on anyway. He offered the bottle to Gallat, but Gallat just politely declined. Gallat was awestruck at the gentleness of Lucifer, and those eight wings sang not of terror but majesty over the heavens.

This Lucifer was not the kind of Lucifer he had come to expect at all, Gruggor had implied that the prince of darkness would be scary and intimidating, but no, he was the most genuine and gentle creature imaginable. Of course, Lucifer had done evil, but Gallat couldn't help but wonder, if just because a person does evil, that makes them evil, or merely a victim of an evil situation.

For despite the many tales concerning the violence of the Battle of Ichor, had Lucifer not been placed in an impossible situation where he had to choose between slavery unto God, and war, he would never of caused the death of many of his brethren otherwise. Was he not caught in an impossible situation, were doing the right thing was totally impossible, for there was no right in the various wrongs that were Lucifer's only conceivable reality.

Lucifer smiled as he looked at Christ. He liked the way he appeared in this world, in that he seemed to be modest, not flamboyant or massively athletic, but he had that intelligent look about him, though maybe this was simply thanks to the glasses. But he had got this far, and he was curious how far his boyfriend's creation could go. Plus since he fiercely loved Ariton, and was also the proud father to all continental life, he felt a great desire to help this being become all it could be.

Lucifer gave Christ a hug and asked, "My beloved child, is there any question you wish to pose to me?"

Gallat looked around feeling quite nervous but Lucifer being omniscient in the minds of those that opened themselves up to him, said, "You can speak freely my boy, none shall hear us, for we are both well alone, I can assure you of that."

Gallat gulped, still a little uneasy, but went on, knowing now was the time to ask it if ever he was going to have the nerve to do so. "I wonder, well, it's come to me, well, really the worry—"

Lucifer put a firm hand unto Gallat's shoulder and said plainly, "Just ask me, my boy, and tell me what is troubling you."

Gallat took in one deep breath and said, "Can I trust Gruggor?"

The question was out of his mouth before he could take it back.

But Lucifer's smile didn't waver and he simply said, "No."

Gallat was relieved that the prince of darkness did not consider his questioning concerning the Arch-demon's honesty and the genius of his so-called altruistic deeds, into question. In fact he was totally unsure what to say to such a direct and unthreatening response, he had expected Lucifer to fry him to death or something or bring out some long whip and begin a torture session. But this Lucifer, was, well, seemingly benign.

Lucifer looked into his glass and wine started to fill it to its brim. He took a sip and then swirled it approvingly before looking Gallat right in the eye, to show the level of his sincerity, and said, "This is very pleasant and warming to my pallet, but if was to suppose that it's the colour of blood that made it allied to all that is battle drawn and unto the destruction of purity, then I would be forgetting that this liquor has its own set of ways and manners by which it might seek to actively influence the course of events into a particular image that is not conducive to the war effort."

Gallat looked at Lucifer baffled once more.

So Lucifer spoke more plainly, "Gruggor, or as I like to name him, William, has had a difficult life filled with initial poverty and abandonment at an early age. He then was thrust into my service a little early if you ask me, for Ariton, bless his damned soul, was eager to get us out of the realm so we could go on a holiday to Cuba and taste the exotic food, he quite likes pineapple, you see."

Gallat just nodded, not quite sure what to make of this talk about pineapples and holidays, but supposing maybe demonic conversation was a little less full of Hebrew and Latin than he previously suspected.

"Well, anyways, William has grown a very hard shell with an unfairly harsh outlook upon the world. He perceives thus me and all my kindred that have followed me, as destructive and dark creatures that wish to overthrow the very throne of God. This is part of what we wish to do, but we are primarily peaceful and would not have slain a single Angel, if only God was not stubborn enough to refuse to come to the meetings to even discuss the possibility of his Avocation.

"Mind you, most of the Luminarzi refused to come to, being good little stooges to the tyrant. But then we were forced into a position where violence was required, as a necessary evil. Not a desired course of action by any stretch of the imagination, well not till I tasted Angelic flesh but that's another story. My point, my child, is this, Gruggor is too filled with hate and anger to truly appreciate the beauty, serenity and love which shines within my plans and designs for the new creation that I shall make, when I am the lord."

Gallat moved his seat a little closer to the table, partly because he wanted to whisper even quieter and still be audible, even though there was no one nearby, and partly because he didn't like being so far away from the profiteroles.

Picking one up, and enjoying the rich choux pastry, he whispered whilst his mouth was filled with Emmerdale crema, "But then why are you letting him lead the orthodox wizards, and not appoint someone who might be a little more sympathetic to your outlook. I mean, like seriously, the way he talks about you and all of hell, makes half of the cotenant too terrified of devil worship to even say hi."

Then Lucifer leaned in a little closer and said, "I shall. In fact, I already have though the Arch-demon knows it not. For I have in my halls a throne below mine and Ariton's, and it shall be held by the greatest wizard of them all, the great conjurer, who shall wield all five of the foundations of magic, and be as a god unto men."

Gallat picked up a choux bun and devoured it with incredible skill before saying in an even quieter whisper (Really, he should enter the Guinness Book of Records for the quietest conversation ever by this point.), 'But this is not possible of a man. Each wizarding master can only hold one, else the conflict of two magics taken to master level would kill him and possibly damage the entire cosmos itself."

Lucifer then smiled in a cunning and devious manner, likened unto his nature, and said, 'No man cannot. But Christ is more than a man. He is the son, the only son of my beloved, Ariton, Angel of the moon. And his son, is my son, so as a father might say to a son sundered from him for long, 'Hail, Gallat, Christ and the rightful heir to the throne of hell, and beloved son of mine'!"

With that the scene before him began to fade as he entered that semi-conscious state in the living world and was less and less aware of the dream world, second by second. But just before everything went dark, and he opened his eyes unto the chamber in Mados Mordrė, did he hear his father Lucifer say unto him, "My child, in whom I am well pleased. Take forth thy rightful place and with magical mastery of the entirety of sapiens Sharir, overcome all who would stand in your path to ascension."

Meanwhile, Gruggor was making much use of Gallat's repose and just as Gallat was awakening, Gallat saw the outline of Gruggor's white teeth, and tasted his fishy breath, as Gruggor leant over him, picked him up and led him to the sacrificial table. Apparently Gallat had also been gagged during his conversation with Lucifer so he could do little but moan. Gruggor then took out the sacrificial knife and stabbed Gallat firmly through the stomach.

Gallat had also been given some kind of mortality numbing magic potion.

He cried, as the blade, once more, came close to his chest, just before the tip was about to hit Gallat's heart. But then all of a sudden, the blade turned into a feather and Gallat just got a little tickled. Then the bands around his arms snapped open and fell limply to the ground.

Gallat shone brightly as he rose like some demon, and grabbed Gruggor around the throat, saying unto him, "I am not to be slain. Neither am I your son. I am Christ and more."

Gruggor spluttered saying, "You can't defeat me! I'm the Archdemon, leader of the people of orthodox wizarding church. Besides, you wouldn't harm your father would you my boy. Now just let me go and all will be forgiven. We just wanted to take some of your blood you know, not much, you know, and you don't need it for your magic. You would be loved and cherished. Now let's stop this foolishness."

Gallat looked onto Gruggor with hate in his eyes and said, "Two things you should know, Gruggor. Firstly, I am not your son, I am the heir to Hell. Secondly, I am the great conjurer, master of all of Sapiens Sharir, and thou cannot best me!"

With that, Gallat broke Gruggor's neck.

He stood in front of the Necromantic order as Arch-demon, Christ and the Great conjurer. And to them, he said, "I shall free my lord. Together, we will free Lucifer from the pits of hell and follow him as he leeks carnage upon the heavens, and be exalted by his side when he takes the very throne of God. Praise be to Satan!"

And with that, my dear reader, doth our story end. Well almost, there is but one more twist in the tale till I bid thee goodbye.

Chapter 32
Lucifer's Worst Nightmare

Ariton was having some sword practice, fine tuning the motor skills of his new form. He found the weight of these flimsy things humans called swords quite comical, and joked about how he could throw it like a javelin at an opponent some hundred yards away. He then proved this by killing an assassin sent by the Barbarian community to begin the overthrow the kingdom and check out its defences. Ariton was becoming a fine knight and defending the realm well.

And the kingdom was ruled by the most absurd women in history these days, professor Triffon, now yes, he had persuaded her to come and Gruggor to command her to do so in hopes she would find the kingdom to her taste and desire to save it. But he had not realised quite how mad this leader was. Tea madness he could deal with, but constantly having to check the palace halls for the presence of mushy apricot was totally unexpected. The apricots were always a hazard which made getting from A to B, twice as long and twice as dangerous, particularly when humans were recovering from that strange state known as sleep.

Ariton often just laid flat, face down, leaving just enough room to breathe when he first awoke. Things in the demon world were much simpler, he would just do things, no need to rest or experience that illogical feeling that having a nap would be the best thing in the world, and no weird dreams either.

Someone had talked to him briefly about the subconscious coming alive during the night but he wasn't quite sure if the person was on drugs. Or if he had overlooked the very important fact that psychology is hardly a reliable science given that most of its hypotheses are completely impossible to verify analytically or give five sigma data for. Ariton liked science you see, and was unwilling to believe in any truth unless it was proved beyond plausible doubt.

Yet he had been forming a premature thing, between Triffon's arrival and Rupert's capture, known as a crush but more so a slight crush on Triffon's lover partly because of her favourable descriptions of him, partly because he was astonished by his kindness when he visited from time to time to check on how the rebel demon's plan was going to keep Gruggor happy. Jasper just seemed amazing and both he and Jasper were of similar biological age, and Jasper was somehow familiar, like he was a kindred spirit.

Ariton had seemingly developed premature feelings for Jasper but didn't know what to do. You see in the demon realm, people have emotions. Very extreme emotions in many cases. But they arise fully formed and at their peak, so simply 'crushes' were not a thing and romantic ambiguity was like a knife blade with no romantic investment on one side and being head over heels for the person on the other. This tickling kind of love was not something Ariton had ever known.

So, on top of all the intricacies of being human, the problems of trying to get the boy to the palace whilst Triffon was continuingly messing up his plans to bring them both to safety (which she always did in a cataclysmically selfish manner), and wondering how unearth to save this kingdom, he now had to worry about the concept of polyamory. For he loved Lucifer with passion, but he also was at the beginning stages of second love. He had never really considered going polyamorous before since he and Lucifer had long been in a very happy monogamous relationship, but hopefully Lucifer would not be too dissatisfied with the arrangement. He could be like Persephone, and visit the physical plane on weekdays whilst having the weekends off in hell.

Triffon, to make things even worse, was having a crush on him. This meant the number of apricots between him and his destinations grew as Triffon became more familiar with the knight's routes and so provided many a refreshing bit of substance in case halfway across the corridor the knight suddenly felt the urge for lunch. Now this knight was not like Rupert, this a true gentlemen. Like all proper knights he spent more time concentrating on his hair and his cooking talents than the arena of the battle field, and didn't seem all that into killing at all.

In fact, that last evening Jasper had seen Ariton baking chocolate chip muffins in the oven. And the smell that wafted forth filled Triffon's nostrils. Jasper also never showed any interest in Triffon these days which surely must mean he was too shy to confront Triffon about the bubbling feelings for Ariton that he was so impressively hiding from the world. Now yes, she kind of loved Jasper still, sort of, well not really.

Jasper for example never remembered to use extra virgin oil, and always went to get the cheapest thing when going shopping in the local market. Such economic sense was distasteful to her.

Yet just as Ariton was about to take off his bronze armour, did he hear round the corner secretive voices talking and his heart fell into the underworld below, metaphorically.

Triffon was standing like a dwarf in comparison to the ridiculously tall creature in front of her. It was skeletal and looked like a soldier's seven-foot shadow, with stretched out hands and a black vortex for a mouth. It was covered in a black garment and had fire blazing where eye sockets should have been.

This creature said in a raspy voice, "Thou is a seer which the black tower could use. For whilst the orthodox wizards focus on expansion and set their sights upon global domination, the nameless ones shall have a golden opportunity to take their prize and wreak havoc upon the world. For we are immortal and alone of the angelic host, free to walk upon this earth. We have only restrained ourselves whilst the Academy of the Arch-demon posed an annoyance unto us, yet now its concerns are spread so thinly as a spider's web, we shall bend down upon it and break its feeble chord."

Then the creature turned to face a guy with curly blond hair, wearing a bright blue top who looked like a pretty cool dude, but standing next to this creature, the dude looked a lot more shifty than he might otherwise. And Triffon burst into tears and hugged him so hard it looked like she was trying to break all the bones in his body. "You have returned from your training, my love! I love mine Jasper," and she kissed him on both cheeks and he spun him around. She had apparently forgotten all about Jasper's poor love of replacing butter with tasteless spreads, for as all know temporary distance does make love all the stronger.

Jasper looked happier than a child at Christmas. And Ariton felt worse than he did that day he had a salt water bath. He would have wept, but he couldn't break his cover now, so he just quietly cried in his shirt as the conversation between the three continued.

Unto Jasper, the creature hissed, "My Lord Michael, we rejoice in your leadership. How well have you lead the nameless ones, and deceived God into believing that thine are under his service. Will you now stand with us and lead us to victory?"

Michael smiled as he did so his Angelic wings that were previously concealed sprang out. Michael then said, "As I trapped Lucifer in his realm, not under the orders of God but desire to clean the earth of demons ready for thine ascension, and as I have taken command of the royal court by the order of Gruggor but will to make this kingdom your playground, so I shall now in my own will take the Cobalt throne of the Black Tower and then lead thine people forth to crush heaven, hell and all creation to rubble!"

Suddenly, things were worse than Ariton had ever imagined. How foolish were they all. For in the battle between demons and Angels, had everyone forgotten those who sort only to destroy and would bring ruin unto them all as they squabbled among themselves. And he was helpless to do much in his weakened state. And the previous Archon, Michael, was leading them. Yes, it was prophesied that Lucifer would have to confront Michael in conflict, but never in a million years had Ariton thought Michael would have the full force of nameless ones behind him. Michael had played the game well, and outwitted God, Lucifer and himself all so horribly.

Lucifer would rise though! For even Michael couldn't prevent that! If only Rupert, Hamfield and Bob all found each other and could be convinced into finding the last of the Septicon, all might still be saved. And God and Lucifer might have to put differences aside, and unite, for what does it matter whose skeleton sits upon the throne of a desolate wasteland that was once creation.

So began, Lucifer's worst nightmare, a union of heaven and hell.

And God, the creator of all looked unto hell from the sphere of heaven and unto the triune son said, "Look, did we not say that all work that is done shall only improve the glory of my work. Now shall reality see the angelic order united under my banner, as they were once so long ago. And Michael's rebellion lead to Lucifer's salvation."

To this the triune son asked, "Then whom shall save Michael?"

God laughed and said lightly, "Oh my dear son, that is another tale for another time."

And thou, reader, may ask yourself why Michael would engage with such a nihilistic group of beings as the nameless ones whilst being so completely naive in the ways of death, and unable to comprehend death itself. Well, it could be that his mental block with regards to mortality was merely a cover up which he used to imitate an angelic like attitude to life to fall God for a while, or else it might have been a real thing.

For often, we do most evil, when we are ignorant of the exact evil we are doing. And in trying to detach ourselves from darkness so extremely, make the danger of not recognising the darkness of our actions all the greater. For evil is never a thing that should be underestimated, overlooked or locked up. For if we do any of these things, we shall ignorantly become the embodiment of it.

So it was, is and will ever be, for ignorance is the one true enemy of both Lucifer and God. And knowledge is the key to freedom.

Yet far down below did Ariton have to flee for there came forth out of the skies Thunderbolt of the mountain dragons. There to barter with king Bartibus. And he sent forth the flame imbued with base magic, which shone gold as the sun. And could blind a mere mortal. Yet though such fire was impossible to extinguish using wizard's magic, as Jasper had now revealed, he was no wizard at all or simple practitioner of Sharir.

He was an Arch-angel, and he stepped into the flame of the dragon unscathed and as his massive wings unfurled, he shot like a bullet into the sky. The dragon, with a slit neck, fell lifeless by Triffon's. All who were not trying to break through the rubble knelt in adoration of the angel. And Michael raised his hands unto the heavens and proclaimed, "I AM THE ONE TRUE GOD, BOW BEFORE ME, YAHWEH AND LUCIFER, FOR I SHALL TURN THINE CREATION INTO RUBBLE!"

And all the inhabitants of Mados, save Ariton alone, sang and praised Michael's name.

Appendix

Conclusion:
A Tale Yet to Come

Dear reader,

The pleasure of putting a furry paw to ink, and then ink onto parchment is one of the joys of life. Yet even more greatly valued is the hope that it shall one day help both furry and furless people smile and enjoy a nice warm mug of tea. So, where, reader, shall we go from here?

Well, there is much more to say for I did not wish to turn you away by making one all comprehensive book, that spans thousands of pages. Take for example the look of a twelve-year-old when the entire bible is handed to him at his confirmation, and the minister makes plane how important it is to read the whole thing and know it even as well as you know yourself. Well, maybe your priest is a little less hard going on the scripture learning, but at least in Wolfish priests of God, knowing the alarming number of weird passages and outdated names, there is yet an inbuilt instinct that they feel the urge to subtly enforce their knowledge upon their congregation.

So, I leave you hopefully with a smile on your facc, and hopefully not being too upset that you must wait till a sequel to have more of the questions answered, if indeed I survive long enough in this chaotic realm with demons, wizards and equally dangerous tree-cutters. Which is no guarantee!

So, will the Dylan work effectively with Lucifer, or shall he escape the confines of hell and stir up the kindness that once existed in Gallat's sheepy soul before Gallat frees Lucifer from his prison? Will Gallat steal or bargain for the last of the Septicon and bring it unto Lucifer or get eaten by Madam Parsley? And will Bob, Rupert and Hamfield all find each other, and joining together be able to reclaim control of Mados from the clutch of Triffon and the nameless ones?

I hope so, my dear reader, I hope so. But as yet I do not know, for these events hath not been resolved and I am no seer. If you don't receive a sequel from me, the likelihood is that I have passed on, have gone mad or developed arthritis of the paw, but there shall be no need to weep, for I may well be in wolfish heaven where the trees are forever green and the carrots, nice and purple, as they should be. If none of this comes to pass, I shall gladly retake my role as narrator, and give to you reader another tale to enjoy. But till then, if there shall be or shall never be a next time, I send many a four-pawed blessing and bless your heart.

John,
Your furry author

Author's Note

Dear reader,

Am writing with many great thanks to all who have supported and helped with this work, both directly through reading and indirectly through simply being wonderful people and inspiring me to think of life differently, and make life worth living, even when it goes on rougher terrain. I am truly blessed to know so many amazing people and this book is as much to give something back to them, as it is to explore and question our beliefs and axioms.

Having had amazing friends, who are genuinely lovely, would like to give all a massive thank you.

To my dad who has been involved in reading a proportion of what you see you before you, and many renditions, some good, some not so, would like to sincerely apologise for the lack of good parent/son bonds in these books. He is an amazing father and far better than was prince Rupert's, and well, all of the fathers in this book.

And for those of you who enjoyed the mathematical or physical references, I have but one last comment of warning to make, never investigate the theory of relativity, else it shall drive you as mad as Triffon who does reflect the state of mind of a fresher coming out a special relativity lecture hall. If despite this warning you do wish to dive into relativity in full, might I suggest taking a look at 'a very light introduction to relativity', which shall go into the full joy of covariant derivatives, tensors and metrics.

But seriously, thank you so much to you, the round ear that is reading this right now, and I hope that something in the tale has brought some joy and happiness to your day, and I give you a high-five and all the blessings my wolfish heart can conjure up.

With best wishes,
Jamie

Glossary of Key Terms

Dissolution: Death of an eternal being (or total destruction of the immortal aspects of biologically mortal forms).

Allarich: Angelic, warrior like priests, who are obedient to God.

Luciferian: Noun relating to any being that serves the will of Lucifer.

Sphere of existence (a realm): A self-contained reality, though it can be affected by the reality and events of other spheres. Realm magic concerns how to bridge, intertwine and block these realms. This is an ability only those of the Angelic order (be it angels of God or demons of Lucifer) can use. The spheres of reality include, the astral, physical (biological), magical, heavenly, hellish and dream realms.

The dream realm: One of the spheres, it acts as the realm of consciousness and subconscious thought. Here all spheres of reality are very close, and dramatic changes that happen here often have effects on the other realms.

Breaking the bridge: A casual phrase used for the charm which an Angel can use to split two interconnected realms as much as possible without doing significant damage to either.

Abyss: A little known realm within hell—it drives that all that beheld it to madness and is said to be an anti-light to Lucifer's light. Many Luciferians in the world believe even Lucifer himself can have his sanity damaged by the Abyss if he remains trapped in hell overlong.

Septicon: The dragon name for the seven scrolls which legend has it can free Lucifer and the demonic armies from the confines of the hellish realm.

Christ: The creation of Ariton, second in command of hell. His birth was named the immaculate conception, due to the lack of a mother's procreative involvement in his conception and his father giving birth to Christ. Ariton's purpose in creating him, was to test the satanic forces on the earth, like creating a light to see how effective and unyielding the darkness is.

Bob the blob: The wolfish name for beetle juice.

Homo sapienist: A creature that views its species as having value above human species or as having some higher inherent importance.

Sapiens: The casual wolfish term for all Homo sapiens and Neanderthal people.

Pentalpha: The reversed pentagram found often in satanic literature, sometimes referred to as the star of Baphomet.

Furry ones: Wolfish name for wolves and feline creatures.

Pointy ears: Wolfish name for themselves as a collective species.

Round ears: Wolfish name for humans.

Fur ball: An affectionate name for a wolf. Often cubs are called fur balls as well as being a common way for a wolf to address another very dear wolf.

Deep Buddhism: The first recorded religion (after the war of desolation), minimalistic version of our 'guru Buddhism'. They adopt many of the service features of the Quakers.

War of desolation: The nuclear war in which almost all life became extinct, occurred 1 billion years before the writing of this story.

Battle of ichor: The name given to the war in heaven in which Lucifer rebelled. Technically this consists of a series of battles, but most when speaking of the Battle of ichor mean the last stretch from the hill of the lamb to Lucifer's bondage, in which Lucifer showed shamelessly his new taste for Angelic flesh.

Sharir: Generic name for the sentient magic which flows through all sentient life. This magic is agreed by all present in the world to exist and is quite undeniable. Some people consider Sharir as like a sentient force of nature, like an additional fundamental force, though this is debatable.

God/Yahweh/the triune God: The creator which Christians commonly refer to as the trinity. It is the source of all reality and has no gender or actual form, for he is equally in all things. However in the form of the trinity, the dove is female, Jesus is male and as for the Father's gender, well there is a lot of debate. Some say his has no form, others that he is a new gender all together and some say he's just non-binary.

Demonic possession: The state where a biologically mortal being is filled with the spirit of a Fallen Angel, and gains some strong control or influence of the being.

Demonic possession of the first kind: Possession where the being is controlled completely leaving the being with no mental or kinematic control over the hosts biological form and mind. With extreme will, and if having significant enough strength which has not been subdued in the possession ritual, the being can break free.

Demonic possession of the second kind: Possession where the mortal is heavily influenced by the demon, but is very aware of their own thoughts and desires distinct from the demon. The sustained will of the host becomes of primary importance and the demon's thoughts and motives, are somewhat revealed.

Moopitarian cake: A cake rumoured to be made by a tribe in the southern lands, the first spice cake (post the war of destruction) to be made upon the cotenant.

Soul-suckling virus: The mythical virus designed to explain why people within the walls of Mados Mordrė, were often found feeling like their very life force and will was being drained out of them.

The horned God/Prince of darkness/Angel of light/King of light: Titles for Lucifer.

Oak tea: The most common type of tea in the northern realms. (within Ontock, a close competitor is peppermint tea.)

Northern realms: The combined term for all Northern human kingdoms (which at the time of writing is Mados and Ontock).

Duke: A member of the inter-kingdom focussed group, which tries (rather hopelessly) to keep all the Northern realms together and unite the kingdoms. In the name of peace they have the power to put in new laws and systems, if they are favoured enough to be given this power by the consent of the entire royal Court. Dukes tend to be very knowledgeable, not always very wise but often claim to have a basic grasp of Sharir to intimidate royalty they dislike.

Madosian: An adverb concerning something being related or originated from, or carrying the essence, of Mados.

The devil's hoof: The secret detectives which seek Lucifer's hiding place and have sworn a life's oath that they will one day set him free.

The five foundations: The foundations of magic which humans can access. They can be thought of as different kinds of Sharir, even though strictly speaking Sharir is one sentient thing.

Emotiavartos: The foundation (or principal) concerning emotive magic studies. This is considered as the most pure form of magic and groups of barbarians which might shun most wizards will on occasion welcome an Emotiavartos master.

Egonounos: The foundation (or principle) concerning Linguistic studies. Sub-magics included runic magic and the structure of the grammar of magic incantations themselves. Egonounos masters often are the wizarding scholars, and focus heavily on studying the theory of magic as opposed to using it practically.

Egomortalarfos: The foundation (or principle) concerning the magic of life, death and resurrection. This is very dark and strongly associated with Luciferian practices and philosophy (though there is no proven direct link). Resurrection magic is the most controversial of all any many of the wizards which practising it beyond the walls of Mados Mordrė are shunned.

Egosphilos: The magic seers use. This is a special kind of magic for it involves the practitioner travelling into the dream realm to see visions of things both distant in time and space in the other realms. The magic is involuntary and allowed by a guardian Angel or demon which guides the seer to the dream realm. For those who do not believe in Angels or demons, they reject seers as phony people and con artists for realm magic is impossible by human magic alone as has already been mentioned.

Druids: Magicians who do not master any of the five foundations of wizardry.

Ammut: The name of the demonic form of Lucifer's handmade dagger capable of killing Angel's. In ancient Egyptian, this translates as 'devourer of the dead', whereas Lucifer often addresses the dagger 'devourer of hearts' due to the way he likes to eat the hearts of rebel angels himself. Since part of him resides in the dagger, he has a very personal connection to it, and only he (or his servants) can wield it.

The Great Conjurer: The legendary sorcerer that is destined one day to master all of the foundations of magic. This will grant him power more like a god than a human. Some claim the great conjurer will be the dove (holy spirit) made incarnate. Others believe this will be a wizard who unites the northern realms. Though whom it shall be/is remains a great mystery and causes a lot of conflict and fighting between religious groups.

Suicidal apricot theory: The theory which proposes that a member of the fruit family would willingly die and be bitten or chopped if it could vote upon the outcome of its life. This was instrumental in getting pro-fruit supporters into the wizarding community, where eating fruit is seen as a sin since fruit is seen as unclean under the eye of Lucifer.

A wizarding master: This refers to a fully qualified wizard who has mastered one of the five principal foundations of magic. All professors within the academy of Mados Mordrė, are wizarding masters.

Black Moor: The name the dukes give to the cave which houses the entrance to hell (only entrance within the physical realm and a one-way ticket to hell).

The knighting of the black flame: This is one of the very well-hidden rituals, practiced within all orthodox wizarding groups. In the ritual a student of magic joins in the contract with magic, which was made long ago by a divine being (the identity of the divine being is much debated). At the end of the ceremony the wizard emerges from the ritual as a wizarding master. Very similar to Christian christening crossed with a conformation. The wizard is given a new wizarding name, and welcomed in as part of the official wizarding community and thought of as part of the wizarding worldwide community.

The valley of passage: The only passage through the wolven forest was one small narrow path which stretched for some ten leagues, and there in it is likely a traveller might be allowed to pass safely as one journeys between Mados and the Barbarian lands. Wolven people tended not to raid along this path as they respected human's need to travel across the cotenant without the constant fear of being attacked or mugged.

Hhai Sharir: Life magic. This allows certain creatures to have certain abilities which are aided by their biological bodies but are only made completely possible due to their bodies internal magic. Examples include dragon's ability to breath Fire, and capacity to fly. Another is the wolf's ability to speak and make use of well-articulated vocal communication.

Spell-caster: A youngling who is known to have magical power, but has not reached magical maturity as yet. They are greatly scouted for by Recruitment officers sent out by Mados Mordrė.

Necromancer: A master practitioner of mortality magic. The term was often used in a dark connotation, with associations of evil wizards though this is not strictly part of the original definition.

High necromantic order: Sometimes referred to simply as the Necromantic order when not speaking formally in rituals or official correspondence to them. This order was led by Gruggor and was in charge of converting Christ to the Luciferian cause as well as enforcing Luciferian vengeance upon angels who came down to help or aid Sharir practitioners who allied themselves with God.

Diralisin's blade: The symbol used to represent the Necromantic order of Mados Mordrė.

Conjurer: A generic name for any being that can make conscious or instinctive use of its magic.

Black tower: A tower built to occupy un-orthodox wizards who neither served God or Lucifer but instead desired total destruction of creation, and were at heart extreme nihilists. They worshiped the nameless ones. As some of the nameless ones abandoned Lucifer particularly after the slaying of Axcat, one of their most respected figures, many never ventured in hell and so were not trapped within it unlike their fellow Luciferian fallen angels. Therefore the nameless ones often visit the black tower, and it is rumoured that some even live there though this is unconfirmed as anyone who ventured into the Black Tower to investigate never returned alive.

White tower: The tower built to occupy unorthodox wizards who actively supported God and who constantly sort out signs for the coming of the Dylan, which they saw as God's prophesied sign of hope for the peoples of the world against the rising powers of Lucifer. They had mixed feelings about Christ as some were appalled at the idea of a man giving birth, others at the idea of a demon so directly creating a human and others were frightened as to what might happen to them if he turned to the Luciferian cause in the end.

Arch-demon: Name given to the holder of the Caduceus of Hermes and wielder of the power of Mados Mordrė. Traditionally he is treated like the headmaster of the Academy, though he is more of a spokesperson for all orthodox wizards, and their representative (chosen or otherwise). His regular meetings with demons in the dream realm altered both his dream and biological self gradually over the years, but after passing a point known as the time of reckoning, his spirit self-ascended in nature to the point where he isn't really human anymore, though still very much bound to the human limitations concerning Sharir.

Cattle madness: The madness that causes a farmer to begin eating his cattle in psychotic episodes, as well as other symptoms, generated by sensory interaction with or observation of the Black Moor.

Magico: The particle which transmits information along the Sharir field.

Triune: The ritual by which to fate opener uses the Septicon to recombine the hellish and physical realms.

Fathers of magic: When used formally this refers to the collection of sapiens which joined in the festivities of hell, celebrating the meeting of Fallen angels with human kind. These individuals came to be very well known by demons and it is said by some, though it is not known to be true, that some of these were actually trapped with the demons in the realm of hell when Michael did his magic to prevent demons from escaping the confines of hell and limit their ability to personally continue their evangelism of humans to the Luciferian cause.

Sharlger: Name of the continent upon which this story takes place.

Hlidskialf: The throne over which destiny can see all events which occur within the five realms.

Madman: The only royally approved newspaper of the northerly kingdom of Mados.

Scythan order: A group of powerful wizards who desired to set Lucifer free but also took an active role in scouting out for spell-casters which might be able to join them in later years, once the students were trained by Westog at the academy of Mados Mordré

Base magic: A name for the underlying magic upon which Sharir is imbedded. Though casually this is also used to refer to draconic magic.

Glossary of Angelic/Demonic People

Lucifer: The first of god's creation. He was the high prince of all angels before his rebellion, in which him and his kindred were cast out of the heavenly sphere.

Cherubim: Angel of great power but not necessarily being given oversight over some operation. Lucifer was himself one of the Cherubim, though in his case, God gave him enormous responsibility.

Seraphim: Angels who forever sang praises and preached. They rejoiced in the spirit of God. There compositions were revealed under all the angelic host on the meal of the sabbath.

Offamin: Angelic guards who solely presided over the protection of Yahweh. Some of them were however dispatched during the heavenly war when Lucifer marched to the temple of the Lord, with the desire to sit on the lord's throne and govern all of creation himself.

Lieutenant of the pits: Originally, this was a title belonging to Lucifer's cousin, and one of his closest friends. Lucifer had planned to make him the chief architect in a new heaven, however Lucifer's cousin died during the heavenly war ere this could be done. When Lucifer made his home in hell however this became a title held by any angel that was in charge in that moment of time, in overseeing the building of Lucifer's cities and temples.

Archon: An angel who presided over some assignment.

Godric-wolf: This refers to the being that was long prophesied by the wolven people, that one day God would hear their pleas to save them from the tree destroys as they name the sapiens people. And the Dylan would help the wolfish kind annihilate the sapiens or make them as slaves. Note that the true Allarich-wolf (at least as my belief goes), actually is trying to unite all the different species of the land to oppose the rising of the kingdom of Lucifer.

Junior angels: Newly created angels, who are under apprenticeships. Their age in human years is typically eighteen to twenty. They have small two-foot wings, and whilst being junior angels can only fly in the heavenly and physical spheres of existence. When they mature passed this age, God gives them freedom to travel in all spheres. They have difficulty comprehending the full light of the high prince, and this was used to his advantage in the heavenly wars. It can be likened to the way fully developed angels struggle to comprehend God's light when shone in its full glory.

Nameless ones: The rebel angels who fall out of favour with Lucifer and worship oblivion or Anarchy but are not conducive to the development of any kind of order or society.

Raphalim: Architects and builders of heaven.

Luminarzi: Angelic princes, leaders of one of the races of the Allarich. Lucifer is sometimes named the Luminite, head of the Luminarzi, though he rejected such a title right before his battle with god's Angels.

Pellanorian winged soldiers: Respected servants of the angelic people.

Angels of the four corners: These are angels who delighted in navigation and were very instrumental in guiding early wanderers with the aid of Astronomical charts and information. Their interest in astronomy and desire to teach Sharir law, was probably how the two became very interlinked. The four angels were, Lucifer (Eastern angel), Astaroth (Western angel), Asmodi (Northern angel) and Beelzebub (Southern angel).

A devil: A lesser demon, i.e., a fallen angel who does not hold the rank of a prince or a Duke of hell. Their numbers are unknown, though it is known they make up a large majority of the angelic forces who rebelled against God in the heavenly war. They are not to be confused with the term, the devil, which the Allarich use to refer to Lucifer after his fall.

Demon kings: The leaders of hell who serve under the banner of Lucifer (and his second in command, Ariton). They often worked with wizards or druids seeking life changing events or colossal personal transformation. They are named is many wolfish tales as Lucifer, Leviathan, Satan and Beelzebub.

Duke of hell: Those chief spirits who govern the demons. They are under the leadership of their respective king. It's much debated as to who the dukes are, but a couple which are known are Astaroth and Asmodi.